FEBRU...

THREATCON
DELTA

Also by Andrew Britton

THREATCON DELTA

ANDREW BRITTON

PINNACLE BOOKS
Kensington Publishing Corp.
www.kensingtonbooks.com

PINNACLE BOOKS are published by
Kensington Publishing Corp.
119 West 40th Street
New York, NY 10018

All Kensington titles, imprints, and distributed lines are available at special quantity discounts for bulk purchases for sales promotions, premiums, fund-raising, educational, or institutional use. Special book excerpts or customized printings can also be created to fit specific needs. For details, write or phone the office of the Kensington special sales manager: Kensington Publishing Corp., 119 West 40th Street, New York, NY 10018, attn: Special Sales Department; phone 1-800-221-2647.

ISBN-13: 978-0-7860-3219-8
ISBN-10: 0-7860-3219-7

First printing: December 2014

10 9 8 7 6 5 4 3 2 1

Printed in the United States of America

First electronic edition: December 2014

ISBN-13: 978-0-7860-3220-4
ISBN-10: 0-7860-3220-0

PROLOGUE
MURRIETA, CALIFORNIA

It was the kind of dusk that made millennia melt away.

Sitting on a boulder on the side of the cliff, 2,100 feet above the Temecula Valley, it didn't feel to Victor Yerby like it was December 4, 2014. A mild wind blowing at his back from the west made the palm fronds rustle above him, a low and lazy, slightly brittle sound. The chill in the clean air was common to nighttime on the edge of a desert, but warmer than usual for December. There was the slightest musky taste to it, the remains of a late-afternoon dust storm that blew through the fringes of the Inland Empire. Yerby had just been waking up when he saw it rolling below, big and billowy, just like it was pictured in the movies.

Now the cloudless black sky was already showing crisply marked stars. He could not hear the sounds of the thinning traffic on the distant Highway 15. On one end of the freeway, about ninety minutes west, was San Diego. Travel three and a half hours east and you were in Las Vegas. Here, well south of Los Angeles in mountains close to the border with Mexico, there was nothing but horse country and remnants of the Old West. Just now there were no planes, civilian or military, passing overhead. There were no sounds on the private road that dead-ended at a cliff. It seemed to him that this dark night could have been plucked from the pioneer days or even further back. It could just as easily have been 2014 B.C.E. in some Middle Eastern desert. The few lights could easily be torches or campfires instead of homes.

Dressed in layers under a black sweater with leather elbow patches he had sewn on himself, with a black baseball cap turned around, the slender six-footer kept his eyes on the target zone toward his right, southeast, while his mind enjoyed the transporting nature of the environment. His borrowed house was a little farther down the hill behind him and all he could see on three sides were boulders, all he could hear were the fronds and the gently swaying high grasses with an occasional off-syncopation sound that he knew was a coyote moving through the brush. For the week he had been here he had not bothered the coyotes and they had not approached him. Perhaps it was the understanding and respect of one predator for another that made them circle wide.

Yerby wondered if someone in earlier times, sitting under the evening canopy, had thought about an even older era. Did people back then think past the generation of their parents or grandparents? Without machines, their days were probably more or less as quiet as their nights. And *night* meant when the sun went down For most of history, that life had been the norm. This life, a life of electricity, was a relative novelty.

Yerby didn't know if he would have been an officer of the law back then, a Texas Ranger in the Old West, a spearman in the B.C.E. Or was it his skill with firearms that had simply led him where he was? No, there was a bowie knife in a leather sheath attached to his belt. It felt right there. It always had. Maybe he just liked justice. Maybe he liked seeing one less bad guy in the world. After all, it wasn't the gun that sent him to the DEA recruitment office when his hitch was done. There had been a—

His thoughts snapped back to the present.

Don't let your mind roam too far, he warned himself. He knew from long experience that snipers on stakeouts had to keep from getting bored, but they also couldn't let their attention wander. He remembered one marksman in his army group, "Swamp Water" Andrews, who used to train in the Okefenokee where he grew up. He'd go into the swamp at dusk and let mosquitoes bite the hell out of him all night while he waited for deer that he knew wouldn't show up until morning. He never allowed himself to swat the insects or scratch and was still motionless and focused when dawn brought his prey.

Yerby did not have that kind of obsession even when he was green. He was not like some Marines he knew who went around thrusting out their chests and admonishing strangers, "Hit me! Hit me!" He was a professional who got the job done without living the part. Even here, he was cautious enough to use a leafy branch to wipe out his tracks. There was no deep,

secret part of him that longed for a face-to-face con-
frontation.

He continued to study the sky as he listened for a
sound that was not flora or fauna. He didn't know which
of the lights above him were planets; the brightest was
Venus, he guessed. He had always meant to get a tele-
scope for the month he was out here in the mountaintop
house. He had an NVWS-4 tactical medium-range night-
vision Gen3 scope on his M40 but he only removed that
when he was servicing the sniper rifle. He had been
tempted to use it to look at the full moon when he first
got here but the light might glint off the optics, off the
weapon itself, and be seen by someone lower down on
the mountain. He had selected this place because he
didn't want anyone to know he was here.

The house, a single-story structure built in the
Mediterranean style, was at the very top of a gated community adjoining the Santa Rosa Plateau. It had been
empty since the California real estate implosion over a
decade before. Members of the property owners' association cut the grasses back one hundred feet from the
structure as mandated by local fire laws, but that was
all they did. Field mice and insects had made the attic
and chimney their home, respectively. Rattlesnakes and
tarantulas moved unchallenged along the cracked concrete of the driveway.

But Yerby did not care. He slept in a sleeping bag
during the day, had a well-stocked pantry for a month's
stay, and kept the lights out at night when he came out
to watch the valley. This was not the desk job a twenty-
year DEA man would have been entitled to had he
wanted it, but Victor did not want that. He wanted to be
in the field, doing what he had vowed to do ever since

his older sister, Ginny, died of a heroin overdose: fight drugs, from the cartels to the mules who ferried the goods across the Mexican border to the dealers who gave them to kids to sell in schools. That wasn't just the situation in Texas, where Yerby grew up; it was the same everywhere.

Satellite surveillance and a series of drone flyovers out of nearby Marine Corps Base Camp Pendleton pinpointed this small town in Riverside County in Southern California as a pinch point for drug trafficking. Immigrants came right through the mountains. The Immigration and Naturalization Service didn't bother them: that was considered profiling. Individual property owners had to make specific complaints against anyone, and they were loath to do that with suspected illegals. Most of the four hundred families who lived on the mountain had kids who stood at bus stops or chased monarch butterflies through the fields or rode horseback or ATVs on the trails. This was also a fire zone. One spitefully flicked cigarette could burn an area the size of Rhode Island. It was better to just look the other way.

Unless you were Victor Yerby.

Yerby sat on a low, flat rock, his rifle lying on a leather carrying case on the ground. Now and then he flexed his hands to make sure they were limber and ready. He watched the ridgeline to the south. That was where storms, fog, and illegals came in. He would see them plainly as they passed, blocking the lights of the spotty homes situated on minimum five-acre lots.

This was where one man in particular was supposed to be coming through: Danny Hernandez. The DEA had tracked him from Veracruz to Mexico City and that was where they lost him. He had gone silent when his private jet landed in the capital city: no electronics, no tickets, no credit card use. But the DEA knew where he was likely to come through since this was the route his mules took. Neither the DEA nor any other federal agency was willing to authorize a legal takedown. An arrest would get them nothing, given the lack of hard evidence against Hernandez. He was careful to keep his hands clean and no one ever ratted him out.

Until now. A tip from a worker in a drug field in Jalapa, the capital of the Mexican state of Veracruz, had brought them here. The worker had needed the cash and got it. Within twenty-four hours the money and the headless informant turned up in several canvas sacks in a Dumpster.

But Danny Hernandez was here on a special mission—special because it would make him an international political player, not just the head of a leading cartel. Intelligence suggested that he was here to negotiate using the mule train to smuggle bioweapons into the United States. Hernandez had hooked up with pro-Islamic radicals in Iran thanks to the orchestrations of Ricardo Ramirez, a Venezuelan mobster whose international ambitions had progressed further and faster than those of his old friend Hernandez.

The Iranians were cautious, however. If they were going to spend millions of dollars to send materials with Hernandez, they wanted to know the goods would be safe. They wanted him to prove the security of the route by taking it personally.

From the government's perspective, this event was too big to risk official intervention. Yerby was with the Special Operations Division, the black-ops group of the DEA. They were the only ones who risked off-the-book activities. It was easier to insulate these players from discovery—and from leaks—if they were all in one secure place.

For Yerby, that place was not Washington, D.C., with the rest of his colleagues. It was El Paso, Texas, from which the war on border incursions was being waged with an eye on arrest and prosecution. That never sat well with Yerby, a bounty hunter at heart who had grown up in Laredo, Texas, in the late 1960s. That was long before *terrorists* became the default word for religious and racial sociopaths. He had seen what fear could do to communities—fear of outsiders who brought desperation instead of hope, who brought illegal substances to stoke the rebelliousness of youth, who looked to infiltrate and erode instead of join and build. People on the outside, the well-meaning citizens in big cities, wanted to embrace and rehabilitate all the floundering souls whoever they were and however they entered the land. That was a nice thought, but that took time and money. And while a few souls fleeing monstrous poverty in Mexico might be saved, a greater number of young in America were lost: All it took was one desperate illegal with a backpack full of heroin to ruin a few dozen lives not just the junkies but the people they robbed to feed their habits or enlisted to share their addiction.

Yerby had escaped from the memories and impotence he felt by enlisting in the army. He had been raised by a widower auto-mechanic father who had a big home garden and taught him to put the eyes out of jackrabbits. Yerby displayed proficiency with long-range firearms and was one of the first snipers to be trained as such. Before that, according to the old-timers who had served in Vietnam, marksmen were just guys who could shoot really, really well. Most of them were singled out for sniping missions only after they were in-country. That changed in the mid-1970s when, following the trail blazed by the Marines in 1969, snipers were recruited, trained, and put in special units. Yerby served in one of those units. He spent time in the Sinai in 1980 as part of Operation Bright Star, training with Egyptian armed forces as a result of the Camp David peace accords signed the year before. There, he readily volunteered to help Egyptian officials capture a hashish boat smuggling along the eastern coast. Yerby liked that work. He liked it a lot. He liked seeing the men tried and hanged for their crime.

After that, he knew what he wanted to do with the rest of his life.

As far as everyone in his office knew, Yerby was on vacation right now. He had just turned fifty and no one begrudged "the geezer" the ample downtime his seniority had earned him. Of course, he was rarely on a real vacation. He preferred stakeouts like this one, where he could wait to take out some of the nastiest smugglers on earth.

Only DEA administrator Ryan Beit and deputy administrator Deborah Brook knew what he was really doing—and even that, unofficially. There were no e-mails, no phone conversations that could be recorded. Brook met Yerby at a roadside diner in Las Cruces, passed along what intel she had, and that was it. Yerby made his own "vacation" arrangements and every expense went on his own credit card, from the gas it took to drive here to renting the mountaintop aerie.

The world was so quiet here, so remote. Yerby wondered if this was the kind of place to which he would someday retire, a place where golden eagles soared and field mice jockeyed for survival.

If you ever retire, he thought. Bad people preying on the vulnerable or innocent would always rouse him from an easy chair —

All his senses sharpened as his eyes, adjusted to darkness, noticed motion on the ridgeline. He saw a short, stubby caterpillar of black, a crawling silhouette of humanity against the slightly dimmer black behind it.

He slid from his rock perch, picked up the rifle, and leaned forward on the boulder. He peered through the scope. Yerby melded almost organically with the weapon. The joints of his fingers, the skin of his fingertips, all found their familiar places on their own. His eye was on the green-tinted figures nearly one mile distant. Ironically, this was how he knew Hernandez: from grainy night-vision images obtained by the Mexican army —remarkably, the only group in that country waging a war on the powerful cartels. And that was really no more than a holding action, since the cartels were growing exponentially in wealth and power, and in the ruthless execution of that power.

Yerby watched the illegal immigrants move slowly. These were not the poor ones who paid an outrageous fee to be stuffed into trucks or the holds of boats. These were the poor ones who agreed to work for the Hernandez Cartel in exchange for safe passage. They were shown where the underground tunnel border crossings were. They were escorted by armed guards into the United States. They were met by guides who transported them to safe houses. Once they were shown the route they were expected to make three years of crossings, carrying drugs. During that time their families were watched back in Mexico. If the drugs did not arrive, the families were made to pay for the loss. Especially the daughters, whose mothers were given a choice: watch them be raped and killed, or have them sent into prostitution. If a mother chose the latter, she was spared having to witness the rape.

One reason Yerby's missions were typically off the books was that unlike drones that carried sophisticated target-ID software, his hits were instinctual. The target could be a decoy double. It could be a coincidental lookalike. That was why he had to act on solid intel that the individual he sought was on the move and in the vicinity. The good news was, right or wrong—and unlike drones—there was never collateral damage.

But Yerby had been doing this long enough to have a good instinct about whether the person in his sights was the person he wanted. No interaction with those around him, suggesting his elevated status. Persons in his group scanning the region for an ambush. A point man some distance ahead watching for tripwires or alarms; this group had two of them. The usual mule train that consisted of only two or three people, typically a man and two women, did not take those kinds of precautions.

Yerby was in no hurry. The ridgeline was the only clear spot to walk. To their left was a steep drop. To their right was a six-foot brick wall and a property owner who knew what took place on the other side and didn't want any part of it. He didn't even have security cameras, though Yerby could see a pair of mountings. No doubt someone had removed them on their way through the mountains at some point and probably left a dead animal in its place. That was the cartel way: offense with a sharp postscript.

Yerby focused on the man in the middle, tracking him as he walked. The elbow pads kept Yerby's sweater from tearing, allowed him a smooth and steady motion. The man walked tall, had what appeared to be new hiking shoes, and wore a firearm under his dark Windbreaker. The outline wasn't distinguishable but the bulge was unmistakable. And he wasn't wearing a backpack. If by some mischance the group was arrested, he could break off from them, say he had nothing to do with the smugglers. That was why Yerby shot people dead. Because guys like Hernandez always had a way of slithering from the fingers of the law.

The monster seemed absorbed in his footing, letting the others worry about his security. Yerby watched the man's gait. He couldn't make out any features, but the walk was the same as in the surveillance footage. The man raised and rode horses. He was slightly bowlegged. Yerby was confident—

There was a sound like a dry branch being snapped over a knee. Yerby felt a small fist of air on his left cheek an instant before his chin struck the top of the boulder. His face was dragged to the side, hard. The rifle tumbled from his grip as he slapped his hands out to brace himself. He tried to push off but found that he didn't have control of his head. It was lopsided and wouldn't move. He reached for it and felt something strange inside. His teeth had somehow shifted; no, they were loose and they were on his tongue—which hurt him. He tasted blood. He coughed as he finally inhaled, and blood clogged his throat.

All of that had happened in a few seconds. His face hurt. He picked up his left hand. It was weak and trembling violently. He let his hand drop to the rock, which felt sticky. He dragged his fingers toward his face.

What the hell happened? His only thought was that a bird may have struck him, possibly an owl thinking he was dinner.

His wriggling fingers reached his cheek, felt something that didn't belong. A beak? There were feathers—

He let his hand drop, tried to move his head but it was too heavy. The wind cooled his flesh, which was wet. But it wasn't raining. This didn't make sense and he found it difficult to focus.

Someone stepped beside him. He didn't know who it was because his face was turned the other way. He heard heavy breathing, as if someone had been running. He tried to turn but his head wouldn't obey.

"Help."

Yerby heard the word in his head. What came from his mouth, though, was just burbling. He saw light in front of him but the source was behind him. There were two flashes. In the distance he saw two pinpoints of light flare in return.

Oh, Christ, he thought. *They had a spotter.*

That was always a danger on these lone-wolf operations. He had to sleep sometime. It left him exposed if the criminal had been tipped off, or was simply overly cautious.

Yerby had done nightly circuits of the perimeter before taking his position. These guys were tunnel diggers, so a foxhole wouldn't have been a problem for them. Still, he hadn't seen anyone. He hadn't smelled food or waste products or tobacco or anything that would suggest someone was up here. He knew his skills weren't slipping. Someone was either better at skulking than he was, or luckier.

Yerby pressed his palms on the rock, pushed hard. He had to get up, get to his bowie knife, and at least inflict a wound on whoever was there.

He felt a hard rubber sole push down on the side of his head. His face was pressed to the stone, slamming the pain in harder. He cried out, but all that emerged was a throaty release of air. It blew a metallic taste into his nostrils: his own blood. He felt his teeth tumbling like hard candies in his mouth with every breath, every involuntary move of his tongue. His eye sockets ached. His eyes felt rigid. He was breathing roughly through his nose so he didn't swallow blood. His brain was finally processing the fact that he had been badly injured. Some corner of his mind was ticking off the little evidence he had. It hadn't been a bullet or knife that had taken him down. It was a shaft, an arrow. Sighted and fired at night, it was most likely a bolt from a crossbow. Cartel soldiers used those when they didn't want to make any noise.

Yerby felt someone feeling around his waist. He made an effort to reach down, stop it, but his hands were like empty gloves, limp and helpless. He felt himself being pulled on his left side, then his right. His cell phone was on his left hip. On his right

He heard a voice speaking a language he did not recognize. He couldn't place the language but he knew the name he heard: Hernandez. He felt spit land on the back of his neck. A moment later his entire body came electrically alive as the tip of a knife, probably his own— these bastards liked using a man's own weapons against him—was pressed to the spot where the spittle had landed. There were more words. He was glad he didn't know what was being said; it allowed him to collect his thoughts. Yerby actually savored the breaths that gurgled deep in his throat, the sudden numbness that filled the lower half of his face as though he were waiting for a root canal. The body was a marvelous machine, a guardian that protected itself from debilitating pain when it could. Except for that point of fire in his neck, he felt surprisingly all right.

But he didn't want to waste his last seconds running a self-diagnostic. His brain flashed to the wonderful people he had known. Juri, whom he would have married except for the fear that he would leave her a widow. Ryan Kealey, the CIA agent who had understood his approach and goals in the drug war and helped him to perfect his black-ops skills. Yerby sent a wordless wish to the agent, telling him how much he respected him, how grateful he was that Kealey's unofficial training of him had resulted in so many successful missions. He smiled, his expression frozen as the words stopped in his mind. He knew he only had a moment left. He made an effort to flop over, to dislodge the foot from his head, to put up some kind of struggle—

Yerby felt a fist of fire punch the base of his skull. The spotter leaned into the knife, the tip reaching to the vertebra of the wounded man. The pain caused Yerby to cry through his broken teeth, made his limbs stiffen and shake. He felt the blade cut downward along his spine, blood spilling over the sides of the wound. This was more pain than his body could handle; it didn't grow dull but just the opposite. Lightning raced to the small of his back, along his rib cage, down through his groin and into his thighs. He screamed horribly and kept screaming, twitching, flopping even as the cutting stopped between his shoulders. However much he wished it, the world refused to go black. It remained a bright, hideous red, like fireworks of blood exploding against the darkness. . . .

2

The killer left the knife protruding from the base of Yerby's neck. It took several minutes for the man to die, his struggles subsiding slowly like a fish in a canoe. It was partly the fault of the knife, so sharp that it made an incision like a paper cut, doing very little lateral damage. The man bled out slowly.

Not that Abejide minded. She had been out here since dawn, going wide of the house by making her way along the steep mountain slope. Though the woman was five foot eight she was extremely thin, moving with snake-like sinuousness below outcroppings and plentiful shrubs. Born in South Africa, as a youngster she had learned to avoid predators both animal and human; unless there was drought or famine, leopards and Cape buffalo were not typically as dangerous as packs of men who had been drinking.

Like many hunters, this man before her had been so confident of his location and arsenal, so sure of the actions of his enemies, so entrenched in his methods that he had not allowed for something outside his experience.

Under a blazing sun she had used binoculars to scan the area around the house. She had seen the spot where the man waited each night. The dirt was darker there, moist subterranean grains stirred by his footsteps. There was also a crushed anthill. She had also spotted a discarded branch where it did not belong, far from a tree and alone in the grasses. It had not been blown there: it had been used to erase the man's tracks.

While the target had slept she had picked her spot to the north. She had discovered the concrete foundation of a house that had never been finished and had lain behind one of the low walls. The huntress did not have any specific intelligence that someone would be watching for Hernandez, but he had enough respect for the DEA—and enough mistrust of his new allies—to be prepared for an ambush. From here, she had been able to watch the mule train's progress from the Santa Rosa Plateau. Another member of Hernandez's personal guard had been eyes-on from the Mexican border tunnel to the plateau, not watching the group but scanning any and all aeries as they made their way.

While the man before her died, the young woman checked his phone. She knew it wouldn't be locked. If Hernandez had changed his plans, someone would have had to pass that information along, and the man wouldn't have wanted to waste time typing or swiping a password.

There were a lot of names in the phone, and a lot of e-mail addresses with government domain names. Hernandez's tech team would find a great deal of value here.

The young woman took a photo with the phone. By the time anyone found the man, animals may have discovered him first. She wanted a record of the moment of death. She looked through the man's e-mail con-

tacts, found one from Homeland Security, attached the
photo but did not yet send. That was for Hernandez to
decide: the photos of the dead man with the shaft pro-
jecting from his bloody cheek, the knife in his back,
would cause a lot of DEA agents to get hot and want
revenge. When they cooled, though, or went home to
their families, they would have second thoughts about
the business they were in. In the end, there would be more
of them than any men and women roused to vengeance by
the murder. And of those who did want revenge, their
need for immediate gratification would cause them to
make mistakes.

She turned off the phone and put it in an aluminum-
lined pocket of her crossbow carrying case. If the phone
had a GPS signal, the metal would block it. Then she took
off her leather gloves. She did not want them to be bloodied. Abejide bent and yanked out the carbon-tipped
arrow. Though she made her arrows herself in their
Mexican armory, she did not want to leave any evidence behind. For all she knew, dirt particles from
Jalapa could have been trapped in the fletching, or
pollen from a plant that only grew in central eastern
Mexico. Why give American law enforcement a road
map?

The young woman said a few more words in Zulu.
She had commended the dying man's courage before
taking his life, a tradition among her people. She did
that even though Hernandez and his creatures found it
amusing. It kept her from becoming cocky and letting
down her guard. All enemies were formidable until
they were returned to the earth. Even a dying skunk
could choke the throat of a lion.

Abejide did not want to linger. She did not know if the man was supposed to check in with anyone, or they with him. She zipped up her case and slung it over her left shoulder. She had her own hunting knife in a sheath on her right leg. Taking a look through her night-vision binoculars, she did a full 360-degree turn to make sure no one had observed her, was observing her, or might observe her—in which case there would be more bodies on the mountaintop before she departed.

There was no one. That was one reason the agent had selected this spot. He could wait for his target in privacy.

Already the nocturnal predators smelled blood. While scanning the horizon she had spotted a mountain lion on the ridgeline to the east. She heard coyotes coming closer in the tall grasses. Insect scouts were beginning to make their way over and even mice were emboldened to leave their shelters under rocks. She wondered if the cat and coyote would fight for the corpse or whether the cowardly prairie wolves would wait until the superior hunter had finished. That was how it worked in South Africa. It probably worked that way here, too.

She glanced back as the big cat approached, alone and uncontested. She smiled. It would be easy to kill it. But that was not her way, as it was with so many so-called hunters. She enjoyed her work, the challenge of her work, and she did not do it for sport.

The hunt was orderly and respectful. It was not only about might and cunning and a complete awareness of one's surroundings. It was devoid of ego, of revenge.

That was why she was alive and this man was dead.

That was the way with true hunters.

Abejide shouldered her gear and set out to keep an eye on her employer's party as they headed for their rendezvous at Lake Elsinore at the foot of the mountains. She was looking forward to the next part of the mission, which would be a much bigger challenge with a far greater impact.

PART ONE
THE TARGET

CHAPTER ONE
BAGHDAD, IRAQ

Dina Westbrook hated the place. From the moment the door of the C-130 had opened two days before and the first wave of diesel-smelling air to now, there was nothing good about this place. Not even the intel she had come here to collect.

Scholars called this region the Cradle of Civilization. To the forty-four-year-old senior agent with ICE, Homeland Security's Immigration and Customs Enforcement agency—and to many of the military personnel who had served here, whose worldview no one ever asked—a different *c* word applied: the cesspool of civilization. That was not a reflection on the people but on the inhospitable terrain, fly-infested humidity with deep sandstorms the color of rust, streets often filled with bomb-sprayed blood and torn flesh that clung to the cobbles and asphalt, their odors baked in by the sun, and hatreds that dated back more than a thousand years.

It was not just a hothouse. It was a madhouse.

She knew she should be grateful that she was here in December and not July when the heat would have felt like rippling waves from a barbecue pit. However, her temporary office, in the section of the Green Zone fortress left to the CIA by departing embassy employees, was only a few hundred yards from the impossibly polluted Tigris River. Even with temperatures in the sixties, she was still being plagued by mosquitoes. The insects didn't keep twilight hours like their American counterparts. The air was quieter during the day and better for flight. The undersized bugs squeezed through the screens and tried to mass hungrily around her face and hands. She could only close the windows for a half hour before a dankness she detested turned the air of the room to soup. She slapped at a bug in the bangs of her short-cropped blond hair, then watched it fly giddily away.

There had been two days of waiting around, confined to the Green Zone because of security concerns. She'd refused to watch DVDs she could see back home. She was unwilling to talk to the remaining embassy personnel and other agents who could not tell her what they were doing any more than she could tell them why she was here. Two days of cursing the interrogations skill set and intuition that had made her reputation. She had almost completely transitioned to working on the American side of ICE's international counternarcotics operations, but her track record still ensured several trips per year to pits like this. Two days of looking online to see what type of work she might find in the private sector when she got back home. Two days of increasing claustrophobia.

Now, at last, Dina had permission to see the de-

tainee she had come to Baghdad to interrogate. It was
red tape that had held her up. The Iraqi Special Operations Forces had brought the man in. Their umbrella
organization was the Iraqi Counter-Terrorism Service.
However, the Service still had not been approved by
the Iraqi parliament after years of attempts, so whenever the Service had a major find of international significance to report, the question of whom to report it to
had to be debated all over again. The Iraqis had become increasingly disinclined to share information
with the Americans because of, according to the CIA's
suspicions, a drip-feed infiltration of the Iraqi military
by Al Qaeda. Their old enemy was newly reorganized
in Iraq and loaded up with weapons filched from the
Syrian conflict on the northwest border.

However, the CIA had allies in the Service, too, and
Dina was about to benefit from them.

The door to Dina's office opened and two Iraqi soldiers entered with the man she had come to see. A
translator entered behind them.

The detainee was an adult, unlike so many of the
prisoners she had seen in this area of the world. Most
of them had been boys still in their teens convinced
that they were in the process of earning their man-
hoods. This prisoner was about forty but Dina knew
better than to assume the age of his character matched
the age of his body. He was an Iraqi, short-bearded and
dressed in an orange jumpsuit. He was handcuffed in
front with a chain that connected to a leather waistband. That, in turn, dropped a chain to ankle bracelets.
The Red Cross had decided that the front-cuffing with
two connected pieces was the most comfortable for captives. Dina had no opinion about that. She didn't think

the man's scowling expression would have been changed by anything except a sackcloth over the head.

That's not politically correct, she cautioned herself. But that was what the new Iraq did to her. The sense of impending failure with this country they had fought so hard to make safe and decent, now rolling back to the same old ways—guns, drugs, and jihads—it stripped her of her training and left only her instincts. And her instincts were leading her away from anything that looked, sounded, or smelled "humane." She wished there were a U.S. military Moses who would emerge to smite the enemy and lead all these kids to the Land of Milk and Honey, once and for all time.

The man allowed himself to be placed in the chair in front of her desk. His dark eyes fixed on her pale, fair, blue-eyed face. The soldiers stood at ease on either side of him. The translator sat in a chair to the man's right, between him and the door.

There was a laptop open in front of Dina. She touched a button but did not break eye contact with the captive.

"You were captured driving a truck full of opium," she said, "on Highway 6 to Basra. Tell me about it."

When the translator finished the man just sat there, still staring.

Dina swung the computer around. "This is your settlement in the marshes near Amara, seen from a drone," she said. "We know there are opium stores. We know the enclave of five huts is yours. We know your wife and sons are home. You will cooperate or the buildings and the bales of drugs will vanish." She exploded her hands, fingers splaying.

The man didn't need the translator. He started talking.

Dina knew that the wetlands near Amara, about thirty miles from the border with Iran, had once been the home of the Marsh Arabs, a society largely ignored or reviled by mainstream Iraqis, especially because of tales of Persian blood in their veins. Having long suspected the quiet people of harboring insurgents, in the 1990s the Iraqi government burned the marshes and drained the water in an explicit effort to drive out the Marsh Arabs. It worked. They were scattered across Iraq, some into Iran, and the environment was devastated.

The Americans, arriving in 2003, decided to do the right thing and restore the valuable wetlands to their former state. The reeds grew high again, boatmen resumed paddling on the waterways, and the old tradition of building huts and houses from the reeds was revived. However, recently it had become apparent that only a small percentage of the new populace were members of the original Marsh Arabs. The others were taking advantage of the wetlands that were impossible to police, the border with Iran, the roads to Basra, and the poorly watched ports on the Persian Gulf, to do some highly lucrative business.

He was not trafficking the drugs, the detainee said, and he had no contact with anyone in Iran. He was storing the opium for the agent of someone who had connections in the Iranian plateau. He did not know who the men were or how they worked.

Dina studied him. The dominant stare was important and it belonged to her ice-blue eyes, not to him. She did not break it.

"I want you to take two of our people to the supply," she said.

The man stiffened, then spoke through the translator: "If I do that, I and my family will be killed."

"If you do not, the drugs will be destroyed. Now." She leaned forward slightly. "Unless you have a name of a contact that I can verify, right now. I'm going to be using this computer for something."

As the translator spoke the man seemed to deflate within his jumpsuit. He asked for water. One of the soldiers held a small plastic bottle with a straw for him. The large bottles could be used as clubs and a glass could be used to inflict wounds. Any bottle, overturned, could damage the computer. Hence, the straw.

The detainee thanked the woman. If he was hoping to gain her sympathy he was wrong. The opium trade helped to fund the Iranian government as well as Al Qaeda. It paid for weapons and it involved cartels that transported those weapons along with the drugs.

"I only know the man who comes to my home," he said. "The agent."

"Is he Iraqi or Iranian?"

"He is from Ferdows," the man replied.

That was a relatively populous city in the Iranian plateau.

"He comes across the border how?" Dina asked.

"I do not know," the man said. "I meet him on the road, Road 13, near the border. He drives a truck."

"And you bring him to your boat."

"Yes, we unload the opium to my boat. Three days later I drive to Basra. I only drive opium. No weapons, no people, opium only."

Dina noted the extra information.

"Describe his truck, the exact meeting place, and when it is due," she said. She turned the laptop around and put her fingers over the keyboard.

"Please," the man said—in English.

Dina grinned. "Don't worry. I won't touch the 'attack' button by mistake."

The man appeared thoughtful, then shook his head vigorously. "If I tell you what you want, they will do unspeakable things to my family."

"Amazing." Dina's expression hardened. "These people will torture your wife and children . . . but you hate us."

"You are *kaafir*," he replied without hesitation.

Disbelievers. It was better to read the Koran and kill other readers of the Koran than to accept help from Christians. This world was mad.

"I understand your concern, and these monsters will not know you've told me anything," Dina assured him, focusing on the task at hand. "The drug traffic will not be stopped and the personnel who run it will not be assaulted. We wish to watch them, nothing more."

"'Watch,'" he said dubiously. "Like an eagle eyes a field mouse."

"No," Dina said. "Like a nation that doesn't want weapons of mass destruction on its shores."

That was true. The route was all that mattered, a route that might one day ferry nuclear materials or biotoxins to the United States, regardless of this pawn's fervent faith that no weapons were ever transported.

The man took a sip from the water bottle. His mouth was twisted, his expression pinched. His eyes said, *If I had poison, I would rather take it than help you.*

"Make your choice," Dina said.

"It is a green MAZ dump truck," he said. "The driver is named Abda Larijani."

The translator confirmed the spelling and Dina typed the information into the computer. MAZ was the Minsk Automobile Plant, where Russia had produced heavy road vehicles for decades.

"When is the next pickup?" she asked.

He hesitated again. "How will you do your 'watching'?"

"I'm not free to discuss that," she replied.

"Your drones . . . are not silent. He will know."

"The driver will know nothing," she said. "This will never be traced to you. Whether you believe it or not, we don't want anything bad to happen to your family."

He nodded toward the laptop. "Is that why you were ready to kill them?"

"We don't want anything to happen to our families, either."

The man seemed to accept that. "He comes the night after tomorrow. Shortly after sunset."

The man described the drop site and Dina sent the information to the 134th Cavalry Reconnaissance and Surveillance Squadron of the Nebraska Army National Guard. They were in charge of RSTA—reconnaissance, surveillance, and target acquisition—for this particular mission. They would have "tail-running" surveillance on the ground by jeep, out of sight from the truck. The truck would also be tracked by satellite. Stops, contacts, and routes would be carefully marked. The truck and everyone who had any contact with it would join the Active Target Surveillance program at the National Reconnaissance Office, meaning there would be eyes and ears on everyone 24/7 until the full reach and activities of the smuggling system were understood. The route would not be obliterated until they picked up a weapon of mass destruction or a component thereof. Squashing them now would only send the surviving players elsewhere.

Dina swung the laptop around so the detainee could see it again. She pressed a button and a green sign that said ENDED flashed across the image. The surveillance went down. The prisoner did not seem relaxed; he had, after all, just ratted out a deadly ally. But he had averted what he thought was a more immediate danger. It wasn't, of course. Dina never had any control over the drone. It had been sent there to coerce their guest, nothing more.

Dina told the man he would be released after his information had been confirmed. She followed that with several minutes of silence while she stared at him. The man, at first relieved to know the worst was over, began to exhibit signs of renewed anxiety. *Still some water left in this bottle,* Dina thought. *Just need to put the straw in the right place.*

"No weapons?" she asked.

He was adamant that never had he transported or seen any weapons, aside from the machine gun that of course the driver must carry for self-defense.

"And no people," she said.

"No, no, no, no," he stated.

She leaned forward. "I think you have been transporting terrorists," she said.

"No, I have not!"

"It's not possible that no people should ever take advantage of this route," she said. "I think we will have to keep you until we hear the truth."

She stood as if to leave.

The man howled. She had a flash of sympathy for him. He was now in a position of trying to prove what could not be proven.

"Only one man," the detainee cried out.

"From Iran?" she asked.

"Yes, from Iran, he was a doctor, one week ago. I drove him to Basra, that is all I know."

She recognized the look of a broken man. She knew he had given her all he had. Her intuition was satisfied. She ordered the soldiers to lead him away.

Alone, Dina exhaled. Only now she realized how much she had perspired, how uncomfortable she truly was, how tense that session had been. She never doubted that she would get the information she wanted; now that she had it, though, she could relax. She alerted Homeland Security's Office of Counternarcotics Enforcement about any Iranian doctors who might be involved in the opium trade; they would get the message to all other agencies. Then she shut down her laptop, planning on finding a shower and some anti-itch ointment.

The phone on the desk pinged. Two seconds and she would have been out the door. She sighed and picked it up. It was Lt. Gen. Alan Sutter, commander of the American army units that were conducting, so they said, training missions in Iraq. It wasn't his aide or a lower-ranking officer, but the lieutenant general himself.

"Ma'am, since we have the good fortune of entertaining you here a little longer, might we trouble you with one more matter?"

They sure were polite when they wanted to skip protocol and ask a favor of Homeland Security.

But before she could decide whether to wiggle out of it, he said, "We've picked up an American soldier who's been lost in Iraq for sixteen years."

CHAPTER TWO

NEW MILFORD, CONNECTICUT

Ryan Kealey stood on the windswept hillside look-ing out across gently moving treetops. This mild weather on the East Coast seemed more an extension of fall than the beginning of winter, so he was dressed in a tweed blazer, his black hair nearly to the collar—though it was not touching the collar just now. It was blowing gently to the left. Beside him was a slender, older woman with deeply wrinkled skin and eyes younger than his.

"See that blue ridge out there?" Ellie Lammer asked him.

Kealey followed her bony finger. Behind the green hills was a faint line of cliffs against the pale blue sky. "I see it."

"Those are the Catskills."

"In New York State?" he said.

Her head nodded beneath the long, blowing expanse of her white hair. "It's the Taconic Range."

"Wow." He smiled. Every night, wherever you were,

most of the Earth's population could see light-years
into space. Yet to see something closer, just a few hundred miles distant, seemed exceptional. Maybe because from here, the view was unique. You owned it.

Kealey had seen the FOR SALE sign while he was
driving south on Route 7, on his way back from forty-
eight hours in Boston. Something about the road
leading up and up called to him. Maybe it was because it was a Saturday morning, an ideal time for
wandering. Or maybe it was the idea of home. The
longest Kealey had ever been anywhere was when he
left the CIA, got a teaching gig, and bought a three-
story house in Cape Elizabeth, Maine. He spent three
years there with Katie Donovan. Unlike this fine Connecticut home from the 1980s with its iron columns
and hand-hewn wood beams, that old place in Maine
defined *fixer-upper*. He had enjoyed doing the work
himself, for himself and Katie. When that ended—

"You didn't say where you're from," Ellie remarked.

"D.C.," he said.

"Ah," Ellie smiled. "The hub of things."

"Yeah, it's the hub of the world all right," he said
with more than a trace of irony. "At least, that's what
they think. Most of them have no idea what it really
means to be plugged into something big. I had a house
in Maine, once. That was nice. But it was more a case
of me taking pity on it and giving myself something to
do with my hands." He looked at the little lady who
was a head shorter than his athletic five foot eleven.
"Tell me—you've been here thirty years. What have
you learned from this place?"

"That I am something big," she replied. "I am a part
of all this. We have fifty acres here and the land behind

us was my late husband's airstrip. He built bridges. He would fly to a job site, then fly home. Even though he was up there in his plane with the clouds and hawks, he said he never felt better than when he was on this ground with the little hummingbirds at eye level. When I flew with him I got—oh, I guess you'd call it some kind of perspective. But it's like an iron, the kind you use for clothes. It has weight and it has potential but until the wire goes in the wall it's not really active."

Kealey had perspective, too. He'd been around the world, in more places of natural beauty and ancient hostility than he cared to remember, from South Africa to Iran. All those journeys left him with was a severe case of dark, clinging cynicism.

"Why are you leaving, then?" Kealey asked. "Memories?"

"No," she said. "Snow. I can't work the damn plow and on social security I can't afford to have someone do it or help keep up the half mile of dirt road. I won't lie to you, it gets rutted and the gravel rolls away when there are gully washers. I'm going to Sedona, Arizona, to join my younger sister in her New Age shop." She glanced at his hand. "If I'm not prying—well, I am—I don't see a ring. You got a girl . . . or a guy? I guess you have to ask that now."

"I'm sort of seeing someone," he said. "She's a psychiatrist but she doesn't want to leave Washington."

"Good business to be in there, I guess."

"Very."

"You want to leave."

"I already have," he said. "I just don't know where I'm going."

"This is a good place to find yourself," she said. "I'm not trying to sell you on it. That's just a fact."

Kealey couldn't disagree. The woods in front of him were vital and nurturing. The house behind him, a boxy contemporary, reminded him of the pillboxes on Normandy Beach, built to keep trouble at bay without making you feel like you were a prisoner. And the airstrip behind the house, though overgrown from neglect, was a long stretch of calm. He had not gone over to the hangar, which reminded him of one of those old airship shelters from the age of the zeppelin. This was the kind of place where, he was sure, if he closed his eyes he would hear the hum of long-silent propeller engines. . . .

"I desperately want to leave D.C.," he said. "I was interviewing for a teaching job in Boston, but I realized I don't want to go from one bureaucracy to another. I need to find something else."

"What kind of work did you do there?"

"Intelligence."

"We could use a good home security store in town," she said. "Not that you need anything up here. I've got a shotgun but I've never had to chase anyone off. Hell, I've never even locked my door."

Kealey took his cell phone from his shirt pocket to take photos.

"Reception's pretty good here," Ellie said.

"You're close enough to orbiting satellites," Kealey joked.

"I'm told I could see them if I knew where to look," she said. "I have broadband and a TV dish on the roof. All the modern whatnots. I also have chipmunks, deer, and you can see thunderstorms coming from up here like no one's business!"

"Yin and yang," Kealey said with a grin.

The breeze and morning sun felt good on his face and scalp. It was strange. The last time he talked to anyone about the Maine house was with Allison Dearborn. They were out at the aquarium at the harbor in Baltimore when the convention center became the epicenter of a terrorist attack. He came alive then, too, but in a different way—prepared to enter a crime scene, weaponed-up, ready to take down terrorists and free hostages.

This way, breathing wondrously clean air, was preferable. It had nothing to do with feeling physically safe. He never expected to be injured when he went into combat; his brain was too adrenaline-pumped for that. It didn't have to do with being in his early forties and feeling a little stiffer after each run through a burning building or wheel-wrenching drive through a kill zone.

Being here even for—what had it been, a half hour?—wasn't about a life lived in response to some monstrous act that a demented soul had perpetrated. It had to do with being in the presence of something larger, as Ellie had said. It had to do with being nourished instead of drained.

Could he stand that? Allison had told him—when they were shrink and patient instead of lovers—that he needed extreme challenges. He didn't know if he needed them but he certainly thrived in that environment. He liked it more than dealing with the directors, deputy directors, assistant directors, secretaries, and undersecretaries in the nation's capital, all of whom were grabbing people and glory as if national security were a game of jacks. It was about power first and the populace second. And then there was the lame-duck administration that had only a few months left of its spotty eight years. Everyone was busy networking for new jobs on a grand scale, looking for work instead of doing it. The district was politically calm but structurally chaotic, like a corpse full of maggots that would suddenly erupt—

He focused on clouds that were changing the light and color on the trees below them. He wanted to think about that right now, not about the mausoleum to the south.

He liked Allison a lot and enjoyed being with her. He liked the work he did because he had just enough ego to appreciate having the fate of a major metropolis or somebody's loved one resting on his shoulders. But after a score of years on the job he was out of gas. And he didn't know where a refill was coming from.

"Would you like coffee?" Ellie asked.

"Yes, thank you," he said. "I also want to ask you something."

"Yes?"

"Can I look at the hangar?"

"Of course. Do you fly?"

"Not a bit," he said. "But I'm thinking this would be the time and place to learn."

They had coffee on the stone patio overlooking the Housatonic Valley and talked about her husband, Douglas, who had died in a fall from a bridge in Tennessee.

"Going that way would have pleased him, if he hadn't hit his head first and been unconscious all the way down," she said without remorse. "We had fifty-two glorious years, partly because he was away so much. I don't say that to be flip or derogatory. We never had a chance to get tired of each other. A few months together and then, bam! He was off somewhere else."

"No children?" Kealey asked.

"We both didn't think it was fair, with him being away so much," she said. "And I didn't mind. The animals in the forest were my babies, just like in a Disney cartoon. I can't tell you how many generations of rabbits I fed in the warren behind the house. Left the dead ones for predators." She shrugged. "They have to eat, too. That also left me free to go with Douglas when it was a place I wanted to visit. I loved taking pictures, scrapbooking—though it wasn't called that, then. It was just putting photos in an album with other keepsakes and labeling them."

That kind of verbal bloat was true in his business, too, Kealey thought. When he came to the CIA, the words *spy* and *spook,* not *intelligence agent* and *surveillance specialist,* were still the common vernacular. He missed those days when people were tracked by eye and not by a GPS in their cell phone. It was also more efficient, then. People on the ground were trained to observe. They came back with more data, more detail, not just an individual's location. The overwhelming reliance on ELINT, electronic intelligence, covered more ground and let fewer people watch more people—like the government did through e-mails and social networking sites. But it lost nuance. Only the Israelis did both in equal measure, ELINT and HUMINT, making sure the faces of trackers were seen so they could become trusted, even embraced by their targets. Terror cells could be broken that way, or by blasting them with a drone missile. The Israeli way made sure there was little or no collateral damage.

Kealey was about to tell the woman he wanted to buy the place when his phone beeped.

"Well, at least you've got reception," Ellie grinned.

"Not sure I want it," Kealey said as he glanced at the name. It was Jonathan Harper, deputy director of the CIA. Kealey's mood darkened and his brain mumbled something about leaving him the hell alone. But he stepped away from Ellie until she wouldn't be able to hear him and pressed Answer just the same, with his bloody damn sense of responsibility.

He suddenly, fervently wished that he was not about to hear the word *situation* used in a sentence. If Harper said that, it meant his call was about something grave, something he did not want to discuss over an unsecured line.

"Hello, Jonathan."

"Morning, Ryan. How're things?"

"I've had a good few weeks," he replied. "How's Julie?"

Juliette Harper, Jon's wife, was seriously injured in the convention center explosion in Baltimore.

"Recovering nicely," Harper said. "She's got a cane but she's walking on her own."

"Glad for her," Kealey said sincerely. "What can I do for you?"

"I need to talk to you about a situation," Harper said.

Kealey inwardly cursed. Outwardly, he said, "I'm retired. For real, this time. I'm about to buy a house."

"Do you remember Victor Yerby?" Harper asked.

"Yeah. He got reprimanded for frying a warlord's

opium field in Bawri, Afghanistan," Kealey said with a proud half smile. The man had guts. "Please don't tell me something's happened—"

"Let's have a face-to-face," Harper said.

Crap. Kealey had been assigned to Yerby as an instructor for a week once, to hone his sharpshooting skills. He'd liked and admired the man so much, he took ten days of vacation to train Yerby in return, taking him through all the black-ops tactics a formal, advanced course would have provided, plus a number of secrets it wouldn't. He knew Yerby was a lone-wolf kind of guy, like Kealey himself, and never expected to hear much news of him after that, but rejoiced when he did. The opium field story was one of his favorites.

But Kealey knew lone wolves had limited futures. Ultimately they were always arrested, taken hostage, or killed. There was never any other kind of life. Since DHS wasn't Harper's bailiwick, Kealey was guessing it was either a hostage situation or the murder of Yerby, something that had international repercussions involving the intelligence community.

"I'll be in your office tomorrow morning," Kealey said.

"Not soon enough," Harper replied. "Where's the nearest airfield?"

Kealey looked behind him. "About fifty yards from where I'm sitting. Small plane or chopper?"

"Whichever you like."

He surveyed the weedy landing strip and surrounding trees. "I think a chopper will have a better time of it."

"I'll arrange it."

"I'll get the details and send them over," Kealey told him.

Kealey was frustrated as he clicked off. A crisis, he could probably ignore. But not the plight of a brother agent. Too many people had helped Kealey, saved his life over the years, for him to be callous.

He walked back to Ellie. "I would like to buy this place."

She smiled.

"But," he continued, "it's going to have to wait a few hours. And I need to borrow your airstrip. Can you give me the address here so I can Google Earth a map to my colleague? And can I leave my car?"

Nonplussed but gracious about it, she told him his car would be welcome and gave him the information, which he sent over to Harper. The deputy director would send a small chopper out of New Haven, most likely. Something with a maximum range of four hundred miles could make both legs of the trip without stopping to refuel.

Kealey told Ellie that he didn't have a check to make a deposit but he noted the woman's bank information and told her he would transfer funds before the day was out. He said he would trust her to get the paperwork in order while he was away. He didn't think he would be gone very long.

"Are you always this impulsive?" she asked.

"Not by choice," he laughed. Kealey thought about the many times he had had to make a decision on the fly that meant life or death for anyone from one to one million people. Yes, he was impulsive. "In this case, I'd call it being certain of something," he smiled. "I don't get that a lot in my life."

"I see."

"Do you always trust strangers with your personal finance accounts?" he asked.

"You just met my airstrip and you're already trying it out. If that's not a sign of loving this place, what is?"

Kealey laughed at that. "I'm guessing you've damned a few torpedoes in your life, too," he said.

"Not as many as I wish I had," she said. "But there's still time left. Well, you've picked a good anchor for a new life." She glanced behind her. "This home has been a rock for me."

They finished their coffee and watched the clouds. Within the hour they could hear a helicopter coming in low from the south. Kealey hugged Ellie good-bye as the Bell 429 set down among the tall, wheat-like grasses. He ran over, climbed aboard, and loved the house and grounds all over again as he lifted off.

Like General MacArthur departing the Philippines, he found himself vowing that he would return . . . and soon.

CHAPTER THREE

BAGHDAD, IRAQ

"He's allowing me to sit in on one of his sessions?" Dina Westbrook asked incredulously as she walked down the hall with Lieutenant General Sutter.

"Gave us permission in writing," replied the compact, impeccably courteous officer. "After he made his decision, I think the psychologist felt she had no choice, so she agreed, too."

"Very helpful of him," Dina mused. "Almost too helpful."

"As if he's going out of his way to show he has nothing to hide?"

"It would make sense if he's been turned."

"I will say, over the past two weeks we confined him to barracks and the mess hall while we discussed what to do, and we did decide that he was a hero, not AWOL. The Pentagon notified me this morning."

"A hero and not AWOL, for sixteen years."

"Yes."

"I'm not sure what I can add to that decision, sir." She was subtly chiding him for wasting her time, and she intended for him to know it.

He picked up on it. "It was a strategic decision, ma'am. If he has been turned, we're more likely to discover that in a man who's being treated like a hero instead of a deserter. That's why he's been in evaluation for two weeks, and we'll be shipping him stateside soon, where he can be monitored by the Warrior Transition Brigade."

"And you want my opinion?"

"Your reputation for reading people is legendary, and I don't use that word lightly."

"All right," Dina said with a smile. He was trying so hard, after all. "Give me the thumbnail sketch."

"In March of 1998 Chaplain Major James Phair left his forward post with the Twenty-Fourth Infantry Division in the midst of a massive assault against an Iraqi Republican Guard tank division. According to what he has told our psychologist, he slipped away to minister to the spiritual needs of wounded Iraqis being carried into an abandoned government office. A bomb exploded on the building. We listed him as missing in action and presumed dead. Apparently, all this time he has been ministering to Iraqis of every stripe. He's been working with Sunnis, Shiites, Yazidis, various Christian sects like the Nestorians. He's learned their customs, faiths, and their languages."

"So if he hasn't been turned, he's a remarkably valuable asset," Dina confirmed.

"Like money can't buy," the lieutenant general said, then smiled at his lapse in military enamel. "Two weeks ago, an Irish Guardsman discovered the chaplain in

Basra, where he was helping South Korean Christian missionaries feed orphaned children. There was a suicide bombing, and afterward a metal detector registered the dog tags he was wearing around his waist. They brought him to us."

"And you made him a hero."

"Personally, ma'am, I think he is one."

He had finally fallen for her bait. That was exactly what she'd been trying to ascertain.

"It's just down this hall," he said, and began to turn a corner. She put a hand on his arm to stop his stride, then faced him in the hall.

"What does the psychologist think about it?"

"She's refused to summarize her assessment until after this last session."

"Any reason why she'd be swayed one way or another?"

"Well," Sutter thought. "I think she's starting to feel guilty."

"For what?"

"Ma'am, have you heard of the controversy about General George Patton's treatment of a certain soldier in 1943?"

"Doesn't ring a bell."

"A battle-fatigued private in Sicily was refusing to go back to the front, so Patton slapped him across the face. Patton was relieved of combat command for a year for it. I've heard Major Dell, the chaplain's psychologist, refer to our pharmaceuticals as a 'slap.'"

Dina nodded. "The Army Medical Corps doesn't have the time or personnel to handle all the PTSD—"

"Experienced by one in four soldiers in Iraq."

"So they medicate."

"One-third are back on the field in a week. One-half are back within a month."

"And it's wearing on her. On you, too."

The lieutenant general looked shocked, vulnerable. Then he sealed the enamel back on. "Major Dell is part of a team that we all are hoping can find a better answer."

"Good, thank you for informing me of her perspective. What medications has she prescribed for the chaplain?"

"None."

"None at all? Has anyone prescribed anything for him?"

"He hasn't appeared to need any."

"After sixteen years in Iraq?" Dina's eyebrows rose.

"In the worst of situations and through repeated traumatic crises, yes, ma'am."

Dina's eyebrows remained raised as she walked with the lieutenant general down the corridor.

"If there's a crash coming for him . . ." she started.

"It'll be off the charts," Sutter finished her thought.

He stopped her at the psychologist's door. She assembled a neutral face before he knocked.

During the introductions, Dina casually but openly regarded Chaplain Major Phair. He was nearly six feet tall, with a slight slump in his shoulders. He was shaved and groomed, his salt-and-pepper hair cut close. He was a little thin, as one might expect after all he'd been through. There was caution in the slow but constant movement of his eyes, which was also to be expected. He had not been among fellow Americans, or military protocol, for a long time. His shake was gentle, also to be expected from a pastor. His hands were badly calloused and that was a surprise to Dina. The lieutenant general excused himself and the majors sat down opposite each other while the agent sat to one side.

"We're going to be talking at greater length in the States," the psychologist said to Phair, "but I wanted to give us one more chance to meet here before we go back."

She likes him, Dina thought. But she also gave credit to Maj Amanda Dell, a dark haired woman with congenital shadows around her eyes, for being shrewd. A patient with the feel of a beloved place around him can remember more details, or drop his guard, however one preferred to view it.

"How long have you been here?" Phair asked the psychologist.

"Three years."

He considered her answer. "That's a long time, if you don't want to be in a place."

"Indeed it is," she said. "I can't wait to go home. What about you?"

"I miss my friends," he offered.

"In America?"

He smiled. "My friends are all here."

There was a strange, halting quality to his voice. He had mostly spoken just Arabic and dialects for years.

Major Dell made notes in a folder that lay open on her desk. Nothing was keyed into computers during sessions. The electricity was too unreliable.

Dina wondered if she was writing about his expressions of belonging and longing. Those were two of the three qualities that suggested someone had been turned, in the lexicon of covert operations. Dina guessed Major Dell would not make explicit mention of that fact in her notes, however. Even a hint of brainwashing or Stockholm Syndrome could ruin a life and career.

"Then you consider Iraq your home?" Major Dell asked.

"It's where I've lived for so long," he replied.

"Do you still regard yourself as American?"

"Of course," he said.

The response, stated emphatically, carried a lot of weight in his favor. Dina watched Dell make another note.

"When the soldiers found you, you asked to be reunited with that family before you left . . ." The psychologist flipped through her notes.

"The Bulanis," he said, smiling.

She found her notes on the subject. "You didn't seem to want to say much about them when we first met."

"I didn't want to say much about anything," he said. "I felt a little lost."

"Will you tell me more now?"

"What would you like to know?"

"Do you miss them so much?"

"That, and I wish I could have helped them more," he said sadly. "They were among the first people I met. I made"—he stopped and seemed to search for the word—"a crutch for their boy. His foot was gone. I made a strong one from two discarded table legs." He smiled. "When he was sitting, he used it like a cricket bat, hitting rocks and shards of brick."

"How old was he?"

"Four, then."

"You stayed in touch during the entire time you were there?"

"We were together a great deal. Raheem is Sunni, originally from Algeria. His wife, Shada, is Shiite. They had to move frequently as militias came and went. We often traveled together."

"When was the last time you saw him?"

"Last month," Phair said. "He is a driver. He has a nice little business, which I suggested to him."

"Whom does he drive?"

"Iraqi soldiers," Phair said. "They go home every week with their pay."

Dell paused to read her notes. "You were not in a good way when the Irish soldiers found you."

"Not physically."

"Yes, I should have been clearer," she said. "You were in the back room of a soup kitchen—"

"That was when the explosion occurred," he said. "They found me in the front room. I was trying to help poor Kim. Have you ever seen a child make snow angels?"

The woman nodded.

Phair said, "That was what she was doing. In her own blood."

The woman stopped nodding. She looked at her file.

Dina put her fingertips to her lips as if she were thinking. The movement surprised her. It was an old tell revealing that she'd had an emotional reaction. She'd trained hard to wipe all such tells from her system and hadn't exhibited one in years. Something about the chaplain was getting to her.

"Before you arrived at the soup kitchen," the psychologist continued, after a decent pause, "your trek to Basra had subjected you to hunger, dehydration, heat, cold, the elements, and occasional abuse. Also malaria and several forms of the flu. And you were nearly killed when someone from a Sunni neighborhood noticed you and followed you."

"Yes, I was wearing the clothes of the Kurdish Peshmerga."

"They took you prisoner and would have executed you, but you escaped."

She paused again. Dina realized that she was trying to find a new way to ask a question she'd tried before. Had he said how he escaped from the Sunnis? If not, that would certainly explain why the military brass doubted whether he had escaped at all . . . or if he had been turned by them and planted back with the Americans.

The silence continued. Eventually Dell asked, "Why didn't you leave Basra after you escaped from the Sunnis?"

"Because I had—a mission," he said. "I was being exposed to the many faces of God. I was not yet finished with my study."

Dell looked over the typed report from the unit that had discovered him. "This says you were found in the street. How did you get there?"

"With help from a Kurd I didn't know who had heard of my plight and risked his life. How ironic," he said. "He never would have helped me thinking I was Catholic. Or American. Yet I am the same person as the man in the Kurdish clothes."

"You would have helped him, though, in a similar situation?"

"Of course," Phair said.

"What happened after that?" she asked. "You could have fled."

"They were looking for me," he said. "I might have fled right to them. So I pretended to be homeless until they stopped searching. So many are homeless now, you see. I knew no one would notice me. But a few days later the Irish soldiers did."

"You were wearing your dog tags," Dell said.

"Yes." He absently rubbed the flat of his fingers across his waist.

"Why?"

"In case anything happened to me," he replied. "I wanted someone to know. They would have been sold in a curio shop and made their way back, eventually."

"You were wearing them on your belt, tucked inside," she noted. "Were you afraid they'd be seen around your neck?"

"That was one reason," he said. "Did you know that Herod the Great carried his bona fides around his waist, and not his throat?"

"I did not," she said. "Was he your inspiration?"

"No. He feared someone would use them to strangle him. I was not. I had a rosary attached to the chain when I first started out. It made me feel closer to God, though I'm not sure He would have appreciated the location. Still, He knew what was in my heart."

"You didn't have the rosary when they found you."

"No," he said. "It broke while I was running from a militia and fell through my pant leg. Perhaps God had the final say after all."

"You still sound as though you wish the Irish Guardsmen hadn't found you."

He sighed. "Part of me was ready to come back. I had run out of resources."

"Physical?"

He nodded. "To have any significant impact here requires money and more hands and hearts. And—something else. I don't know what." The forty-five-year-old grinned. "It certainly requires someone who is a little more rested than I am."

"You can continue to do your original job, now that you're back."

He managed to sustain the grin. "Do you think they'll let me?"

"That depends," she said.

"On what?"

She replied, "On how badly you want it."

"That is the question, isn't it?" he said. His eyes slid to Dina Westbrook.

Later, after the chaplain left, Dina discussed the situation with Major Dell.

"Spiritually," the psychologist said, "I have never met anyone who is more plugged in. He has squeezed every bit of religious and cultural juice from the sects he has encountered, but without taking on any of the political pulp. I would say that of course he feels lost, being removed from what he perceives are his spiritual roots."

"But is the air of being lost just a cover for patience and a plan?" Dina queried.

"I don't think so, but honestly, it will take much more time to find the bottom of this man. He is a deep well."

"All right," Dina said. "How about we make sure you are assigned to the Warrior Transition Brigade when you get back to the States, so that eventually you can continue to work with him?"

"I would very much appreciate that." It was clear that Dell was covering an even more enthusiastic response.

They shook hands, and the psychologist walked Dina to the door. "Do you believe him?" Dell ventured.

Dina started to raise her hand to her lips but stopped. "I'm prepared to withhold judgment," she said, almost to herself. Then she smiled brightly.

CHAPTER FOUR
LANGLEY, VIRGINIA

The old reality was back.

It only took a few minutes for the chopper to rattle the magic dust from Kealey. His thin mantle of peace fell away as they followed Route 7 and then picked up I-95 and traced it south. The noise and shaking weren't bad as helicopters went, and the fuel smell was no worse than he could have expected. But the sight of the traffic, the industry, New York and Philadelphia— they were all the world he had wanted to leave behind. The change from power-down mode to plugged in felt like he was pulling a dusty, ratty, indigent coat from the closet. It fit like a second skin but it wasn't what he wanted to be wearing.

By the time they touched down at Langley Air Force Base in Virginia, Kealey was back at war with himself: this-is-my-duty versus I-don't-want-to-do-this-anymore. Only now that he had tasted clarity, the cacophony was maddening. The sound of the aircraft arriving and departing, the vehicles roaring and thumping across the tarmac, the haze in the air where he knew the city of Washington, D.C., was lurking—all of it was oppressive. He felt Ryan Kealey starting to backslide into ryan kealey, a mere cog in a big machine. He had to pull that old coat around him, button it up, polish up his skills and achievements like the coat's buttons, to retain a sense of his personhood.

It was a necessary machine, his left brain reminded him. A machine that keeps totalitarianism at bay.

His right brain felt only burnout. Allison had warned him about this day.

Kealey was surprised to find Harper waiting for him on the tarmac. The deputy director had a golf cart and a civilian driver. He looked ten years older, thirty pounds lighter, and a couple of inches shorter than the last time they had been together. The toll of the convention center attack was different on him than it had been on his wife, Julie. And then there was the pressure of the job. . . .

"No luggage?" Harper asked.

"Back in my car," Kealey replied. "It was my to-go bag."

That was the bag Kealey kept packed for sudden trips. Its contents duplicated all the essentials he had at his place down here.

"We're only going over to the JIB," Harper said.

Kealey did not ask, "And then . . . ?" Whenever a government official met you at an airstrip, it meant they did not intend for you to stay very long.

Kealey did not want another mission. By God, he did not want one.

The JIB was the Joint Intelligence Building. During the Cold War, the nondescript, two-story brick structure was a staging area for Emergency Rapid Responders. That was a relatively benign name for the flight crews designated to evacuate key officials from the capital to secret bunkers built deep in Maryland's Blue Ridge Mountains. With the fall of the Soviet Union and the downsizing of the air force, evacuation operations were consolidated at nearby Andrews Air Force Base. The building at Langley was given over to DHS.

The two upstairs floors were for monitoring everything from e-mails to cell phone calls to websites and blogs. Only two desks were needed to monitor news sources worldwide, down from half a floor just two years before. The basement, formerly the communications center for the ERR teams, was where the influx and analysis of joint field intelligence operations took place. That was where Harper took Kealey via an elevator, the shaft of which was built to withstand a nuclear detonation, literally. They went to a small conference room that had dark monitors on every wall. There were laptops on the rectangular table. None of them were turned on. The only other object on the table was a briefcase.

The driver had accompanied them and Harper asked him to get coffee.

"What can I get you, sir?" the driver asked Kealey.

"A Get Out of Jail card," Kealey smirked. "I'm okay, thanks. I had a water on the chopper. What's your name?"

The young man snapped a look at Harper to make sure it was okay. "Solomon Gill," he said.

"Pleased to know you," Kealey said with a knowing smile.

"He's a good man," Harper said when the driver had left. "Wants to be a field agent."

"What is he, twenty two?"

"Twenty-three," Harper said.

"Fresh out of which Ivy League school?"

"Princeton," Harper said. "Doing a lot of recruiting there now."

Of course, Kealey thought. Director Robert Andrews went there. "Well, it's good to see the bright, enthusiastic new blood. Remind you of you?"

Harper grinned. "I wasn't hungry, I was patriotic."

Harper had begun his career as a young analyst working the Soviet desk, but it wasn't long before the smart, intuitive young man had found his way into the Operations Directorate. By the mid-1980s he was running agents behind the Iron Curtain and arranging for the safe passage of a few defectors whose positions within the Committee for State Security made them valuable assets to the CIA.

"You were pretty ambitious back then, too," Harper noted.

Harper had intentionally understated that one. Kealey had joined the U.S. Army as soon as he was able and fast-tracked it to the rank of major in eight years. He had a chest full of medals to show for it: the Distinguished Service Cross, the Legion of Merit with one Oak Leaf Cluster, the Bronze Star with two Oak Leaf Clusters—the list went on. He led an A-Team in Bosnia and became a Company man all before his thirty-first birthday. He spent the next three years with the Special Operation Division, putting out wildfires in places no one else could get to, in ways no one else had even considered—or dared. He had been so busy it never occurred to him, then, how accurate the SAD acronym had been. Kealey kept shrugging off the atrocities he saw and the things he did until the cumulative weight of it could no longer be ignored.

Gill arrived with the coffee—already prepared the way Harper liked it—and shut the door. Harper opened the briefcase with a thumbprint on the top panel. It hummed open. He removed a tablet, turned it on, handed it to Kealey. There were photos of a dead man, one after another. The resolution was sharp enough for Kealey to see the flies on his stab wounds and bird droppings in his dried blood. The eyes were gone, probably not from the attack itself.

"Two days ago, Yerby was watching for a mule train that Danny Hernandez was part of," Harper told him. "He was hooking up with Iranians who want to use his resources to transport WMDs into this country."

"His orders were—?"

"Removal. The permission slip was verbal, eyes only, DEA administrator Ryan Beit and deputy administrator Deborah Brook. I know them both. No paper trail and there's no way they told anyone."

"Who watches the watcher?" Kealey asked.

"Exactly. Someone had protective eyes on the party and spotted Yerby," Harper said.

"Crossbow and knife," Kealey said, examining the photos of the wounds.

"Yes, and it was surgical. The killer wasn't one of the typical message-sending thugs."

"Footprints? Trail?"

"They found some broken grass, crushed bugs," Harper told him.

"Urine?"

"Not a trace. There were a couple of partial footprints, enough to give us a size 8D boot," Harper went on. That would fit what little intel we have about the cartel, that it's gender-blind."

"It's easier for women to recruit females as agents, especially girls that lost their mothers," Kealey said. "It's probably the same in that trade."

"Worse," Harper said. "For many of them, from poor villages, the only other option is prostitution. Which these guys force on girls who refuse to carry for them."

It was a stinking business. There was nothing ideological that a bleeding heart could use to defend it. This extreme human abuse was about greed and power, nothing more.

"Okay, so you're involved because of the Iranian connection," Kealey said. "Why do you need me? You've got a lot of good people and for that matter so does the DEA."

"The Iranians have some bad people on their side, too," Harper told him. He retrieved the tablet and opened another file. He handed it back to Kealey. There were computer-enhanced photos of several people.

"Crap," was all Kealey said.

Several of the images clearly showed the features of Dr. Hanif al-Shenawi in a hotel. Two of them, time-stamped in the early evening, showed him sitting in the backseat of a sedan with dark windows.

"We were tipped off by a DHS agent in Iraq, Dina Westbrook."

Kealey chuckled.

"You know her?"

"I've heard they call her the 'Icebreaker.' Haven't met her, though."

"She was interrogating a driver on an opium route from Iran through Iraq to the Gulf. He mentioned that an Iranian doctor used the route about a week ago. We put the system to work and computers pulled these images through the sedan window and matched them with an old surveillance photo. Once we had those pictures, we grabbed a few more along his itinerary."

Kealey examined the partial profile shots of the physician in the hotel. A lifelong jihadist who had spent time in an Egyptian prison, Dr. al-Shenawi treated the highest-ranking Iranian officials—but, while that high-profile position was legitimate, it was also a cover. Attending medical conventions around the globe, he was a top recruiter for Iranian intelligence. The man was said to oversee a terrorist training center in Kyrgyzstan, in caves that were part of the Tian Shan Mountains. United States intelligence had never been able to pinpoint the location.

"He's never needed secrecy in Iran," Kealey pondered. "He flies direct from Tehran to whichever international conferences are convenient for his plans. Why would he smuggle himself out with an opium driver this time? Was he showing someone that the route works?"

"It's possible. The images of him in the sedan were taken by a pair of state troopers who were working with DHS to test low-light, high-speed, license-scan software on I-15 in Fallbrook. That's a few towns out from where Yerby was killed later on the same day. Several hours after these photos were taken, al-Shenawi showed up in security footage at the airport in Ontario, California, for a flight to San Antonio. We cannot account for the hours in between."

"So he may have met Hernandez."

"Yes."

"Hernandez may have been proving his end of the route works, too. Any idea whether they met to talk or to make a pickup or drop-off?" Kealey wondered.

"That's a damn good question," Harper said.

"Did the doctor fly commercial to both destinations?" Kealey asked.

Harper nodded.

"So it would have been stupid to carry anything into the country," Kealey said. "And if he were picking something up he could have driven to Texas to avoid airport security. No, this was a classic meet-and-greet." That was not so common with terrorists, who preferred to work through couriers carrying coded messages, but drug dealers were different. They wanted to look into the eyes of their top-level counterparts in any new arrangement.

"Agreed," Harper said. "The worry, obviously, is that something from Iran is en route to Mexico and al-Shenawi was there to solemnize the new relationship with Hernandez."

"Do we know if the Iranians contacted Hernandez or whether the cartel wants them for something?"

"We do not know."

"And why San Antonio?" Kealey went on. "Who or what is there?"

"We don't know that, either," Harper said. "And we have no way of finding out."

Kealey suddenly understood why he was here. "You lost the doctor."

"The SOB went to worship at a mosque on San Pedro Avenue in San Antonio. The FBI was watching him using existing video equipment in the street. They got eyes-on inside the mosque, a woman disguised as a worshiper, within three minutes of him going inside. They never saw him inside or coming out."

"A disguise?"

"Possibly," Harper said. "Over four dozen people have gone in and out since he did. Any one of them could have swapped clothes, head scarves, or beards with him."

"Or he may still be inside. Thermal scans?"

"No hidden rooms," Harper told him. "That said, we do not have visuals on several chambers and listening devices tell us nothing. He might be communicating with others by handwriting."

"The Alamo is in San Antonio," Kealey said thoughtfully. "That would be a hell of a target."

"Agreed," Harper said. "It's right in the middle of the city, accessible on all sides, heavy with bus tours. There's also the River Walk, the top tourist attraction in Texas. One of our think tank guys said it would be a coup back home to turn it red with blood, like the Nile."

"Payback some thirty-three hundred years later?"

"These boys have long memories," Harper pointed out. "They're still pissed about the Crusades, about El Cid tossing them out of Spain. And there are other moving parts here."

"Such as?"

"There are two local DEA offices that have been long, sharp knives pointed at Hernandez's side, preventing a full-scale expansion into Texas," Harper said. "One is the El Paso division where Yerby was assigned and the other is the San Antonio District Office. There's concern that Hernandez used himself as bait to see what key assets showed up and to take them down."

"So he may have enlisted a terrorist group to help him and not the other way around?"

"Possible. Very possible."

"Which means we need to find al-Shenawi."

Harper nodded.

Kealey had been to San Antonio about a decade before and liked it, a small-size city with big-size character. Kealey had also been on cold-trail hunts and he liked those, too. There was an inescapable thrill knowing you could pretty much go where you wanted, talk to whoever you chose, knowing that a phone call would back up your right to do so.

But he sat there staring at the photos without seeing them. He didn't want to do this . . . not even to get the doctor who had recruited so many terrible killers.

Kealey looked up. "Jon, this is gonna sound cold, but I'm done with all this."

"So you've told me. Then why'd you come?"

"An old friend asked me to. And he sent a helicopter."

"I'll send you to Texas in a jet," Harper said with a grin. The smile faded quickly. "You knew the old friend would ask you to do more. I repeat: Why did you come?"

Kealey thought for a moment. "I honestly don't know. I've got my pension and I liked it where I was. Everything you're telling me—it's nothing new. Washington has known the cartels were making a push into Texas and has done next to nothing to seriously amp up border security. Washington has known that terrorists were looking to hook up with drug czars for years and has done next to nothing to infiltrate the cartels. No HUMINT where we need it."

"Agreed."

"Now I'm supposed to fix that?"

"DEA has run a few names up the flagpole but no one with Middle Eastern savvy, except you. If you don't go, we may just be sending agents to an ambush."

"Jesus, Jon. Guilt?"

"I have to try," Harper said. "We've got one, possibly two nasty men within our borders. Finding the doctor could lead us to Hernandez."

"Do you think he's still here as well?"

"We don't know," Harper admitted. "What we don't know is staggering, in fact. The surveillance of Hernandez was hazy. He's not stupid. He traveled by night and kept to wooded areas. He apparently moved around by tunnels as well. For all we know, the meeting was about getting him to Iran for sanctuary. There may be a drug war percolating in the south. Mexico is not so well informed. But here's something my gut and the circumstantial evidence tells me: We have a perfect storm to take out two monsters."

"Texas has FBI, DHS people. Experienced ones."

"They do. Top people. They want to be set loose."

"But they aren't getting the go-ahead," Kealey said.

Harper gave him a look that said, Of course not. A mob of angry, vengeful agents standing shoulder to shoulder with bayonets bared, so to speak, would be spotted by the kind of expert bodyguard who killed Yerby. This mission required HUMINT by someone who knew how to track and keep his distance—or move in for the takedown.

Kealey sighed miserably. Allison had told him, as a psychiatrist—before they scuttled all kinds of professional ethics and busted a few of the Commandments to boot—that Kealey found it difficult to say no since doing so could result in death. That was the burden of being a peacekeeper in any capacity.

"How much time do I have to kill?"

"Estimated time of departure, an hour and a half. Thank you, Ryan."

Kealey waved it off, not looking in Harper's eyes.

Harper went to an office and left Kealey with one of the laptops. Kealey transferred the funds for the house to Ellie's account and considered calling Allison. He decided against that, too. She was as much a part of his former life as Harper was. He cared for her but he did not want to immerse himself again emotionally. Agreeing to take on this mission—which he had, even though he hadn't—was enough of a step in the wrong direction.

Kealey went to the small officers' mess a short walk from the JIB. It was a pleasant walk in the late afternoon, reminding him of how many tarmacs he had crossed in so many cities over too many years.

He chose a Cobb salad, sat in a corner, and watched as men and women began filing in for early dinner. He remembered when officers seemed so much older than he was. Now Kealey was at least in the upper twentieth percentile of age.

And most of these guys don't have to get physical the way I do, he thought as he looked over the rainbow mix of in shape, slightly out of shape, and some who would never make it through boot camp today. They also weren't mostly white men. Maybe half of them were. The rest were women and a rainbow of races. It seemed as if the world had come to Kealey. Yet here he was, ready to go out and fight it again. He wondered how many of these people identified themselves as hyphenates? Asian-American, Latino-American, Gay-American, Muslim-American. There was a time, even at the height of the "melting pot" in the early twentieth century, when someone was American first. You were Irish-American or Italian-American pretty much just one day a year, when there was a parade. He wondered how many of these people identified themselves as Americans first. He wondered if it would be politically incorrect—or even perceived as "hate"—if he dared to ask those questions aloud.

It was a pretty good salad, though. Better than the prefab-tasting meals in "his" day.

He didn't mind waiting in the mess hall but a couple of cafeteria workers were hanging Christmas decorations before the real dinner rush started. The scraping of ladders edged closer to Kealey's seat until he realized they were probably going to displace him and left. *At least they waited till December to decorate,* Kealey thought. He especially loathed the new trend of decorating for Christmas even before Halloween.

He didn't have a badge to go walking around the base, so he returned to the JIB. He watched aircraft of all stripes coming and going.

This mission has got to be it, he decided. The last one. He was too jaded to keep going. He did not tell himself he needed rest, because he knew too many people who grabbed some premature rest from a bomb or a bullet. But he did need peace. Like a mystic who had seen too much horror in the world, too many territorial squabbles on the world stage and on the political stage, he needed to find something new sitting on that mountaintop in Connecticut. Next Christmas, he promised himself, he was going to spend the day flying in his own little plane over his own secluded home.

He stopped still at the thought, just before he was going to enter the JIB. He whipped out his cell phone and called Harper.

"Don't tell me you got lost on base," Harper answered.

"It's Christmas," Kealey said.

"You've got a couple weeks yet—"

"Jon, it's Christmas in Texas, too."

There was silence on Harper's end. Then Kealey heard him wrench a door open and start running.

CHAPTER FIVE

SAN ANTONIO, TEXAS

San Antonio is one of the oldest settlements in the Southwest. The Payaya Indians, who lived along the San Antonio River, were among the first indigenous peoples encountered by Spanish settlers in the region. The colonists constructed forts, trading posts, and Catholic missions in the eighteenth century—including the famed Mission San Antonio de Valero. Today, this building is better known as the Alamo, the Spanish word for the cottonwood trees that grew there. American settlers wrested San Antonio from Mexico in 1835, and the following year the Republic of Texas was founded. The Mexicans retook San Antonio twice in 1842 but each conquest was short-lived. Texas was granted statehood in 1845.

Clean, sunny, and a mecca for tourists, San Antonio is the jewel of Texas, even though the inhabitants of Dallas, Houston, and other great Texas cities demur. The disagreement is polite, however, since it is still a treasure of the Lone Star State.

Dr. Hanif al-Shenawi did not know or care about any of this. He had never been to Texas and had no interest in it; he was here in the mosque on San Pedro Avenue for one reason, and it was not to pray.

The short, balding fifty-six-year-old sat in a room that had been constructed beneath the *mihrab,* the semicircular niche in the wall that faces the direction of the Sacred House in Mecca, the direction in which all worshipers should face. The room was used to store prayer books and had been constructed after the mosque was completed. The imam and his followers never anticipated committing or abetting acts of sedition against the United States. But to many of them it was, after all, only a host nation and not a home. Mecca was their home, and the mosque was its representative on any shore.

This was a new experience for al-Shenawi, who had never been compelled to go into hiding anywhere. Not in Yemen, where he was sought by undercover Israeli operatives for organizing local radicals into hit squads; not in Egypt, where he had recruited military marksmen for assignments overseas, right from under the noses of their secular commanders. In those and many, many other instances the physician had been able to make getaways in ambulances, by using disguises, or by slipping into an embassy. He not only held a passport for his native country but also forged documents for Chechnya, Turkey, and Spain.

The doctor lay on the cot that had been brought downstairs for his comfort. Food and drink had been provided and sat on a tray table beside him. The imam had been cordial if not friendly; so many clergymen did not like being drawn into political matters. But it was a political world and theirs was a politicized faith. There was no escaping the demands of the modern world.

The irony was that al-Shenawi was not here for his own safety. He was in the mosque simply to be here, in this city, at this time. His job was to remain hidden until the action was concluded.

Lying here with books and dissertations he had brought with him for entertainment, al-Shenawi felt like he did when he was a student at the School of Medicine of the University of Tehran before it became the Tehran University of Medical Sciences and Health Services. Once again he was in a small, mostly airless room, sitting on an uncomfortable bed, reading medical texts and drinking water, eating bread and fruit—which was all he could afford at the time. Now, it was actually a pleasant experience because he knew it was only temporary. Al-Shenawi did not sit here and think, I am an honored physician to the leaders of a nation, I should receive first-class accommodations. Instead, he was reminded of how far he had come, the son of a bus driver who had surpassed his modest ambition to become a doctor and practice in his home city of Zanjan.

He was content.

He perused a text about the latest developments in laproscopy. *Soon,* he thought, *medicine will merge with religion.* Except perhaps in the matters of accident and trauma. Instead of minimally intrusive surgery, doctors would heal without entering the body, by laying on hands and manipulating tissue. In the future there would be very little distinction between doctors and clerics. Perhaps if patients learned to self-heal, they would need neither.

We would all, then, truly be like unto the Prophet, Allah praise Him and those who follow in His radiant footsteps.

The doctor shut his eyes. He was tired, jet-lagged, exhausted. He reclined and savored the passive part he was about to play in events that would shape the world.

The doctor smiled a little. The fact that his role was passive made this even sweeter. All he had to do was be seen arriving in this city and in this mosque, but not leaving. All he had been required to do was grab the attention—and the eyes of law enforcement. The only other thing on his itinerary—and this was more a nod to decency than anything else—was not gloat when he finally walked through the front door of the mosque.

CHAPTER SIX
SAN ANTONIO, TEXAS

The woman arrived in San Antonio in a station wagon driven by a man she did not know.

Buddy Anthony, the thick, middle-aged man plumped behind the wheel, had never met nor heard of his passenger. There was no reason he should have. His one-person car service had been engaged online in Phoenix to make a pickup in Southern California and drive to San Antonio. He was given half of his fee in cash by an agent in Arizona, the motel rooms were paid in advance, and he would receive the other half of his fee when his passenger arrived in San Antonio.

The fee was exactly Buddy's asking price, one thousand dollars with a hundred-dollar surcharge for higher gas prices. There was no haggling—which was unusual. And a very generous tip was promised.

Buddy's passenger was uncommonly quiet. She did not eat with him when they stopped for the night in Gage, New Mexico. She went right to her room at the Motel Pyramid and did not emerge, at least while he was awake in the room next door, until the following morning. The woman was young and attractive, not rude or distant; just someone who kept to herself. He tried engaging her at the start of the journey, telling her the always reliable story of his brother Ricky who lived on a boat in Connecticut—even when it was stored in a friend's garage during the winter. She didn't bite. She didn't even nibble.

Which was fine with Buddy. He listened to his music, chatted occasionally on the phone with his wife, who never asked whom he was driving or where—she was too busy doing needlepoint and selling kitten pillows online—and enjoyed the open, uncrowded highways. It made him feel like the rebel he thought he was back in the 1970s when he hot-rodded and then motorbiked his way through the desert and across the unpopulated Southwest. He never wondered what his life would have been like had he joined his friends in their car and bike clubs. Most of those guys were in prison or dead. No, his two daughters were grown and happily married and he was okay with his life, with being his own boss, with the occupation he loved as a young man still available to him.

They arrived in San Antonio in the early evening. He dropped his passenger at Main Plaza, where it looked like there was some kind of Christmas shindig going on. She paid him in cash, then walked over to a pushcart selling snacks. She bought a pretzel as Buddy fingered through the hundred-dollar bills. There were two extra. That was a handsome tip.

Whoever these nameless, faceless people were who hired him, Buddy pulled away hoping they'd need him a few more times this year.

Though he had opened the door for the woman and then checked the backseat to make sure she hadn't left anything, Buddy did not look under the passenger seat. If he had, the vendor was watching and things would have happened a little sooner.

Because Buddy was not so diligent, Abejide did not have to hurry after making her purchase and walking away from the vendor.

Plaza de las Islas, or Main Plaza, is one of the oldest features of the city of San Antonio. Located a walkable half mile from the Alamo and a stone's throw from the San Antonio River, it was planned by its Spanish founders to be the heart of the city, and placed immediately to the east of the white stone San Fernando Cathedral, some of whose walls are now the oldest standing structure in Texas. The founders hoped, of course, that this arrangement would keep the state of the citizenry's souls foremost in their minds as they gathered and socialized in the plaza.

A hundred and sixty years later the dark red sandstone of the Bexar County Courthouse was added south of the square across Dolorosa, and gradually other lots nearby grew buildings and lost them and replaced them according to the style of each era. After some decades of disuse as San Antonio's suburbs grew apace with the rest of America's, the plaza was reclaimed in 2006 by urban planners who saw its potential for outdoor events and a cheerful marketplace. It was refurbished to be an extension of the life gathering in the new restaurants, bars, and hotels along the nearby River Walk. Now the city puts together a calendar of events for each month of the year with activities designed to bring together the diverse cultures and peoples of San Antonio, from music festivals to food fairs. But the city saves the best events, some would argue, for last.

Every year on the day after Thanksgiving, over a hundred thousand Christmas lights of all colors are turned on along the River Walk. Festooned on branches and storefronts, they turn San Antonio into a kind of candy land. Main Plaza erects a Christmas tree in front of the cathedral, nearly as tall as the church itself, bursting with red, yellow, blue, and purple lights. Holiday market vendors are invited to set up temporary shops, and on the first Saturday of December chairs are arranged in the plaza for the free "Silver Bells" concert. The performers vary from youth orchestras to mariachi bands but Santa Claus, in person, is there every year.

Today was the first Saturday of December. Kids were still running around the shops but the adults had mostly taken their seats, waiting for the concert to start. A wave of applause suddenly swept through the crowd: Mayor Isobel Garcia, the youngest Hispanic mayor in the nation, had just walked up from her SUV on East Commerce Street. She, her twin sons, and her husband, Manuel, a patent attorney, were taking their seats in the first row. Mayor Garcia waved and smiled and shook the hands of everyone seated near her.

No one noticed the young black woman with a bag slung over her shoulder. No one paid attention to the snacks vendor facing East Commerce Street, who suddenly moved his cart to the east, opposite the direction in which Buddy's car was headed. When surveillance images from the plaza were studied later, he would just be a man who was moving his snacks closer to the high school brass band waiting to perform. Surveillance would also find nothing unusual when the vendor, leaning into his cart to get up some speed, pulled a cell phone from his hip. A number had been programmed into the memory of the phone. He pretended to make a call, laughing as he walked, watching and waiting until Buddy's car was just passing another crowd of performers waiting for the concert to start. Then he moved the phone to the side of his head away from the cameras, slipping a thumb between his ear and the phone.

The ensuing blast ripped the station wagon in half, blowing both ends nearly fifty feet from one another. It sent nails, pieces of the car, glass from the windows, and then bodies and body parts flying in the direction of the plaza and the cathedral. The explosion and the ground-shaking roar punched a crater in the street, in the day, and in the lives of everyone who survived.

CHAPTER SEVEN
LANGLEY, VIRGINIA

Kealey ran into the open center of the uppermost floor of the JIB, where Harper had already shaken the wasp's nest to life. All the intelligence agents and support staff were shouting into phones or typing furiously, screens flashing.

"Silver Bells," Harper told Kealey.

The Bing Crosby song started playing in the back of Kealey's mind, warped by the sounds of anxiety all around him and his own urgency.

"It's one of their earliest Christmas events on Main Plaza, giant tree, choir concert, mariachi band, Santa Claus, and it's about to start in a few minutes."

"Security?" Kealey asked.

"Local police and the mayor's detail, also police."

"Was the mayor's presence announced or spontaneous?"

"We don't know but she's front and center with her husband and two boys. They're getting her men on the phone for me."

But as an agent was motioning Harper to pick up a desk phone, Solomon Gill called out, "Sir! Explosion in San Antonio city center!"

Everyone in the room heard him. A half second later and they resumed their activities at a frenetic pace, trying to get details.

"How do you know?" Harper asked.

Gill held up his phone and said, "Twitter."

Harper picked up the desk phone, said, "Officer! Officer, hello?" He dropped the phone. "He's gone. That's good, they'll be hustling the mayor and her family to a secure location."

"Probably separate locations," Kealey said. "I need a map."

An anonymous voice called across the room, "Confirmed car explosion on East Commerce Street!"

"Give me a magnification of the plaza!" Harper called. "And the feeds from the security cameras!"

Hands slid three laptops onto the table in front of him and Kealey. One had a street-view map of San Antonio, zoomed in on the cathedral and Main Plaza. Another had feeds from six cameras pointing in different directions across the plaza. They showed people running, crouching, screaming, chairs overturning, all in silence. One camera was almost useless, half-obscured by the lights of the big Christmas tree in front of the cathedral. The third laptop showed the white façade of San Antonio City Hall a block away, blank and empty, no activity.

"Confirmation, Mayor Garcia is alive!" called an agent.

"Alive and safe? Alive and wounded? Alive and

with her family? Alive and what?" Harper shouted back. There was no answer.

A fourth laptop slid onto the table, showing the Alamo. Police were locking down the area but there was no panic, no running, no sign of trouble, just precautions.

"Anything happening on the River Walk?" Harper called out.

A voice answered, "Nothing on the stretch near the square, we're checking on the rest of it!"

"Damn it, what else," Harper muttered to Kealey. "Am I missing anything?"

"The church." Kealey stabbed his finger at the cathedral behind the big Christmas tree.

"Anything on the church?" Harper shouted.

A voice called, "Some of the crowd is running into it."

"That's all we need, a sanctuary from one bomb exploding with another," Harper grimaced, then ordered the room, "Tell the local force their first priority is to secure that church, get the people out of it and the place shut down."

Kealey motioned at the map and said, "The good news is, if they were after the church they probably would have driven the car off the street onto the plaza and into the building."

"Hope you're right," said Harper. "What else?"

"Those are the identifiable targets," Kealey said. "Anything else is blind darts."

They heard, "Confirmation, no unusual activity anywhere on the River Walk!"

"Could it just be the car bomb?" Harper asked quietly.

"I don't know," Kealey said, staring at the screens, "but he came all the way from Iran for this."

"Update on the mayor!" Harper yelled at the room.

"Working on it!"

Kealey and Harper watched helplessly as the security cameras recorded the terror of San Antonio's citizens.

"I forgot it was Christmas," Harper murmured. "The weather was so warm."

"Me too." Kealey said, thinking, *the mountain was so high*.

CHAPTER EIGHT
SAN ANTONIO, TEXAS

Abejide had determined there were only three direc-tions the police could take the mayor. North was not an option as the explosion would take place at the juncture of East Commerce Street and the plaza. This was almost the exact location, it turned out, where the mayor's SUV dropped her and her family for the con-cert.

East was a possibility but a slim one. Holiday shops, vendor carts, and trees congested the path across the plaza to the river. The panicking crowd would hit several bottlenecks there and make the area even more difficult to pass through. However, on the off chance the mayor's security detail did choose that direction, Abejide had planned the fastest route to run ahead of them and jump down into the small, sunken park between the plaza and the river. Once there, the spot would actually be helpful for her. The park was full of stone blocks of dif-ferent sizes, creating crannies Abejide could tuck herself into. The stones were low enough that she could maintain a sightline, curl around a stone block, and aim. They would make an exit trickier, but she knew she would have a spare second no matter where she was located. Without the sound of a gunshot, the mayor's security detail would react first to the result of Abejide's action, which would be the mayor falling to the ground. There would be a moment of recognition that something was wrong before anyone looked up and around, and in that moment Abejide could join the crowd of frightened, running citizens.

East was a remote chance, though, so before the bomb exploded the young woman had already circulated through the assembled seats toward the tall Christmas tree and the cathedral behind it.

West was a distinct possibility. There were two exit routes leading west out of the plaza, on either side of the cathedral toward City Hall. Reviewing the territory a month earlier, Abejide had ruled out the northern exit as it was too close to the planned explosion site. The southern route was a short passageway between the cathedral and the neighboring cathedral center, a two-story, white stone building with red timbering supporting the roof, frequently used for wedding receptions. The passageway would not be overly obvious to stampeding citizens. Since fewer people were likely to notice and use this route, it was very possible that the mayor's security detail had already pre-selected it in case of emergencies. The short passageway opened into a small courtyard with a fountain before continuing past the cathedral to the street.

The advantage of this route for Abejide was height. She could accomplish her task while standing on the ground, but it would be easier and more effective if she were either lower than or elevated above the mayor. Being higher was preferable and it didn't have to be by much; she did not need a roof. The scalloped stone edge of the fountain would provide about a foot-high boost but better yet, there were usually outdoor chairs and tables placed around this courtyard. A chair would elevate her by two feet and be easy to jump on and off from.

However, this route made her own exit significantly more difficult. She could not count on there being enough of a fleeing crowd to melt into. Her precious moment saved by not using a gun would be spent on jumping down from her chair. The cathedral center had columns she could run and dodge behind but she would probably be noticed and the columns would obstruct her sightlines. She did not intend to switch from hunter to hunted all in an instant. She decided that if this was the route they chose, she would follow her jump from the chair by squatting and cowering. Since she was a woman and no weapon would be visible, it was likely that the mayor's security would look at every other person in the courtyard and up on the roofs as well before their eyes would come back to her. By then she could have scuttled in pretended fear to the building, behind the columns, giving herself enough of a lead that when she stood and ran she would not feel like there were crosshairs on her back.

But the most obvious choice for the mayor's security was south. A straight, broad stretch of plaza pavement led past the cathedral and cathedral center to Dolorosa. The path would be full of the escaping crowd, yes, but in the short time required to jog it, the security guards could call the mayor's SUV. Since it had so recently

driven away, it would not take long for the driver to circle around and approach on Dolorosa. The safest location near a bomb site was a vehicle that could speed
away from it. Abejide could not afford to let them get
too far down this route, which meant her optimal window for accomplishing her mission was just after the
moment security hustled the mayor away from her seat,
during their rush past the cathedral.

Which was why Abejide was already standing next
to the tall Christmas tree before the station wagon exploded. The tree was positioned visually in front of the
cathedral but still in the plaza, so that the mayor and her
security would have to pass between the tree and the
church. The red, yellow, and blue tree was surrounded
by what she believed was called a "white picket fence,"
consisting of movable sections a few feet long. The rails
that capped the fence sections were a good size for a
hand to grip and were festooned with ribbons and gar-
lands. Apparently someone was scheduled to give a
speech next to the tree, since a microphone and chest-
high sound speakers were positioned there and wired.
Abejide had already visually followed the wires to
check for the person responsible for running the sound
equipment; his table was established behind a tree. It
was not likely that his first thought would be to save
his speakers.

A thin lamppost with a security camera stood just
outside the white fence but close to the tree, ensuring
that from one angle, at least, the view of the camera
was blocked. Abejide stood in the blind spot, pulled her
weapon from her pocket, and carefully removed the
small, hard plastic cover. It was so small that to anyone

watching she would look like she was handling a phone or similar gadget. But now—pre-loaded, highly sensitive to any pressure at several different points, and in the hand of its maker—the weapon was extremely dangerous.

The bomb exploded.

Abejide flinched, screamed, acted horrified for whichever cameras might see her. She put on a perfect display of terrified paralysis, looking this way and that to see where she could run but unable to choose any direction. She held her hands to her chest as if trying to hold herself together, hold back screams, but was actually creating a cocoon for the weapon in her hands, protecting it from the jostling she was receiving from the frightened concertgoers. And wherever her head turned to look, she moved her eyes so that she was seeing nothing but the mayor.

Immediately after detonation, Mayor Garcia and her husband flung their arms and torsos over their sons sitting between them. They stayed in that position until the three policemen of the security detail reached them and leaned over them, supplanting their human shield with their own bodies. Standing up but hunched under a dome of uniformed chests and arms, the Garcia family hurried in the direction the guards guided them, south toward Dolorosa. The thin screams of one of the twin boys seemed to pierce through all the wailing of the crowd.

Abejide saw the family's faces clearly. The mayor was arguing with her husband and the reason became quickly apparent. One of the security guards was already trying to peel the mayor's husband and sons away from the mayor's side. The guard was leaning to the right and Abejide knew instantly that he was going to steer the family west through the courtyard while the mayor was escorted to Dolorosa to meet the SUV.

It had only been seconds since the explosion. The Garcias were about to pass the Christmas tree. Everything had to happen very fast now.

The world took on a kind of silence for Abejide. It was not soundless; as an excellent hunter she still needed all her senses to be sharp. The sound of an approaching shouting voice could indicate that someone was about to get too close to her, notice her, or accidentally disrupt her plan in some way. The sound of a table scraping could be the worker of the sound equipment coming unexpectedly toward her instead of away from her. The rattle of a chair could be a sign that one was going to fall in her direction and interfere with her footing. She was aware of all of these possible sounds beneath the screams and cries, but she did not sense them viscerally. They registered on her consciousness abstractly, as if they were diagrammed on the sphere of her auditory world. In this way it felt like silence. Separated from her senses but even more alert, she was free to move as if she were in a bubble, smoothly and timelessly carrying out the sequence of events she had planned.

As the Garcias passed the tree, the security guard pulled the mayor's husband and children toward the cathedral, already placing them on the trajectory for the courtyard. The mayor gave an extra squeeze to the last hand she held, one of the sons'. Then she grabbed one of her two security guards and pushed him in that direction as well. He resisted and there was a very brief argument and a bigger shove from the mayor. The guard jogged after the family. Now the mayor had only one policeman with her, but the pause had been the real fortune for Abejide.

The young woman held on to the lamppost and stepped up on the nearest white picket fence rail, steadying herself with one of the sound speakers. The fence rail was only the width of one of her feet and its decorations were slippery, but it would suffice. Wrapping her arm around the lamppost, she brought her other hand to her face as if calling desperately for someone. She was careful to use the hand that would block her face from any security cameras pointed at the cathedral and the tree. Looking like she was struggling to keep her balance, her arm around the lamppost reached farther and grabbed the weapon that she had placed on top of the sound speaker.

At Langley, Ryan Kealey suddenly stabbed his finger at a laptop. "What the hell was that?" he said.

Jonathan Harper looked at the array of security camera feeds. Kealey was pointing at the feed that was mostly obscured by Christmas tree lights. "I wasn't looking," Harper said.

"I barely caught it and it's gone now," Kealey said, "but I could swear it was a sleeve." He yelled to the room, "I need eyes on the Christmas tree, right now, cameras, anything!"

But by the time someone communicated with the police arriving at Main Plaza, it was too late.

* * *

The mayor's remaining security guard was visibly unsure of what to do with four sides of a woman to protect and only himself to do it. He switched to the mayor's right side, trying to create space for her to move by holding out his arm against the crowd surging in the same direction. That left her open to the tree. The guard's other arm was around her shoulders and she had adopted the universal posture of the besieged, shoulders up, head down, back of the neck exposed.

Abejide hugged the lamppost tightly, to all appearances for balance, but actually to steady her arm and hand. Bare-fingered—she had used surgical gloves during the preloading so no fingerprints would be found on the arrow—she squeezed the trigger of the crossbow that was the size of her palm.

In one of the odd coincidences that have run rampant through lives of inventors in every era of history, Abejide had been working on her own miniature crossbow three years ago when the news broke that an Israeli jeweler had completed a fully functional model. His was made of silver, gold, and steel. Hers was similar only in the steel bow and string, but the result was the same: an arrow half a finger long could be shot ten feet, silently, with severe impact. The arrow was only about the size of three matchsticks clumped together so Hernandez had doubted the efficacy of the weapon, despite the convenience. After all, wouldn't the skinny arrow simply pass through its target altogether, leaving a remarkably clean hole? It would land a body in the hospital but it wouldn't kill.

Her answer was to spend more time on inventing the arrow than it had taken to craft the crossbow.

Now, standing next to the Christmas tree, she knew before the arrow hit that her aim had been not perfect, but satisfactory. Perfect would have been hitting the jugular vein, but she had designed the arrow so that would not be necessary. Keyed to such sensitivity that the entire crossbow had to be shielded in hard plastic until just before use, the arrow tip would react to the slightest pressure, such as meeting the skin of a neck. Upon impact eight triangular, razor-sharp carbon points exploded from the body of the arrow, making a much bigger hole than the tip could cause.

Five feet away from Abejide, her arrow tip lodged in Mayor Garcia's muscle. One carbon point pierced her windpipe and another pierced her jugular. Without a sound she dropped to her knees. The guard felt the drag on his arm and tried to catch her. There was no exit wound in the mayor's neck, so blood was spilling from her mouth.

Abejide screamed and jumped down from the fence rail. She grabbed the first person within reach, pointing and pushing at him to look. "The mayor!" she shouted. He hurried to the fallen woman and several other people followed him. By the time the security guard looked up he had three or four faces gathered around the tragic figure. Abejide was not one of them.

Still acting for the cameras, she looked around wildly, holding her shoulder bag with one hand, the crossbow hidden between her hand and the strap. She put her hand to her face as if calling again for a missing person, then gave up in desperation and ran from the plaza, south to Dolorosa, where an SUV had just pulled up to the curb. Abejide never looked at it, only kept running straight past the courthouse. Several turns and backtracks later, she headed for the appointed location to meet with the pretzel vendor's contacts. The world of sound came back to her, but all it contained was distant sirens.

CHAPTER NINE
LANGLEY, VIRGINIA

Five hours later the upstairs room at the JIB was still quietly buzzing with coordination efforts, but everyone was despondent. Twelve people had died on Main Plaza, including a ten-year-old who had played guitar for the mariachi band slated to perform. A further twenty-two were wounded, some now in critical condition at the hospital. San Antonio's citizens, unable to access the plaza or the cathedral because of police cordons, were creating a memorial for their young mayor on the lawn of City Hall, filling it with flowers, candles, photographs, and handwritten notes and prayers. The lawn was fairly small, so the memorial was spilling all the way around the white stone building, and mourners unwilling to go home were sitting on their parked cars on every block nearby. On the plaza, someone had turned off the lights on the big Christmas tree.

Jonathan Harper could not have taken it harder if he had lost someone personally. The deputy director sat with his chin propped on three fingers of his hand, watching the videos, photos, and reports roll in. He had devoted one laptop screen to coverage of the growing memorial. Kealey could see by how rigidly he held his neck that he was raging inside at the nearest target: himself.

"Jon," Kealey said quietly, "you know if you'd warned them earlier, any safety precautions they would have taken still wouldn't have mattered. They couldn't have closed down streets without information that we didn't have. They wouldn't have checked cars for bombs without clear evidence pointing that way. They could have limited entry and exit points for the plaza but chances are, they would have used that particular corner. And even if they'd kept the crowd a yard or two away from the street, some people would still have died."

Harper only nodded.

"And you don't know if the mayor would have consented to dragging around more security guards than she already had. Frankly, more men in play probably wouldn't have made a difference."

"We'll see what the autopsy says," Harper said, locked in his guilt.

The autopsy results were e-mailed to him a quarter of an hour later. The first photo showed the tiny arrow, half the length of a finger with open slits along the side. It had been placed on a white towel and had not yet been washed, so there were streaks of blood on the arrow and smears on the towel. Arrayed next to it were eight carbon points soaked in blood.

"That's almost impossible," Kealey said. "The spring mechanism would have to be so sensitive, it would go off if it hit a raindrop."

"Not much rain in Texas," Harper muttered. "What

on earth would have propelled something like that? A blowpipe?"

They shook their heads, incredulous.

"Whatever it was," Kealey mused, "the person holding it must have had preternatural muscle control. To launch something that sensitive with a panicking crowd all around, very little time to aim, and such a small target . . . that's not someone with some military training under his belt. That's someone who's been practicing his whole life."

"And did it in a way that he wasn't noticed, either," Harper added with a sigh.

They had spent the last five hours reviewing the feeds from the security cameras over and over. Neither one of them had seen anything suspicious. Rather, they had seen everything suspicious and nothing even remotely conclusive. They'd spent ten minutes repeatedly watching one girl hop the Christmas tree fence just as the mayor was passing by, but she was so obviously trying to get out of the way of the crowd, making no movements that could be read as taking aim . . . At that point they had realized they were burning out and seeing ghosts where there were only bedsheets. The people nearest the mayor at time of death had been detained by the police and questioned, but all they said was that they saw everyone else looking at the mayor after she fell so they ran over to help.

Harper scrolled back to the photograph of the miniscule arrow and its multiple heads. "I hate assassinations," he grimaced.

"You know who could have done this?" Kealey said. "The archer who took out Yerby. Victor was one of the best, yet he was outmaneuvered."

"The archer with the size eight shoes," Harper said, staring at him.

They quickly found the security feed with the view of the tree and the cathedral. Unfortunately the camera was placed across the plaza so figures were small. Again, they watched the young woman with the shoulder bag hop onto the fence and cling to the lamppost. She was distraught, calling out into the crowd. In the moments before the explosion, she had been simply standing by the tree and waiting.

"It's obvious," Harper said. "She was waiting for her friend or her boyfriend or whoever, the bomb exploded, she was terrified her person had been caught in the explosion or in the crowd, she stayed as long as she could get herself to stay there, and then she ran."

Kealey nodded agreement. He watched the tape again. "There's just no way in hell anyone could shoot with that precision from that position with that much motion going on. Aside from the fact that she had nothing to shoot with."

"Although it is a security camera feed," Harper said. "Lousy on detail."

"And we don't have a view of every corner of that plaza," Kealey said. "But I'm still willing to bet that Yerby's killer and the mayor's assassin are one and the same."

"I'm not disagreeing with you," Harper said, and fell silent to prove it.

"I'm willing to bet my new house on it," Kealey said.

"Thank you, Ryan," Harper said, recognizing that Kealey had just offered his foreseeable future to the operation they would rapidly roll out.

"To clarify," Kealey said, "I want Hernandez."

"I know you do." Harper rubbed his eyes.

Damn it, Kealey thought. He had openly stated his objective because somewhere deep down, he'd already known that Harper would say no.

"The DEA will take Hernandez," Harper said. "We need you on the doctor."

"The DEA hasn't done the job so far on Hernandez—" Kealey started.

Harper cut him off. "You have the international experience, Ryan. You take the international job."

Kealey didn't argue further, just watched the memorial flowers and candles fill the lawns of City Hall. Finally he stood. "I'll report to you tomorrow morning," he said. "I've got to pick up my car. You'll let me know if the doctor leaves the mosque?"

Harper nodded and the battle-scarred old friends shook hands.

"Take the chopper," Harper said.

Kealey left the building wondering what he was going to tell Ellie about her refuge on the mountain. He could already feel his operational mind hardening over his feelings of disappointment. When people like the mayor's husband were telling his kids that their mom had been killed, people like Kealey put their feelings to the side.

PART TWO
THE WEAPON

CHAPTER TEN
JEBEL MUSA, SINAI PENINSULA
June 26, 2015

A hot wind swirled a six-foot-high dust devil into life, a pillar of air carrying sand and dead foliage across the plain. The airborne flotsam gleamed red in the noon sun. The fast-spinning funnel passed behind the beefy man in khaki shorts before colliding with a steep hillside and exploding.

"There is a great deal of wonder in this land . . . and gold in this ground," Oxford professor of archaeology Desmond Wesley confided to the high-definition TV camera, conspiratorially tapping his walking staff on the hard, pale plain. Small, rosy pearls of sweat plumped the caked makeup on his balding head. But the greater heat was the one in his eyes, a fire possessed by so many outsiders for this land, its history, its mad prophets and worthy martyrs.

"The gold deposits come as no surprise, since the ancient Land of Midian was renowned for its deposits of precious metals," Wesley went on. He gestured behind him, to a card table that held a device that looked like a megaphone attached to a small microwave oven, the front of which sported an LCD display. "But we are not here on a prospecting mission, per se. In this broadcast, we will use a molecular frequency generator to scan the strata and distinguish between whatever lumpish indigenous gold lies beneath our feet and any carefully worked trinkets and statues carried by the Children of Israel when they left the servitude of Pharaoh. In that fashion, we hope to be able to find the first *actual relics* of the Biblical Exodus."

As the professor spoke, a small figure swathed in a dirty black burnoose appeared on the white-graveled foothills some three hundred meters behind him. Wesley was unaware of the intruder, but a production assistant raised his binoculars to make sure it was just one of the pilgrims or holy men who frequented the holy mountain and not a terrorist. He did not seem to be a threat, though this pilgrim was different from the few others they had spotted since the *Archaeology HD* jeep caravan arrived the night before. The man was moving quickly, as though he were running from—or to—something. No bother, as long as it wasn't them. More likely he was hurrying to the Monastery of St. Catherine, which sat behind them in the foothills of Mt. Sinai.

The host noticed the stares of the crew and turned to follow their gaze. He shielded his eyes with his hand.

"Those are the robes of a monk of the monastery," Wesley commented.

"Maybe a snake bit him or something," suggested a production assistant.

The veteran camera operator continued to record as an Egyptian bodyguard traveling with the group unshouldered his MISR assault rifle and walked forward cautiously.

"*Esmak eh?*" the Egyptian shouted.

When the man failed to identify himself, the bodyguard raised the weapon waist high, pointed toward him, and repeated the question.

The newcomer waved his arms over his head and shouted something back. Wesley struggled to hear it but couldn't quite make out the panting Egyptian.

The bodyguard managed to hear him and shook his head. "*Mesh mumk'n!*" he yelled with a sneer.

The man, now about fifty meters away, slowed to a trot and held both hands up as though he were surrendering.

Standing behind the camera, the director frowned uncomfortably. "He said something about Allah. That's not good, is it?"

"It's all right," the bodyguard said, relaxing his weapon. "He was simply swearing that what he told me was true."

"What did he tell you?" Wesley asked.

The bodyguard gestured toward the top of the holy mountain with his weapon. "He said that he has just seen the *Gharib Qawee.*"

"Did he now?" Wesley said with some astonishment.

"Who's that?" the director asked.

"The Remarkable Stranger," Wesley replied.

"And who is *that*?"

Wesley said, "It's a Byzantine usage that references Exodus 2:21–22, the Stranger in a Strange Land."

"I'm confused," the director said.

Wesley told him, "This fellow insists that he has just seen the prophet Moses."

CHAPTER ELEVEN
FORT JACKSON,
SOUTH CAROLINA

It didn't happen often, but *infrequently* is not *never*.

The Department of Defense assigned Maj. Amanda Dell to Fort Jackson, home of the U.S. Army Chaplain Corps. While Maj. James Phair was assigned to teach a course in Chaplain Officer Basics to new recruits, she was asked to make a more thorough study of him. It came as Administrative Directive 703 ID—Intelligence Detachment—and cc'ed one Deputy Director Jonathan Harper at the Central Intelligence Agency. The AD gave no reason other than to say that "the cleric," as Phair was called, was a "subject of interest." The description told her nothing she hadn't gleaned from the assignment itself. The fact that the CIA was involved told her that it wasn't so much Phair as his walkabout among the Iraqi people that was of interest. She had not been instructed to probe him on any specific points, however. That was uncharacteristic of the military. Also to her surprise, Dina Westbrook had not been cc'ed on the AD.

Dell was instructed by the head of psychiatric studies at the Pentagon not to make him her sole patient. They did not want him to feel special, put him on guard. She e-mailed the HOPS that he was already on guard because of his experiences in Iraq and asked if that mattered. They said no. They reiterated that this was simply a six-month project that might be followed by what they called an "Evaluation of Impressions," which was bureaucratese for "What do you think of him?"

Goals and priorities were still shielded at worst, vague at best. But at least the air-conditioning worked here.

This was session number nine since she arrived early in the spring. Phair had come here in January to give him time to settle in.

"How's the teaching?" she asked as he settled into the armchair across from her desk. He had been training up-and-coming clerics for two weeks.

"They're eager and devoted to God and country," he replied, though his terseness suggested that he had more to say.

"Is that wrong?" she asked.

"No," he said behind an out-thrust lower lip. "Not conceptually."

"In practice?"

"I don't know."

She was flipping through notes. At least the cleric's speech patterns and enunciation were getting back to some level of pre-Iraq confidence. "Have you been keeping a journal?"

"That hasn't been working for me."

"Why not?"

The lanky Phair leaned into his lap and looked down. "The words just aren't there."

"The words or the feelings?"

"Oh, I feel a lot," he said. "I just can't seem to isolate one memory or reflection from another."

"How does this hodgepodge make you feel?"

"The hodgepodge itself is frustrating because I feel like I'm stuck on flypaper," he said. "I have this sense that I was 'found' while I was away and 'lost' now, though there wasn't a day out there that I wasn't scared."

"For some people, fear and chaos are a familiar and therefore natural and more comfortable state."

"If they'd lived with it before," Phair said. "I hadn't. I had a very stable life."

"Which you tossed away when you left your post to minister to the wounded Iraqis."

Major Phair remembered that he had told the psychologist that he had been intent on ministering to the spiritual needs of the Iraqis. He realized later, after he'd moved to Fort Jackson, that although he had gone to the Iraqis for their aid, it had really been more to assure himself that in the shadow of death, sectarian distinctions were nothing and spirituality was everything. He had to let the wounded men know—and himself, as well—that while men made war over fine religious print, that all vanished as one stood poised to turn himself over to the care of God.

"Let's talk about how life was simpler before you began your independent work in Iraq," she suggested.

"My 'independent work,'" he smiled bitterly. "Some of my superiors have called it desertion."

"Their information is incomplete."

He gave her a long, searching look. "Are you helping to fill it in?"

"I am not," she replied. "I'm here for you."

Phair grinned a little. "I'm sorry," he said. "There has been so much spin—that's a new word I've learned since I've been here. Very useful." He settled back. "Do you know that one of the commanders in Baghdad wanted to write my work up as a black-ops action?"

"To help you?"

"Are you kidding?" He shook his head. "It would have helped him, added to the tally of proactive maneuvers as opposed to defensive tactics."

"Do you believe it was desertion?" Major Dell asked.

"No. I was compelled to do what I did out of love of God, not from a lack of patriotism." He took a long, slow breath and looked at her with searching eyes. "But I will tell you this, Major Dell. My life was very much simpler before I left that hole in the ground."

Phair had already been on his way to the abandoned government office building, following the wounded Iraqis, when his unit began to withdraw. Intelligence had just been received that the insurgents were using the building as a base. The unit was pulled back and the American forces bombed the building. Since Phair knew the phone lines would be secure inside underground concrete conduits, and help could be summoned—which had been the point of taking the wounded there—Phair hid with several Iraqis in a bomb shelter, where he tended to the bodies and souls of two wounded Sunni fighters. They remained for more than a day, under attack from the air and from artillery fire. A subsequent sweep of the town failed to locate him or his young companions. In the small hours of the following night, Iraqi militiamen who knew of the fortified room dug them out. The assault left the clergyman frightened and disoriented, initially fearful of anyone except those who had gone through it with him. The Iraqis who rescued him would have killed him, but for the interference of the men who saw how he helped their comrades.

"Do you ever think of your emergence from the cellar as a kind of rebirth?" Major Dell asked.

"No," he said thoughtfully. "It was more like mitosis. I split off a new me."

The sixteen years that Phair had stayed in Iraq, learning from Sunnis, Shiites, Yazidis, Nestorians, and other religions, he felt his devotion to Catholicism had been enhanced. He had affirmed that the goals of charity and good were fundamentally the same from group to group, as was the ultimate destination of a beatific afterlife.

As was the desire to foster one faith over all others, often through violent means among the radical elements.

While Phair found the rituals and hierarchies instructive and inspiring, he came to believe that no one group had a monopoly on the Way. Not even his own. It was no different than when he would watch the soldiers train in various martial arts disciplines. Judo was different from karate was different from kung fu. All were valid and the end result was the same: self-preservation. Understanding this, there had been no need to question his Catholic faith. It served and continued to serve as his unfaltering conduit to God.

"This new you," Major Dell said in a way that suggested a weighty preamble. "How much overlap does it have with the old you?"

"In what respect?"

"Any."

"Let me answer that bass-ackwards," he suggested. "I can guess the reasons for these ongoing sessions. The DoD wants to know if I've been brainwashed, either by design or association. Correct?"

"If that's a concern, it's not mine," she answered semi-truthfully.

"How does the military view me?"

"I can't speak for them," she replied.

"You know they debriefed me there," he said.

She nodded.

"They prodded me to recall everything I'd seen and heard as what they wanted to call their 'undercover observer.' They wanted to know about the unguarded lives of Iraqi citizens, what the black market was like, how often and in what way the Iraqis were bullied by insurgents or the police or the military and how they responded. I saw a lot of that. I told them what I could remember. That the people are afraid. Of insurgents, of local authorities, of Americans, of despots, of anyone from outside their villages. They shook my memory like they were panning for gold and frankly, I remembered things I had forgotten."

"Except for the first few weeks you were away from your unit," Major Dell said.

"That's right."

"No dreams or fragments or déjà vu that might indicate what happened?"

He shook his head.

It bothered her superiors in the Army Medical Corps that Phair seemed to have been brought back from post-traumatic stress—literally shell shock, from the hammering he took in that cellar—by fraternizing with "a population that might include enemy sympathizers or activists." Phair remembered coming out into dusty daylight from the shelter beneath the bombed building. He remembered hearing an argument among the Iraqis about sparing his life, but he recalled little else until three weeks later, when he was learning Nadji Arabic from a schoolteacher.

The question that remained to be answered was: had he "gone native"? Had he begun to assume the prevailing view of Americans as invaders? He didn't appear to have done so. By identifying with their spiritual rather than political needs, he regained his own center. Though he stayed in Iraq to educate himself and others, he remained fundamentally the same James Phair who was last seen running off during a firefight—but now his own twin, with a new set of experiences and influences.

What would happen if he went back? That's what the top brass wanted to know.

"Are you having difficulty remembering aspects of your stay that used to be clear?" the psychologist inquired.

"The details are still clear," he said. "It just seems a little odd to me that I don't think in Mesopotamian Arabic or Kurdish or Farsi the way I used to. When I look in the mirror I see sunburned skin and silver hair where I once saw pale and brown, but I have seen that before, as a teenage volunteer working in different missions. I could just as easily be looking at one of my faces from Veracruz or Ethiopia as one from Mosul. The original James Phair is back. It doesn't feel as though I've been away."

"That's because your core beliefs didn't change," she remarked. "You collected ideas and experiences without being altered by them. You made them subjective instead of objective, though those can be reversed by changed circumstances. We have a medical term for that."

He looked at her with a look of patient, clerical inquiry.

"We call it 'the switcheroo,'" she explained. "Faith *can* move mountains."

He smiled back. "I am a modern-day Mohammad. Shall I change my name? Would the DoD appreciate that?"

A twisted grin was her answer.

"There is actually some truth to that," she went on. "These experiences have made you more connected to those distant prophets. They had moved among people who were very much like the ones you met. Their awe was your awe, their humility your humility. The difference is, all the faiths you encountered were cumulative in you. Each of those old prophets only received what each of them carried. They had an agenda of stamping out multiple faiths."

He settled back in the armchair, his mind skipping back. "You asked about my teaching post. The one thing that has changed since I started is how I feel about the students."

"How do you feel?" Major Dell asked.

"I see me as the old me, but I see the students as religious militants."

"You effectively began your career in the clergy as a teenager," she said.

"It was a haven."

"Were you a militant?" she asked. "I'm sure you saw and felt passion when you studied at the St. Charles Seminary. Isn't faith your own backbone and heart?"

"I felt safe there, and wanted," he said. "And I had faith but not certainty. These young people—and I have not been around them since I was a young enlistee here—but they seem to be not distractible in their beliefs, just like the Iraqis. Enlistment in the Chaplain Corps is up. I think, or at least I suspect, that some portion of the American youth is hungry to become zealots. Maybe that's a response to what they consider a threat to our way of life from the Middle East—I don't know."

"Perhaps they only seem that way against a backdrop of war," Major Dell suggested.

"No, these kids are different," he insisted. "They 'blog' about polarizing community issues and they get angry about things they read in other blogs. They bring cell phone cameras to rallies and post recordings of objectors on video websites. All of it is not only legal but they say it is justified, given the fervor of an adversary who challenges their faith and homeland."

"You're saying they target Muslims and you feel uncomfortable about that?"

"They target everyone, Major. Sikhs, Buddhists, atheists. This environment that should be inspiring is very un-settling."

"Any religious collective goes through phases, influenced by charismatic people or events," she said. "Students or acolytes in particular tend to be reactionary. We've seen that before, dating back to the Crusades—"

"They were waged with swords and arrows," he said. "The Inquisition, horrible as it was, was waged with primitive implements in a geographically narrow realm. But you're right. My students are like Raymond IV, Godfrey, and Tancred. They possess a level of aggressiveness that makes me feel like an outsider, or somehow a betrayer of the faith."

"Do you find yourself emotionally drawn to their side? Or are you being pulled in the opposite direction?"

"I'm paralyzed," he blurted. "I guess that's what bothers me. I can't move in any direction. I don't *want* to root for one side over the other."

"You want everyone to get along, like the truest Christian."

"Yes."

"Have you been to confession since you've been back?"

He nodded.

"How did that make you feel?" She wouldn't ask what he had said, but hoped this question would tell her.

"Like I was back in that Iraqi bomb shelter," he said. "I closed the door of the confessional and I sat down and I wanted to scream."

"Why didn't you?"

"It was a packed chapel, and only the priest is required to honor the seal of confession."

Major Dell scowled out a question. "Is that why
everyone whispers in the confessional?"

He nodded.

"I never knew."

"Make a note for your superiors," he added. "That's
the only religious secret I know."

The analyst gave him a disapproving look but let it
pass. It wasn't the confessional that had made him feel
trapped, she suspected. But what situation weighed
most heavily on him? The students? Being home and
bound to the base? The sixteen years he'd been lost and
wandering? Or sixteen years of feeling not lost at all?

This was going to take a while.

He looked at her. "That wasn't a joke, Major. Is the
army still worried that I've been turned?"

"I honestly can't say."

"You know, maybe it's not the captivity that scares me."

"What do you mean?"

"Well, as a kid, the church and my faith provided
fuel to keep me growing. While I was in Iraq, I needed
others to survive. Now that I'm back, the army has decided to give me everything I need until I don't need it
anymore or they don't need me. What happens when I
become self-sustaining?"

"Let's not fly before we've poked our beak over the
edge of the aerie."

"Am I that bad off?" He laughed self-consciously.

"Not at all," she replied. Then, trying not to sound
augural, she added, "But let's not assume that the army
wants to toss you, okay?"

"Okay," he said, looking at her with a little smile. "Though that's one thing that is very different in Iraq."

"What's that?" she asked with interest.

"The people were provincial," he said with knowing eagle eyes. "No one ever had to pretend they didn't know more than they knew."

CHAPTER TWELVE
ROCKVILLE, MARYLAND

Ryan Kealey was standing in his living room with the TV remote in his hand and his mouth open. He was staring at Dr. Hanif al-Shenawi on his 4K television. The channel was Al Jazeera America, which he'd reluctantly flipped to after catching a brief flash of the doctor on CNN. He figured they'd give the bastard all the coverage they could. Only the most basic facts would be reliable but this was a definite basic fact: the man who disappeared into a San Antonio mosque just before the mayor was assassinated was now going to be the top-level manager of a nonsectarian hospital in Basra that would be under joint stewardship of Iraq and Iran.

The news coverage did not include an interview with the doctor, only footage of him walking around the large, flat, dusty vacant lot where the hospital was going to be constructed, chatting and smiling with his colleagues, motioning in the air at future wings and floors. News of the hospital would have been staggering enough. News that the man who traveled an opium route out of Iran through Iraq only six months ago was going to be the public face of this project . . . Kealey wanted to sit down and spend the rest of the evening researching this, but the doorbell rang.

He was expecting her. After a few perfunctory phone calls, the courteous coolness of which made it clear that Kealey did not want to rekindle anything with Allison Dearborn, it had come down to the stupid, unavoidable fact that he still had a pair of her earrings. They were emeralds, they were antiques, they belonged to her grandmother, and she would have been heartbroken if anything happened to them in the mail. Even overnight mail couldn't be fully trusted. It made simple, aggravating sense for him to hand them to her, and since his neighborhood was on the way home for her from the office, her stopping by was preferable to being caught up in dinner somewhere. Kealey had no patience for small talk these days and an aversion to anything deeper, and dinner with her would surely strike deep. With this arrangement, even after the doorbell rang his mind could still be hovering on the broadcast, barely thinking of her.

He opened the door of his newish townhouse, virtually identical to every other townhouse in the area, brick in the front, vinyl siding in the back, no exterior decorations. In this neighborhood, it was a fair bet that any house without a summer flag in front or a red-white-and-blue-ribbon wreath on the door or children's toys out front or out back was the residence of a CIA employee. They were temporary leasers, counting down until they were reassigned as if the neighborhood were a helicopter pad, and Allison knew it. There was a trace of pity in her expression when he opened the door. He could have told her that he now owned the property on the mountain in Connecticut but he chose not to. The ownership was abstract. He hadn't set a foot on the land since the day he wired the down payment. And telling her might have complicated their simple ending.

"What's wrong?" she asked.

He shook his head, unwilling to engage in surprise that she could still read him so easily. He just walked back over the newish, beige wall-to-wall carpet to the living room, letting her close the door and follow him to the TV. The channel was now showing footage of Dr. al-Shenawi clucking over the crowded, unsanitary conditions in an existent hospital in some remote location in Iraq.

Allison looked at Kealey's face, looked at the TV. "It can't be the hospital that's the problem, so it must be the man," she said.

"I've been trying to find him for six months," Kealey said, choosing his words carefully as always to avoid giving too much information. "He was in a hot zone, let's put it that way. And he vanished. Even factoring in the help of his extremely powerful friends, the complete absence of clues for how he got out and where he went has been. . . ."

"Disappointing?"

"It's been a kick in the teeth. And suddenly here he is, fully publicized. We had no hint he was involved in this."

"So this is good, you found him."

Kealey laughed shortly and Allison glanced at him.

He had never laughed at her for any flash of optimism before.

"The hospital is a problem," he said.

"Because it's Iran working with Iraq? It's surprising for old enemies but surely it must be a good omen."

"Iraq and Iran have been cozying up for a few years now," Kealey said, his eyes fixed on the screen. "It was one of the unforeseen consequences of the sanctions against Iran for their nuclear program. They started to realize that they needed at least the semblance of friends and allies, so they started courting Iraq as soon as our troops pulled back. They started with one of the richest offerings they could make: natural gas."

"A trade agreement?"

"More fundamental than that. They ran pipelines into Iraq to make the exporting as easy and cheap as possible. Mutual assistance has been proliferating ever since. This isn't even the first joint hospital. The Iranians have been building clinics for their pilgrims to certain Shiite holy sites in Iraq."

"So this is a problem because our foreign policy has been assuming a natural state of distrust between the two of them?"

"Our foreign policy doesn't assume anything. Look, there have been instances where Iran has worked together with Al Qaeda. That's like yoking a shark and a crocodile together and watching them pull a plow. They hate each other, yet it happens, every now and then. So there are no illusions being shattered here. A hospital in Basra, a hub on a major opium route? No heads spinning over that one, either. But Iran publicly, proudly helping to build a nonsectarian hospital? That's a problem."

"Why?"

"Because it doesn't make sense. Iran still throws non-Muslims into jail for years whenever they feel like it. Christians and Jews are barely tolerated; everyone else is tormented at will. The regime isn't going to back off of that any time soon. So why? What are they gaining? What do they think they're doing?"

"Maybe Iraq made it a requirement of the joint partnership?"

"Sure," Kealey said, in a tone of voice that said, *not likely*. "And then they put this man at the head of it."

"He could be involved in opium?"

"A bit more than that."

Kealey abruptly turned off the TV, strode to the air conditioner gauge and turned it off, strode to the table next to the door where he picked up Allison's earrings, and placed them in her hand without looking at her. He refused to allow his mind to observe, at any level of remove, that this was a woman he'd once come very close to loving. He cut his mind into manageable surfaces like her emeralds.

"You're heading out, too?" she asked.

"I need to access some databases."

He reached for a cap from the coat-closet shelf. She put a hand on his other arm. "Ryan, I've never seen you like this. I've seen you in mission mode and this is different. You are locked off and locked down."

"I'm focused, Allison, that's all."

"No, I've seen you focused, too."

He made a move toward the front-door handle, but she stopped him.

"I don't need a Cassandra, Allison. I know what terrors the world holds in store."

"Yes, and you also know how you respond to them, which is why it's important for you to know when you're responding differently. If I had to guess, I would say that you are deeply confused at something, by something, over something . . . whatever it is, it is eating at you at your very core. And you look like you're going to pick up a ball-peen hammer and smash it because you don't understand it."

Again, he would not let himself feel surprise at her insight, but this time it was harder to sequester the reaction. She really was outstanding. He wanted to tell her about Hernandez, about Isobel Garcia. He wanted to confess to her that yes, it was driving him crazy, trying to figure out why the hired killer of the drug dealer would have assassinated the youngest Hispanic mayor in the United States. They had checked Garcia's history and it showed no reason why Hernandez would have any particular grudges against her, no indications that somehow she would be a more formidable opponent for him than anyone else had been. No connections at all. It was possible the killer was a mercenary and had simply been hired by someone else, but then Dr. al-Shenawi had been in San Antonio, too, after just meeting with Hernandez. The drug dealer had to have been involved. None of it made sense and they had no leads, because Hernandez had disappeared as completely as the doctor had. Every day Kealey cursed his assignment because he should have been the one to go after Hernandez. Instead he had wasted six months only to find another unfathomable event.

"I'm only useful when I'm locked down," he said.

"I understand why you feel that way," Allison said. "But be careful about—"

"Be careful about what I smash?"

"Yes but also, be careful about what hammer you choose."

She broke eye contact and put her earrings in her purse, signaling that he was free to go now. He hesitated. He wanted to, not give her something, not reward her for her insight, but let her know that he had heard her even though his decisions would probably be based on a thousand things other than her advice. It was still sane advice.

"As a psychiatrist," he said, "if you had to send someone over there to . . ."

"To keep an eye on things?" she said, smiling at how close he was edging on saying things he shouldn't.

"Yes. What kind of person would you send? I'm assuming not a surgeon, not an administrative type, maybe a nurse?"

"Well, to a nonsectarian hospital being run by two countries that may not completely grasp the meaning of the term? I'd send a man of God."

He half smiled. "Which god? Assuming that an American imam, for example, would be under suspicion because he could be turned."

She shook her head. "You live in a cold and brutal world, Ryan Kealey."

She put her hand on the door handle and let herself out.

Kealey watched her walk down the cement path toward her car. He stepped out, closed the door after him, and followed the same path to his own. After all they had experienced together, been with each other, they simply half raised their arms in good-bye. Then he followed her taillights out of the suburb.

CHAPTER THIRTEEN
JEBEL MUSA, SINAI PENINSULA

Until today, thirty two year-old Lieutenant Bassam Adjo—a five-year veteran of Egypt's elite Task Force 777—had never spied on his own country. On and above the borders looking outward, yes. On unauthorized aliens coming in, yes. But never on Egyptians in Egypt. That was the job of the Mubahath el-Dawla, the General Directorate of State Security Investigations, which reported to the minister of the interior and spied on everyone, including the minister of the interior. They were useless, the information they collected serving as a deterrent to anyone within the government acting against anyone else within the government. The result was the same as if no one had any intelligence about anyone else. That was all nonsense. But this . . .

Spying on ordinary citizens made him uneasy, as if the precious democracy he supported—an oasis in a desert of theocracies and dictatorships, so incredibly hard won after the years of Egyptian Spring and subsequent falls of several governments—was starting to dry around the edges once more.

Perhaps, though, this mission was not without justification, he told himself. At least he hoped so. He loved and respected his organization too deeply to imagine its mission changing.

Based northeast of the capital in a nondescript hangar at the Cairo International Airport, the seventy-man Task Force 777 typically patrolled the outer regions of the ancient nation in a fleet of Mi-8 and Westland command choppers. Now, however, a commando group under Lieutenant Adjo was crouched on a ledge 1,920 meters above Wadi el-Deir, the passage that connects Mt. Sinai to the Plain of el Raha—the Plain of Rest, where the restless Israelites awaited the return of Moses and built themselves a calf of gold to worship.

Adjo was lying on his belly, the sleeves of his leather jacket fluttering as he stared at the Mountain of Moses through night-vision goggles. He was studying a black cave at the summit of the sacred mountain. It was in this cave that the prophet was said to have dwelt for forty days while he communed with God and crafted the tablets of the Ten Commandments.

Beside Adjo, Cpl. Kek Massari was listening to an electro-acoustic amplifier. They lay in silence until, with a heavy sigh, Massari removed the headphones.

"The wind is too severe," Massari said, pulling the hood of his jacket over his ears. "I can't make out anything."

"I can't see very much, either," Adjo admitted. All he had seen since they arrived three hours before, shortly before dusk, were the thirty or so pilgrims milling around the mouth of the cave.

Adjo rolled on his side and motioned to a radio operator who was crouching by his equipment outside a
tent, the canvas flaps whipping in the cold mountain
air. The young man hurried over and dropped to his
knees beside the officer.

"Tell the pilot we're staying the night," Adjo said,
cupping his hand by the private's ear.

"Staying the night," he repeated. "Yes, sir."

The private ran back to his radio and transmitted the
message. The helicopter that had ferried the four men—
the fourth member, huddled inside the tent, was a veteran climber in case they needed to reach a different
vantage point—had landed on an outcropping on the
other side of the mountain, some three hundred meters
down, where it could not be heard or seen by anyone
on Mt. Sinai. Theirs was a delicate reconnaissance due
to the nature of the reputed individual they were seeking and the ramifications of whatever he might be
doing.

"Did you tell him we're staying?" asked Massari.

Adjo nodded.

"We are among the fortunate," Massari said sarcas-
tically, rolling his eyes heavenward.

"We have warm clothes, at least," Adjo said, taking
another look at the cave. "Not like those robed devils.
Take a break until the wind quiets."

"I don't mind waiting with—"

"Grab it when you can get it," Adjo admonished
him.

Massari gathered his gear to go to the tent as Adjo
continued to watch the cave. He had never been to Mt.
Sinai. Due to the high tourist volume and the fact that
three major religions revered Moses and had to com-

mingle here, this region was a joint protectorate of the Egyptian government and the United Nations. Though he was not a particularly religious man, Adjo was not immune to the power of these ancient sites. This place was not like the pyramids at Giza, which were the handiwork of men. Here, the hand of God had been felt. His voice had echoed through the very crags at which Adjo was looking.

That was a lot for a man to comprehend. He didn't know how Moses did it. He was a prophet, yes, but still a man. Did one just accept that the finger of the Almighty had touched him? Did events simply carry him along, events whose tides and currents the shepherd could not resist? Perhaps both. Or perhaps he was a man big enough, wise enough, strong enough to believe that he could do what, after all, God had appointed him to do.

Maybe it was just as well that he had this assignment. The lieutenant could not afford to be swayed by what he sensed, by what he wanted to feel, only by what he saw. The mission was too important for misinterpretation.

The powerful binoculars sat on a small, squat tripod that prevented the equipment from shaking as Adjo's hands trembled in the cold. A stubby antenna jutted from between the two eyepieces and pale white numbers scrolled along the bottom left of the green, glowing image, a time-stamp and file reference numbers for the digital recording being made on a laptop in the tent. It was a very different age for surveillance compared to when Adjo first joined the army in 1998. Back then, the big transition was still replacing the aged Soviet equipment with new infantry combat vehi-

cles from the United States. When the war against jihadists began in 2001—a slow-burning World War III
to those who were inclined to take a long, large view—
more and more sophisticated electronics were added to
the arsenal. The son of a fisherman who hated the
water—it was too restricting for him—Adjo was excited
to transfer to 777 when the opportunity arose. He loved
the adventure but that was the least of what motivated
him on patrols in the dry, baking desert and now the
mountains. He loved being a part of one of the most
honored divisions of the oldest military force on the
planet. Whereas most of his comrades had joined the
military as a way to make a living—and there was certainly nothing dishonorable about that—the weight of
Adjo's responsibility had inspired him to levels of performance he had never imagined. His commanding of
ficer had two brass paperweights on his desk which
no longer held paper, merely these sentiments: one
said, "The Army Makes Men," the other, "Men Make
the Army."

"Which is the truer?" Lieutenant General Samra
would ask newcomers.

In twenty years, according to the officer, no one had
ever been able to choose.

After another hour there was movement outside the
cave they were watching. Adjo clacked two rocks three
times their prearranged summons—and Massari hurried
over. Everything he heard, like everything Adjo saw, was
also being digitally stored. As Massari rolled up the hem of
his wool cap and slid the headphones on, people were
emerging from the cave, incongruously holding battery-
powered lanterns.

If this was the work of God, the bushes would burn,
Adjo thought, comforted by his own clear grasp of the
situation.

He watched the group of men, now forty-odd strong,
most of them wearing dark, loose-fitting *djellabas* with
the hoods drawn up for warmth, as they formed a semi-
circle, their backs to Adjo. They were looking at the
mouth of the cave.

Suddenly, something fell among the men, landing
heavily at their feet. The three men nearest the object
flinched, taking backward steps that kicked up a fine
layer of sand.

Adjo studied the object. It appeared to be a pole about
two and a half meters long. Though the dust partially obscured Adjo's view, what he did see confounded him.
The pole appeared to expand width-wise at one end, as
though it were a child's balloon inflated with a single,
long breath. This fattened end shifted slightly from
side to side and appeared to rise slightly, all under its
own power, it seemed; while the bulk of the pole, still
earthbound, twitched once in S-curves along its length
and back again. After a moment, the serpentine shape
lay down and was stiff again. Hands emerged from the
darkness of the cave to retrieve the object.

"They seem to be chanting," reported Massari. His
voice was calm; in the darkness, he had seen nothing
of what had transpired.

Adjo raised one of his companion's earphones.
"What are they saying?" he demanded.

Massari replied, "The Stranger has returned!"

CHAPTER FOURTEEN
WASHINGTON, D.C.

Jonathan Harper had loved Washington, once.

When he had first arrived years ago, he'd felt profoundly that if he didn't work in government he would have worked at a café or sold tickets at Union Station or driven a cab, just to be around all this. It didn't only feel like the center of the world, it *was* the center of the world. What was decided in every office had ripple effects through every other office and thus, through all of civilization.

Then down through history, he thought as he drove toward Capitol Hill for a meeting with a senator.

And the city endured. Washington and all it represented had weathered the extremes of Joseph McCarthy and Jimmy Carter. It had survived wars and terror threats, impeachments and assassinations. And it would always endure. As the old joke went, "Show of hands, all those in favor of abolishing democracy!"

He still loved his job but now he was no longer sure whether he deserved to love his job, having failed it.

He was supposed to be protecting the nation, and Isobel Garcia was dead.

It was nine a.m. and he was stuck at his fifth red light in a row when he received a secure text message from Ryan Kealey:

EN ROUTE TO FT. JACKSON

Always full of little surprises, Harper thought. And sometimes big ones.

Rather than text him back, the deputy director waited until he could access a secure phone line in the Russell Senate office building. Simultaneously, he opened his tablet and pulled up the IACA file on the base. The Inter-Agency Cooperation Assessment file rated the affiliations and loyalties of every military, intelligence, and industrial resource in the world. It was the equivalent of pledged delegates in a political contest. Fort Jackson's commander, General Emory Farrell, came up with a cumulative tag of intelligence cooperation at 41 percent.

That was a good ranking for a military officer. One hundred percent, for example, would be if the president ordered everyone on the base to a war zone. General Farrell would, of course, comply. This rating—based on past experience with organizations other than the military—meant that a petitioner asking for military cooperation on a nonmilitary undertaking would have a near-even chance of getting a favorable response. Considering that Farrell's cooperation with the navy was rated at 32 percent, that was encouraging.

What Harper didn't know, of course, was what Kealey was hoping to accomplish at Fort Jackson. Kealey was pretty independent, with Harper's blessings, but at least he kept his superior in the loop, even now when Harper knew he was continuing to rankle over Hernandez.

"What have you got?" Harper asked when Kealey picked up.

"Someone who would be perfect for the trip," Kealey said. "I wanted to get to him before someone else does."

"Name?"

"Major James Phair."

"Isn't he the AWOL who did the Iraq walkabout?"

"That's the man," Kealey said. "Only I'm not convinced he was AWOL. Not strictly speaking."

"Sure sounded like it when I read the repatriation debrief summary," Harper said.

"Well, if you want to look at it *that* way, it sounded more like treason, aiding and abetting an enemy combatant," Kealey said.

"Right. That's much better."

"But I don't think 'sounded like' is enough to base a decision on. Anyway, that's why I want to get a measure of the man himself."

"Shit," Harper said to no prompt in particular. It was a general, all-encompassing utterance.

"I know," Kealey said.

"This trip of yours already has more potential holes than surface," Harper said. "I have no budget, no support. We have no evidence the doctor was involved in San Antonio, no firm, justifiable reason to suspect his motives and actions with this hospital in Iraq—"

"So, fine. We're on our own, trying to stand on balloons," Kealey said. "What else is new?"

"Balloons?"

"Something I saw at a circus in Shanghai," Kealey said. "Too much weight in one place, they pop. Lean wrong, you fall. But if you center yourself exactly, neutralize your downward impact the way this Chinese acrobat did—"

"I see."

"Look, we need someone who can read the situation in terms of both practical logistics and theological analysis. It's going to be tough finding a nonsecular national we can buy or a local we can train. We might as well look at someone who has had a foot in both worlds and is still a federal employee."

Harper had to agree with the reasoning—the logic of compromise—even if he didn't relish the reality. He rubber-stamped the visit to Fort Jackson. Sincc Kealey's logged itinerary was filed at six a.m., showing he was catching a seven-ten flight to Columbia Metropolitan Airport, his feet were probably already on the ground in South Carolina, anyway.

Kealey told him he would text as soon as he had additional information, though the deputy director knew him well enough to know this: whatever he received would probably be after the fact. In this case, though, Harper didn't blame him.

They had no strong reason to be tracking Dr. al-Shenawi, so the less Harper knew about it before Kealey did anything, the better. The agent's diminished level of communication with his old friend, which had been notable since Texas, saddened Harper but didn't surprise him.

CHAPTER FIFTEEN
CAIRO, EGYPT

On the books, the two hangars at the Cairo International Airport were a training center for the Egyptian Military Academy. But it was an open secret that this was a staging area and barracks for Task Force 777. The government had chosen this site for that reason. They wanted emissaries from other nations, especially countries in this region, to see the comings and goings of the airborne soldiers. They wanted outsiders to know that Egypt was watching its borders, that gunships were prepared to take action against expeditionary forces. They wanted the world to know that their internal affairs were settled and strong enough to withstand any scavengers who might be thinking Egypt had been weakened over the past few years.

After the helicopter had returned to collect them as scheduled, Lieutenant Adjo and his team had gone directly to the debriefing center in Hangar One to make their report. It was a small room with ivory-white walls and a small wooden conference table in the center.

There was a computer, a phone, and a pitcher of water with a glass. There were folding chairs, which the men opened for themselves. They were not permitted to go to barracks, however much a shower and change of clothes would have been welcome. The lieutenant general liked his information raw, unwashed, without a cleared head. He feared that minute, important observations could be lost or memories freshened as traces of the site itself were washed away.

Adjo was not looking forward to the meeting. He disliked failure, disliked it more than his superiors. But that was small comfort. He had confirmed that something was going on up there, but that was all. He had been unable to identify anyone and had chosen not to go to the cave to reconnoiter. That was outside the mission parameters and he did not want to risk scaring away whoever was there.

Adjo gave the memory sticks containing the audio and video data to a staff sergeant who loaded them into the computer just as Task Force 777 commander Lt. Gen. Adom Kaphiri Samra arrived. He had dark eyes, a trim moustache, and a crisp uniform that was nonetheless sweat-stained under the arms. He had been working hard. He had been *worrying* hard.

The men stood and saluted. Samra motioned for them to sit. "What did you find out?" the officer asked eagerly.

"Sir, we should talk after you see the data," Adjo said.

Samra frowned. "Is a picture worth so much or is your data worth so little?"

"Both, sir."

Samra continued to frown—directly at Adjo now—

as he motioned for the sergeant to run the recordings. Adjo had spent the three-hour return flight trying to figure out exactly what to say to his superior. That wasn't it. Yet Samra—who was a fierce nationalist—would probably like the next part even less.

Adjo and Massari had bookmarked sections where figures were active and noteworthy events transpired. That was roughly five minutes of merged video and audio. After watching the section with the serpent four times—which was the bulk of the recording—the commander rose so that he could see the men. His expression had gone from displeased to puzzled. It matched that of Adjo.

"I see what appears to be a stick becoming a snake and then a stick again," the officer said.

"That is what appears to be happening," Adjo agreed.

"What did your *eyes* tell you?" he asked.

Adjo was silent.

"Sir," Massari said, "I was watching the cave without night-vision glasses and I saw nothing but the lanterns and their immediate vicinity."

The dark eyes of the senior officer shifted slowly from the acoustic engineer back to Adjo. "You heard nothing?"

"Only the wind, sir."

Samra steepled his fingers on the table and leaned forward.

"I had men on the scene who saw and heard very little," he said. "Yet people who were not there know much."

"Sir?" Adjo said.

"Between last night and my coming here, Internet

discussion of this man has quadrupled," Samra said. "In just the last hour, visa applications from our sister countries have increased"—he tapped the keyboard and looked at the monitor—"sevenfold. We can slow the processing of these applications, but that will not stop many from crossing the borders illegally. Either they know something we do not—which, I needn't point out, would be rather an embarrassment as this is an intelligence division—or they are being misled. Either this man we were not quite observing is the prophet Moses returned or he is not. So. What do I tell the commander in chief? What does he tell the supreme commander?"

The four men were uncomfortably silent.

"Should we infiltrate the cave with the next wave of pilgrims, who are bound to arrive presently?" Samra asked with growing impatience.

"I am not sure that would produce useful results," Adjo offered.

"Why is that, Lieutenant?"

"If this man is not the *Gharib Qawee,* no one will believe us," Adjo said. "Besides, an effective disinformation program would take days if not weeks to mount. Conversely, proving that to be so would accomplish nothing. We would still have the problem of what to do with him and the crowds he is bound to attract."

"Do you have a constructive next-step offer?"

"Perhaps," Adjo said. "I read the daily intelligence packet on the ride back. It contained an interview with the English professor Wesley, who first observed this phenomenon last week. Did you see it, sir?"

"I have not yet read the transcription," Samra told him. "Perhaps you can summarize it?"

"Sir, he referred to this as a 'throwback' to ancient days, when what he described as 'a movement through the grasses' elevated remote desert and mountain hermits to the level of holy teachers and *mahdis*."

"This 'movement through the grasses,'" Samra asked. "What does that mean exactly? Like a snake?"

"No, sir. It means a force, like a wind stirring the land," Adjo replied.

Therein the problem with all religious translations; the true and crucial meaning is in the subtleties. "So it's more like a wildfire?"

"That is a fair translation, yes, sir. In this case, since the fire already exists, the question is how do we douse it?"

"Can we evict him as a religious agitator?" Massari asked.

"That might cause the flame to grow brighter," Adjo suggested.

"And if this is real, we must be careful," said the radio operator, who seemed anxious. "I mean, sir, it was real once in history. Could it not be again?"

"I don't believe that," Samra said. "I won't."

"If this man is real, we probably won't succeed in stopping him any better than we did the last time," Massari said.

Samra shot him an angry look.

"I still say it doesn't matter," Adjo insisted. "Even if we were to capture this man and his magic rod, he could say that his is the only hand that can make it work and he can decline to do so. Even if he is a false prophet, the believers will continue to believe."

"We don't even know who he is or what he looks like," Samra pointed out. "I wonder if he was hiding from you or from his own people."

"Why hide from his own people?" Massari asked.

"The unseen is more powerful than that which is in the open," Samra told him.

"Which is what I was leading up to," Adjo said. "If we *can* get a look at him, perhaps we can trace his movements back to where this started. We might be able to attach him to a cabal of some kind. Perhaps some foreign military. That might undermine his credibility with the common people."

"I'm not sure such a connection exists," Samra said. "Before you arrived I was reviewing images taken over the past week by the GRU's Bliska-3 satellite."

The GRU—Glavnoye Razvedyvatel'noye Upravleniye, the KGB's rival and survivor—was Russia's General Intelligence Directorate. The Kremlin had a mutual support pact with Egypt that gave Cairo access to Middle East satellite data and Moscow the use of Egyptian airspace for sorties to protect tankers entering the Mediterranean from the Black Sea.

"I wanted to try and determine if we were dealing with an individual or a group," Samra said. "There do not seem to be any unusual patterns of group traffic. Image-comparison software suggests that every tourist who went up the mountain as part of a group came down as a group. I examined bus records. No missing persons were reported. My presumption is that an individual arrived, perhaps on foot or by taxi, went up at night to prevent being spotted from above, and began his ministry."

"How, sir?" Adjo asked. "Did he simply start throwing down his stick to the ground and wait for people to notice?"

"Why not?" Samra asked. "Prophets don't think the way we do."

"You just told us the Englishman likened this to the way prophets made names for themselves in ancient times," Massari asked. "This would fit well with that idea."

Adjo nodded but he didn't buy it.

"Lieutenant, I agree that we must investigate every angle," Samra told him. "But we mustn't simply assume there is a conspiracy. If we are facing one crazy or ambitious individual, that would be better than having to deal with a larger, well-organized plot. It would certainly inform our tactics going forward."

Massari shrugged. "The man could just disappear from his cave one night."

"Sir, I would prefer if your scenario were correct," Adjo said to the lieutenant general. "But I can't believe the video crew just *happened* to be there when a pilgrim who *happened* to see someone who said he was the prophet just *happened* to come down the mountain."

"They were at that site for fifteen hours," Samra pointed out. "To see one man in that time is hardly a miracle. I'm not saying this so-called prophet may not have accomplices, which is why I want you to go there, Lieutenant. See what you can discover, find out whether this is the work of God or men."

"Yes, sir," Adjo said. He was still chewing on what Samra had said. It wasn't going down. "And what then? Time may not be on our side."

"I honestly don't know," Samra admitted. He watched the recording again. "I'm going to send this out to allied intelligence services and see what they make of it, what they suggest."

From where he was sitting, Adjo could see the screen. The image was green, grainy, inconclusive. Adjo the military officer wanted to know what was happening out there. He wanted to keep his country safe. But Adjo the man wanted to know as well. He was not a Muslim of great faith and yet something had touched him out there. He wanted to make sure it was the mountain, perhaps the shadow of history, and not the man they were investigating.

The lieutenant general removed the memory stick and put it in his shirt pocket. He faced his men and they stood.

"We'll have this computer-enhanced, but I doubt it will tell us much," he said. "You know, I'm informed that the priests of the pharaoh were able to duplicate this miracle using simple catches and releases set inside a painted tree branch."

"I myself have seen street corner magicians perform similar tricks, causing canes to sag and stiffen," Massari remarked. "The transformation itself means nothing."

"To us," Adjo said.

"You're right," Samra told him. "And I hope to keep it that way."

"What do you mean, sir?" the radio operator asked.

Samra turned to go and the team saluted.

"I mean I truly hope this man is a fake," the commander replied as he left the room. "I've had boils and I don't like them."

CHAPTER SIXTEEN
FORT JACKSON,
SOUTH CAROLINA

It was Major Dell's dream that one day she would have an orderly. That had not yet happened. Here, though—unlike Iraq—she had a buzzer. When someone came to the door, she didn't have to shout.

She expected the callers and let them in. Ryan Kealey was tall, in his forties, and dressed in civilian clothes. General Emory Farrell was a head shorter, some ten years older, and barrel-chested. The officer shut the door behind them.

"Thanks for seeing me," Kealey said, shaking her hand after she'd saluted the general.

"Your call intrigued me."

"Plus, I ordered her," Farrell said. He didn't sit but stood fidgeting anxiously as he gestured for the others to be seated. Only Major Dell did.

"So?" Kealey asked her. "How about the major?"

"He's all right," she said.

"Define 'all right,'" Kealey said. "And be specific.

Please." He was impatient. He wanted answers, not the usual bureaucratic dance.

"The major is feeling a little lost, a little alienated, a little claustrophobic—"

"The first two I got. Would you care to explain that last one?" Kealey urged.

She sat back. "Major Phair is being choked by the support system he needs here—"

"Here as in 'Fort Jackson' or as in 'the United States'?"

"Both."

"How does that manifest itself?" Kealey asked.

"General restlessness," she replied. "He's been used to free-ranging, not sitting. He *wants* to be somewhere else without making a complete break, so having both feet in one place upsets him."

"A straddler? Indecisive?"

"No," she said emphatically. "He's more like a kite. One that wants a long string and just as much tail as is required for stability."

"Who doesn't?" Farrell asked.

"Which is why your call interested me," she went on, ignoring the other officer.

"I didn't really tell you anything," Kealey said.

"You're with the CIA and you're asking about a cleric who spent well over a decade in the streets of Iraq," she said. "You have an operation that requires his skills, his experiences. It doesn't take a profiler to figure out that one."

"Maybe you should hire her," Farrell snorted.

"Maybe I will," Kealey said. He smiled, a little too disarmingly to be sincere. He used it like a surgeon's knife. "I have to know, yes or no: can we rely on him?"

"That depends."

"That's not yes or no."

"Do you want him abroad? Working domestically? Using his mind, his body, his faith? I can give you a yes or no to each of those, but there are a lot of combinations and variables."

"That's fair," Kealey replied. "Has he gone over?"

"No," she said. "He has not."

"But he's been living among Americans," Kealey said. "What happens if we send him back?"

"He'll no longer be living among Americans, sir," she replied.

The general smiled sweetly. "Until there's a drawdown, I'm not so sure of that."

"Touché," she said, embarrassed to have misstepped in front of Kealey. She moved on quickly. "Sirs, I've been looking for lingering psychological tripwires. I haven't found any."

"Do we know if he ever left Iraq during his time there?" Kealey asked.

"He says he didn't, and there are no fingerprints of Iraqi IAM," she replied.

"IAM?" Farrell asked.

"Input And Manipulation."

"She means 'brainwashing,'" Kealey said.

"That's right."

"What would those fingerprints be?" Farrell inquired.

"You can't remake the brain without psychological scarring," she said. "We've been studying subjects who have been held in Iran, for example, for five or more years and pulled out by special ops teams."

"Subjects?" Farrell asked.

"Tourists, soldiers, people we've allowed to be kidnapped."

"Helluva commitment on their part," Farrell said.

"It's the only way to do it," Kealey told him.

"Because the captives have been retrained by and spoken only with Iranian indoctrinators, they forget, and tend to trip over, colloquial phrases, both saying and comprehending them," Dell said. "That's because the psy-ops personnel in Iran were educated in English or American universities where they tended not to socialize with local students and did not pick up jargon."

"So the subjects are thrown by cadences and usage that jar with deeply planted overwrites," Kealey said.

"Repetitive overwrites," Maj. Dell said. "The key to IAM is repetition in circumstances of sensory deprivation."

"That's all they have to focus on," Kealey added.

"Right."

"I understand that Major Phair freaked out in a confessional," Kealey said.

His words were like thrown ice. "How do you know that?"

"I stopped in the chapel on the way to see the general, told some of the kids I was an old army buddy looking to surprise him," Kealey said. "They're a little green, you know."

"I think we need a base-wide directive," General Farrell said.

"I did give Major Dell a chance to divulge that when she said he felt claustrophobic," Kealey said.

"That information was privileged," she said.

Kealey didn't seem to care. His eyes remained on the major. "Would a man who was held, say, in a steel cage in somebody's desert cellar flip out in a situation like that?"

"He would display a wider range of anxieties," the psychologist said sternly.

"Beyond freaking out in a confessional," Kealey said.

"That's right. He would be prone to express rage whenever he felt trapped, not just physically but emotionally. He would be uneasy in cafeteria lines, a standing automobile, an elevator."

"You've had no reports of that kind of behavior?" Kealey asked.

"Major Phair was not held in a cage and brainwashed," Major Dell replied.

General Farrell shook his head slowly. "You know, Mr. Kealey, I'm not sure whether my decision should address your needs or his. He sounds a little iffy. And before you plant the 'national security' flag, sending an incomplete man into the field doesn't exactly help that cause, either."

"There will be a lot of eyes on him," Kealey assured him.

The general took a long breath and looked at Major Dell. "The part I would need you to sign off on is whether or not you think he's a security risk."

"General, I'm sure you remember the incident with Col. Tina Meadow at Fort Bragg," the psychologist replied. "She wasn't a security risk until her mom was about to lose her house and someone offered Colonel Meadow a suitcase filled with hundred-dollar bills."

"You can always expect the unexpected," the general said. "Our job right now is to consider the odds."

"Consider the situation," Kealey urged patiently. "I

need a cleric who speaks Arabic and knows the Iraqi people. I need someone who knows how to win their trust. The risk of inaction is worse than the slim chance we're taking the wrong action."

"How do you define a 'wrong action'?" Major Dell asked.

"James Phair causes World War III," Kealey said. "Short of that, he can't do a worse job than we're doing in the area of counter-theocratic operations. The jihad isn't dying, we may be looking at the start of a new push within it, a new alliance, and I need someone who can help me reverse that."

The Stalin Maneuver, Major Dell thought. Five years ago, during her fourteen-week Army Medical Department training at Fort Sam Houston, one of the instructors warned the class about the inevitable clash between intuitive psychological care and checklist military procedure. "The worst part won't be the disagreements," Col. Naomi Griss had warned her, "but the fact that your patients are commodities. Just don't succumb to the Stalin Maneuver, which the Russian dictator employed during World War II, which is to throw anyone and anything at a problem until something works. That cost him three million lives."

"At least let me talk to the man," Kealey implored. It was the first time he'd made a request that didn't sound like a demand.

"That's tantamount to turning him over to you," Major Dell said. "You'll work the claustrophobia, offer him space."

"No," Kealey assured her. "My ass is on the line, too."

General Farrell sat in the armchair opposite the desk

as he considered the request. In the distance, church bells sounded eleven a.m. That seemed to decide him. General Farrell pushed himself up using the armrests.

"Your patients have a more comfortable chair than I do," he told the psychologist. He quickly became serious. "Has Major Phair been off base since he arrived?"

"Only locally," she replied. "He goes to the movies, eats with students once in a while."

"So this could be good for him, too," the general said.

"It could."

"Can you say that with more conviction, Major?" the general asked.

"Sir, ideally I would have more time to make a determination. Absent that, I can only guess."

"And your guess is as good as his," the general cocked his head toward Kealey, who stood like a car in neutral, idling with an occasional rev in his eyes.

"Mr. Kealey does have one advantage," she said. "If he is allowed to take Major Phair from the base, at least he will be present in Washington to perform any midcourse corrections." She regarded him. "If the major goes to Iraq, will he go alone?"

"I don't know," Kealey said. "In any case, he wouldn't go unprepared. I don't want to lose him or jeopardize my work."

"Well, he's been instructed to wait in his apartment in the event he was needed," the general said. "I guess the next step is up to him."

Major Dell rose. "Then I've said all I can." She saluted the general and offered the other man her hand. "Good luck, sir."

Kealey thanked her, smiling somewhat more sincerely than before.

The men left together, leaving Dell feeling as though she'd been used. It was a Kabuki-like drama that Kealey had clearly intended to go a certain way. The fact that General Farrell had come here personally suggested that he was under some pressure from Washington to comply. She didn't see any point fighting it, and the general was correct. She had no good reason to dissent. If Phair proved reticent, he could be sent to some remote post like Fort Greely, Alaska, or on a typhoon-watch in the Republic of Palau, where soldiers had nothing to do but study radar screens and watch DVDs, and the clerics had less to do than that. If Phair opted to retire, he could be pressured by the threat of a dishonorable discharge or even a court-martial. Because the cleric had acquired a unique talent set in Iraq, his actions during and subsequent to the battle had never been reviewed by a military conduct panel. That was still an option. The DoD could still destroy him, professionally and spiritually.

She hoped that it would not come to that, though she wondered—even at the risk of personal peril—whether Phair would accept a position that might exploit the citizens he had lived among.

It wasn't her problem, though Dell knew what she would counsel if Phair asked.

Take it. Not from fear, not even from patriotism, but because the Middle East needed people of conscience.

Washington, too, she thought as the men's footsteps faded down the hall.

CHAPTER SEVENTEEN

FORT JACKSON,
SOUTH CAROLINA

Making things happen in government was like trying to put out a wildfire with spit. It's possible, but
just barely. And unless you dance while you're spitting,
you're definitely going to get burned, inhale smoke, lose
your bearings, and maybe lose your house if there's a
sudden change in the wind. Which is why, when Ryan
Kealey made up his mind to do something, he started
spitting . . . and dancing.

Kealey left General Farrell at the front of the medical building, where the general's driver met him and
brought him back to his office. The general did not say
much after they left Major Dell's office, other than to iter-
ate that he would honor Phair's own wishes in this matter
and abide by the psychologist's findings—which did not
seem like an endorsement to Kealey, but an avoidance of
committing to one. The psychologist saw no reason to
believe that Phair was a risk, but offered no real evidence that he was not.

If Kealey's field operatives gave him reports like that, the nation would be in the gravest peril.

It was a pleasant afternoon and, having secured directions from the driver on how to get to the new residential block, Kealey decided to walk.

The air was scented with freshly cut grass and diesel fuel, and there were a few patches of late tulips along his walk. The orderly layout of the base, the passing columns of vehicles and marching recruits, the clean, emphatic lines of the buildings, all spoke to the kind of organization that went completely to hell outside these walls. Kealey had been to Iraq and Afghanistan several times and—though he'd never say this to General Farrell—he would take a questionable, free-ranging operative over a mechanized brigade any day. The way to get these guys was to undermine them from within, like decay, not hammer them from without. It was great when a couple of five-hundred-pound bombs took out a terrorist leader. By their nature, however, those weapons also took out any civilians, residences, shops, and passersby who happened to be in the blast radius. Unavoidable, but a real spreader of ill will. The Iraqis had more respect for a combatant who pulled some bastard warlord from a hole in the ground by his hair, as they did to Saddam. In the end, in this struggle, combat was just a distraction. The real work was on the inside, the erosive stuff.

And who's the greater boon to the national goal? he thought. *A morally numbed reservist on his third consecutive tour of duty, or an American cleric who can, hopefully, still distinguish between an opportunity and a target?*

The salmon-colored homes with identical lines and sidings lay behind neat squares of lawns, which were tucked behind wide cement sidewalks and litter-free streets. It was a perfect, economical little community, and he wondered if that was an architect's vision or someone's compromise. Did someone think we'd all be better off living in giant ant colonies?

Is it a joke on the super-patriots? he wondered. *Are the people in charge inevitably Communists at heart?*

Sprinklers watered the small, identical lawns up and down the street. Kealey glanced at the numbers painted olive green on the curb. He squinted into the sun and saw Phair sitting in a folding lawn chair on a small patio at 323, away from the spray of the sprinkler. He recognized the cleric from his dossier photo. Phair was dressed in jeans and a military-issue short-sleeve shirt. His silver hair was cut short and he was clean-shaven. In the photos from Baghdad, it had been long and he'd worn a thin beard which had prevented his cheeks and chin from turning bronze.

Kealey raised his left hand in greeting, Phair raised one in acknowledgment—like two Native American braves meeting unexpectedly and warily on the trail—and the agent turned up the narrow cement path that bisected the lawn perpendicular to the sidewalk.

"Sorry to keep you hanging around like this," Kealey said, extending his hand. It was always good to open an attack with an apology for it. That softened resistance. "I'm Ryan Kealey, special agent, CIA."

The other man rose easily and accepted the hand. "James Phair." Phair's grip was strong. His brown eyes were wary but unflinching.

"Pleasure to meet you," Kealey said.

Phair was studying him. "You don't look like a Company man."

"How so?"

"Those boys are all hungry, like bees in the morning. You're relaxed."

"I'm—well, let's just say I'm not one of the regulars and leave it at that for now."

"A defrocked priest who still has faith," Phair said, warming.

"Something like that."

"You want to talk inside or out?" Phair asked graciously. Either he had good manners or was looking to put Kealey at his ease for a counterattack.

"Here is fine," Kealey told him.

"I'll get another chair."

"Don't bother," Kealey said, leaning against the rubbery vinyl rail, putting the sharp afternoon sun behind him. "I don't much care for being on my ass."

Phair sat back down and squinted up at his guest. "What kinds of things do you do when you're off this ass?"

"Nice try, but as I just suggested I'm not going to talk about that," Kealey said with a smile. "Interesting work, though. I like to think it's important."

"Do you enjoy it?"

"That's too strong a word," Kealey said. "Let's call it 'necessary.' What about you? Do you enjoy what you're doing here?"

"Oh," Phair sighed. "I'm guessing you know the answer to that."

"Actually, I don't," Kealey told him. "I know what you've said to others and what they've said to me, but I don't trust hearsay. Everyone has an agenda, even if they don't realize it. Facts get spun. Let me be more specific. Do you enjoy teaching here?"

"The work is challenging," Phair said carefully.

"Rewarding?"

"To a point," he replied.

"Would you ever consider doing anything more challenging?"

Phair was still being cautious. "Such as? And please, Mr. Kealey. Don't go fishing on me. What do you need?"

Kealey liked that. He had been waiting for a sign of the real Phair, and there it was. "Iran and Iraq are getting together on a nonsectarian hospital in Basra. We're worried about the opium route, about why Iran would suddenly start promoting nonsectarianism, a few other things. We're thinking about putting someone on the inside," Kealey said. "I need you on it. Maybe to go inside, maybe just to plan, but definitely to be involved."

Phair chuckled. "Wow."

"What?"

"I spent sixteen years among a nation of hagglers," he said. "The only people who were as direct as that had their faces covered with black cloth and carried Iranian weapons."

"Well, at least you're on the same side as *this* radical," Kealey said with a mirthless little laugh.

He watched Phair's reaction carefully. The cleric pursed his lips and nodded. He did not look away. "Thank you for that," Phair said.

At that moment, Kealey saw a surety of purpose. He believed he could trust this man.

"You're welcome. The heart of it is, I'm offering you a job, Major, a more interesting one, I hope, than what you're doing now. But before I say more, I must know if you're interested. There are security issues."

"I'm interested in helping people spiritually, Mr. Kealey. I'm not clear how spying fits in with that."

"That's a ratty little word," Kealey said with distaste. "Private eyes looking for adulterers 'spy.' We collect data."

"My apologies," Phair smiled.

"To answer your question, this is a larger task of intelligence-gathering and interpretation. With perks."

"Perks?"

"We have a license to kill," Kealey said.

Phair looked at him with horror that came on like a quick, summer thunderstorm.

"That last part was a sort of a joke," Kealey said.

"Thanks for clarifying," Phair said with a nervous laugh. "But you're not kidding."

"Major, like you, we're interested in protecting the innocent, whoever they are. Anyone who is vulnerable to terrorist activity."

"When I was in Iraq—"

"You hung out with some pretty rough *hajiis*," Kealey interrupted. "And survived. Few Americans can claim to have done that."

"I had to prove myself in ways"—Phair stopped, swallowed—"ways of which I'm not terribly proud."

"Such as?"

Phair's eyes dropped. He stared at the vinyl slats underfoot. "I once noticed men yelling at women and children just before an improvised explosive attack," he said quietly. "That's not uncommon, but after the street exploded beneath an American convoy I asked the on-

lookers if the men who were yelling were the men who
had rigged the IEDs. They said yes. They said the men
were telling them that if they warned the Americans,
they would be killed in their beds. When the rest of the
American convoy searched for the perpetrators, I remained with the children and said nothing. One of the
bombers was still watching. I could have identified
myself and left with the convoy, but these people could
not. They would have been killed."

"Tough call," Kealey said.

"What would you have done?"

"I probably would have encouraged—no, *urged*—
them to talk and offered them protection."

"Where? In some other town? Would *you* want to be
relocated from Washington to Havana or Cape Town?"

"Some days, yes."

Phair smiled a little. "The point is, they wouldn't have
left and coalition soldiers couldn't protect them forever.
Jihadists have long memories. They're still angry about
the Crusades." Phair's faraway expression suggested
there was something more.

"You gave the locals advice afterward," Kealey said.

Phair's eyes snapped up. "How did you know?"

"It's what priests do. What did you tell them?"

Phair took a steadying breath. "That if they saw the
insurgents again, to thank them for not harming the
children."

That surprised Kealey, though he didn't show it.
"Why?"

"The security of their families is the only blessing
they can realistically hope for," Phair replied. "They
must protect that, aggressively. And—looking ahead,

the Iraqis need more children who are going to grow up with reasonable voices based on generous spirits, not bombers."

"Some people would say you were teaching them appeasement."

"I would call it goodwill," Phair said. "Feed an angry dog often enough and it may one day cease to be angry. That works for the spirit as well."

Now he sounded like Major Dell, conjecturing and extrapolating. Kealey preferred facts: a dead terrorist was better than one who might be rehabilitated. Still, he understood where the cleric was coming from.

Phair looked toward the apartment. "Would you like a drink? I've got water and Coca-Cola."

"I'm okay," Kealey said.

"I'm going to get myself something," Phair said, rising.

Phair went inside and Kealey looked out at the flat, chocolate-colored roofs across the street. There was a glint in the window of one, a prismatic sliver from behind a vase filled with hydrangeas. Kealey smiled. Somewhere in the distance he heard a lawnmower. Farther along the street someone was grilling hamburgers. There was a small garden to his right, just in front of the patio. The simple comforts and security Phair had described as lacking in Iraq were abundant here. Instead of enjoying them for himself, he was still clearly lamenting that others didn't have it. That reinforced Kealey's impression that the man would do what was necessary to bring peace to the land. He just had to choose the right time to tell him about Dr. al-Shenawi, the main purpose of the mission.

Phair returned with a plastic bottle, which he set be-

side him as he sat. His hand remained around the bottle.

"Does it remind you of Iraq?" Kealey asked, indicating the bottle.

Phair chuckled. "How'd you know?"

"Coke is big there. Plus, the bottle is safe here, but
you're holding it. Lot of quick thieves over there."

"You're a one-man intelligence agency," Phair said.

"And a stockholder in Coke," Kealey said. "Amazing what you learn about national habits from local
bottlers. So, Major Phair. What do you think?"

"I don't suppose I can have a day or two to think
about it," Phair said.

"My cell is on silent."

"I'm sorry?"

"That's a development you missed," Kealey said. "It
vibrated five times since I've been here. I didn't answer it. In modern parlance, that means I'm serious
about this."

"I see."

Kealey positioned himself casually but strategically
between Phair and the street. "Would it help you decide if I told you there's a woman using binoculars to
watch and lip-read in the living room of number 324?"

Phair frowned. But he didn't look over. Iraq had
trained him not to look at potentially dangerous people. Men like those bombers he had seen didn't like to
be identified later, even by the design of their clothes
or the shoes they were wearing. Not with American
soldiers arresting anyone who might be a bomber.

"How do you know?" Phair asked.

"You spend a lot of time on the patio. The sun, Iraq,
good memories—they comfort you, just like the Coke.

The sprinklers would drown out audio, so I looked for someone eye-level with your chair and found her."

"Damn."

"That's why I'm sitting with my back to the street."

"I just got that," Phair said.

"Your apartment is almost certainly bugged, so if you do stay here I would ask you not to say anything about what I just told you, any of it, to anyone."

Phair shook his head. "How do I know it's the general doing it and not you?"

"Well, there you have it."

"Pardon?"

"The difference between spying and what we do," Kealey grinned. "We engage people face-to-face."

"I suppose it could be Homeland Security, too," Phair said.

Kealey was surprised and showed it.

"You're not the first agent to take an interest in me, Mr. Kealey," Phair answered his unasked question. "Shortly after I was brought back to the base in Iraq, there was a woman who sat in on a session with me."

"By your permission, I hope."

"Yes, of course. I forget her last name but her first name was Dina."

The Icebreaker, Kealey thought. Phair was right, that could be one of her agents across the street behind the hydrangeas. He doubted DHS would bother to send someone to shadow the cleric in Basra, but it was a possibility, and there could be some red tape and turf-squabbling as a prelude. Unless he snuck the cleric out but sent the Icebreaker the equivalent of a polite note, letting her know the man was now under Kealey's care.

"I had never heard of Homeland Security before I was introduced to Dina," Phair said. "I was somewhat removed from the news. On September eleventh I was half a day's travel from a television."

"They had cleaned up the broadcasts then, by the time you saw any of them," Kealey said.

"Yes, but I'm accustomed to imagining stories left untold," Phair said. "Such as a person's last choice between a wall of fire and an open window. I believe that one of the greatest achievements of Jesus was simply his journey among people whose stories were ignored, to reveal and honor their suffering with the hope that it would then be changed. He saved them from the eraser of historians with too little time and too few pages. That was an act as divine as any other."

"I suppose you could say that about any prophet, as well as the messiah."

"In nearly every faith," Phair said.

"I'm curious, did you have conversations of this kind in Iraq?"

"You're asking, did I express my Catholic faith freely?"

"Yes."

"It was so clear to me that I was there to learn, Mr. Kealey. The sound of my own voice would have obstructed my ears. But yes, there were certain moments with certain people, when there were no feelings of suspicion, that I discussed my faith, too."

"Your awareness of those feelings of suspicion, of being able to gauge the emotional tenor of a situation, that was what I was guessing would make you a good candidate for me."

"I am not foolproof," Phair said. "I was told, and shown, that I was being watched and I did not change my behavior."

"But you're sharpening up right now."

Phair took a swallow of Coke. He held the can in front of his mouth while he used his forearm to wipe his brow. "They're that worried about me?"

"That cautious."

"Mr. Kealey, I love this country and I love those poor, besieged people. If I have to decide right now—if I can help one without hurting the other, I'm in."

"We want the same thing," Kealey assured him.

"I won't harm innocents on any side," Phair insisted. He lowered his arm, revealing his lips to the surveillance. "Nor will I put them in jeopardy."

"Life is never so clean and clear-cut, and war is less so," Kealey said. "I will try not to put you in that position. But I would also point out that, with me, you will be in a position to help those same people. And you will lose your guest across the street."

Phair glanced at the house opposite, then at the sky. "For sixteen years I kept reminding myself that wherever I am, I'm beneath God's sky. In the remotest village with the crudest of resources, I would look up and feel that I was home." His eyes drifted back to the house at 324. "I liked it better when it was just God and His angels watching me."

"Don't be too hard on General Farrell," Kealey said. "His higher authority is not as compassionate as yours."

Phair took another draft from the bottle, then stood. "I'll need about a half hour to pack."

"Take your time. The plane doesn't leave for two

hours and I've got a chopper waiting to take us to Columbia Metropolitan."

"We're flying commercial?"

"Anonymity is our middle name."

"What's our first and last name?" Phair asked, half in jest.

Kealey replied earnestly, "Trust and No One."

CHAPTER EIGHTEEN
JEBEL MUSA, SINAI PENINSULA

From a distance, it is difficult to tell where the Monastery of St. Catherine ends and Mt. Sinai, situated to the north, begins.

The ancient walled compound is named after an evangelical who was beheaded in 307 C.E. after trying to convince the Roman Emperor Maxentius to stop persecuting Christians. Her remains were carried to the mountain, it is said, by angels. The monastery has the greatest religious library outside of the Vatican and includes the Codex Sinaiticus, one of the oldest extant copies of the Bible.

Lieutenant Adjo had seen the monastery from the air, where the eye roved unstopping over the sprawling gardens outside and the seven structures and small, ordinary wells and staircases within. From the ground, it was all about the wall, which varied in height from twelve to fifteen meters with sides ranging some seven to ten times that in length. Rather than being dwarfed by the mountain behind it, the structure seemed to gain stature from it, as though the walls had been poured from heaven, down the slopes, and forged at this spot.

Though time was crucial, so was caution; Adjo came as a tourist, complete with a floppy white sun hat and camera. To watch any creature in its natural state, an observer could not himself be identified and watched. Besides, at this point, any group of tourists might include pilgrims journeying to the cave.

The night before, Adjo drove along the Gulf of Aqaba to Dahab, then stayed at an inn. The next morning he boarded a bus for the long drive to Mt. Sinai. Though there was no air-conditioning in the vintage 1970 vehicle, a hot and mildly refreshing breeze came through the windows as they passed through villages where the main trades were goat herding and tending fruit orchards.

En route, the only restrictions, their guide informed them, were that no one could go up the mountain without a guide. They were told that the military had planted land mines.

"To keep enemies of the state from attacking our guests," the young guide said as they pulled up, pointing to razor wire that ran up the side of the mountain behind the gardens.

To keep animals from eating the fruit, Adjo thought. If there were government-sanctioned mines here, Task Force 777 would have known about them. This was a fabrication told for commerce, to make sure people paid for the guided tour.

The bus heated quickly as it stopped. Everyone hurried out.

"What do you know of the Cave of Moses?" Adjo asked the guide as he climbed into the searing afternoon sun. He felt the contours of the hot rocks through the softened soles of his shoes.

"It is closed at present."

"Oh?"

"There are patrols," he said.

"Egyptian or United Nations soldiers?"

"I do not know. I was only told that they watch for terror."

Ah, Adjo thought. *The fearsome catchall designed to get the general citizenry to obey any edict, however unjustified.*

It was another lie. Adjo had not seen patrols as they drove up, saw no military vehicles, saw neither the glint of polished metal nor the clouds of dust that accompanied the movements of any unit out here.

The guide said that walking tours were only going a short way up the mountain to look out across the Plain of el Raha where the Israelites rested while they waited for the prophet. Adjo thanked the man. He did not act guarded, like someone who knew more than he was telling. In all likelihood he was simply repeating what he had been told.

Adjo caught up with the group as they passed through the gardens to the massive main gate on the western wall. Up close, the pale orange walls of the monastery were clearly different from the fields of red and gray rock that surround them. It was also much busier than it seemed from above. It was late morning and hundreds of tourists were about, brought in by the dozen or so buses parked by the gardens or by taxicabs from Dahab. The visitors far outnumbered the twenty Greek Orthodox monks who lived here full-time. Most of the monks seemed tolerant of the intrusion, which lasted only from nine to noon each day. Once the gates closed, the only shelter came from the snack shacks that lined the mountain path. In this heat, Adjo knew that none but flagellants would be willing to make an unbroken three-hour trek to the summit.

Adjo moved among the tourists, looking for any who didn't seem to fit the profile provided by the Ministry of the Interior; everyone seemed to belong because no one did. It was a melting pot of nations, ages, and affluence. The only common factor seemed to be awe.

Inside the compound, the officer made his way to a monk who was just entering a room that the tour map said was a library. The black-robed figure was looking down, a hood pulled low over his forehead. The monks were famous for not speaking to tourists, but Adjo decided to give it a try. Intercepting him, Adjo asked if he spoke Egyptian.

"I do," the man said without looking up.

"Your worship," Adjo said, "I have been told there is a holy man on the mountain, a son of the prophet Moses. Have you heard of such a one?"

The man did not reply but the hood turned slightly and he seemed to study Adjo from beneath its shadowy folds.

"You do not look like a pilgrim," the man said.

"How should a pilgrim look?" Adjo asked. He touched his chest with his fingertips. "In here, I am a seeker."

The hood lowered and the man turned toward the wooden door of the small, sand-colored stone structure.

"Your grace," Adjo said, "I have come far and I must know if this man is *the* man of God, the *Gharib Qawee*?"

The monk entered the building and closed the door behind him. For the moment it was open, Adjo could see nothing but blackness inside. He understood why the brothers kept their hot hoods on as they moved from place to place. In that way they wouldn't be blind when they got inside.

As Adjo stood by the door he heard a bolt being thrown. That seemed excessive. He hadn't made any move to suggest he'd follow.

Something wasn't right here.

As he turned back toward the interior structures, he felt something sting his ankle through his jeans. He heard a crack in the distance, like one rock hitting another, and thought nothing of it at the moment. He looked down, expecting to see a hornet that had lost its way from the garden. He saw a chipped piece of rock. Nearby he saw the fresh, white wound in the cobblestone from which it had come.

The sound had been gunfire.

"*Là-bas!*" one of the tourists shouted, pointing toward the mountain as he moved his wife into a doorway and stood in front of her.

Adjo looked over, thought he saw the last remnants of a chalky cloud.

Tourists were running from the mountain side of the compound, crouching low and protecting their heads with backpacks as they hurried to the perceived shelter of eaves and corners. Adjo hugged the arched entranceway, still scanning the peaks, looking for a glint that might indicate a weapon or sunglasses—anything. He felt naked without his binoculars.

Several thoughts came at once.

First, this was unlikely to have been a coincidence. Someone must have been watching—or listening to?—what was going on here. Perhaps Adjo had been pointed out by the tour guide, possibly for asking questions, or maybe for stopping the monk and asking about the prophet. Perhaps he was being watched simply because he was traveling alone. That was careless; virtually everyone else was in pairs or groups.

Second, the gunman had intended to miss. Otherwise, there would have been another shot. They did not want Adjo dead because they did not know who he was. The local police were corrupt and could probably be bought, but if he were an investigator for a group like the al-Mukhabarat al-'Ammah—the General Intelligence and Security Service—that could cause problems.

Third, the shooters were not likely to be terrorists, as the guide had said, for there had been virtually no precedent for that here. Even jihadists respected this site.

Then why take this step?

Urged by guides, tourists were returning to the garden and from there to the buses and taxis. Adjo lingered. Feeling sufficiently immune to assassination, he looked around for the bullet and found it, a crushed shell that looked like it came from an assault rifle. From the flattened remains, there was no way to tell what kind.

Adjo made his way to the monastery gate, thinking

he might jog to St. Catherine's village, which lay a quarter-kilometer away on the road to the monastery. In his backpack was an STU-III. He would use it to call Lieutenant General Samra. The secure phone was larger than a regular cell phone and he did not want to take it out where anyone watching from the mountain might see. Whoever had fired that shot still could not be certain he meant them harm. He did not want to give them any reason to change that opinion.

As he jogged down the stone path, looking for a suitable place of concealment not only to make the call but to lose himself, he had a stabbing sense that he was going the wrong way. That truly great men went up this mountain.

I'll be back, he assured himself as he headed toward the red clay tiles of the roofs below.

CHAPTER NINETEEN
WASHINGTON, D.C.

James Phair hadn't been on a commercial airplane for nearly twenty years. It was a disappointing experience.

The interiors were plastic; the seats barely reclined and were narrow, thinly cushioned skeletons much too close to those in front and to the side; the in-flight meal had disappeared along with the in-flight movie, which was now an in-flight television broadcast; and the stewardesses were flight attendants and not as attentive as they once were.

The engines were quieter, though. That was something.

Security, too, was very different. It seemed thorough on the surface, though Phair had seen nimble-fingered Iraqis deftly raid pockets, fruit stands, and café tables for flatware. Someone who was trained and determined could easily mislead these disinterested TSA souls with one hand while concealing something in another, then passing it back like it was a card trick. He probably could have brought down the plane himself. They scanned him with a metal detector, found his dog tags, and thought nothing of allowing him to keep them and the chain. He could have gone into the restroom, used the ID to unscrew the fan casing, and fed the chain between the blades to cause a spark, thus simulating an electrical short-circuit. That would have thrown a breaker and affected the linked navigational systems and stabilizers. He remarked to Kealey that he had overheard that scenario being discussed by two men at a bus stop in Mosul. Later, while he was in the lavatory, Phair realized he could have smashed the mirror and transformed a shard into a perfectly functioning knife.

Phair was surprised that Ryan Kealey didn't talk to him more and resisted any efforts at a get-to-know-you exchange. Kealey spent most of the short flight working on his laptop and organizing his expenses. There was something mundane and somehow reassuring about curled paper receipts scattered about the keyboard. Whether Kealey kept apart to maintain professional objectivity—in the military that was called "emotional distancing," the idea being that a commander wouldn't ask a friend to cover a retreat, knowing he might die—or because he simply didn't care remained to be seen. This early in a professional relationship, it was discouraging.

A nondescript black sedan met them at the airport, one of many parked along the curb.

"D.C. is like Vegas," Kealey said. "Only the tourists take cabs."

"I've never been," Phair remarked.

"I know," Kealey replied.

The driver opened the door for them. Inside, a glass partition separated the front seat from the passengers. The dark windows made it impossible to see in; looking out, Phair saw a world in monochromatic blue, carefully delineated but without subtlety.

"I wonder if all your employees feel this naked?" he asked.

"You mean knowing you hadn't been to Vegas?" Kealey said.

"Not only knowing it, but remembering it," Phair said.

"The people of America pay me to be on top of things," Kealey told him. "We've been burned in other parts of the world by interpreters and informants, nationals mostly, because we didn't know enough about them, let alone everything. The stakes are too high for that."

"They weren't Americans."

"Did you report what you heard those men discussing at the bus stop in Mosul?" Kealey asked.

Phair felt betrayed by the question and did not answer, except with embarrassed silence. In the future, he would remember not to offer any information. Maybe that was why Kealey avoided small talk.

Phair looked out the tinted window. He saw the Washington Monument and Capitol Dome near and then fall away.

"It's been two decades, but I'm pretty sure we needed to turn off back there," he said.

"Not to go to McLean, Virginia," Kealey told him. "That's where CIA HQ is located."

"Not Langley?"

"One and the same," Kealey assured him.

"Why didn't we just fly military point-to-point?"

"I wanted to make sure no one was watching for you."

"Who? General Farrell's people? Or Homeland Security?"

"Anyone."

"You mean Iraqis? Hell, if I'd wanted to tip someone off I could have sent a coded e-mail right from my airplane seat, tell them where I was going! Wouldn't that have been simpler?"

"Only if you knew," Kealey replied. "This isn't a fucking game, Major. There's no room for hurt feelings."

That was the last they spoke until they reached their destination.

The car let them off at the security entrance. As they passed through the metal detector and bag check, Kealey acted as he had back at Fort Jackson, affable and welcoming, as if their last exchange had never happened. Phair wasn't sure whether he admired or resented that. He only hoped that he himself could overlook it.

Once they were inside, crossing a wide lobby and headed toward a bank of elevators, Kealey said, "We had a man of Iranian descent, twenty-eight, born and raised in New Jersey, who we sent to Iraq in 2005. His job was to contact Iranians who were part of the insurgency and learn about their personnel and supply routes. It took about six months for him to decide that these killers were his people and that he wanted to help them."

"I see. But he was of Iranian descent——"

"Theology is a tricky business," Kealey said. "Holy man to holy man can be a strong bond, too."

That hadn't happened to Phair, but he had to admit the theory was sound. "How did you find out about your defector?"

"When we stopped hearing from him, Centcom in Iraq sent a special-ops team to find him," Kealey explained. "You can't have people who know your secrets going to the other side. They brought him back so his family could bury him."

Phair couldn't tell whether that was meant to impart information or a threat. Again, he decided he had to look past it. That traitor wasn't him.

They took the elevator to the sixth floor. The place had the feel of a kind of mad newsroom, people rushing here and there from cubicles, studying video monitors on the desks. Phair was still getting used to the proliferation of LCD screens in every house, office, or store he entered.

"You didn't lose a lot of weight in Iraq," Kealey said.

They were weaving through the maze in a pattern Phair could never have repeated. The cleric's mind snapped to attention. They'd had several hours to discuss this. Why now?

Because you're distracted, Phair told himself. *He wants to catch you off guard, see if you hesitate.*

"The populace tends to be generous with holy men," Phair said.

"India is that way, too," Kealey said as if he had expected the answer. "You told Major Dell that you earned some money teaching English and helping men haul goods to market."

"Is there a question?" Phair asked.

"Who wanted to learn English? Young people, mostly?"

"Mostly, and typically men," Phair said. "A lot of merchants saw the GIs as potential customers—at least, when insurgents weren't there, threatening to kill anyone who did business with them."

"Them?"

"Us," Phair said.

"Did you ever have encounters with American soldiers?"

"No."

"You didn't want anyone asking about you, entertaining ideas about bringing you back."

"That's right. Not until I had experienced everything I could."

"If you hadn't been spotted, how much longer do you think you would have stayed?"

"I honestly don't know," Phair said. "I'll admit to being homesick for a soft bed and a fast-food hamburger."

Kealey smiled. He seemed satisfied.

They walked through a secretarial office into a larger office beyond. Kealey smiled at the young man behind a desk. He introduced "Major Phair" but didn't stop, so there was no handshaking.

Kealey shut the door behind him.

"Major Phair, I believe you're a good man and you're certainly a patient one," Kealey said. "I believe you're a patriot and would be an asset to us. But we need to have an understanding." Kealey stepped behind his simple glass-topped desk and folded his arms. "The military had reasons for making you a hero and not an AWOL, but I don't. If you are in the field and go off mission for any reason, you will come back like our friend from New Jersey."

Phair's heart rate jumped. He'd gotten reprimanded before, especially during the Gulf War. He had witnessed a lot of excessive zeal among commanders who felt that pockets of resistance were better blasted out and buried than smoked out and imprisoned. They had deadlines to meet. Phair had been vocal in his disapproval of the hammer-down approach, and that was one reason he'd gone to help the wounded Iraqis on the day he became separated from his unit. He believed that his presence offered them a little protection. Kealey's tone wasn't what bothered him, and the threat of death didn't get to him. He'd faced that daily in Iraq. What troubled Phair was the recurring doubt. Every time it seemed to retreat, back it came in full, ugly flower.

"I do try to be a good man and an understanding one," Phair said. "But I have to tell you, Mr. Kealey—you push me on that. Leaders who rule by doubt and denunciation are never as effective as those who govern by trust and hope."

"Your personal and philosophical priorities may change when thousands of lives depend on every decision you make, when you worry that you've missed a clue that can cause the next World Trade Center attack or Madrid train bombing," Kealey said. "When you have the resources at your disposal to destroy a village just to get one particularly nasty radical, it's tough to keep from lashing out like the angel of fucking death.

"But thanks for the sermon," he added pleasantly as he sat and gestured toward the sofa. "It's something to shoot for."

CHAPTER TWENTY
MCLEAN, VIRGINIA

Back in his office after his meeting on Capitol Hill, Jonathan Harper felt a momentary thrill at the sight of an OD request—Open Door—from a foreign intelligence service.

This one came in via secure e-mail: just seeing that subject line in his mailbox gave him a frisson of excitement, a chance to pit himself against a fresh and unknown challenge. He liked having new perspectives, new contacts, even new enemies. Or at least, he used to. His thrill quickly lapsed. He supposed he had always enjoyed OD requests because deep down, he enjoyed showing up anyone outside the country's borders. He respected the intelligence services of a few other nations, but he regarded most as inferior. Now, however, he was no one to be throwing stones. His glass house had broken because he had failed to remember the completely obvious—Christmas.

The OD was from Egypt; Harper's interest waned a

little further. If one of the tougher units, like Israel's Mossad or Britain's MI6, had needed assistance, that may have meant a project big enough for Harper to forget himself in.

At least it wasn't Interpol, he thought. Those international flatfoots asked for help at least three times a day. It wasn't even personalized anymore. Harper's contact in Barcelona said they sent "eyes only" requests to over twenty-five intelligence services a day. It was surely a symptom of their laughably small annual budget, but still, they should have some pride.

He ran the request from Egypt's Task Force 777— even the name was uninspiring, the numbers coming from the month and year they were chartered—through the decryption and translation programs. He knew he shouldn't be so hard on them; they were a good bunch in Cairo, understaffed but committed to fighting terrorists at home and abroad, and they had navigated the military's struggles with the Muslim Brotherhood with a notable disinterest in jockeying for power. But they, too, were so underfunded that anything that could be outsourced, was.

The official read the request from Lt. General Adom Kaphiri Samra.

"Shot fired at agent. Possible jihadist at Mt. Sinai. Passive intel and surveillance requested. We will take necessary action."

Passive intel. Harper sighed. What they wanted was up-to-the-minute satellite images. Their Russian friends probably didn't cover the area with the frequency of the National Reconnaissance Office. The NRO would handle that, if they were so inclined. But there was something else about the request that made Harper instant-message his executive assistant in the next room:

Wasn't there something about Sinai in a recent intel summary?

The cut-and-pasted segment came back within seconds.

"BBC television crew records man who claims to have encountered an individual who is the embodiment of the Biblical Moses. Internet chatter suggests groundswell of interest among moderate Muslims. Recommendation: Watch for possible influx of foreign destabilizers among the pilgrims."

The video clip was attached. It was tagged item 35-599, 900-2. The numeral prefix designated the visual medium, in this case Internet. The second number identified it as one of more than a half million video clips pulled from the Web since that library was started in 1993. The acquisition team consisted of twenty-eight full-time employees, and the collection was growing exponentially—three hundred a day, up from one hundred a year ago. Clips were accessible by several different searches: keywords, location, individuals, date, and danger level. The final number was a "heat" reference. On a scale of one to ten—Ned Hull, head of the Computer Access Division, had once described ten as being Osama with a Russian nuke—this video clip had been marked a two. Only clips eight and above were sent to everyone on the internal intel mailing list.

Harper watched the thirty-second fragment twice, then went back and paused on the man who came down the mountain. The team had been shooting in high-definition, so he was able to get a clean blowup of the acolyte's face. Harper dropped it in a file that analyzed facial characteristics such as a taut mouth for fear, wide eyes for shock, even corneal reflections to make sure that what was seen in the subject's eye coincided with the surroundings, thus eliminating the possibility that a head was photographed elsewhere and superimposed.

The findings declared the photograph "93 percent authentic"—the view of the location was not in the database and therefore unavailable for comparison. The subject was profiled using keywords drawn from expression- and movement-based templates in the program: "non-aggressive, transfixed, aimless."

"A crazy man who doesn't want to blow something up," Harper muttered. "Yet."

He asked another program to identify the individual by nationality and location, if possible. The result came back: "Ethnicity: 89 percent Eastern Hamitic; age: late thirties; wardrobe: indigenous but inconclusive."

That meant he was almost certainly a native Egyptian, not one of the infiltrators the evaluation had warned against. Of course, the video had not yet been disseminated. Who knew what the situation would be like now?

The request from Task Force 777 seemed rather temperate in light of the potential threat. Harper recategorized the clip as a four, given its coincidence with the date and location of the Egyptian alert. Had the individual been identified as likely a Syrian or Lebanese, Harper would have raised the alert higher, since that might have suggested an early border-crossing and possible insurgent activity.

He checked his watch, then called Ryan Kealey on his cell phone. The agent should have gotten back from South Carolina by now. He might even be in his office in the same building. But instead of dropping down to see him, Harper called.

"Good morning, Jonathan," Kealey said.

"Good morning. Everything going smoothly?"

"Yes. You got my e-mail?"

"I did." Kealey had written earlier to say that General Farrell had given his blessings to seconding Major Phair to the CIA, and that Phair was coming to HQ. Harper said, "I'm sending along something for the both of you to look at. I'd be interested in your new man's impressions of it."

"Related to the hospital?"

"No, but definitely in his field of expertise. It won't take much of his time."

"How urgent is this?"

"I don't know," Harper said, forwarding the file he'd compiled of the video clip, the photo analysis, and the request from Task Force 777.

"We'll have a look as soon as we receive it," Kealey promised.

Harper made appropriate signing-off comments, then hung up. There seemed to be no point in trying to warm up the coolness between them. He knew it wasn't personal; Kealey was simply burying himself in his work to avoid his own sense of helplessness, as Harper wished he could.

CHAPTER TWENTY-ONE
MCLEAN, VIRGINIA

Kealey caught up on e-mails while Phair sat and looked helplessly, absently, at a gadget Kealey had given him—something called an iPad.

The cleric's mind was elsewhere. He had decided that he was not going to let the passive-aggressive displays from Ryan Kealey get to him. When the initial shock passed—he hadn't been dressed down in many, many years—he understood that the questions and comments were not personal. Moreover, Phair well understood the root of Kealey's concerns.

Even before the chaplain went to the Gulf, the intelligence services were criticized for all the things they *didn't* know, for relying too much on electronic surveillance and too little on human intelligence—eyes and ears on the ground, among the people, which gave you a more accurate read of the mood of a place. Phair's own experiences among the Iraqis could attest to that. No doubt that was one of the reasons he had been seconded to a civilian group.

After the World Trade Center attacks, the Saddam-controlled press was filled with mockery of the CIA and their inability to stop what was described as "Islamic justice." After the Iraq invasion, the Iranian press picked up the torch. Returning home, Phair saw more of the same in the American press. It had to be debilitating to people like Ryan Kealey.

The truth was, American intelligence was superb. The fault lay in the lack of protocols to share and analyze the assembled data.

Men like Ryan Kealey were the answer. They cared less about ego than about the process running smoothly, whoever and whatever it took to do that. Upon reflection, he realized the man was not a self-serving autocrat and, just hearing one side of his conversation with his superior, Phair could tell he also wasn't an ass-kisser.

"Making any progress over there?" Kealey asked.

"Working on it," Phair lied. He focused on the device. He had seen others using them and BlackBerrys and iPhones at Fort Jackson, but he was still getting used to the idea of personal computers and cell phones.

"James."

Phair looked up. It was strange to hear his first name barked. Kealey was still staring at his monitor.

"Moses and Islam," Kealey said. "What's the connection in twenty-five words or less?"

"Muslims believe that Adam was the first prophet, a spokesman of God," Phair said. "Mohammed was the last and greatest. Between them were Noah, Abraham, Moses, and Jesus."

"Perfect. So if he were to return and proclaim Islam the one true faith?"

The idea was proposterous, but Kealey seemed serious.

"That would be a problem. Has Moses returned?" Phair asked.

"Someone seems to be doing miracles with his staff up on Sinai," Kealey said. He clicked on another e-mail from Harper. "A newspaper in Lebanon, *Al Fasulya,* is calling any Muslim who believes that to be 'a child.'"

"That's a Christian newspaper," Phair said. "I'm sure they meant 'child' as in 'immature,' an insult, and not 'child' as in 'youth.'"

Kealey grinned. He seemed pleased that Phair knew that.

"Is that kind of name-calling common enough that it won't cause a row?" Kealey asked.

"It is uncommon in a religious context," Phair said. "But it's a very, very mild deprecation."

"Not fightin' words?"

"Not yet."

Kealey returned to the original e-mail. He sent the file to the iPad and told Phair how to access it. "Have a look at the data, let me know what you think."

Phair did as he was instructed and read through the material after enlarging the type. He hadn't realized he was leaning so far forward until he settled back.

"Is it that serious?" Kealey asked.

Phair was confused.

"Your expression," Kealey said.

Phair hadn't realized he was frowning so deeply, either. He relaxed, then lapsed unwittingly right back into a scowl.

"This is similar to the concept of the *mahdi,* the

Messiah who will appear at the end of days in Sunni Islam," Phair said.

"How similar?"

"Actually, what's important here is the difference," Phair said. "The concept of the *mahdi* suffered a setback with the rise and fall of the last pretender, Mohammad Ahmad, who seized Khartoum from the British in 1885 and died five months later—due, in part, to pestilence spread by his slaughters." Kealey's eyes wandered back to the computer, and Phair realized he'd lapsed into professor-speak. He tried to get back to the twenty-five-words-or-less approach. "The movement went away, but this is worse. Someone who proclaims himself to be an incarnation of the deliverer-prophet, but stops short of declaring himself a messiah, attracts a following and the resultant power while removing the burden of actually having to liberate anything."

"I get it. But if this fellow is proclaiming himself the new Moses, why wouldn't Christians and Jews embrace him?"

"Some may," Phair said. "But they'll be coming to the party too late."

"How do you figure that?"

"He was introduced to us by an Arabic title, *Gharib Qawee.* That has already marked him as their own."

"Is the label really that powerful? A Moses by any other name—"

"It defines him by his relevance to the Muslim world," Phair said. "Moses is a prophet in that he was given the laws, by God, to give to us. For Muslims, he is revered for that, not as the deliverer of Israel. The people who have the most immediate access to Mt. Sinai are Arabs, and they're coming to see *Gharib*

Quwee. They will claim him as the lawgiver. They will revere him as a forebear of Mohammad. Whoever organized this was very clever."

"A cabal? I didn't think clergymen were cynics."

"Only when it comes to the actions of men," Phair said.

"Assuming you're right, couldn't some religious brain trust have cooked this up to win over Muslims and some Jews and Christians, to foster peace?"

"Doubtful," Phair said. "The original Moses, the real Moses, was not backward about being forward. He didn't hide in a cave. He came down, he announced the fact of the Burning Bush, Aaron threw the staff at the feet of Pharaoh and it turned into a serpent, Moses brought down the plagues and parted the sea. Someone will quickly ask to see some miracles. As soon as someone does that, an *Al Fasulya* or some TV reporter, that puts the Muslims in a position of having to defend their reincarnated prophet on principle, not on evidence."

"The goal of any conspiracy must be to make the man himself the issue," Kealey said.

"The question is what will happen next," Phair said. "The Egyptians had no other information?"

"Not that they're sharing right now," Kealey said.

"Are you saying they'd withhold information?"

"Would and probably are," Kealey told him. "Many intelligence groups tend to parcel it out as needed. The more data they control, the more likely they'll be the ones to break the case."

"I can't believe it. *That's* more important than a quick resolution?"

"They're both important," Kealey said. "Getting the Nazis out of France was paramount during World War

II, but the Allies often waited to make a final push—subjecting local populations to the Germans' brutal parting abuses—so that French troops could be the first ones into liberated territory. Image matters."

That wasn't a revelation. But Phair felt how different it was when the drama and danger are unfolding than when they are cold, detached history, where you know how it all worked out.

"So what do you think will happen next?" Kealey asked.

Phair forced his mind back on track. He was enjoying this. "Given the importance of religion to the local Arab population, and their mobility—there is little to hold them to their jobs or homes—my guess is that pilgrims will begin descending on the desert by the thousands, perhaps by the tens of thousands."

"Creating a humanitarian crisis for Egypt," Kealey said.

"Yes. From an anarchist's point of view, I don't see the value in that."

"I do," Kealey said. "Egypt is one of the few stable republics in the Islamic world, but that stability is recent and vulnerable. Radicals would love to see that go away." He started typing. "I'm writing up what we just discussed and sending it to my superior, Deputy Director Harper."

"What will he do with the information?"

"No idea," Kealey said.

Phair suddenly realized that Kealey's wavering affability might be related more to his job or his superior than to Phair.

"I may have something to add to your report," Phair

said, using the iPad to look something up on the Internet. He was surprised by how easy it was.

Kealey waited, then grew impatient. "I'll send it in a follow-up e-mail." He tapped at his computer. "Unless you can be more specific right now?"

"It might get people a little agitated," Phair said absently, absorbed in his iPad.

"Why?"

"I'll let you know when I'm sure I've got it right."

CHAPTER TWENTY-TWO
JEBEL MUSA, SINAI PENINSULA

Acting scared, Lieutenant Adjo jogged through the Minaret Gate toward the gardens that spread from the compound. Tourists were still descending from the mountain. He didn't want to call attention to himself by being the last tourist out. He ran past the buses toward the village, jotting down license numbers on his palm as he passed, then paused by a clump of olive trees that shielded him from the lower slopes. Not far below were the first tile rooftops of St. Catherine's Village. Crouching behind a boulder at the foot of one tree, the young officer reached into his backpack and withdrew the STU III—Secure Telephone Unit, Third Generation—surplus acquired from the United States military. The lieutenant selected the "secure voice mode only" since he wasn't sending data. That burned up less battery and he had no idea how long he'd be out here.

Lieutenant General Samra answered at once. "What's going on?" he demanded. "We're getting reports of gunfire."

"One shot from a high-powered rifle about two hundred meters up the mountain," Adjo said. "It was meant to intimidate, I think. I was asking questions and may have been ID'ed."

As he spoke, Adjo looked around to make sure no one was listening. The old streets behind him were filled with tourists hurrying toward buses.

"Do you have any idea who the spotter might have been?" Samra asked.

"No. He could have been a tour guide who heard me talking with one of the monks or someone watching from the slope. It might even have been one of the monks. Do you have any additional information?"

"Nothing yet," Samra replied.

"I'm watching the tourists as they get on the buses," Adjo said. "It looks like a broad mix. Everyone is scared. The guides are looking up, down, and around—no one seems to be relaxed."

"It has to be one of them, and he would have to leave with the other tourists to avoid drawing suspicion," Samra said. "I don't see the Greek Orthodox monks supporting snipers."

"I can't see why they would," Adjo agreed. "But I don't see what anyone would be protecting in this place—unless the entire *Gharib Qawee* matter is a cover for something else."

"Or it might be as simple as supporters fearing for the safety of the prophet."

"Why would the chosen of God need a bodyguard?" Adjo asked.

"The chosen of God have a way of meeting unhappy ends," Samra said. "What are the license numbers of the buses? I will have someone check the passenger manifests."

Adjo read them off his left hand. Then he reached into his camera case. His digital camera had a strong telephoto lens. Adjo moved cautiously from behind the rock, snuggled the phone between his shoulder and his ear, and looked through the lens.

"I'm checking the slopes now," he told Samra. "There are strings of tourists coming down from the summit. They look confused." He took photos; computer analysis might turn up a case large enough to hold a rifle. Then he scanned the peaks, searching for movement or a glint among the rocks. He saw nothing.

"Sir, I'd like to go up there and reconnoiter."

"That's not a very good idea," Samra said. "You're unarmed, and if you were the target—"

"They could have killed me before."

"Shooting you in the midst of a crowd would have forced an investigation," Samra said. "But if they draw you in and cut your throat in the mountains, you will never be found."

"They must earn that privilege," Adjo said.

"I just checked several of the tour sites," Samra said. "They all say they're sold out for today."

"Shooting tourists raises their insurance rates," Adjo said.

"My point is, you'll be up there alone—no crowds to get lost in. And if the U.N. Multinational Force blockades the road, you'll get caught up in their bureaucracy if you try to get out."

That was true. The MFO stationed in the Sinai desert was responsible for helping to patrol and secure the region, and they took their duty very seriously. Whenever

U.N peacekeepers closed off a region, their charter mandated that everyone inside be considered a threat until proven otherwise. The paperwork could take days.

Samra didn't have to waste battery time spelling the rest of it out. He couldn't send the helicopter to Adjo. If the sniper was a vanguard of a larger force, they might have rocket-propelled grenades. The appearance of a partisan military force might trigger a deadly incident, not just a warning shot fired into a crowd. That could start a larger conflict, not to mention exposing the usually secretive activities of 777 to public scrutiny.

"I want to stay," Adjo decided. "I'll find a safe haven if need be and wait it out. You will hear from me when I'm able to call."

Adjo clicked off to conserve power, then found a spot where he could hunker down until dark. He had water, he had a sandwich and a candy bar, he had shade. For now, he would simply watch to see what happened next before deciding how to proceed. If past field experiences were any kind of guideline, "next" would be like nothing he could presently envision.

CHAPTER TWENTY-THREE
MCLEAN, VIRGINIA

Kealey sat down opposite Jonathan Harper in Harper's office. Half an hour had elapsed since he had sent the deputy director the summary of Phair's opinion about the events at Mt. Sinai. He'd heard nothing since then, which he'd expected, until Harper called him to his office, which surprised him.

As Kealey entered Harper had nodded but continued typing, staring at his computer screen with a level of intensity Kealey hadn't seen since Texas.

"Quite a head on those shoulders," Kealey said.

"The chaplain?" said Harper. "Yes, I'm impressed. The thought occurred to me that for an emissary of America wandering around Iraq for sixteen years, we may have lucked out. He might have been better representation for us than we're used to having."

"Better? That's quite a judgment call, Jon."

Harper neither looked up nor looked apologetic, only saying, "Better suited, then. We got another e-mail from Task Force 777, by the way. I'll forward it to you but it just says there is now video 'in house' that shows a staff becoming a serpent."

"But not the video itself."

"Preempting a request, Lieutenant General Samra says he will share the clip when it has been cleared by his superiors."

"They've probably had it for days," Kealey said. "They probably didn't want to admit that they can't verify whether or not it's authentic."

"You sound a little dismissive of all of this, Ryan."

"Just keeping my focus," Ryan replied evenly. "After hearing Phair's opinion I can certainly understand the possibility that this would blow up into a sizable problem for the Egyptians, and they have my sympathy. They've been through enough over the past few years not to need a false prophet appearing on Mt. Sinai. Hell, they probably don't need a real one showing up, either. And I can't imagine the Muslim Brotherhood getting behind this kind of tactic, but that doesn't mean they wouldn't take advantage of it."

"That's analysis. I was referring to your personal feelings about it."

"Personally, I can also see how this could be a tempest in a teapot, one kook in a cookie jar, and I have other things on my mind. An Iranian terrorist, whom we can't bring in because we don't have the proof, is gaining international political traction as well as local leverage in a city with a major smuggling route running through it. Frankly, I'm waiting for you to tell me to pack my bags for Iraq, and Phair's, too."

"The Israelis asked for a presence on Mt. Sinai," Harper said abruptly.

Kealey's eyebrows rose. "They're forbidden from taking part in U.N. activities on Arab soil."

"Which is why the United Nations turned down the request from the Israeli government. They had asked for an Israeli observer to be temporarily assigned to the Multinational Force."

"They're taking this staff seriously, then."

"Seriously enough."

Harper didn't have to point out that the Israelis didn't always share their suspicions or data, at least not directly. Only through requests like this. Kealey already knew.

"If they're that concerned, then we should be that concerned," Kealey said.

"I agree."

"But you didn't have to call me up here for that. You could have just forwarded me the e-mails."

Harper looked back at his screen.

"Jon," Kealey said gently, "you don't need my assurance. You don't need a backup brain. Let Texas go as the unpreventable surprise that it was, forgive yourself, and move on. Your decisions are sound."

Harper shook his head. Kealey had missed the mark. "Danny Hernandez contacted the DEA," he said. "He wants to talk."

Kealey was on his feet before he knew he was standing up. Adrenaline surges he knew, but this was on the level of a solar flare.

"Where is he?"

"The DEA hasn't provided any details about where he is or how he got in touch with them."

"Are they taking tutorials with the Egyptians now? Shit!" Kealey nearly pounded the desk. "Are they sure it was him who got in touch with them? Is it proof positive verified?" Harper started to speak. Kealey rolled over him. "And assuming it's him, how the hell did he do it without being noticed by anyone in his cartel? Never mind evading the other cartels that are all spying on each other. Do we have an informant in his cartel, did he figure out who it was and approach him? And why?!" Kealey leaned over the desk. "That's an even bigger question than how. He got away with it, Jon. We lost him. Why would he be willing to talk to us, knowing that we are going to find a way to hang his ass out to dry for Isobel Garcia?"

"I don't know," Harper said wearily.

Kealey paced. "Did his new friends turn on him? Is he feeling heat from the Iranians, running to the coattails of Uncle Sam? But he wouldn't choose us for that even if that *is* the case. He has Mexico and half of Central and South America to call on for shelter and protection. This doesn't make sense, Jon, I don't like it. I want to know where he is and I want a flight there today."

Kealey hovered over the desk. Harper half expected to see steam float from his nostrils.

"Because if it's a trap," Kealey said, "I trained Yerby and I have a good idea of what I'm walking into and you know the DEA doesn't have anyone who can hold a candle to me. I want to be in on the first phone call, the first pickup, the first meet and every contact after that. I want to be planning it and I want every team answerable to me. If Danny Hernandez blinks, my fingers are going into his eyes."

"What about Iraq?" Harper asked quietly.

"It's a hospital. They've only cleared the ground, they haven't even broken it yet, much less started construction. We'll have a good idea of where the doctor will be for months, or at least where he's going to visit regularly and frequently. Our people there can keep an eye on him and someone else can run Phair until I'm done with Hernandez. Get Dina Westbrook from DHS, she can run him, she's already met him."

Kealey finally stopped and observed the look on Harper's face. What he saw there made him sit down. He was going to *hate* what came next, he knew it.

"I need you to go to Egypt," Harper said. "With Phair. Whatever the Israelis know and aren't telling us, it's clear that this matter has become urgent."

"One of the top drug lords in the western hemisphere," Kealey said, "that is urgent, too."

"Hernandez is smart. He'll drag out the waltz before we get him face-to-face."

"No. Hernandez *is* smart and that's why he'll come in as fast as he can figure out a safe, secret way to do it, to mitigate the possibility that someone finds out what he's done."

"It can't be you, Ryan."

"You think my feelings will compromise me? You think I'm blinded with revenge."

"I don't think that at all. Your international experience makes you essential—"

"I'm getting sick of hearing that."

"And it appears that you have Phair on your side. You can't walk away from that attachment without jeopardizing someone else's attempt to replace that attachment, should you break faith and cause that to be necessary. He is obviously the right person to send to a place where religious fervor might be starting a global firestorm and beyond that, a situation where people are possibly being emotionally and spiritually manipulated. He goes, you go. I'm sorry, Ryan."

"But . . ."

Kealey did not finish his thought, *but what about the doctor?* He had said it himself, they would have a good idea of where the doctor would be for months to come. He had said it himself because Harper had asked the right question at the right time, setting him up.

It was only Kealey's memories of the Baltimore Convention Center, of Julie Harper struggling to regain her confident stride, of Jonathan staring miserably at the footage of candles and flowers being placed around San Antonio City Hall for Isobel Garcia the night of her death, that kept Kealey from calling him an SOB.

He walked out of the office.

CHAPTER TWENTY-FOUR
MCLEAN, VIRGINIA

Kealey had been gone for forty-five minutes, walking himself into a sweat outside, when he finally rejoined Phair in his office. Phair's first reaction at seeing his face was to put down the iPad. He recognized the facial expression. He'd seen it on teenagers when they were angry at God. Not the teenagers with relatively ordinary lives who, through broken hearts or parents' divorces, were learning for the first time that the world would not always conform to their plans for it. No, this was the expression on the face of an abused kid, one whose emotions had been shut down for years and then, after patient work with a trustworthy adult, was starting to feel again—and what was felt was all-consuming rage at the Almighty, because the teenager didn't feel safe enough yet to be angry at the abuser.

But Phair checked himself before offering any assistance. He barely knew Ryan Kealey. He might not know him well enough to read him accurately. The man was an agent, which Phair presumed meant that he had to sort and manage his emotions in a somewhat different way than most people, a way that Phair was unfamiliar with. And Kealey had not been doing patient work on himself with Phair's guidance. Their trust of each other was new and thin. Nor did Kealey seem to be a man who would discuss his feelings under any circumstances. By no interpretation did Phair have an invitation to extend help.

He knew what was coming next and indeed, Kealey's expression began to resolve into a hard, intelligent surface, absolutely practical for accomplishing tasks, strategizing, even socializing, up to a point. Revelations of feelings happened in waves and it took many cycles before someone could start to reclaim their life from their past, whatever that past was. Right now Ryan Kealey needed to work, and the best thing Phair could do for him was to help him work.

"The Staff of Moses," Kealey said, now faultlessly professional. "What should we expect from it? Or to put it another way, what should we expect the faithful will expect from it?"

"Well, so far the behavior of the staff is certainly predictable," Phair said, picking up his iPad again. "The apparent behavior, that is." The cleric recognized that he was toning himself down so as to match Kealey's impervious mood, but the truth was, he felt energized in a way he hadn't been since returning from Iraq. He hadn't realized how cocooned he'd become until the pieces started to chip off. "According to the Bible, the first miracle with Moses's staff was God transforming it into a snake. Later, in the presence of Pharaoh, Moses used the power of his staff, channeling God, to turn the staff of his brother Aaron into a serpent. When the sorcerers of the pharaoh duplicated the feat, the serpent of Aaron devoured the Egyptian snakes."

"I remember that from Sunday school," Kealey remarked. "But the trick could be faked or this video the Egyptians say they have could be doctored."

"That doesn't matter," Phair said. "If word of the miracle spreads now, it doesn't matter how many people saw it, or didn't see it. Rumor becomes fact in the telling. That dates back to the oral tradition at the dawn of these civilizations."

"A foolproof plan," Kealey reflected. "It doesn't even matter whether the staff is real."

"Actually, it might," Phair said, typing into the iPad. "These people may have screwed up."

Kealey prodded him with an inquisitive look.

"This probably isn't the work of a Muslim holy man," Phair went on. "According to the Koran, the staff is simply said to have swallowed 'falsehoods,' which the serpents represented."

"Why is that a problem?"

"It's a metaphor," Phair said. "The staff wasn't supernatural. But the people behind this appearance of the staff have presented a case that it is."

"Can't it be both?"

"Not to Muslims," Phair said. "They may rally at Mt. Sinai to judge for themselves, they may come carrying hope, but they will be less impressed by tricks than by a feeling. They will want to know that the man and the relic are holy."

"How will he prove that?"

"By what he says, not so much by what he can transform. Our problem is that most of these people are so disenfranchised by tyranny, poverty, war, and tribal conflict that it won't take much to convince them that the *Gharib Qawee* is a leader worth following, even if they have doubts about his pedigree."

"But you're saying there's a good chance this staff is a fake," Kealey said, "and that by presenting it as a miracle worker this prophet has, perhaps inadvertently, announced that fact and left it vulnerable."

"Right. He did what was expedient. He got the attention of local Muslims, and that was perhaps more important."

"Do we know what is supposed to have happened to the real Staff?" Kealey asked.

"According to the Bible and historical texts, Moses gave it to his successor, Joshua, who gave it to Phinehas, the grandson of Aaron, who buried it in Jerusalem. That much is probable, or at least plausible. What's less likely is that the Staff was later unearthed by Joseph, who took it to Egypt, where it made its way into the hands of James, the brother of Jesus. There, it was supposedly stolen by Judas and used as the transverse beam of the Cross."

"It makes a good story," Kealey observed.

"It makes the events seem predestined, part of God's great plan," Phair said. "The more so if you accept that Moses's Staff, originally his shepherd's staff, was hewn from the Tree of Knowledge in Eden."

"Do you believe that?"

"No, but I want to," Phair admitted.

The cleric closed the Web address of an academic archaeology site. It did not have what he wanted. He had actually gone to this site before, in Iraq, while trying to identify bricks beneath a building that had been bombed in an airstrike. He discovered that the kind of straw used had been discontinued at least five centuries before. It saddened him that it took a war to unearth a treasure. And that might prove ironic before their work here was done.

Hunting and pecking, Phair continued the search he had started before Kealey was called away to his superior's office. After another false start—he was directed to the personnel managing an art collection endowed by a philanthropist named Moses—he found what he was looking for.

"Heiliges Geheimnisvoll Produktprogramm," he read in adequate German.

"I recognize *product* and *program,*" Kealey said.

"It's the Occult Relics Program of the Nazis," Phair read. "It was organized by Heinrich Himmler in 1937. Agents were sent in search of artifacts to give them a supernatural edge in world conquest."

"You mean that wasn't just in the movies?"

"It was very real," Phair said. "Part of that undertaking was to find ancient religious items that could produce similar effects."

"You mean like the Ark of the Covenant or the True Cross, which was supposed to do—something."

"Protect the army wielding it from all harm," Phair said. "It says here that Himmler's SS itself was modeled after the Knights Templar, the religious warriors who were thought to possess the Holy Grail. The identification is more than just symbolism," Phair read thoughtfully. "The Grail was said to have once held the blood of Christ. Blood—as in *bloodline,* the cornerstone of the notion of the Aryan master race."

"What about the Staff of Moses?"

"It was one of the objects they reportedly sought."

"With no indication whether it was found."

"It says here that Himmler established a meeting-house-slash-museum for the Occult Relics Program in the castle at Wewelsburg in Westphalia," he went on. "After the war, the Allies examined every stone and floorboard for evidence of tampering. The grounds were searched and X-rays taken. No significant religious or occult artifacts were found. However, the fact that we knew to go there suggests something else."

"What?"

"That the Allies found at least one of the people who was involved in this highly secret program and debriefed him."

"Sixty-plus years ago," Kealey said.

"There may be files, records, maps," Phair said.

Kealey considered this for a moment, then went to the landline. He punched a single number.

"Sir," Kealey said. "We're going to need some information."

Phair noticed the *sir* Kealey used, and the faint twist he put on the word. But for the rest of the phone call he was a paragon of a busy agent, recapping what Phair had told him. He said he wanted any data pertaining to the Allies' debriefing of anyone involved in the Occult Relics Program and one thing more.

"I want to know if there are any survivors," he said.

CHAPTER TWENTY-FIVE
WASHINGTON, D.C.

Chief Librarian Trey Dunlap was pouting.

He loved his job for three reasons. The first was that he could help people. Not "outside" people, the ordinary citizens whose lives and security depended on what they did here, but "inside" people—his coworkers, the men and women who could actually pat his back and boost his career and inflate his ego. It was something a nerd needed in order to define his uniqueness as an asset instead of a liability.

The venue was the second reason he loved his job. He sat in a small, private, out-of-the-way room, with low overhead lighting illuminating a team of six people cramped in small cubicles, four men and two women who were uninterruptedly lit by the glow of their computer monitors. It was like ruling over a hell of information. But he *was* the lord. Though it was not permitted to make political statements through stickers, buttons, or even coffee mugs, he had a Libertarian

Party symbol—the Statue of Liberty on a blue field—
with the name boldly written in Klingon.

The Devil was supposed to be devious, after all.

Finally, the thirty-six-year-old loved his job because
it gave him access to information that few people knew
or could know. He had read, for example, the scanned,
redacted, original draft of the Declaration of Indepen-
dence handwritten by Thomas Jefferson, with marginal
notations and cross-outs by John Adams and James
Franklin. He had read a file called "Rollover" which
was compiled in 1939—a list of secret information
about journalists to be used against them if they ever
reported on the fact that President Franklin Roosevelt
couldn't walk. Then there were the files on Roswell,
New Mexico. It wasn't a weather balloon or a flying
saucer that crashed there. It was an airborne listening
device monitoring Soviet nuclear tests.

The requests that came to him were varied and were
made available based on a three-part number. First,
there was the level of security clearance: one was highest, five was the lowest. Second, there was the division
number: one was the Oval Office, two was the State
Department, ten was the Department of Housing and
Urban Development, the Federal Reserve, and other
specialized divisions. Finally, there was urgency factor: five was this week, one was yesterday.

This request was 101. The 'zero' indicated it was
from your own team.

This one was for Ryan Kealey, okayed by Jonathan
Harper, and it was about Nazis. Which was why Dunlap was pouting. The information that Ryan Kealey
needed was not information to which he had direct ac-

cess. That meant Dunlap had to go to someone and ask a favor. It meant that now *he* was a number, and not necessarily a high one. He hated that, and he hated how it made him act and feel when he had to ask.

No, beg, he thought ruefully.

Most of the records of the Nazi regime had been given to various Holocaust museums around the world. But many of the more sensitive debriefings were still on file with military intelligence, mostly those that dealt with aborted weapons programs. Dunlap had seen some of those. The U.S. government did not want to give potential enemies access to the most devious minds of the Third Reich, men and women who had come up with notions like acoustic cones that would deliver jolts to fault zones, typewriter ribbons that would release airborne bacteria when struck, and chemically treated roads to compromise rubber integrity and cause blowouts.

With a sigh, Dunlap sent an urgent e-mail to his counterpart Wendy Norris at the Directorate of Intelligence, the wardens of sensitive military information stored by and for the Joint Chiefs of Staff. The records dated back to 1903, when the Joint Army and Navy Board was first established. An official request for information had to be in writing. Archived, the e-mail would constitute that. Then he videophoned her.

"Is this for a TV special?" the young, pretty woman asked suspiciously.

"Not this time," Dunlap replied. A movie and TV buff, he was also the go-to guy for U.S. military and espionage history by any number of documentary filmmakers. If the Communications Division approved the script, the government provided those services for free on a low-priority basis. Dunlap bumped the priority up because it got him invites to parties and premieres.

"There's not a lot on Hitler's Occult Relics Program," Wendy said. "The menu doesn't say anything about individual discoveries, only about the history and organization of the program."

"What about debriefings?" Dunlap asked, checking his own videocast to make sure he looked his best. He was sweating despite the robust air-conditioning, and his thick features stared back at him moodily. He mollified his expression slightly, absently pushed hair onto his forehead to give him that virile man-at-work look. One day he might even ask her on a date.

"The overview says the data is mostly operational details from maps and logs, primarily geographical areas the five SS units covered," the woman said.

"They were all Schutzstsaffel?" Dunlap remarked.

"Apparently," she said. "I'll read the July 1945 summary. 'The captured enemy does not say much, which is not surprising since they were Hitler's most elite and trusted soldiers. Neither Hitler nor Himmler would have wanted to put such power in the hands of those who might use it against them.' This is interesting," she remarked. "The interviewer goes on to say, 'The interviewee wasn't boastful but seemed almost sad. I got the impression they finally did find such objects but never got to use them in the service of the cause.'"

"Wow. I wonder if they found the Holy Grail or Excalibur or any of those things," Dunlap said.

"Are you looking for something in particular?"

"I was told to try and find out about the Staff of

Moses and anyone who might still be alive who had a hand in this program."

"There's nothing about the Staff," she answered, running a search, "and there are only three prisoners mentioned."

"Status?"

"One committed suicide in 1946, one died in 1998, and the other was still alive as of 2005—the last time the file was updated."

"Name?"

"Nope. For security purposes, in case of Soviet moles, they were listed as Subjects Alpha, Beta, and Delta."

"How do they know Delta is still alive?"

"He made a computer transfer from a long-standing Swiss bank account to another in Germany," she said. "There was obviously a tickler on his account number and this transaction was registered. The transfer was recorded in the minutes of the United Nations War Crime Commission."

Dunlap *ugh*ed. The UNWCC was a seventeen-nation body that had investigated Nazi atrocities from 1946 to 1949, and still updated their files as news—typically filed by Israeli law enforcement agencies—became available. Unfortunately, their findings were sealed and accessible only in the face of a clear and present danger. While Israel maintained that the existence of extremists represented just such a peril and demanded the files be opened, the United Nations would not participate in what they described as a process of "harassment and persecution of octogenarians or their families who may have knowledge of criminals, but who may not themselves have committed illegal acts." The United Nations was historically anti-Israeli. However,

Dunlap wondered if they might not be willing to provide the name of this individual if Egypt requested it.

Dunlap noted the name of the bank and transaction number, though he felt a little like the impoverished young fairy-tale lad who had been sent to sell the precious family cow for money and returned with a handful of beans.

He thanked Wendy, asked what she planned to do that night, and utterly failed to follow up when she said, "watching TV with my dog." Deflated and perspiring even more, he sent the banking information to Deputy Director Harper along with an evaluation of the available DOI—depth of information—which he rated one out of a possible twenty. There was nothing about the specific artifact, very little about the program itself, and only one clear option for potentially acquiring additional information. That was about as unhelpful as things got.

As he composed the e-mail, Dunlap didn't have an opinion about the Staff or the Nazi operation, though he did have a thought about faith.

If there really is a God, He'll have Wendy undergo an epiphany, e-mail and ask what I'm doing tonight, and when I say, "Nothing," she'll ask me over to watch TV with her.

It didn't happen.

Exhaling displeasure loudly through his little domain, Dunlap forwarded the bank information to Ned Hull at the Computer Access Division. He had a feeling that would be Jonathan's next stop.

CHAPTER TWENTY-SIX
NEW YORK, NEW YORK

On his way to a General Assembly meeting, Egypt-ian ambassador to the United Nations Osman al-Obour went to the fourteenth-floor office of the United Nations War Crimes Commission. The current director of the committee was Asef Shiyab of Jordan. Shiyab had only been in America for three months and the men did not know each other very well.

That didn't matter.

Al-Obour was directly descended from a merchant who had negotiated trade routes for the Eighteenth Dynasty four thousand years ago. His brother Arab, Shiyab, once remarked that his own ancestors had worked that route selling timber and probably knew al-Obour's forebears. Whether or not Shiyab was being even remotely truthful, the men had bonded over the idea. Kinship, like reli-gion, did not always need archaeological records to make it a de facto reality.

As it was in the days of horse-trading, personal contact was the most effective tool of any diplomat. Honored by the visit, Shiyab stopped what he was doing and checked the files.

"The holder of the bank account is Herr Lukas Durst, who lists his residence as Berlin," al-Obour was told. "However, that is simply a mail drop at the post office on Schillstrasse."

Indicating for al-Obour to wait, Shiyab phoned the German ambassador seeking help in tracking the owner. Ambassador Hirsch regretted that issues of privacy made that prohibitive, though Shiyab had expected nothing more. At a cocktail reception honoring a new children's initiative in Africa, Shiyab learned that the German ambassador was descended from aristocrats who had warred on Shiyab's own forebears in 1918 as advisers to the Ottoman Empire. A new world it might be, but old battles were constantly being refought.

Shiyab had simply wanted to show his brother Arab that he had made every effort.

One day, Ambassador al-Obour knew, he might be asked to return such a favor.

"It does not seem like much of a lead, but it is something," the Jordanian apologized.

"It is more than I entered with," al-Obour said graciously. "I will pass this information along."

En route to the General Assembly, al-Obour texted the information to the Egyptian minister of defense in Cairo. He promptly sent the information to the CIA in Washington, D.C., attention Deputy Director Jonathan Harper, who had made the request.

Both al-Obour and the minister imagined they were doing the American a favor, and Harper was annoyed to hear from the minister how flattered they were that the powerful American organization had made an OD request of them.

He let it pass.

One day, he knew, he would get to tell them the truth.

CHAPTER TWENTY-SEVEN

MCLEAN, VIRGINIA

It was what Kealey called "orderly disorder."

True to Kealey's prediction, Task Force 777 had sent over a grainy, night-vision video of the Staff of Moses turning into a serpent. To him, the miracle was inconclusive. Shrunk in size, posted on the Web—he had every confidence it would somehow make its way there—the effect might be more persuasive.

Kealey left Phair studying it on a laptop when he received a call from Hamish Dean of the CIA Linguistics Lab.

"The text does seem to say 'mail drop for Lukas Durst in Berlin,'" Dean informed him.

"That's it?"

"In its entirety," said the caller.

Kealey had forwarded the e-mail in question, that was in coded Egyptian, to Dean nearly a half hour before. It wasn't simply a matter of translating the words but ascertaining the exact meaning and context. For example, *mail drop,* translated to Egyptian and then to

English, could have been a *mail box* to begin with in its native German, which would have been an entirely different thing.

Kealey thanked him and hung up.

As he was talking with Dean, Kealey had received an e-mail from Ned Hull letting him know the names of all the current businesses that were likely to use this bank over another. It was possible that this Lukas Durst worked for, or had a relative who worked for, one of those establishments.

The connection that caught Kealey's attention was the Venezuelan embassy, which was right next door to the bank. South America had always displayed a welcome mat for former Nazis and their money.

Kealey punched in Ned Hull's speed dial number. It occurred to him there was another way to approach this matter. If so, Hull would find a way in. The MIT graduate had been arrested for hacking CIA records to find out what they knew about him. The fact that they "knew something" had been floated as a lure to see if he could get in. When he did, they offered him a job. Now he was the head of the Computer Access Division.

"Ned, what kind of access do you have to current census data, specifically Venezuelans living in Berlin?" Kealey asked.

"Not so *bund*erful," the technician joked after checking the index of previously hacked files to which he still had passwords. "That information is recorded and kept by the immigration bureaus and released as simple number amounts, not as specific individuals. Why?"

"Many expatriates need to keep ties with their homeland," Kealey said. "We saw that with Iraq under Hussein,

Iran under the Ayatollah, and certainly many Nazis who fled Germany. If the guy we're looking for lives in Venezuela, he may be related to someone who works for the foreign service whom he trusts to go to a bank and withdraw the money he needs to live."

"I've got a way to do that," Hull said. "If the family member is Venezuelan, he probably has credit cards from a bank there. Those numbers are all nationally distinctive. I'll just check to see who's spending what in Berlin."

"Brilliant," Kealey said.

"Who's the ultimate guy we're looking for?"

"Lukas Durst. Age, in his eighties."

"Hang on," Hull said. "He doesn't show up in tax records of either country."

"No surprise," Kealey said. If Hull could hack these files, so could the Israelis. Former Nazis had a clear interest in staying off those records. South American tax officials were renowned for looking the other way if there was a generous donation to their personal economy.

"But I've got a lot of unlocked bank records so we can watch money laundering," Hull said.

Kealey waited while Hull went to work. It was a brief eye of the storm. He took the moment to catch his breath.

"I have seven names charging expensive dinners and clothes in Berlin," Hull said. "Give me a second to compare them to the Venezuelan tax records."

"I thought you said there wouldn't be any—"

"For the Nazi," Hull jumped in.

"Right. Not his family."

"Got him," said Hull. "One Cesar Montilla. Let me

just search him and—here it is. Just building the yellow file."

A yellow file was a program that distilled data into chronological order. It was the computer equivalent of a highlighted textbook with all the nonessential data eliminated.

"Okay," Hull said. "Montilla is Durst's son-in-law. Durst had a wife, Dita, married 1961, a daughter Nina two years later. Nina doesn't appear after 1981 and the mother has no mention after 1994."

"Daughter turned eighteen and the mother died," Kealey speculated.

"Right you are. Public death records show that Dita Durst died in the Hospital de Clinicas on August 8, 1994."

"Which is located where?"

"Caracas, Venezuela," Hull replied.

"Can you get those files?" Kealey asked, typing.

"Checking, but I doubt it," he said. "Nope. Many of them still aren't computerized down there."

"What about a marriage record for Nina Durst in Venezuela?"

"Newspaper account," he said, reading down the yellow file. "She wed the son of the comandante general of the Guardia Nacional in May 1986. That's our Cesar Montilla and he's a courier in the diplomatic corps."

"You have an address for him in Venezuela?"

Hull looked it up in the directory and gave him the number of a house in the Altamira district. "Hold on, though. He's got a second house registered. Let me look that up. . . . Uh, okay, Cesar Montilla has a second house in Alto Hatillo."

"You sound bemused."

"Alto Hatillo is one of the wealthiest neighborhoods in Caracas. Chock full of millionaires and probably a few billionaires, too. Our little courier has a house there—well, technically it's just outside the neighborhood but it would still be money—but he doesn't live there."

"Are you sure it's the same Cesar Montilla?"

"Same phone number listed, must be a cell."

"So who's living there if it's not him? Is he split from his wife?"

"Let's see what the utilities bills say." Kealey heard Ned singing under his breath. It sounded like "Electric Avenue" but way off-key. The singing stopped. "Electridad de Caracas, the local power company, says a Carla Montilla is paying the bills. Cross-referencing . . . says she is the daughter of Cesar and Nina and she's a physical trainer. Which means she's not paying anything *but* the electric bills on a house in that neighborhood."

"Married?"

"No," Hull said. "Hah!"

"What?"

"Reading her electric bill," Hull said. "It's a fat one. Unless she's running the dishwasher 24/7, it's too much for one person. She could have roommates or a boyfriend, I guess."

"Or her grandfather bought the house, put it under his son-in-law's name, and he's living there with his granddaughter," Kealey said. "That could be the one we want. One more question. What have the Israelis got on Lukas Durst?"

"I already looked that up and the answer is not much," Hull said. "Born 1923, joined the SS age eighteen, activities unknown, whereabouts unknown. Do you know how high in the ranks he climbed?"

"No, but I'm guessing he wouldn't have been at the top or someone would have heard of him by now."

"Then he probably couldn't afford this house, either. Even if he hoarded his SS salary, even if he didn't spend much of it getting to Venezuela and making the necessary bribes, even if he lucked out and bought the land decades ago, not guessing that it would become so exclusive. And even considering this house is just outside the Alto Hatillo instead of in the middle of it, SS underlings just didn't make that kind of money."

"Maybe he's being paid off by someone? If he has useful information—or maybe he had something priceless when he arrived that turned out to have a substantial price after all, and a willing buyer."

"Or he's being paid off by Ricardo Ramirez."

Kealey gripped the phone. "What?"

"The mobster. Our locations analysis for this neighborhood has red flags all over it. It's believed Ramirez has a house in the Alto Hatillo and it's known that some of his closest cronies do. A man living just outside the neighborhood beyond his obvious means could be a valued employee or source."

"I don't know if you just made my day or ruined it," Kealey said.

"I aim to please," Ned said. "One thing's for sure, there's going to be hefty protection all around that area. You might want to go in with a white flag, if going in is what you're thinking about."

Kealey thanked him, got the number of the house in Alto Hatillo, and hung up. He told Phair what he had learned.

"Is it possible he took an occult relic or two with him to Venezuela and sold them there?" Phair mused.

"Perhaps including the Staff of Moses?" said Kealey.

"I'm betting Durst's superiors wouldn't have invested time or energy seeking this particular staff," Phair said, indicating the video from Egypt. "It's really nothing."

"You're going to find that we live in an era of video nothings," Kealey told him. "Someone on YouTube crying about something stupid or arguing with an ex can make them a star."

"YouTube," Phair echoed sadly. "And we're fighting to make the Iraqis more like us?"

"Something like that," Kealey replied. He drummed his desk thoughtfully, then moved his fingers to the keyboard. "I'm asking my superior if we have any maneuverability with or around Ramirez," he said, tapping out an e-mail. Again, Phair noticed a twist on the word *superior*. "But with or without him . . ," Kealey murmured, still tapping. "Let's go."

Phair rose. He was excited. "To Caracas?"

"To dinner," Kealey replied.

Phair deflated.

"Ricardo Ramirez has a reach as deep as it is wide," Kealey said. "If we don't have some kind of protection or connection and we go after one of his favorites, we won't even get a cup of coffee with him. We're officially in hurry-up-and-wait mode." By the tone of his voice, Phair could tell that he had mentally finished that sentence with *again*. "In the meantime, I'm hungry. Let's grab a hamburger."

Phair shook his head. "It's strange to say this, but Iraq feels well-ordered compared to what I've experienced the last few hours."

"Simple survival is always simpler."

"It isn't just that," Phair said. "All the technology, the data—I feel like I've just gone through the looking glass."

"You have," Kealey said as he headed toward the door. "But only a very, very little way."

CHAPTER TWENTY-EIGHT
JEBEL MUSA, SINAI PENINSULA

There was a saying in the Task Force: Armed prey is dangerous, but only if you are reckless.

Adjo was not reckless as he watched the compound empty, the gate shut, and activity on the mountainside cease. Except for the observer and the occasional hum of a distant aircraft, it could have been an earlier millennium. A few bedouin boys came along, tugging camels, having given up on finding a brave tourist to rent one for the ascent. That only enhanced the sense of time out of sequence.

Then there was the holy man on the mountain. As much as Adjo tried to hold to rational thought, the site lent its weight to the claim that he was the *Gharib Qawee*. If Adjo felt that way, he could only imagine what more susceptible men might feel.

Then, what he had been expecting occurred. He heard the familiar growl and would have to decide now what to do.

Four jeeps came chugging through the village. The

United Nations Multinational Force and Observers had arrived. The MFO had been established by Egypt, Israel, and the United States in 1981 to keep this holy region from becoming remilitarized. The MFO was comprised primarily of Egyptian peacekeepers under the supervision of Egyptian, Jordanian, Saudi, American, and British officers. Their mandate was to provide defense and deterrence, not to engage in combat operations. Pulling up to the front of the gardens, the white-helmeted soldiers set up blockades and multilingual signs advising traffic not to enter the area. Their only protectorate was the defined roadway, paved and labeled on a map. Pilgrims were free to find another way up, and locals were still permitted to use the peaks for sheep grazing and olive groves. The United Nations presence was strictly to control what was defined as "commercial visitation and passage." Truckers or buses seeking to use the route would be stopped and questioned. If the interviewer suspected they might be delivering arms or reinforcements, or in this case, helping the gunman flee—improbable though that was, since no one would be searching for him and he could stay on the mountain till the MFO left—they had the right to detain him or turn him back. Many of the soldiers could be bribed. It was a big, ineffective gesture that satisfied an international mandate for peacekeeping but accomplished, in fact, very little.

According to protocol, absent a second attack, the MFO would treat the shooting as an aberration. If another shooting did not occur within twenty-four hours, they would withdraw. If there were another attack, Task Force 777 and other special operations units would be permitted to undertake "cleansing activities" under MFO supervision. Lieutenant General Samra had once said that the mandate prevented genocide but not murder. He was absolutely correct.

Because Adjo had anticipated their arrival, the lieutenant had marked possible trails up the mountain in his memory. He did not want to use the tourist routes, which were relatively level and clear of rock. If this were a plot of some kind, then the men who felt they now commanded the mountain would be using those paths. He wanted a route that would overlook those arteries. The moon would be nearly full tonight, and there would be ample light for observation—and, he hoped, for the climb. His only considerations were that the slope of the area be gradual so that he could walk or crawl rather than climb, which would tire him quickly, and that there be no steep falls from either side, something he might stumble from in the dark.

Adjo had half a bottle of water and now only a well-melted candy bar. The tourist paths were dotted with small shacks that sold tea, snacks, and Coke. Even if they were open, he didn't dare approach any of them. He rationed the water but ate the chocolate before it had to be licked from the wrapper. For the last hour of daylight, he stayed in the dark shadow of the tree where he was less likely to be seen and where it was at least ten degrees less—*cooler* was not really a word that applied here—than the 120 degrees in the sun.

The sun was finally swallowed by the peaks behind him, vanishing in a murky pool of red and violet. The moon was climbing above the mountain's southern peaks; a pie-shaped wedge cut by a promontory diminished as it rose. Before the blue-white light could illuminate the ruddy, darkening peaks, Adjo set out. He walked along the monastery wall, which concealed him from the ghostly glow that swiftly swept the mountainside. The path he had selected was littered with irregular, fist-sized chunks of granite left by ancient excavations. The rubble had slid into a stable, triangular sheet that barely shifted under his tread. It rose for some fifty feet, the top half of which he took in a spidery walk, his hands spread before him. He felt like a boy again, playing in the ancient quarries near his home in Wadi Kom Ombo. His father was a carpenter who worked for a small boat maker on the Nile. Adjo was the youngest of three children and he hid among the rocks to keep from going on the water. It frightened him because no one ever knew when it would leave the riverbed and consume land, homes, cars, and people. He did not want to work on boats. Even at the age of five he liked wrapping his fingers around stone, knowing that it could be used to build or fight or stand on. In school, when they read the stories of the ancient gods, he always wanted to hear more about Geb, the earth god, who was not part animal like the others but was a man the color of mud and flowers. Adjo drew pictures of him, at one point painting his own body with mud from the riverbank. He liked the notion that the night god, Nut, came to bring him darkness and rest, that the snake-headed water god, Naunet, feared him.

Bassam Adjo joined the army to protect the land he had loved—first as a physical thing, then as an ancient political concept. He was drawn to 777 where he could soar above the waters and occasionally see the place on the river below where his father and brothers toiled. He liked the freedom and also the control. But being here, like this, was also good. It was like visiting his boyhood home, the place where he was born.

The rocks felt familiar, the night air invigorating. The evening was cooling quickly, and by the time he reached the top of the mound there was a distinct chill in the air. At the top of the rock apron he moved to the right, where waters—perhaps from the time of Moses himself—had carved a waist-deep gully in the mountainside. Adjo's Nikes provided a strong cushion where the V-shaped cut was insufficiently deep for him to touch bottom. Sure-footed, he made his way in a zigzag course to a small ledge some fifty meters above the monastery. The gunman would have been at a nine o'clock position laterally from where he was standing.

The rock cut ended and Adjo continued along knobby outcroppings of varied size and uneven surface. This was more of a climb, and the shadows the rocks threw made it difficult to see anything on the left side. He didn't want to stop in the open and there was no point going back, so he had to feel his way before committing to a handhold. Here, his thick soles were a hindrance. His feet themselves weren't very happy, swelling from the heat and exertion. But he was not in a rush and it still felt good and right to be among the rocks.

When the sniper's post was below him, Adjo paused and turned his back to the rock. He took a swallow of water—he kept the plastic bottle in his backpack, whose metal clasps he'd covered with dirt lest they reflect moonlight—and looked back at the gunman's perch. The tourists' path went right by it, about ten meters away, meaning the gunman could have come from above or below, day or night. There were no security cameras looking up from the monastery, so he wasn't concerned about being spotted. Still, he wasn't sure it was worth going to investigate at night—especially if the shooter was still in the vicinity.

Adjo looked up the slope and decided to make for the next outcropping, one which would give him a good view of the tourist road at sunup. He wasn't tired but he was cold and shivering, the long afternoon's perspiration cooling everywhere on his body. The desert wind had come up, carrying not just a chill but sand. The puffs of grit got in his eyes, in his mouth, and clung to the sweat on his exposed hands and face.

I wonder if Moses had to brush his beard and hair and shake out his robes when he reached the summit. That may have been why it took the prophet so damn long to carve the Ten Commandments.

The next forty or so meters took three times as long to negotiate as did the first fifty. In addition to the wind, the rocks were larger, rounder, and had steeper faces than those farther down. Gripping them was a problem. Also, the wind had a deep, whistling quality that made it difficult to listen. If anyone were waiting up there, Adjo would have to see them, not hear them. But he made the ascent without incident, and was surprised to see that fully three hours had passed since he set out. It seemed much shorter. Nestling between two rugged projections that jutted like thick, flat arms from the side of a boulder and provided some protection from the wind, Adjo had a good view of the tourist path and below, the sprawling, open plain beyond the foothills. At one point during the long night he thought he heard voices. But they sounded distant and muffled, as though someone had left a radio on in one of the tea shacks. He hadn't seen any pilgrims, which didn't surprise him. This was not a journey a novice would take at night. The noises he did recognize on the peaks were not human, whether it was underbrush stirred by the wind or the scratching of a large lizard crawling among the rocks. He was also alert for wolves and mountain lions, though there was enough game and trash so that they almost never attacked humans.

Not unless their natural hunting grounds are disturbed by an influx of pilgrims, he thought, casting a cautious look around.

Adjo wondered what his family, and his father in particular, would think if they knew he was working on the Mountain of God. They were not religious, but they would fear to tempt God by showing disrespect to one of his temples. Nor would they understand how a man could be paid to sit outside, on his bottom, and watch for people who might or might not show up. That would seem like stealing to them. And the fact that Adjo enjoyed it would have been doubly mystifying to his father in particular. To Youssef Adjo, playing checkers or watching action movies with friends was something for a man to enjoy.

The stars were clear and Adjo could clearly see the Milky Way. If God had not actually summoned Moses to this spot, Adjo could see how a man would come here to be inspired, how it would help him to search his soul for a means of organizing a rabble into a law abiding people.

The young man closed his tired eyes. The shrieking wind and the cold prevented him from sleeping for very long, but he was comfortable enough otherwise. Only occasionally did he hear one of those muted, far-off murmurs, never close enough to concern him.

When the inside of his eyelids went from black to brown, he opened them and watched the new dawn break. Feeling neither tired nor rested, he shifted to a crouch so he could see over the northern arm of his resting place. He moved slowly and purposefully on limbs that were stiff from sitting and sore from the climb. He had a headache from trying to see in the darkness; he was accustomed to having night-vision glasses. But he stretched his mouth and eye muscles to a semblance of alertness and poked his head above the rocks.

The discomfort and fogginess were shoved aside when he saw an encampment at the base of the mountain. It must have been set up just after sunset, for he had not seen it when he began his climb.

There were more than a thousand people below. They weren't tourists, for there were no cars or buses. They were lying under blankets, their heads on bundles. Some were already going about their morning devotions. Others were still assembling at the far western section of the camp, at the fringes of the desert.

They were pilgrims, and Adjo knew that his mission here had suddenly become irrelevant. The sniper had wanted to shut the mountain down for a day, make sure that no one got in the way of these people. He didn't want tourists or shopkeepers to see them and report them. And with the MFO in the field here, 777 would have stood down for the evening.

Brilliant.

Adjo took out his phone and called Task Force headquarters. As much as these pilgrims worried him, he

was far more concerned with something else: the likelihood that they were only the first wave.

And something more dangerous that he couldn't
even begin to consider: what would happen when the
prophet came down to engage his flock?

Or, perhaps worse, Adjo thought. *What if he does
not?*

CHAPTER TWENTY-NINE
ARLINGTON, VIRGINIA

Kealey drove Phair to a small restaurant in Arlington where Kealey was known—at least to the hostess who seated them and to the waitress who took their order. Phair didn't note the name of the place and didn't remember what he ordered after he'd ordered it. His mind was scurrying about the puzzle of what was happening in the Middle East, interspersed with flashes of the dramatic events that had brought him from a firefight in Iraq to a restaurant in Virginia poised for a mission to Venezuela that might or might not involve a mobster. It was the antithesis of the first half of his life, which had been a testament to order.

The future cleric had grown up in Germantown, Pennsylvania, outside Philadelphia, where his father had been a railroad conductor. His mother, with whom he spent the most time, was a volunteer at the local church, organizing everything from bake sales to prayer groups to disaster-relief drives. An only child, young James sought fellowship among other children at the church and found himself repeating to them the lessons he had learned in Sunday School and from his mother. He rarely got them to listen, but it made him feel good to take the side of the Lord. And when he was inside the church on Lincoln Drive, he felt as though he were *at* the side of the Lord.

He was sixteen when his mother died from a heart attack. He had to be there for his father, who was lost and lonely. James never resented it, and there was no question then what he would do with his life.

Talking to his priest, young Phair decided that he wanted to minister to people under stress, like his father had been. He enlisted in the military and found his calling.

Be careful what you wish for, he told himself as a salad and a plate of fish and chips were placed before him. *The fate of the Middle East could end up resting on your shoulders. That's a lot of people who need help right away.*

"We won't find a lot of affection in Venezuela," Kealey said as he peppered his fish. "Regardless of Ramirez. The Venezuelans think Americans are bullies. Did you find that in Iraq?"

"Not so much," Phair said, rising from his disjointed reverie.

"Really?"

"Many of them, especially among the young, want what Americans have."

"You mean possessions or freedom?"

"Possessions," Phair replied. "A lot of them don't seem to know what to do with freedom—at least, our notion of it. They don't require gay marriage or the right to publish pictures of Mohammad. They don't want cruel dictators, but they've belonged to groups, to tribes, for thousands of years. They like that sense of community and interdependency."

"What about free speech? Freedom of religion?"

"They have always grumbled among themselves," Phair said. "They don't need others to hear it. A few firebrands do, but mostly those who are looking to subvert the system we've been trying to install. As for religion, they are free—within their own communities. Outside of that," he shrugged helplessly. "That is something we will probably never change."

Kealey chewed thoughtfully on a fry.

"There is something about the Venezuela trip that is worrying me," Phair said.

"Only one thing?"

"I trust you will take the necessary precautions with the obvious obstacles."

"Thank you."

"But my worry occurred to me when we first discussed this course of action. The excitement of the chase pushed it aside—but not far enough, I guess." Phair hesitated. He knew going in how it would be coming out. But he had to say it just the same. "Are you familiar with the debate over Josef Mengele's research?"

Kealey nodded gravely. "Submerging healthy men in tubs of ice water to study hypothermia or injecting them with malaria to find effective treatments."

"Among many other experiments," Phair said. "And much worse. We had an ethics class in the seminary where the question was asked whether doctors should use findings obtained in such a fashion. I was against it. I listened to all the arguments about how the victims would have died in vain or how good can come of evil.

But the odor of evil was still present for me in the process. I would have felt a part of it."

"I understand. That didn't stop us from going to the moon using rocket science perfected when the Germans bombed England," Kealey pointed out. "The facilities used to study and construct the missiles were built by slave labor. The Soviets readily embraced the research and the captured hardware. Had we not used what we obtained, Mr. Khrushchev may have nuked us from space."

"It feels like there's a difference," Phair said, searching to find it as he picked at a dish of coleslaw. "Perhaps it's the fact that one was done while looking into a man's eyes."

"It's an old debate," Kealey said as he crunched on a piece of fish. "The Abu Ghraib prison in Iraq—I'm sure you heard about that."

"Sadly."

"Over here, the uproar was less about the acts—which were mild compared to what Saddam had done—but the fact that America was doing them."

"The Iraqis were used to torture," Phair said. "It was the American angle that soured everyone over there."

"It's unfortunate but I would argue that, faced with the insurgency, we were pretty temperate. One can certainly understand why Saddam ruled the country the way he did. It was the only way to hold all those mad, suicidal factions together."

"He was a sadistic despot, not a nationalist," Phair said, a little surprised.

"No argument, and Abu Ghraib is nothing I'm proud of. It's also a result of war. People—kids—are gonna pop from that kind of pressure, lose perspective."

"Well, there's a price to pay for that," Phair said. "You asked if the Iraqis saw Americans as bullies and the answer is—not at first. They do now, most of them."

"It's an imperfect, sick world," Kealey said. "The good—or bad—thing is, at both Abu Ghraib and in the prison at Guantanamo Bay, we've obtained operational data about the insurgency that has saved American and Iraqi lives."

"From *every* man tortured?" Phair asked. He'd needed a second to digest the fact that Kealey seemed to be endorsing it.

"Of course not," Kealey acknowledged. "But you can't know that going in. My point is, should we have discarded the information we did obtain? Right now, somewhere in the world, attacks are being planned in secret little meetings against good, innocent people. Not just in the Middle East but in Africa, Indonesia, Latin America. Is it wrong to pressure individuals who attend such meetings for information?"

"I believe it is," Phair said. "You can't pre-punish."

"I can," Kealey admitted. "I haven't got whatever charity muscle it is that drives you. If we obtain information from this Nazi prick, I have no problem using it."

Phair let the subject drop. The other Kealey was back, the Mr. Hyde who wanted to stay on mission and would defend whatever that required. Perhaps he had misread Kealey earlier; perhaps he was only a teenager who would throw a tantrum when the world wouldn't behave the way he wanted it to. The cleric took a sip of water; his mouth made it taste like metal. He picked at his salad. He was hungry, but felt guilty eating.

"Maybe he won't know anything," Kealey said. "Or

maybe he'll be dead. Then we won't have to worry about it."

There was sarcasm in his voice. Obviously, that wouldn't help them or the situation. Maybe that was why Phair had been drawn to religion as a kid. The rules were very, very clear.

"Life was simpler once," he said, not having meant to say it aloud.

"When?" Kealey asked. He warm and calm once more.

"Among people whose only goal was to raise a family in safety and some comfort, to pray in accordance with their traditions," Phair said. "There were no larger matters to consider. I was color-blind when I left my unit to minister to the wounded Iraqis."

"Humanism and patriotism are not always compatible," Kealey replied. "I accept that, and it only underscores the point I was trying to make that few things are ever clear-cut. Certainly not in our present situation."

Phair still didn't agree, and he felt nauseous. Maybe it was the oil in the salad dressing or maybe he was trying too hard to swallow a reality that didn't want to go down.

Kealey's phone buzzed. He checked the caller's name, then answered it. Phair watched the man's hand holding his fork become perfectly still. He was listening so hard to his phone, he looked as if he were going to drill it through his ear. All he said was, "I'll be there in twenty." He tapped his phone off and shoved it into his pocket, dropped his fork with a bite still speared on it. Standing, he pulled out his wallet and dropped forty dollars on the table.

"Was it something I said?" the chaplain tried joking.

"You have no idea," Kealey said, shaking his head. "You have no idea. I'll send a car to pick you up and bring you back to my office." With that, he was gone.

Mr. Hyde has left the building, the major thought. Nervous though he was about being tied to this agent for a mission of such urgency, in his absence Phair felt his appetite returning. He was able to finish the salad and made a decent showing on the fish. It helped to recall all the times in Iraq when he was hungry, having given whatever food he had to children. Since returning, not a bite had passed his lips when he didn't feel guilty for having eaten it. Instead of thanking the Lord for His bounty, he found himself asking why He didn't provide to those who truly needed it. They were not Christians, most of them, but that was beside the point. They were His children. They were Phair's brothers. Patriotism was only a part of it. Those poor Iraqi families, orphans, the elderly, the wounded; they had caused a crisis in faith that he was still struggling to reconcile.

And soon you'll be consorting with a Nazi, he thought.

It was strange and disconcerting to think that repatriated, asked to help prevent a possible war, he felt as far from his core as he'd ever been.

CHAPTER THIRTY
MCLEAN, VIRGINIA

"It was a convenient time." The phrase was repeating in Ryan Kealey's head like an unanswered insult. It felt much like one, too. He knew it was the adrenaline pumping through his system that was making his brain catch on to the phrase and worry at it. He was willing to admit that his rage had something to do with it, too. If he admitted his anger he had a chance of cooling himself down before the conversation began.

He was sitting in the Automat, which was nicknamed after the old vending machine as high and long as a restaurant wall that, in exchange for your coins, would open one of its glass pockets and present you with a sandwich or a beverage. At Headquarters, the Automat was one of the windowless rooms the size of a walk-in closet that was used for maximum-security conversations. There were no cameras. There was nothing on the white walls that could provide a surface for a bug. The walls had been treated with a substance similar to the paint-resistant veneer used on subway trains to prevent graffiti, but this version of it prevented any adhesion, not just paint. The floor was a single smooth sheet of white linoleum, also treated to present the same slick surface. There was one chair and one square desk the size of a night table. They were made of glass. The room did have Wi-Fi, so anything that transpired on a laptop could be monitored, recorded, and traced, but the system in place was designed with the same high level of security as the computer systems that hacked China's networks. This was the one location that best guaranteed that only other CIA employees could access what was discussed here.

Kealey knew there was no way this conversation should have merited the Automat. The call should have been witnessed by umpteen people, not least of which would be his boss, Jonathan Harper, so that someone would be there holding the reins on Kealey and guiding his side of the conversation if necessary. Placing him in the Automat was a gesture of faith that Kealey did not need supervision. He knew Jonathan was apologizing, in a way, by giving him this privilege. That did not stop him from giving Kealey a look as he held the door open for him that said clearly, *Don't blow this for the rest of us.* Danny Hernandez could be a veritable Fountain of Youth for a number of federal agencies, but only if he kept talking. One ill-considered question or intimation from Kealey and Hernandez would run right off the grid again. He would never look back.

"It was a convenient time." That had been Hernandez's explanation for why he contacted the DEA today, telling them he was interested in cooperation, and less than two hours later was going to sit in front of a computer and prove it. Kealey was going to be the proof. If

Hernandez helped him out with his specific dilemma, Harper would then pick up the relay baton and discuss terms for an ongoing informant relationship. The implications were breathtaking. Inside information from the head of an international drug cartel would change the game entirely, even if half of what he delivered was calculated bullshit, as they all assumed it would be.

The price of the deal was going to be amnesty for all past, present, and future crimes, including the death of Isobel Garcia.

Kealey sat with the blank blue screen of his laptop on the glass table, waiting for the secure video call like it was a phone date. His pulse was running so hard he could feel it throb in his neck. He pressed one thumb on the tabletop in a sequence of prints still greasy from the french fries. *I am at his convenience,* he thought. Everything in him revolted at the idea.

The DEA agent had been a new face in San Jose, California, which explained why Hernandez had chosen him to approach. The agent hadn't specified how Hernandez had done it in a secure way, only that it was secure, which probably meant the drug czar had caught him in the john. Hernandez had told him to lose himself in the city for two hours, then meet him—carrying whatever technology he preferred for contacting HQ— at a specific parking space in the underground parking garage of the Hilton Hotel on Almaden Boulevard. The agent had arrived to find a BMW with smoked windows and no driver. Hernandez was sitting in the backseat. "It was a convenient time."

Like he knew we would drop everything for him, which we did.

Chaplain Major Phair had been so prescient it was

almost scary. The CIA was about to enter a long-term relationship whereby they would collect the wages of sin and reinvest them for the greater good. It was information laundering, to put it plainly. And there were plenty of people who were going to continue suffering lives of misery, pain, and degradation because the agency was going to use Hernandez's business instead of putting him out of it. Ryan Kealey, personally, was going to benefit. *No,* he corrected himself, *my mission will benefit. Not me. Not even a mission I wanted.* But a new front in a holy war led by a false messiah could become a global problem—so he was not allowing himself to think of San Antonio.

His computer warbled, and without preamble, Danny Hernandez's face filled the screen. He looked like a dad. Kealey was used to seeing faces that had been warped by lives of crime, whether frown lines cut into the forehead by shows of fierceness, or the sleek skin resulting from facials and grooming, sometimes plastic surgery, for the bosses. At times he wondered if a man's face could be born looking criminal and therefore lead him to the illegal life, with everyone's assumptions about him shaping and dictating his options and opportunities until only crime was left. This man, though, with streaks of gray in his black hair, cheerful eyes, and the slightly heavy cheeks of a fifty-year-old mostly in shape but a little loose in the middle, looked like the manager of a supermarket.

He smiled. "You are my pieces of eight," he said.

Keep it short, Kealey thought beneath his neutral expression. *Keep it brief and you won't stray into the danger zone.* "I'm Agent Adams," he said, using one of his old standby identities. "And I'm sorry, I don't get your reference?" *Play dumb, play inferior.*

"I present the silver coins and swear there's gold to follow, a pirate ship of treasure." He could be reading a child a bedtime story.

Kealey was in no mood to chatter but apparently Hernandez liked to feel companionable. "And only you can lead us to it," Kealey said. "I'd say that's about accurate."

The video feed was freezing and skipping a bit, probably caused by the underground parking garage. Hernandez looked like a string of photos, smiling like a Christmas portrait.

"Do you know a man named Lukas Durst?" Kealey asked.

"The name is not familiar."

"He could be associated with Ricardo Ramirez?"

"*Ay, papi,*" Hernandez said. Now his smile had a burnt edge to it. "You want me to help you go after *him*? You trying to rape my quinceañera?"

Kealey threw a blanket over his anger. *Keep it short.* "No, no," he said. "We only want to talk to Lukas Durst."

"Sure, only talk to him. Maybe you can't find his phone number, is your problem."

"We know where he is. We don't know how much protection Ramirez has provided or would provide."

"You show up dressed like FedEx, you want to know if you're going to get shot?"

"We'd like to know we wouldn't. He lives in Ramirez's neighborhood."

"That is not an easy thing you're asking. He would want to know why I'm making this request. Maybe I'll just shoot this agent sitting next to me, drive to the ocean, and dump this computer there."

The DEA agent wasn't visible on Kealey's screen but Hernandez's eyes slid to the left. The kid must have reacted involuntarily. The smile never changed. He had built his empire on the difference between his Best Dad Ever face and his Worst Nightmare words.

"What neighborhood?" Hernandez returned his eyes to Kealey.

"The Alto Hatillo in Caracas."

"Okay, I'll do this for you. You call or visit this guy, you won't be bothered."

"Without alerting Lukas Durst that we're coming?"

Hernandez shook his head no in a condescending way. Kealey realized that the gesture was a comment on Kealey himself. Hernandez *wanted* someone smart. He would only tolerate playing with the little boys for so long. Either Kealey had to put Harper on the call pronto, or Kealey had to be one of the big boys.

"What did she use in San Antonio?" Kealey said smoothly.

Hernandez started laughing and leaned into the laptop like he wanted to pat it. "To kill the mayor? I don't have enough secrets of my own, you want me to tell hers? You're more interested in her than me? You're breaking my heart!" He was still laughing.

"Why did you have the mayor killed?"

"To get your attention."

"The attention of the government?"

"So that when I contacted you, as I am now, that you would be listening."

"You didn't have to assassinate a mayor to do that."

"Didn't I? Mr. Adams, I brought an Iranian bad guy,

a very bad guy, into the United States and showed him one of my routes, and you sent a solitary sniper. One man! I question your priorities."

"But judging by the movements of the Iranian, you had San Antonio planned before you discovered our sniper."

"Yes. I mention the sniper because it's indicative of your choices for the last ten years or so. Either you are not taking my industry seriously or you are . . ." He pursed his lips and shrugged.

Incompetent, Kealey finished his sentence. He dug one of his thumbnails into the quick of a fingernail. *Play smart.*

"I think you're just telling yourself that. I think the assassination was the Iranian's idea."

"No, no, all mine. He was a nice little packaging—again, so you wouldn't miss my message." He laughed. "My message was shooting the messenger. Very compact. I am efficient that way. Agent Adams, I don't expect you to understand this when I say I love my country. So I will say it another way. I love my business. I want it to continue without any wild shocks. A little bit of disruption is good for my business. A lot of disruption is not. The Iranians wanted a route for their extremely disruptive industry. If it had not been me, it would have been someone else, so I decided it would be better to exert what control I can. Which is why I am talking to you now. I will be your insurance and you will be mine."

Kealey put his thumb over the camera lens in his laptop. He knew he couldn't control his reaction to this.

A drug czar had smuggled a terrorist and killed a mayor because he knew—he knew without doubt—

that the American government would play the game his way as soon as he offered them a chance. He was saying that the American government was so predictable, so reliable, that he could use them as a strategy. Not on a local level—on a national and international level. Danny Hernandez was saying that America was no longer a worthy adversary, and he was proving it.

Kealey removed his thumb and said, "My superior would like to speak to you now."

"My pleasure," said Danny Hernandez.

Kealey exited the room. Harper entered. Kealey did not acknowledge him, or anyone he passed on his way to his office. He was moving and functioning by default, a state he had only ever experienced after severe physical pain.

When he walked into his office James Phair, sitting and waiting, recognized the sea change. Kealey was no longer angry at God. He had decided that God did not exist.

CHAPTER THIRTY-ONE
JEBEL MUSA, SINAI PENINSULA

Concealed among the rocks, Lieutenant Adjo had become stone himself, peering down for more than an hour at the wide, arid plain and watching the size of the multitude grow. There were at least two thousand people camped at the base of the mountain, with more trickling in from all sides below the MFO checkpoint. As a Task Force agent, he was outraged by the intrusion. He also didn't know what they would— or could—have done about it. You can't stop a human flood with a helicopter and Jeeps. Rubber bullets and tear gas would only have caused panic and anger.

Maybe it's just as well things developed as they did, he thought. But the intrusion still caused him to bridle.

Adjo used the last of his battery to send a picture of the crowd. Perhaps the photo-analysis team could find something useful in the image—pockets of people with organizers, or perhaps food and water that had been hidden days before. The question that bothered him most, however, was who was behind this? Anti-Arabs?

Pro-Arabs? Anti-Egyptians? Were they jihadists or anti-jihadists, using snipers and the threat of violence to keep away anyone who challenged their activities?

He spent a total of two hours watching the influx of people, most of whom came on foot. The arrivals stopped as the sun rose higher; people had obviously planned to travel when the day was coolest. When the sun afforded little shade or cover, Adjo marshaled his energies to explore the mountainside. He had come here to find a sniper and that was still, in his mind, his prime objective. He would be exposed, but then so would anyone he was seeking.

At first, Adjo's overtaxed legs were unwilling participants in the resumed climb. But once he started moving in earnest, picking his way around wide boulders and along precipitous ledges, his body quickly readjusted. Fresh, warm perspiration was added to the musky film that already coated his body; he thought he smelled as a goat should, which would prove helpful if a sniper happened to be downwind. Of course, that could work both ways.

I will beware of goat smell, he promised himself.

But there was no one, as far as Adjo could tell. Cautiously, in an arcing transit across the face of the mountain, he made his way to the site where the sniper had been concealed. As he descended upon the site he would move a few meters, listen, then move a few more. The wind cooperated by being silent, blowing against the backside of the holy mountain.

The absence of wind also helped him to see, since the desert sands remained where they belonged. He held his breath as he approached the perch. He didn't want to miss a thing and once more turned to stone as he reached the site. He wasn't sure a footprint would tell him much, but a shell casing might. That was where many manufacturers put their mark. That might help them to trace a militia, since different nations were known to provide arms to different groups.

But there were no casings, candy wrappers, or other pieces of detritus. There was, however, something that caused Adjo some concern: ribbed markings in the sand that had blown through the day before.

The impression of a prayer mat.

The gunman was a Muslim who knew he would be here for several hours at least, Adjo thought. Of course, the conspiracy corner of his brain—they were trained never to take anything at face value—poked him with the notion that the evidence could also be a plant—the Israelis? Perhaps he'd been fired at to draw him out, to find the evidence, to blame his fellow Muslims. It wasn't inconceivable.

What would the Israelis gain?

It could even create a schism, many Jews joining Muslims to welcome the prophet. Maybe *that* was the goal, Arabs framing the Israelis to cause a rift in the Jewish state—

Enough. For now, it was just the impression of a prayer mat probably left by a Muslim. Adjo examined the imprint closely. There were four depressions in the midst of the woven design. Someone had been kneeling here, facing southeast—the direction of Mecca. Someone who was here long enough to pray at least twice, meaning at least seven or eight hours.

Adjo decided to accept the evidence as it appeared. When the road in any investigation forked, or even potentially headed in other directions, Lieutenant General Samra did not like his men to waste time speculating. He preferred to take the most likely path—based on instinct, if nothing else presented itself—and be on the alert for additional information. That approach had been embraced by Adjo and the team.

Right now, instinct told Adjo he was seeking a fellow Muslim.

Finishing the last of the water, Adjo made a final scan of the site, looking under shrubs and finding nothing— not even a cigarette butt.

The world is upside down when even terrorists are health conscious.

It wasn't that, of course. A struck match or a lit cigarette would burn like a streetlamp in night-vision glasses. But there was a time, not long ago, when smoking was a sign of manhood, the habit starting when a boy was eight or nine. Even Adjo had smoked until one of the team members was killed on a nighttime stakeout. When Sargent Samahi lit his cigarette, the anarchist in the house he was watching—who was also watching him— knew that he had set down his gun. The Syrian chose that moment to emerge and throw a hand grenade at the sergeant. Adjo stopped smoking the next morning.

Adjo's mind snapped to attention when he heard rocks crunching above. His limbered legs folded unwillingly now into a crouch as he retreated toward the slim shadow of a higher ledge. His heart was slamming against his throat but he forced himself to breathe as silently and shallowly as he was able. He had nowhere to move and nothing with which to defend himself. Yet a part of him welcomed whatever came. Knowledge, keenly desired, often came at a price.

A man strode around the edge of the cliff. He was

wearing a red beret and dressed in shorts and a shirt with brown and green leaflike designs. It was the uniform of an Egyptian desert corpsman. On his shoulder was the distinctive white dove on an orange field—the insignia of the MFO. On his shoulders was a backpack.

The man stopped on the ledge, raised a pair of binoculars, and looked out at the plain filled with pilgrims.

"Lieutenant Adjo?"

The young officer held his breath. He was paralyzed and dumbstruck, the capacity to reason entirely gone.

"Yes," Adjo replied, for there was nothing else to do.

The soldier let the binoculars drop around his neck, shucked off his backpack, and set it on the ground beside him. He turned. He had a wide, squarish face with small eyes. Adjo did not recognize him.

"From the lieutenant general," the man said, quickly withdrawing two packages and sliding them over. The newcomer took a swig from the canteen he had placed in the grip, a covering action in case anyone was watching.

"Thanks," Adjo said. "Any messages?"

"Only this, from me," the man said. He took another swallow, then replaced the canteen. "Don't stay up here for very long."

"Why?"

"We're getting indications about a big event," the man said.

"Here or separate from this?"

"Here. Something other than this rally. During the night, shepherds were told by voices at their windows to stay off the mountain."

"Someone doesn't want collateral damage."

"We're told that even the field mice are leaving."

"Mice?"

The man nodded. "We don't know what it's about, but we're going no closer than we are."

"Then I can't leave," Adjo said. "I'm here to collect intel—"

"Collect it somewhere else, if you're smart," the man said, standing and turning. "Just friendly advice from a fellow soldier."

Adjo thanked the man, who took a last look through his binoculars before disappearing around the bend. It was as strange an encounter as the young officer had ever experienced, though he appreciated Samra's far-sightedness.

Adjo pulled the packages toward him hungrily, like some mountain scavenger. He opened the largest one. There were clothes, a goatherder's *jalabiyya* and *kufiyya,* along with a pair of leather-soled sandals. Adjo would have to rub the robe and headdress in the dirt to make them seem used. There were also baggy trousers and a fresh shirt. The markings were those of the Bani Rasheed—a smart acquisition. The tribe had a large population in Egypt and few of the members would know one another. Adjo was guessing that Samra intended for him to go down and mingle with the pilgrims. But he had other ideas.

The second package contained a cell phone, a calfskin water pouch with warm water, and several wheels of soft bread and unpeeled carrots. There was no weapon, which seemed strange. On reflection, maybe Lieutenant General Samra was afraid that Adjo might be found and searched. There was nothing, not even the cell phone, which a man of his station would not normally possess.

After burying the wrappings under a rock, he ate the

vegetables hungrily and examined the cell phone. It bought him another twenty-four hours, maximum. He knew that Samra wouldn't call him, lest the ringtone or vibration be overheard. Adjo decided to call later in the day; he hoped by then to have something to report. Conversely, if Samra didn't hear from him he'd know that nothing was new.

After finishing his modest meal, the lieutenant turned to the clothes. He broke twigs from shrubs and used their thorns to catch and rip the hem of his robe. He used sap to stain the cloth and rubbed his own perspiration on the underarms. Then he scrubbed the knees of the trousers hard with a rock to make them seem prayed in. After dressing, he edged around the slope. There was no point going out among the pilgrims. Finding anyone who knew anything about a plot would be virtually impossible. But there was something else that interested him.

Why would a sniper have been watching the compound? Perhaps it was just a coincidence that he had been fired upon. Perhaps the goal, all along, was to bring in the MFO to keep the tourists out.

But what if someone had been told he was asking questions? What if the shot had been fired to scare him off? What if there was something going on in the monastery that related to this?

Finding a nook under a large overhang, Adjo settled in with a mental apology.

Sorry, sir. This is a fork that merits consideration.

CHAPTER THIRTY-TWO
CARACAS, VENEZUELA

Coming into the capital by air, the impression Phair had was that someone had opened a box full of pearls, with the brown velvet lid open on one side. The brown was the Avila, a 2,600-meter-high mountain, whose peak was hidden in clouds as the plane dropped below them. The pearls were the walls and windows and tile rooftops of the city, luminous despite the overcast day.

It wasn't the worst flight the major had ever endured. The C-130 that had ferried him to and from Iraq all those years apart—possibly the same plane, given the threadbare seat and rattling superstructure he'd endured on the ride home—was colder, louder, and bumpier.

Kealey and Phair were traveling as Foreign Service Specialists with the State Department. That meant flying coach, row 33.

"I thought high-ranking officials flew business class," Phair had asked.

"They do," Kealey replied. "And the Dirección de

Contrainteligencia Militar scans business class for government employees to harass when they disembark. I'd just as soon avoid the bugged hotel room and hookers who knock on the door with, 'Oh! This isn't my room! But, say, you're cute!'"

"Has that happened to you?"

Kealey shook his head once. "I'm unmarried and straight, not much of a target for blackmail. You would be, though, being a priest. That's the real reason the DoD never wanted gays in the military. They weren't afraid they'd consort with other soldiers. They were afraid the boys would be compromised."

They'd been airborne for a total of eight hours, with a two-hour layover in Miami. Phair slept for some of it and read up on the Heiliges Geheimnisvoll Produktprogramm for the rest. He did not require government files for that; he had printed public Internet files. It was a wonderful thing, the World Wide Web. Like a Library of Alexandria that no Caesar could destroy.

Some of the information he knew but most he did not. Hitler was a devout believer in the supernatural. That much was evident from his selection of the swastika as the emblem of his movement—a symbol of religious power formed by the ends of the arms of a Greek cross being bent at right angles. Phair had known that Hitler possessed what was believed to be the Spear of Destiny, which had been used by the Romans to pierce the side of the crucified Jesus. It was said that he who owned it would control the fate of civilization. Hitler personally took the spearhead, which was all that survived, from the Hofsburg Museum in Vienna in 1938. Certain that the fall of Austria and his acquisition of the spear was an omen for future conquests, he

charged Himmler, the head of the Gestapo, with organizing a group of his most devoted soldiers to find
other holy and occult relics. Several units fanned
across the world searching for items that ranged from
the Holy Grail to the lost prophecies of Nostradamus.

The fact that Hitler was defeated did not, in the minds
of his followers, diminish their belief in the Spear or the
occult. Hitler's suicide was regarded as a blood sacrifice, an acknowledgment of his own failure and not
that of the supernatural. April 30th, the day he took his
life, was the eve of *Walpurgisnacht,* which celebrated
the Canaanite deity Baal—the most sacred day of the
supernatural calendar.

There was no record of the Nazis ever finding anything as significant as the Spear of Destiny. Most of
their discoveries were at the level of a few saintly
skulls from Rome and witches' brooms from the Black
Forest.

"How could they have reconciled finding a Jewish
artifact?" Kealey asked, looking over Phair's shoulder
as they made their final approach.

"You mean the jawbone wielded by Samson to slay
his enemies or David's slingshot?"

"That's right."

"I believe the desire for power would have trumped
any other consideration," Phair said. "Jewish, Hindu,
Chinese, Eskimo—I don't think they would have made
a public display of it, of any of these items, but they
would have studied them to learn their secrets."

"Do you believe any of these objects had special
powers?"

"I don't know," Phair said thoughtfully. "I think if I
were holding a piece of the True Cross, nothing would

frighten me. I might not believe it would stop a bullet, but I wouldn't be afraid to die."

"You think you would know if it wasn't just a splinter of wood?"

"I'm not sure," Phair admitted. "I can tell you this, though. I'd be out there in the desert with the other pilgrims, eager to have a look."

The plane touched down at Simón Bolívar Airport in the seaside city of Maiquetía. It was a modern, nondescript facility of plain, ivory-white stone and girders. Inside, it reminded Phair of Veterans Stadium in Philadelphia, where his father would occasionally take him to Phillies games. People were hurrying here and there on different levels, each the center of their own cosmos, but overlapping and interrelated. He had lost that vertical scale in Iraq, where it was all about the individual in a single spot, on a single mission. He was finding it difficult to readjust.

They had only one carry-on bag each and went to the curb where they waited in line for a taxi. They took one to the Hotel Humboldt, where Kealey went to the information desk, selected a flyer for the cable car trip up the mountain, then went to a wheel of armchairs arranged around a table. Kealey sat down to read.

"Aren't we checking in?" Phair asked, taking the chair to his right.

"No," Kealey answered without looking up. "We're being met."

"On top of the mountain?" Phair asked.

Kealey shook his head.

Phair did not press for further information, nor would there have been time to provide it. A few seconds later someone sat in the chair to Kealey's left. The newcomer was in his early thirties, with a frowning and intense expression. He took off his sunglasses. That appeared to be a signal of some sort, since Kealey leaned toward him and held out the brochure.

"Have you been here?" Kealey asked.

"Often," the man replied.

"Mr. Aguirre?" Kealey said.

The other shifted the weight to his right elbow. "Mr. Kealey," he replied, while looking at the brochure.

Contrary to those complex, non sequitur phrases Phair remembered from spy movies—"The bird has flown the coop," to which the response might be, "I hear the view from the clouds is intoxicating"—this was apparently the extent of the validating password exchange. With people moving all around them, talking into cell phones or to each other, and music playing from overhead speakers, it would be difficult for anyone to eavesdrop. Phair could barely hear them himself, though he did not lean over to join in their discussion.

"We checked the granddaughter's house in Alto Hatillo," the newcomer said, pointing to a photograph as though he were discussing something in the brochure. "An elderly gentleman does live there. We saw him sunning on a porch in the back this morning."

"Did he seem alert?"

"He was reading a book, eating toast, applying sunscreen."

"The granddaughter?"

"Carla is a fitness trainer," Aguirre informed him. "She was home. We have a flyer she left at a local gym. She holds classes four days and three nights a week."

"Do you have a German interpreter?"

"Marta will be on a two-wheeler down the block but

you may not need her. We found a newspaper article about Carla Montilla. She became interested in diet and fitness while studying languages at the Universidad Central de Venezuela—probably to please her father, the career diplomat."

"Nice job," Kealey said. "Thanks."

"I assume this is talk and not take?"

"For now," Kealey answered.

"We're prepared for the other," Aguirre assured him. "There's a forty-one-foot yacht in the harbor with a CAT 3126 engine. She'll outrun anything. We have a navy frigate out of Aruba on drug patrol, ready to assist if necessary. Ironic, no?"

Kealey didn't laugh. "We'll go over to the house after I use the restroom," he said. "Keep watching the place. If I come out walking ahead of my companion—this is Major Phair, by the way," he said without pointing, "we're going back tonight."

Aguirre did not look at Phair, who did not acknowledge him, either. He gathered the man worked for the embassy. He guessed that the reference to "talk or take" meant they were prepared to kidnap Durst, if necessary.

Now this is more like a spy film, he thought.

Kealey thanked the man again and rose. Phair followed him across the lobby to the public lavatory.

"I'm confused," Phair said quietly. "Why didn't this fellow just meet us at the airport?"

"Embassy employees are watched as they go to and from the airport," Phair said. "I didn't want any surveillance video of us getting into a car with him. That would have put our faces in a database that is shared around the world."

The men entered the restroom. They were silent inside. Phair was surprised that Kealey really did have to go. When they left, Aguirre was talking on the house phone. To no one, Phair surmised.

"What if he was followed here?" Phair asked.

"If anyone questions him or me, all I did was ask if he spoke English and if he'd ever been on the cable cars and when they were least crowded," Kealey said. "He told me a little about the best time to go and how long we should allow."

"And what if someone *is* watching him, saw us talking, and sees us head in another direction?"

"Our destination could be interpreted as being on the way," Kealey replied. "That's why we agreed before we left to select that particular brochure. It'll all look kosher."

"One more thing," Phair asked. "Why couldn't he have just given you this information on your cell phone? Then we could have gone directly to the house. Less exposure, no?"

"Pickpocketing is the number one crime at this particular airport, with over five hundred cell phones lifted in the last year," Kealey replied. "I didn't bring it. Too much sensitive data on mine . . . and a new one, with no data, would be suspicious, even to a pickpocket. He might turn it, and me, over to the airport police. We're accepting the hospitality of someone who would not appreciate our attracting the attention of the police."

Phair felt as though his skull was going to explode. He didn't know how Kealey kept all of this straight and how he appeared so unperturbed by it. He forgave the man's little outbursts even more. He needed a vent or his head would burst, too.

They got into a waiting cab, and Kealey gave the

driver the address. They pulled into the early-morning traffic. Phair felt comforted by Kealey's attention to detail, but he still couldn't relax and enjoy the new scenery. They were still on a dangerous assignment, and Phair knew from experience that the most deadly bombs were often those hidden underfoot, where they couldn't be seen, imagined, or planned for.

CHAPTER THIRTY-THREE
CARACAS, VENEZUELA

In 1997, a group of Shiite radicals opposed to the rule of Saddam Hussein planned to attack an oil pipeline in Basra, the first of a series of disruptions designed to weaken the tyrant's finances, his prestige, and ultimately his hold on power. They were being provided with funding and technical assistance by members of the French ecological activists PDT, Protecteurs de la Terre, which opposed the exploitation of natural resources.

James Phair was not yet fluent in any Arab tongues, but he knew enough French from school to understand the intent of the group with which he found himself resting during a trek from Baghdad to Basra. When he came to understand their plans he tried to discourage them, insisting that reprisals would be severe and that violence was not the best way to effect change. He left before their attack, but not before the Mukhabarat—Saddam's secret police—had infiltrated the group and taken pictures of everyone in and around the camp. Most of them were imprisoned over the next few days, and the attacks never occurred. Copies of the photographs were sent to the police of other oil-producing nations in an effort to stem petro-terror as a means of protest and destabilization.

Venezuela's Dirección de Contrainteligencia Militar received copies of the photographs, which were tagged *Prioridad Una*—Priority One. They were sent to every police station in the country. The nation's economy was driven by oil, and no effort was spared to protect that resource. In 2007, the photographs became part of a database linked to facial-recognition technology that was deployed at the country's international airports. The face of everyone who disembarked was scanned at the gate and compared to images in the library. A flagged individual was not apprehended at the airport but followed, in the hope that he or she would lead authorities to any cells operating within the country.

When he landed at Simon Bolivar Airport, James Phair's face caused a computer alarm to sound. Before he left the airport, a security guard was following him to the street. The number of the taxi he entered was noted, its destination was obtained from the dispatcher, and hotel security was told to watch the man. The plainclothes guard saw him as he was leaving the lobby and watched him get into another taxi, whose destination was obtained in a similar fashion.

Operatives with the Metropolitan Police Force were dispatched to Alto Hatillo to intercept what they presumed was an American undercover plot against their oil. As if to ensure their guilt, the occupants of the taxi had not provided a specific address. They asked to be left off at the end of the street.

While two cars headed for the street, desk officers

looked up the records of all the houses on the street. They informed the mobile unit they would have to reconnoiter before taking any action, since there were no likely candidates for anarchy—in fact, quite the opposite. Ricardo Ramirez was a fan of the oil economy; some of his biggest clients were oil tycoons. He had also been known to be opinionated about the decisions of local, national, and international police forces.

CHAPTER THIRTY-FOUR
JEBEL MUSA, SINAI PENINSULA

There were at least four potential outsiders in St. Catherine's Monastery. At least, that was what Lieutenant Adjo had decided after three hours of careful observation and census-taking.

Sitting on the mountainside, hidden from view by rocks and scrub, Adjo had identified the possible outsiders not by their robes, which were identical to those of the monks, but by their movements. All walked with speed and purpose that was not to be found in the others. They came and went from St. Stephen's chapel, which, according to his tourist map, was also the home of the archives. He noticed a satellite dish on the side of the building. Even monks needed Internet access, and he surmised that was how they communicated with the outside world.

Or God, he thought with a grin.

There didn't seem to be any pattern to the comings and goings. The four he was focused on communicated only with themselves, not with the other monks. What's more, the rest of the clergy were acting as though these people were invisible. That was uncommon. When Adjo was down there, the monks had busied themselves in and around the structures but always kept a protective eye on them.

I need to find out who they are and why they wanted the monastery shut down for a day.

Adjo decided the best way to do that was to talk to one of the men who at least acted like a monk. If the others were unwelcome guests, perhaps one of the clergy would tell him. Adjo didn't want to wait until the tour reopened. Whatever these people were doing, they had obviously planned events so that they'd be ready when the MFO pulled out and the buses were allowed back in.

He studied the wall below and saw a spot where he could use a tree to move over onto one of the slate rooftops. Adjo was unconcerned about the sniper; he had accomplished his mission and was probably long gone. Moreover, a gunshot now would cause the place to be shut down indefinitely. He didn't think they wanted that. What's more, if he *had* been the target, he had different clothes now. For all the organizers knew, he was a different man.

I am the same, he thought, *only more.*

If there was a plot afoot and Egypt was the target, he intended to stop it. Adjo's biggest fear was that someone wanted to undermine the new, vulnerable sovereignty of a secular Egypt. After poverty, that was the government's biggest concern and it was the primary focus of 777.

If this situation with the Staff of Moses got out of hand, Egypt could not necessarily rely on help from the United Nations. That could be an advantage, as the

United Nations sometimes concerned itself with policing international borders to an extent that blocked the efforts of a nation trying to cauterize the reach of an international threat. But it could also be a disadvantage. When Egypt's army in 2013 put down the oppressive Muslim Brotherhood regime that had taken its democratic election as a license to install a nondemocratic system, some divisions of the army had shown signs of power madness. The results were bloodier than they should have been. The persons responsible in those divisions were weeded out, but perhaps if Egypt's army had to deal with an internal threat again so soon, more of its officers would go mad. That would be a scenario where assistance from the United Nations could be stabilizing and supportive.

Adjo decided not to inform Lieutenant General Samra of his plan. The lieutenant general would probably order him to stand down. The monastery was not Egyptian property, and the matter was too volatile for anyone to go poking around.

Both of those reasons suggested why the plotters might feel immune and would not expect him. Making sure his phone, water, and a pouch of food were secure deep in his pockets, Adjo started down.

The descent was not as easy as he'd expected. Gravity worked against him, pulling him along slopes of broken, unsecured stone. More often than not their steepness prevented him from walking. He had to crawl down backward, stiff-legged, his head craned toward the foot of the mountain.

The north face of the monastery wall was lined with fruit trees, part of the large exterior garden that helped feed the monks. These were set back behind the smaller, intervening wall that Adjo could use to reach a large branch that came close enough to make the crossover. Whether he could do it without being seen or heard was the question. If Adjo were caught, he could always claim to be a pilgrim who was eager to see the prophet. Even Bedouins had cell phones these days.

Heights in the darkness were misleading. Climbing the meter-high outer wall, Adjo still had to reach the lowest branch from a standing jump. His hands raw from the descent, he found it difficult to grab and hold the limb. He made several attempts and on the last, the cell phone hopped from his pocket and clattered loudly on the ancient granite cobbles. Adjo scurried back down. Though the phone was undamaged, the noise attracted the attention of someone on the inside. The young lieutenant heard the gate squeal on its large, iron hinges.

Deciding to play his part, Adjo shook the tree hard, hoping to dislodge an apple. One fell just as a monk came around the corner, his robe swirling angrily behind him. Though the monk bunched up his robe quickly as he approached, Adjo saw what he never expected to see.

Unless the order had undergone a radical change, Adjo did not think the monks carried firearms in shoulder holsters.

CHAPTER THIRTY-FIVE
CARACAS, VENEZUELA

The houses in the Alto Hatillo were angular three- and four-story structures, well kept and discreetly hidden behind trees and large shrubs. The curving residential street seemed out of place in the gleaming city, which was no doubt what made it desirable to the rich and titled. Phair imagined that the home had been in the family of Guardia Nacional Comandante General Montilla for many, many years.

Just like in Iraq, Phair thought unhappily. The homes there were one or two rooms, made of stone or bare wood and corrugated tin. The families simply couldn't afford to go anywhere else. He found it unsettling that his frame of reference was that, and not the Philadelphia suburb where he grew up.

The men exited the taxi down the street and walked over.

"I assume we got off here to make sure we weren't followed," Phair said.

"I'm sure we're being followed," Kealey said. "The

idea is to be followed only by Ramirez's employees and not the police. Also, car doors slamming have an injurious effect on the psyche. People assume it's the police or bad news and are automatically on guard."

"But everyone answers a doorbell," Phair said.

"They may keep the chain on, but they'll see who it is," Kealey replied.

The men walked along a sidewalk and came to the white-painted iron gate of the house Ned Hull had cited. There was an intercom system, a small camera, and a locking mechanism on the gate at which Kealey peered. To Phair's surprise, Kealey simply pushed the gate—and it opened. Either someone living there was absentminded, or the assistance Kealey had negotiated for had come up with one hell of a beautiful lie. Kealey did not look grateful. He looked stern, almost angry. Now at the front door of the house, Kealey pressed the bell. Phair heard it buzz inside. He heard a woman talking in Spanish, probably on the telephone. The voice came nearer, still talking.

"Is your wallet handy?" Kealey asked.

"Yes."

"Get it out, keep it hidden in your hand."

Phair obeyed. He wasn't sure why. He hadn't had a driver's license in years.

"If it's the granddaughter and not a housekeeper, I want you to ask to see her grandfather," Kealey said.

"What?"

"Tell her you have a theological question."

"How will I know if it's her—"

"The shoes," Kealey said. "Housekeepers wear simple, inexpensive brands. When you ask, tell the truth except who we work for. You're a seminarian and I'm the librarian."

"No, you're crazy!"

"Improvise!" Kealey snapped. "Uneasiness is disarming."

In that case she'll be putty, Phair thought. Kealey had planned it this way. He was a formidable man, damn him.

The door opened and a young, wary, very pretty face looked through the screen door.

"¿Si?"

"I am Father James Phair," he said, swallowing hard as his voice cracked. "Do you speak English?"

"Yes. What do you want?" Her eyes shifted suspiciously from Phair to Kealey. "How did you get past the gate?"

"The gate was open."

She pursed her lips in irritation.

"We're seeking help, ma'am. On a religious matter."

The woman's eyes returned to Phair. Her expression was still guarded. "Are you sure you have the right house?"

"We are—we do," he said. "This is a little awkward—"

"Say it," she said impatiently.

"Someone claims to have found the Staff of the prophet Moses," Phair said, forcing out his words on the back of a big, deep breath. "We do not believe this to be the case."

He stopped. She said nothing. That was a good sign. At least she wasn't denying that there was someone there who might be able to help.

"We have files in our library, of which my companion is the curator, which suggest a gentleman named Lukas Durst, at this address, may have information which can help," Phair said.

The young woman's eyes shifted to Kealey. "*You're* a librarian," she said.

"Senior librarian," he corrected in his softest voice, with a disarming little bow.

"Where is this library?" the woman asked.

"In the United States. Philadelphia," Kealey answered.

"Do you have identification?" she asked.

"I'm not a member of the clergy, but Father Phair has his ordination card—if that will do."

Phair opened his wallet and took out a white card with black type and a gold seal showing a church spire against the sun. The card was laminated; despite that, it looked every year of its two decades. It caused the woman to relax. The fact that he had his wallet out, ready for her inspection, showed that he had anticipated—and respected—her caution.

The woman studied them a moment longer. "*Azor miyad,*" she said.

The men looked at her blankly.

"I'll be right back," she said, and closed the door.

"Hebrew," Kealey said from the side of his mouth.

"What was she doing, testing us?"

"Exactly," Kealey said. He looked casually up and down the street. "An Israeli agent looking for Durst might have slipped up and answered, or at least indicated that he understood."

"You know, I don't appreciate how you handled this," Phair said. "You used me."

"It went fine."

"It might not have."

"You spent years doing this in Iraq," Kealey told him. "I knew you'd be fine."

Kealey's eyes lingered on the north side of the street for a moment. Then he turned back to the door.

"I don't know how much time we're going to have," Kealey said. "There's a car parked across the street with two people inside, just sitting. They weren't there when we arrived."

"Couldn't they be ours? Or Ramir—"

Kealey cut off the name. "Not in the open like that. Given the old money on this street, I'd guess that marked and unmarked police patrols are fairly regular. Not all the residents here are under our friend's protection and they would want some vigilance on the part of the city."

"And if these are not the regular patrol?"

"We won't have a lot of time to get what we came for," he replied vaguely.

"What about the translator?" Phair would have looked himself but was afraid to turn from the door. He didn't want the occupants of the car to see the fear in his expression.

"She arrived on her bicycle shortly after we did," he said. "She's sitting on the curb drinking water and checking cell phone messages."

Carla Montilla returned. "My grandfather is on the patio in back," she said through the screen. "Go around the side. I will meet you there."

Kealey and Phair turned to the right, following the slate path.

"I wasn't expecting open arms," Phair said.

"Men in hiding tend to be bored as hell here."

"Her reaction surprises me more than his."

"Did it ever occur to you that she may believe us?"

Phair looked at the clean, sandy red bricks of the house and the ivy-covered lattice fence to their right. The house and grounds were extremely well kept.

"Also, I never pictured these expatriates living in luxury," Phair said with a hint of distaste. "Whenever I read about them in the press, I imagined remote farms or huts in a jungle somewhere."

"The Eichmanns and Mengeles had to live like that," Kealey told him, "the ones who had to go deep under-cover to avoid justice. The others, the functionaries, simply went here because that's where the wealth of the crumbling Reich was smuggled for them to draw on while they waited to be called to action. Of course, our host apparently found additional income."

The thought gave Phair a chill as they rounded the corner.

A tall, white-haired man was stretched on a chaise lounge. He had on tan shorts and his legs and bare feet were bronzed from decades of sun. He wore a white T-shirt and an amber visor. He rose as the guests came over.

"Welcome," he said, his English thickly accented with his native German inflection. "I so seldom have visitors."

"You speak English, sir," Kealey observed.

"My late wife has taught me," he said, extending his hands to Kealey and to Phair simultaneously. "She was a journalist." His grip was surprisingly strong. He re-leased their hands and gestured toward a group of folded wooden chairs leaning against the wall of the house. "I am told by my granddaughter you have a matter involving the Staff of Moses."

"Yes, sir," Phair said.

"Records of some manner suggested to you that I can be of assistance?"

The men opened chairs and arranged them near Durst. "Declassified documents indicate that during the war you were part of a group that traveled the globe in search of religious relics," Kealey said.

"*Ja,* that is so," Durst replied as he eased back onto the lounge. He looked from one man to the other. "Who is the superior? You seem the elder," he indicated Phair.

"We're a team," Phair said thinly.

"Teamwork is everything," Durst said.

Carla Montilla emerged from the house carrying a tray with a pitcher and glasses. She set them on a table, poured iced tea for everyone, handed a glass to her grandfather, and opened a chair for herself.

"What exactly is the situation that brings you so far from Philadelphia to discuss?" the German asked.

"Mr. Durst, someone—we don't know who—has placed himself in a cave atop Mt. Sinai and claims to have the Staff," Kealey said. "He apparently transformed it into a serpent, which has attracted a large following in the Middle East."

"Stupid dogs," Durst said with a dismissive wave of his hand.

"What do you mean?" Kealey asked, simultaneously calming Phair with a glance. He knew the comment would not sit well.

"They follow a scent here, follow it there. Whatever camel smells the best. It has always been so. Do you have a picture of this supposed Staff?"

"We don't," Kealey said.

"Well, it is unlikely to be authentic," Durst said.

"Why, sir?"

"Because we found it and buried it," Durst replied with a little laugh. His hand waved again. "A useless piece of wood."

"How do you know you found the authentic Staff?" Phair asked. The revelation had blown past his distaste.

"It was with the authentic Ark of the Covenant in Ethiopia," Durst said, still chuckling.

"How did it get there?" Phair asked.

"It was shipped by the old Jew king—what was his name?"

"Solomon, grandfather," Carla said.

"*Ja, ja.* He had troubles and sent it with his son by the whore of Sheba," Durst went on. "It was hidden for centuries in a church and the Jews never knew it."

"How did you find out about it?" Phair asked. "Were there records?"

"We interrogated the locals, everywhere we went," he answered. "They talked to us. And when we had the objects we took them to study and do you know what we found? Science, not the supernatural! The surface of the Ark was—*goldblatt*?"

"Gold leaf," Carla said.

"Yes, still all of it there. It was covered with a woolen blanket and carried on wooden poles. You see what that did?"

"Not really," Kealey said.

"*Hin und her, hin und her,*" he moved his hands back and forth. "The blanket created a charge. Anyone who touched it would be killed by the *statisch*. Sixty thousand volts of electricity was created by this chest!"

Phair was dumbfounded. "That was the fire of God?"

"Not God," Durst said. "The bearers!"

"Where did you put these artifacts?" Kealey asked.

"The chest is gone," Durst said. "We needed gold to continue our search and so we heated it. The wood beneath it burned. We buried the other thing, the Staff, in Morocco while we searched for the true cross. We intended to recover the Staff later for tests. As far as I know, the trunk that held it is there still."

"You burned the Ark?" Phair blurted. "It is one of the greatest treasures in the history of humankind!"

"To whom?" Durst asked.

"That gets to the problem we have now, sir," Kealey said. "You see, we believe this new prophet is looking to use his false Staff to help start a mighty jihad in the Middle East. One that will cause trouble throughout the world."

"Who exactly are you?" Carla asked Kealey suspiciously. "Why would seminarians care about this?"

"He is no librarian," Durst laughed. "This one is a Catholic priest, that I can see," he indicated Phair. "But this one has been outside. He keeps the other one at bay with his eyes and is skilled at asking direct questions. He has done this before."

"You are correct, sir," Kealey said. "I am no librarian. I work for the United States government in the capacity of a jihad preventer."

"You fight these people?"

Kealey nodded.

"You could have been honest with me," Carla said angrily.

"I'm sorry, there wasn't time," Kealey said. "The situation overseas is tense, and I didn't know how much time we would have for this interview. Our countries are not on the best of terms."

"But we, you and I, have a common foe," Durst said proudly. "The Jew, the Arab, the African. Christian America has never been our enemy."

Phair was deeply silent as he glanced at Carla.

She said, if not proudly then without apology, "We have agreed that my grandfather's ideas are his and mine are mine."

"My unfashionable ideas," her grandfather said, lightly baiting her.

She only shook her head at him. Her refusal to explicate further bespoke what must have been a history of arguments. Apparently they had valued their relationship more than winning their debates, for there was peace and affection here.

"We need to get the Staff." Kealey regarded Durst. "Will you help us?"

Phair felt the eyes of every Iraqi he had encountered, shared a meal with, spoke to, slept beside, burning into his soul and branding him a coward and a traitor to humanity. Phair didn't like Durst, but at that moment he liked himself even less.

"They are people, not stupid dogs," Phair said.

Durst and Kealey both looked at him. They suddenly seemed to have a common enemy. Incredibly, Durst's expression seemed milder than that of Kealey.

"That is entirely beside any point," Kealey said sternly.

"I'm sorry, but you're wrong," Phair said.

"Herr Kealey, it is not necessary that the priest and I agree," Durst said. "I am here, in this country, because my ideas are so unwelcome elsewhere. I learned that during the time I spent in Europe and then in Australia after the war. I don't take offense. I don't care, quite honestly, what others may think." He put his palm on his chest. "I know to be true what is true."

Phair looked from Kealey to Durst and then to Durst's granddaughter, and remained silent.

Kealey said, "I apologize for my colleague's remarks."

Durst laughed. "You are a gentleman and, very clearly, a diplomat. Who *do* you work for?"

"An intelligence agency. That's all I can tell you unless you agree to help me recover the Staff," Kealey said.

"I will help you to stop the Arabs," Durst said. "Jews are bad enough but at least they are educated. And neat, except for the bearded ones."

"Thank you," Kealey said.

Those two words caused bile to fill Phair's throat. He had never felt like hitting someone, not even in Iraq. He felt the desire now. He was actually angrier at Kealey than he was at Durst. Kealey should know better.

"Mr. Durst," Kealey said, "were there any records of your quest, any maps or reports or letters?"

"*Ja*," he replied. "We sent pouches with top-secret maps and dispatches to Berlin. I knew the couriers. They were never intercepted."

"Where in Berlin?" Kealey asked.

"Our office was part of Himmler's complex at the Chancellery."

"The Russians ate that place up," Kealey said. "Your data could easily have fallen into their hands."

Durst dismissed the notion with a wave of his finger. "The Soviets were interested in rockets and bombs, nothing more. I was held in a makeshift prison—in a church basement—by those godless peasants. I told them what I had done during the war. They were so disinterested in my work that they sent me to the Americans as a show of comradeship. I wasn't worth feeding."

"That doesn't mean they didn't read your reports."

"Doubtless they did," he agreed. "Some poor, underpaid drunk who probably thought our work was a joke and tossed the files in a fire rather than carry them to Moscow. They were more interested in carting spoils than research."

"Assuming there's no record," Kealey said, "what can you tell us that will help our search?"

"Tell you?" he said. "Nothing. I will help by going with you abroad and taking you to the real Staff."

Kealey and Carla both looked like they'd run into each other, their shoulders moving forward involuntarily.

"Sir—"

"Grandfather!"

"I wish to go. I insist upon it," Durst said. "I once traveled the globe, going where I pleased, where I was needed, yet I have not left this country for longer than Carla's mother has been alive. I will go to finish what we started, to collect items that will save the human race from *scheize*."

Phair didn't need a translator to know what that meant. Durst practically spat the word.

"I really don't have time to debate it," Kealey said.

"*Nein*. And—you will be going, will you not?" Durst asked Phair.

"I work in Washington—"

"He'll be going," Kealey said.

Phair glared at him.

"He'll be going because this is more important than bruised egos or personal feelings," Kealey said, glaring back.

"*Sehr gut,*" Durst said. "I am glad. I have not had such a stimulating friend in years."

"I will go, too," Carla announced.

Kealey shook his head once. "This is a clandestine operation, not a holiday—"

"Then you cannot afford to leave me here," she told him. "I might slip and tell someone." There was an implicit threat in her tone. "Besides, I will not let my grandfather go alone. That is out of the question."

There was a scraping of metal and shouts from the street. A moment later a woman was apologizing in English. Men were yelling in Spanish. Phair heard the word *detención.*

Kealey was already moving toward the side of the house. "Carla, would you come with me? I may need your help."

"Why? What did you do?"

"Nothing," he replied. "Yet."

Carla followed, with Phair close behind.

So much for clandestine operations, the cleric thought as he jogged along the slate path.

CHAPTER THIRTY-SIX
JEBEL MUSA, SINAI PENINSULA

"What are you doing?"

The monk flicked on a flashlight and approached Adjo from behind its thin but powerful beam. He was about thirty meters away. The young lieutenant shielded his eyes. He was effectively blind and had never felt so exposed.

"I was hungry, your grace, and the concession shacks are all closed down," Adjo said.

"That does not give you the right to steal our fruit or prowl about in our garden!"

The monk was ten meters off now. Adjo could see his feet and he was approaching along the wall with swift, long-legged strides. Adjo was bowing from the neck, his arms across his chest, a portrait of supplication. He supposed he could run without being fired upon, but that wasn't what he came to accomplish. Now that he was convinced this was no monk, he needed to know more.

Adjo took a quick, furtive look at the top of the wall. His face was overwrought, twisted with fear, as though he were imploring God to save him. That was all for show. His panicked, searching eyes scanned the summit. No one was there. His fingers splayed in front of his eyes and he looked past the flashlight. No one was coming around the corner.

Adjo was startled back to the moment when the man grabbed his right shoulder. Adjo immediately slapped his own hands on top of the man's hand to keep it there. Simultaneously he twisted his torso and snaked his right leg around the outside of the man's right leg. He hooked his heel hard into the back of the man's knee joint. The impact bent the knee forward. Then Adjo stepped down hard on the back of the man's lower leg. The man dropped to that side. At the same time Adjo twisted the man's hand so it was palm-up, causing him pain. He grunted but it was all happening too fast for him to realize he should be shouting. Adjo's control of the man's hand allowed him to swing the man around as he fell. The lieutenant dropped him hard on his back on the stone path and swung himself in an arc so that he ended up behind and on top of the man. Adjo drove a hard knee into his chest to knock his breath away and prevent the coming, belated scream. He also broke two or three of the man's ribs, causing him to suck air back painfully. By that time, though, Adjo had slapped his left hand on the man's mouth, simultaneously pinching his nostrils shut. While the man struggled weakly for air, Adjo hauled out the man's gun with his right hand. It was an MPT-9K submachine gun.

It was Iranian, but that told him nothing. Tehran sold

arms to countless local militia, whatever their affiliation. Anything to destabilize the region, allowing them to be an anchor.

His knee pinning the man like a butterfly, Adjo felt for additional magazines. He found two in a pouch and took them. Then he shoved the barrel of the gun into the man's ear. He removed his left hand, allowing the man to breathe.

"There is a saying where I trained," Adjo said. "'The man who turns a gun on an unarmed man is cocky. The man who takes that gun should not make the same mistake.' Help me and live. Defy me and die."

"Shoot me and others will come!"

"Nine hundred rounds per minute can do a lot of damage," Adjo growled. "And it will force the MFO to shut down the region."

"*Allah Akbar!*" the man shouted.

That was not what the young lieutenant wanted to hear. This man was willing to die. Further interrogation would be pointless and allowing him to go would be deadly.

Adjo couldn't shoot him. He set the gun down, grabbed the man's hair, and slammed his head hard on the stone path. The man grunted thickly. There was a crack as Adjo brought the man's head down a second time. The man wasn't unconscious, but he was dazed. Adjo rose and dragged him against the wall. He was in this now, up to his chin, and the clock was ticking. He searched the man for ID, found none, then picked up the gun and hurried in the direction from which the man had come. He also tucked the flashlight under his arm.

The gate was ajar. The man obviously hadn't expected to be out for very long. Adjo crouched. Swinging the flashlight inside, he took a picture of the interior of the monastery with his cell phone.

"Darius?"

"Yes!" Adjo replied.

"Okay," said the other.

Adjo was glad he'd used the flashlight and not the flash. He glanced at the picture. It was dark but he could see enough to make out one monk standing by the door where he'd been shot at, outside St. Stephen's Chapel. Otherwise, the narrow streets were empty. Taking several quick, shallow breaths to get his adrenaline flowing, Adjo ducked around the gate, making for the first hiding place he saw: a stairwell to his right leading down. He didn't know where it led, but unless someone was on the wall they wouldn't be able to see him. He stopped on the fifth step down, his eyes at street level. After studying what he could see of the compound, he went down two more steps and called Lieutenant General Samra.

"You disobeyed orders," Samra said angrily.

"I showed initiative," Adjo said.

The lieutenant was annoyed by his superior's attitude even though he understood it. Samra would have to explain this to the minister of defense, who had to keep the MFO from finding out lest they be cited by the United Nations for infracting the Territorial Jurisdiction Agreement of 1998. Still, this situation seemed more potentially dangerous than that.

"In any case, I am here now," Adjo said, "where the problem lies."

"What's your plan?" Samra asked.

Adjo used the light of the cell phone to check the small tourist map he carried. "I'm on the stairs leading down to St. Stephen's Well. Everyone seems to be coming and going from St. Stephen's Chapel. I need to get inside."

"How?"

"There's a guard in a robe," Adjo said. "I need to take him out and then take his place."

"The man who came after you—did you take his robe?"

"No," Adjo said. "His clothes were white. I felt the black robe would help to conceal him if anyone went looking."

Samra was silent for a second. "All right. Check in when you can. I've just learned there is an American team investigating this matter from another direction. I may have information."

Adjo acknowledged and clicked off. He quietly ascended two steps, intending to watch the road he could see and pick his way over to the chapel, moving wall by wall, shadow by shadow.

A moment later—earlier than he would have liked—he heard shouts from a window overlooking the garden. Someone had spotted the unconscious body of the false monk. Adjo was about to make a bolt for the chapel to find out what was in there when that plan was rendered moot. Men dressed as clergy came rushing from the chapel, holding automatic weapons.

Adjo ducked back below street level. He moved so fast that he lost his footing on the well-worn stones and thumped down several steps, landing ungracefully on one knee at the bottom. The other was in the air, with the rest of his leg; he was leaning forward on both hands. Breathing as shallowly as he could, he lowered his leg and waited, pushing aside the many throbbing pains, listening to see whether anyone had heard him. Adjo felt around for the flashlight, which had clattered from his pocket as he fell. He found it just ahead and wrapped his fingers around it. Incongruously, he had a flashback to his days as a fresh recruit, racing against his fellow cadets. He was literally in a sprinter's position, baton in hand. He hoped the muscle memory was there as well.

For a few seconds, he couldn't tell whether it was his heart throbbing in his ears or footsteps pounding in his direction. Someone had to have heard him fall—

Footsteps thudding on cobblestones. Coming nearer.

He couldn't see much in the dark. There were low arches to his right, an open, musty area to his left, and a dark corridor ahead.

Lights came on. A string of naked bulbs trailed from his position, disappearing behind a bend.

Of course there would be lights down here, Adjo told himself. He hadn't suddenly slipped into the sixth century.

He looked back and saw a monk. The man was carrying the same weapon as Adjo. There was a radio on his left hip. Adjo was completely exposed.

The Task Force lieutenant didn't think the I'm-just-a-goatherd gambit would work. Not with him on the inside and an unconscious guard on the outside. That left just three options: fight, surrender, or one other.

With no time to waste, he took the third option.

CHAPTER THIRTY-SEVEN
CARACAS, VENEZUELA

Kealey hurried toward the front of the house, followed by Carla and Phair. He slowed at the corner of the house to see what was happening. The police were in an argument with the woman with the bicycle. She had obviously collided with one of them as they crossed the street.

"Are they here for us?" Phair asked, sidling up to Kealey.

"Probably, or our friend there wouldn't have hit them to get our attention," Kealey said.

One of the officers glanced over at the house. He saw the two Americans.

"¡Permanezca donde usted está!"

"He wants you to stay where you are," Carla said from behind the two men.

"We don't have much choice," Kealey said. Phair had heard him happy and angry but never openly annoyed.

"Are you here legally?" the woman asked.

"With papers to prove it," Kealey said.

"Then why are they here?"

"I don't know," he replied honestly.

Apparently, they had been watching them—either before or after the hotel meeting, Phair guessed. Were they checking on every American who entered the country? Or just those who met someone in a hotel lobby? That was improbable, but he couldn't think of where else they might have been discovered.

"*¿Es usted James Phair?*" the officer asked as he neared.

"What do I tell him?" Phair whispered to Kealey.

"The truth."

"Yes!" Phair called out, smiling and raising his hand. "*¡Sí!*"

The officer unbuttoned the flap on his holster. "*¡Salido donde puedo verle!*"

"He wants you to come out where he can see you," Carla said.

"Now what?" Phair asked anxiously. He hadn't felt this fearful since his earliest days with the army in Iraq.

"You must have showed up on some kind of watch list," Kealey told the cleric.

"How?"

"I don't know," Kealey said. "Go to him."

"What are you going to do?"

"Go with you."

"Won't that tick them off?"

"Just go."

Raising his hands, Phair walked onto the front lawn. Kealey followed a long pace behind. He was watching the bicyclist. She stood on the far side of the street as the officer came over to join his partner.

There were sirens in the distance.

"Backup," Kealey speculated as they grew louder.

"We haven't done anything," Phair said. "What can they do to us?"

"Whatever they want," Kealey said. "This isn't America. At least we know these aren't the efforts of our protector, or else they would have come after me."

A van tore around the corner so quickly that it reached the front of the house even as the police were turning to see where the screeching tires had come from. Two men in black trousers, black sweaters, and black baseball caps jumped from the back of the vehicle. They were holding AK-47s and trained them on the two suddenly motionless Venezuelan officers.

The driver's window had come down. "Let's go!" the driver shouted at Phair and Kealey.

It was Aguirre. Kealey turned to Carla. Her grandfather was just arriving from inside the house. Kealey looked at him.

"Will you come with us, sir?" Kealey asked. "We don't have much time—"

"You have none," Durst suggested.

He was right. Two police cars sped around the same corner as the van.

"We're coming," Durst said, after exchanging a look and a smile of thanks with his granddaughter.

Kealey stepped aside so the two could go ahead. Durst paused by the gate and positioned himself in front of the camera. Kealey watched impatiently as Durst waved his hands in front of his chest in an "I'm going" gesture, then raised both his thumbs and grinned. Having left his message that he was leaving voluntarily—presumably for Ricardo Ramirez, which reduced Kealey's irritation—Durst ran toward the van with the others. He even managed to mount some speed. Kealey waited and fell in behind him but he needed no help.

When they were all inside the van, the gunmen and bicyclist jumped in the back and Aguirre sped off.

Kealey turned to the embassy personnel. He thanked them for their assistance, then asked, "How did this happen?"

"Haven't a clue," Aguirre said. "They couldn't have organized a tail after our meeting. There wasn't enough time."

"They asked for me by name," Phair said, shaking his head. "It must have to do with Iraq."

"Did you have anything to do with terrorist organizations or oil companies over there?" Aguirre asked.

Phair continued to shake his head. "Not that I'm aware. But it isn't like they wear name tags or badges."

"We can figure that out later," Kealey said. He turned to Durst. "Thank you for trusting me."

"Herr Kealey, I trust no one except my family," he said frankly. "But I have been waiting years for a reason to go from here. I did not want to miss this."

"I am curious about something," Carla said. "This van—it was waiting nearby, yes?"

No one answered.

"I see," she said. "Would you have taken my grandfather had we declined your invitation?"

"It was an option," Kealey admitted.

Carla did not seem pleased with the answer. "Thank you, at least, for not insulting my intelligence," she replied icily.

She looked away, her face stone. Durst did not seem

upset, and Kealey didn't appear to care whether or not they were offended. As Phair had noted before, Kealey could be cold, too.

Kealey looked at Durst, who was sitting between himself and Phair. "What were you doing inside the house?" Kealey asked.

"I was getting our passports," Durst replied. "If we elected to join you, I thought we might need them."

"You won't, but I like the way you think," Kealey said.

"When you run from people, you learn to do it with your documents handy," Durst said.

Carla was sitting opposite her grandfather. As she looked through the dark windows behind him she said warily, "This is not the way to your embassy."

"No," Aguirre responded. "The police are not stupid. They may think to intercept us."

"It is not the way to the airport, either," she said. "Where are you taking us?"

Aguirre replied, "To your stateroom on the USS *Liberty Bell*."

CHAPTER THIRTY-EIGHT
CARACAS, VENEZUELA

Aguirre was being droll. Their first stop was actually a local fishing boat where they were hustled unceremoniously onboard. Aguirre had phoned ahead and the vessel was readied within minutes. The ship was already in motion as the slick, slimy gangplank was being pulled onto the deck.

"What will you do?" Kealey had asked Aguirre as the others were boarding.

"We've got a mutual-protection pact down here with the Brits," he said. "We'll wait at their embassy until it's safe to go back."

Within fifteen minutes the forty-year-old vessel was outside the territorial waters of Venezuela. There it stopped while the four passengers boarded a motorized dinghy that took them to the navy vessel. There, all but Kealey were bundled into a small white conference room in the aft section of the vessel, which had only about a third more space than the back of the escape van. A guard was posted outside, ostensibly to see to their needs. Food and beverages were provided.

"I do not think we are here for a conference," Carla said.

The only sound was the hum of the distant engines and the slight wheeze in Durst's breath. It was moderated somewhat by the coffee he drank.

"I wonder if the fishing vessel will return to Caracas," Durst thought aloud. "I doubt it. The police will figure this out. Perhaps they will go to Grenada. They will find safe haven there. And good fishing," he added with a chuckle.

You don't have a right to laugh, Phair thought, and wished the man would just stop talking. He wished the man would stop breathing altogether. And he didn't feel guilty thinking that. Lukas Durst had supported a monstrous cause and he did not deserve the respect or courtesies he was being shown. Phair also envied him, more than a little, his doting granddaughter. Phair did not have that from family, friends, or congregation. He had borrowed it from day to day in Iraq, especially from the Bulani family—but that was gone now. He did not feel sorry for himself, but he did yearn for that sense of belonging.

Kealey had been gone about a half hour when he stuck his head in the door.

"James?" he said, motioning him out with a cock of his head.

Phair stepped into the narrow, gunmetal corridor. His flesh was moving like a tuning fork due to the proximity of the ship's engines.

"You were on an OPEC-backed 'no-admit' list for oil-producing nations," Kealey told him.

"How is that possible?"

"You were photographed with petro-terrorists in Iraq," Kealey said. "They didn't have a name, so it didn't show up on our background check. Those police knew you on sight, so I figured it had to be a photo trigger of some kind facial recognition technology, probably at the airport."

"Why didn't the information show up when we boarded in the United States?" Phair asked.

"We don't use that kind of software yet," Kealey explained. "When you're basically a one-industry nation like Venezuela, you need to protect your assets. I'm relieved."

"No Ramirez."

"More than that." Kealey stepped closer. "I was concerned that Carla had ratted us out while she was inside."

Phair considered that. "This doesn't mean she didn't. She might have come along simply because her grandfather insisted."

"Unlikely, but it's a possibility I'm not quite ready to dismiss," Kealey admitted. "But if that was the case, I don't think it was us or the mission, per se. She may have been afraid for her grandfather's health or security. Still, we're going to have to take precautions that she doesn't try to run to the authorities somewhere— and also to make sure you don't get photographed anywhere else."

"I hope you're not suggesting a fake beard—"

"A real one didn't protect you in Iraq," Kealey pointed out. "The Venezuelans still ID'ed you."

Phair had been joking. Kealey was not. Phair wondered if the man was done with joking permanently.

His tight, grim façade seemed more hardened by the hour. He was perhaps lacking that sense of belonging even more than Phair.

"We'll get you a chip that generates a local electromagnetic field," Kealey was saying. "It will create just enough holes in the pixels of a camera image to prevent registering sufficient points of similarity."

Phair wasn't sure whether he felt relieved or concerned because he'd be undetectable. If this technology were available to him, it would conceivably be available to terrorists.

"Anyway, we're going to Honduras, where we'll be provisioned with fresh clothes and then flown to Jacksonville," Kealey said. "The NSA has chartered a plane to take us to Rabat."

"Why Honduras?"

"SOUTHCOM—the United States Southern Command—maintains bases in the region to patrol Latin America and the Caribbean. The facility in Soto Cano has a significant air force presence to fight drug trafficking."

"I assume we're not mentioning our connection with Ricardo Ramirez, then."

"No."

"Considering who we're working with to fight would-be world conquerors, I'm not sure who is worse," Phair said.

Kealey only nodded.

"Speaking of which, are you concerned that Durst may show up on a list of fugitive Nazis?"

"The truth is, they're older than yesterday's news," Kealey said. "No one's watching anymore. Look what we had to go through to find him." He started toward the conference room. "Let's go. I've got an update."

Kealey entered, followed by Phair. The cleric was slightly relieved to learn how they'd been caught. At least the Venezuelans hadn't been after him for something careless he'd actually done, only for the company he may have accidentally kept. That was unfair, but there was an oddly reassuring competence to it. Maybe there was hope for international security.

Gathered around the table—Kealey and Phair sitting across from Durst and his daughter—the agent cracked open a water bottle and sat back.

"I've just been informed that there are now several thousand pilgrims gathered at the base of Mt. Sinai, but still no actual sightings of this supposed prophet," Kealey said. "I'm told there is an Egyptian operative inside the monastery, which appears to be a staging area for whoever is behind this. We do not know yet what he may have discovered."

"How could such a well-visited compound be a staging area?" Phair asked.

"Its popularity works for it," Kealey said. "Anyone can come or go without raising suspicion. Mr. Durst, can we talk about the location of the Staff? Specifically, how sure are you that it will still be accessible?"

"I believe it is or I would not have come," Durst said easily. "But before I tell you, I wish you to tell me—are all of your operations conducted with as much, what is the word? Holes?" He looked at his granddaughter. "*Porös?*"

"Porousness," Carla said.

"What happened in Caracas was unfortunate and unforeseeable," Kealey said.

"Yes, yes, we have all experienced such setbacks," Durst agreed. "But we are dealing now with a quest and a relic where we must anticipate all things, against people who are undoubtedly far more ruthless than our dear Caracas police. We cannot retrieve this object and, in so doing, deliver it to the hands of the very forces we are trying to discredit."

"We are going to move forward with extraordinary care," Kealey said. "As I was just explaining to Major Phair, we were thrown into this without being able to clear everything from his record."

"What infamy was on the record of a priest?" Durst asked.

"He was inadvertently mixed up with French ecoterrorists," Kealey said.

"Ah, the French," Durst said. "Individually resourceful, yet strangely useless as a whole."

Carla slipped her slender hand over the large one of her grandfather, clearly a familiar gesture intended to remind him he was with company. He raised his thumb from beneath and held her hand.

"In any case, the matter has been cleared up now," Kealey assured him.

"If only I had had such support," Durst sighed, reaching over and patting Carla's hand.

Phair didn't know whether he meant Kealey or Carla. It didn't matter, not when considering the millions of lives destroyed by the Nazis.

"You did all right," Phair said, ignoring the look Kealey fired him.

"'All right'?" Carla replied. "Living in one's native land, free to move about, earning a living in your chosen field —that is 'all right.' You have those things. My grandfather did not."

"I was on the losing side in a war," Durst reminded her. His gray eyes shifted to Phair. "I am lucky to be alive. But do not confuse that for contentment."

"Getting back on topic," Kealey said, "where are we going?"

"The Staff is buried in the desert," Durst said, "in a chest in a well."

"A well," Kealey said.

"That is correct."

"I've been to wells in the Iraqi deserts," Phair said. "Most of them are fragile stone holes that are quickly covered with sand."

"And some last for centuries," Durst said. "The area we chose has not been covered or irrigated. I look from time to time on the Internet."

"Can you actually see the chest that contains the Staff?" Kealey asked.

"No," Durst said. "But it is there."

"Why didn't you try to recover it yourself?" Phair asked. "You could have made a great deal of money."

Durst shrugged. "It is just a piece of old wood. And to sell it—that would have raised too many questions. It was better to leave it."

"I suppose that if the Staff had been recovered, someone would have heard about it," Kealey said. "It would have been offered for sale somewhere."

"I assure you, it is unlikely to have been touched," Durst said with a smile. "And so you don't worry unnecessarily, while you were out I told my granddaughter everything you need to know to find it. I whispered it," he added, turning a finger around the room, "in case there are microphones or cameras in this chamber. Should anything happen to me, should I suddenly perish from all of this excitement, Carla will have the information you require."

"Nothing's going to happen to you," Kealey assured him.

"One never knows about such things," Durst replied. "I am not young, and hate has a long memory."

"Hate has done a lot of damage to the world," Phair agreed.

"Major, be clever on your own time and not around me," Kealey snapped. "Mr. Durst, so that I can make arrangements, where in Morocco are we going?"

Durst savored the quiet moment of victory before replying, "Marrakech."

While Durst and his daughter ate sandwiches that had been brought in, Kealey motioned for Phair to join him outside.

"I'm not going to have any further outbursts from you," he said. "This isn't a war crimes tribunal—"

"The man is an unrepentant Nazi!" Phair charged.

"I need him. I need you. End of discussion."

"No," Phair said. He didn't care which Kealey this was. Durst was a racist creature, a heartless thing. He meant to say so.

He didn't get the chance.

"That wasn't a recommendation, it was an order," Kealey barked, angrier than Phair had seen him. "The world is on fire and I don't have time to piss on Major James Phair. You have been seconded to the CIA under my command. Failure to honor that instatement, duly executed under CIA Charter Regulation Nineteen, will result in an invocation of Regulation Thirty-Seven, which states that you will be fucked by me, up the ass and out the mouth. If you impede my mission in any way, said counteraction to be defined by Regulation Forty-Two and personally observed by me, I will have you tried for treason, I will make it stick—your past record of desertion will not help you, I guarantee—and you will meet your God before we are through. So, Major, let me know right now if any of this is going to be a problem for you."

Phair did not reply. The only response to the hyperangry Old Testament figure before him was New Testament charity. Ruling the roost was obviously important to Kealey, probably because in all those unseen moments with his superior, it had been made abundantly clear that he didn't.

Kealey turned and left Phair in the corridor while he entered a room marked "Communications." The cleric did not reenter the little conference room but stood where he was, staring at the gently swaying floor. He didn't know how much of that speech was bluster and how much could be made to stick. That wasn't the point. Kealey was right about the country needing them both. The question was whether Phair's personal ethics, once compromised, would ever snap back. Kealey was correct; technically, he had betrayed his country once before by deserting. Morally, however, it had been the right thing to do.

For now, he would give Kealey what he needed: cooperation and silence, nothing more.

CHAPTER THIRTY-NINE
JEBEL MUSA, SINAI PENINSULA

Lieutenant Adjo sprinted ahead, chased by the man from the stairs. The pursuer spoke into his radio as he ran. It enabled Adjo to hear the man's voice and to learn if there were any passwords when calling in.

There weren't. That could come in useful, if he lived.

The corridor curved severely, no doubt dictated by the rock the engineers had encountered long ago. To the left were two-meter-high arches every few meters, where clay vases no doubt held water at one time. Now the spaces were empty. Adjo found one that would serve. It was just shy of an S-curve in the corridor and he pressed his back to the wall on his left. When his pursuer was near, Adjo tossed his gun ahead—as though he had been rounding the curve and dropped it. The pursuer stopped a few paces before the arch, listened, then hurried ahead.

As the man passed his hiding place, Adjo extended his right arm, bracing the inside of his bicep with his left hand. The "clothesline" caught the man in the chin and threw his torso back as his legs moved forward another step. The instant the man landed on his back on the uneven stone floor, Adjo leaped from his hiding place and punched him hard in the right temple. One blow was all it took to daze him. Adjo patted the man's pockets until he found a wallet. He put it in his robe, then took the man's gun, radio, and flashlight. He recovered his own semiautomatic—the toss hadn't seemed to damage it—then stuffed it in his belt. He switched the radio on as he continued along the corridor.

"I have him cornered," Adjo whispered in a fair representation of the man's voice.

"Going silent."

"We're right behind you."

"No," Adjo barked. That meant there would be no doubling back. "Hold position until you hear from me. Over."

"Where are you headed?" the voice on the other end asked urgently.

Adjo would have been happy to mislead them while he searched for an exit, but if this was a paramilitary operation—as the guns and radios suggested—the compound was probably divided into sectors with code names. He turned off the radio since the enemy might be able to use it to triangulate his position. The good news was, the question had told him that this tunnel led somewhere.

Where it went immediately was down, which surprised him. Perhaps the ancient builders had been seeking a water table below. That proved to be exactly the case: it ended in a rough-edged channel that millennia of runoff had cut in the rock. It was barren now and Adjo hopped into the dust-dry waterbed, the walls of which were less than a meter high and steeply angled. The lights ended here and he turned on the flashlight. The path turned upward, as he had expected, and the ceiling sloped lower and lower. Water did not need much headroom. He bent, then crawled, and after a few minutes he was wriggling on his belly. His robe snagged and tore on ridged outcroppings and his sleeves were pulled back, leaving his forearms exposed to the rock and bleeding.

Perhaps this is where the Biblical river of blood originated, Adjo thought. He wondered whether some long-vanished, pre-Dynastic people had ever offered sacrifices here like the peoples of Mexico on their pyramids. Perhaps that dark history was one reason this channel was not mentioned on the tour map.

Adjo had no idea how far he traveled, or for exactly how long. Occasionally he was able to crawl, never walk; mostly, he had to worm his way forward. It was difficult to breathe in the narrow chamber, not just because it was so confined but because the heat from the daytime was trapped here, and rising with the addition of his own body heat. While there was no going back, going ahead was uncertain. Finally, a faint, milky crescent appeared where the stone wall curved gently to the left. It grew as he neared, getting wider. He suspected there might be an opening, not only because it was light but because the air became noticeably less stuffy and hot.

In a few moments he saw what was allowing the air and moonlight to enter: a narrow vent, about a half meter wide and two meters deep, cut in the rock. He stopped below it. Using the light from above and his fingertips, he examined the walls. There were chisel marks, with the gouge-end pointing down. The air vent had been cut from above.

So that people could breathe, or so they could come and go unseen?

The gouges were extremely symmetrical. They appeared to have been cut by a power tool.

He continued to shimmy upward. Darkness returned, unwelcome and deeper than before. He had to feel his way lest he belly up onto an opening and tumble in. Curiously, there were mice in the chamber. He could hear their distinctive scratching on the rock, feel their fur as they brushed his exposed skin. Their presence didn't make sense. There clearly hadn't been any flowing water in this arid passageway for quite some time— millennia, perhaps. There was food to be found in the monastery, but it was a long way to go when there were seeds, bark, and insects on the mountainside.

It is a riddle for some other time, the young officer decided. There were more pressing matters.

Adjo wore holes in the knees of his pants and then in his knees. His wrists turned gummy with a mix of blood and clinging particles of minerals. It was an effort to face ahead, to keep his chin from dragging on the rock. Occasionally, he felt his head begin to sag and jerked it up, only to hit the top of his skull on the low ceiling. He distracted himself by recalling all those years he had spent in cramped helicopters and on stakeouts where movement was often extremely limited and patience was the key to success. He remembered one mission in particular, his first year with 777, when he and then-Colonel Samra were trying to discover how gunrunners were getting weapons into the country. A treetop stakeout one night revealed that the arms were being tied to the underbellies of sheep, like the famed Greek warriors from Troy. To determine who was receiving the weapons, Samra and Adjo had to follow the sheep along two kilometers of dry, shallow, scorpion-infested creek bed. The entire operation took ten hours. And then they had to deal with the smugglers and the sheep.

This mission was worse because there was no Abort button. He couldn't just flip himself over the side of a gully or climb down from a tree. Still, without those experiences, the closeness of this place would have been unendurable.

Finally, Adjo saw shadowy light ahead—ruddy, not moonlight—and emerged at the base of the wall of a much larger tunnel. He poked his head through the opening to his ears—there was not enough light to see—and listened.

He heard footsteps approaching and ducked back inside. The steps echoed through the cave, then came over and past him. When they were gone, he slipped from the tunnel, jumped to his feet, and turned on the flashlight—first wrapping it in his big sleeve to diffuse its glow. Immediately, he noticed fresh, lighter-colored scrape marks on the dirt floor of the cave. He crouched and looked at them closely. Something had been dragged from the tunnel opening to the left. He bent closer and saw faint tread marks. They looked like dolly wheels.

Adjo followed them quickly, ignoring the complaints from his ragged knees. As he did, he checked his cell phone. Not surprisingly, there was no reception here. It would not be enough to reconnoiter. He had to see what was going on, then get outside and make his report.

He heard voices behind him from the main tunnel, not the one he'd used. They seemed agitated. He assumed the worst: that the unconscious man had been found and the enemy had figured out where Adjo had gone. He hoped this system of natural caves was complex enough for him to elude them, even hide if necessary. If there were people up here, possibly the prophet himself, they wouldn't be able to smoke Adjo out with fire or tear gas.

Unfortunately, the cavern was comprised of this single passage and it did not go on much longer. It deadended in a large nook. Worse than that, however, was what the cranny contained.

He *had* to get out of here and make his report.

CHAPTER FORTY
MCLEAN, VIRGINIA

When Jonathan Harper received a briefing from Ryan Kealey, he immediately went from his third-floor office to the Satellite Imaging Center in Basement Three. It had always amused him that the division with the highest reach was at the lowest point of the building, but then simple ironies had always held a dark humor for him. Like the fact that instead of embracing a religious figure who emerged from a Biblical desert, they were trying to discredit him.

No different than what the Romans did two thousand years ago, Harper told himself.

But this new Moses could very well be a fake, created as a form of crowd control. *Of course, if that were true,* he thought, *what about the original Moses?* Did he sit up there on the mountain for thirty-nine days, trying to figure out how to rally the mob before finally hitting on something and carving it on the fortieth day?

It was possible, he told himself. The idealist inevitably becomes the cynic, as the Democrat becomes the Republican—and the agency becomes the collaborator.

Harper swiped his ID card to activate a keypad that allowed him to input a code to get to the basement. The code changed each day, a random, computer-generated run of five digits that was only available by secure landline to his computer. He swiped the card a second time to enter the SIC bay. It was actually called the SIC Analysis Laboratory, but he found amusement where he could. There was so little of it elsewhere in this job.

Beyond the door was an L-shaped corridor with four offices located on the left. On the right were a series of slim cabinets, the machine-workings of the computer system. The computers located in this bombproof bunker ran everything from the CIA's phones to the downlinked surveillance equipment.

He passed Trey Dunlap's office and knocked on the door of Paul Schuyler, the chief surveillance analyst. There was a buzz and a click and the door popped open.

Schuyler had been pouring himself coffee that perked on a typing table that hadn't seen a typewriter for a quarter of a century. He swung his wheelchair back to the desk. Crippled by an artillery blast in Afghanistan where he was an undercover operative during the Soviet invasion, Schuyler was a grim and single-minded man. At fifty-three he was what press director Sarah Knute had succinctly described as "a pill." Schuyler had no life, other than to root out suicide bombers, truck bombers, terrorists, and supremacists of any color, stripe, or location.

Not that it was an unfulfilling life, Harper had to admit. In just the first six months of this year, Schuyler had rooted out a plan to crash a bomb-laden mini-sub

into the United Nations in New York and a plot to fire
Stinger missiles at the Mt. Rushmore monument. He
had uncovered a plot by snipers to terrorize Chicago an
hour before the seven gunmen were set to open fire. He
was an idealist who had cycled through bitter cynicism
and come out the other side, reborn.

"Sahara Desert," Harper said. "I need wells with
anomalies."

"What kind? Metal? Wood? Radioactivity?"

"Probably not radioactive," Harper said. "Other than
that, I don't know."

"How old?"

"At least sixty-four years, going back to the dawn of
civilization. I've got nothing, Paul."

"I noticed."

Schuyler input the request to his master file.

"I assume you want nongeological only?" Schuyler
asked as he scanned the rows of listings.

"What do you mean?"

"In a desert of sand, one might consider the black
ash deposits of the Waw an Namus volcano in Libya an
anomaly—"

"Man-made," Harper agreed. "Limit it to Morocco
to start."

Harper wasn't entirely sure he trusted Durst about
the location: the group might get to Rabat and the German could head off in some other direction. In the end,
the expatriate might be an idealist, too, one who might
see an opportunity to revisit his own lost cause.

"We've mapped a lot of old stone structures, mostly
abandoned way stations and wells," Schuyler said.

"Which project was that?"

"I'm embarrassed to say," Schuyler said. "It was called WC."

"Water closet?"

"Worse," Schuyler replied. "They were mythical groups called Well Cells. That was back right before you were promoted. We thought terrorists might try to connect close-proximity wells with underground tunnels and create a network through the desert, the way they did in the West Bank."

Schuyler was referring to the fact that the Israelis couldn't simply bomb regional terrorists out of existence because they lived with families in underground tunnels constructed for shelter and refuge.

"Wouldn't it be pretty suffocating, a few hundred feet down in the desert?"

"A lot of the underground streams in that region flow through wide, ventilated shafts," Schuyler said. "Computer simulations showed that circulation would be pretty good. Visual and ground-penetrating thermal scans didn't find anyone, though. So. What are we looking for today?"

"Some kind of chest," Harper said.

"Wood?"

"Presumably."

"A well would be a good place for that," Schuyler said.

"Why?"

"Organic matter left in the desert dries out and crumbles within two or three years, depending on how it was processed," he said. "But even a nonproducing well would generate enough distillation to keep it moist." He examined the file menus and ticking clock icon. "It's going to take two hours and seven minutes to search the geophysical and photographic files for everything the size of a steamer trunk."

"It could be larger than that but probably not too much smaller."

"Was the object deliberately buried or lost?"

"Buried."

"When?"

"About sixty-five years ago," Harper said.

"World War II," Schuyler said. "By the Nazis, or someone who was running from them?"

"SS."

"You know, that region was Rommel's bailiwick," Schuyler said. "The Germans had a lot of matériel in the region."

"How does that help us?"

"Why bury something unless you were afraid of being caught with it? What was inside?"

Harper told him what Durst had done. Schuyler was intrigued.

"That's the kind of artifact one might use as barter or to raise money," Schuyler thought aloud. "A lot of it."

"To live on or to revive a cause, that's what I was thinking."

"Maybe one of his cronies sold it?"

"That's possible, of course, though it would have had to be a while ago," Harper said. "They're all dead. And Kealey seems to believe him."

"You wouldn't just put it in a well where someone could stumble on it," Schuyler said. "Especially in a region where someone might grasp its significance. And you'd want to mark it somehow so you could find it later."

"How do you mark something in the desert?"

"Exactly," Schuyler said. "Lawrence of Arabia blew up trains during the First World War and the only way to find one of those is to locate a surviving segment of track and follow it."

Schuyler typed in two words. The search was immediately narrowed to six places. He cross-referenced those with charts from the CIA's Center on Climate Change and National Security, specifically charts showing underground channels. Those records had been used to hunt for the mythical WCs. After the cross-referencing, only one place remained. Schuyler accessed the CIA's photographic database of the Middle East and selected the coordinates indicated by his search. He magnified a dark spot in the midst of the tawny sands.

"Could this be what you're looking for?"

CHAPTER FORTY-ONE
JACKSONVILLE, FLORIDA

Kealey's group was airlifted to Florida onboard one of the navy's MH-60 antisubmarine helicopters.

Before leaving Honduras, Carla had been permitted to phone her mother and explain that she and her grandfather had accepted an invitation to take a trip. A Spanish-speaking officer was present in the communications center as she explained that a project had suddenly been offered in which her grandfather felt he needed to be personally involved, and that she had insisted on going with him.

"He will not tell me where we are going," she said. "You know how secretive and headstrong he can be." Carla added that the police had misinterpreted the American officials as terrorists, but that everything was fine.

"The police showed us a photograph of one of the men with terrorists," Nina Montilla protested. "Why would they lie?"

"They made a mistake," Carla insisted. "He is a Catholic priest on a mission of peace."

"They have had terrorists in Northern Ireland, too," Nina pointed out.

Carla assured her that Phair was a man of peace and promised to phone them in a day or two to tell them when they would be returning.

"I hope that wasn't too difficult," Kealey said as they headed toward the deck where Durst and Phair were waiting.

"My mother is not a delicate flower," Carla replied. "My father often goes here or there unexpectedly, often with people from various nations and backgrounds. So it is only a little shock that my grandfather would do so."

"What about you?"

She laughed. "I am often gone for days, hiking or biking. If not for the fact that the police came by, asking questions, she might not have noticed we were gone for another day or two. Though I assured her Major Phair is a gentleman, I am not myself convinced of this. He lacks a certain charity. How well do you know him?"

"Not very," Kealey admitted. "He serves with the United States military. He left us for a while—sixteen years, in fact—to wander among the people of Iraq and minister to them spiritually."

"A Catholic priest in a Muslim nation?"

"Major Phair believes that God is God, whatever He's called, and he let that belief sustain him. There is evidence that he did a great deal of good in communities across the nation, even when he found himself forced to associate with those who had antisocial agendas."

"Do you believe that my grandfather has an antisocial agenda?"

Kealey chose his words carefully. "I don't agree with everything he says, but I don't agree with Major Phair on all things, either. Men often serve nations without subscribing to their less noble aims. I am only interested in what your grandfather does now."

The answer seemed to please her. The conversation ended as the group boarded the helicopter for the nearly four-hour flight. The cabin of the helicopter was spartan, with rows of floor-to-ceiling equipment, canvas-covered floors, and thinly cushioned fold-down seats. The aircraft was stripped down to extend its range from the typical 1,200 miles to around 1,500—often critical in tracking the actions of potentially hostile vessels. The passengers all wore headphones to block the drumming of the powerful rotors. Durst and Phair slept. It was too noisy to argue and there was nothing else to do. Carla read a book someone had left behind, a western, which seemed to engross her. Kealey checked his e-mails, most of which were cc's of material that had been requested by or sent to Harper. They weren't making progress quickly, but they were certainly looking under every stone.

Harper also assured him that since Ramirez was unperturbed by the police attention to Kealey's visit, Danny Hernandez wasn't spooked in the slightest, either. Their agreement was progressing. Kealey deleted that e-mail with rancor. Then he undid the action and filed the e-mail in the proper folder.

After landing at the U.S. Naval Air Station Jacksonville, Phair was given a cross with an electromagnetic chip to protect his identity. It struck Kealey as ironic that the necklace would, truly, be a shield to him.

The four were driven to Jacksonville International Airport, where a Gulfstream V was waiting. Before they boarded, Kealey received a call from Harper. He took it in the terminal, sitting in a quiet corner and making notes. He rejoined the others after they had already boarded.

They sat in uncomfortable silence as the jet taxied and rose into the twilight. Now that he had time to reflect, Kealey was annoyed at how ham-fisted he'd been while getting this mission on its feet. He should never have given Phair the freedom to say, ask, or question anything. That was not how Kealey had run field operations in the past. Here, he had let protocol slide because this was not a team that had trained together. He had wanted them to find their own rhythm, to interlock in a way that was comfortable. In the field, even seasoned operatives reach for instinct over training. A good leader teaches them how to work with that rather than waste time and effort trying to resist it. That hadn't worked here, which was why he'd had to lean on Phair aboard the cutter. They didn't have time to find what the field commanders liked to call "an organic mesh." Phair had to play ball. After they had the Staff, Durst was expendable.

"You do not wear a ring," Carla said. It didn't sound like a come-on, just a woman's observation.

"I'm not married," he said. "You don't wear one, either."

"No," she said, looking at her hand. "I almost married several years ago—to a client, the son of a shipping magnate. Then he was kidnapped, held for a year. When he was finally freed, he left the country."

"That's—different," he said, hiding the annoyance he felt. That information wasn't in the file they'd made for Carla. He opened her dossier on his laptop and forwarded it to Trey Dunlap with the subject line *Hole in the Bucket*—meaning they needed to figure out new ways to collect relationship data when engagements were not announced in newspapers. He suggested Facebook and similar sites.

"You seem to be very much involved with your work, even now," Carla said. "What else interests you, Mr. Kealey?"

"All sorts of things," he replied. "I play chess, read biographies of historical figures."

"Don't you get lonely?"

"Never," he said. "Look at how many new friends I've acquired in just twenty-four hours."

"That's not what I mean."

"I know," he said. "The truth is, I'm never home and it wouldn't be fair to subject a family to that."

"It isn't easy," she replied. "Relationships, I mean. Many people pull away when they find out about my grandfather."

"I didn't think that would matter so much in your country."

"Why?" she asked. "Are we not part of the world? Are our people less judgmental?"

"You were not much involved in the war, except to produce oil for the Allies," Kealey said.

"We were taught in school that the Germans intended to conquer Venezuela as a prelude to invading the United States," she said. "That did not earn them much support—except, we were told, among bankers who were happy to take their money. To this day, my grandfather gets nasty looks and sometimes verbal abuse when people hear his accent, notice his age."

"I'm sorry for that," Kealey said as sincerely as he could manage. "What matters is that it didn't bother your father."

"My father is a diplomat," she said. "Most people are like Mr. Phair. Sometimes . . ." she started, then stopped to collect herself. "Sometimes it is difficult for me, too, when he says the things he does. But I know he is not an evil man. Not like the ones who put those ideas in his head."

"What was your grandfather's situation when he joined the SS?"

"His own father had been maimed in the First World War," she said. "He lost his sight. My great-grandmother worked as a baker's assistant and did not make enough money to support them. She took ill, she died. My grandfather was only eight. He robbed pockets and tills and trash cans so they could survive."

"Did the Nazis offer hope or revenge?"

"Both," Carla admitted. She looked over her seat to make sure her grandfather wasn't listening, then sat back heavily. "Mr. Kealey, people judge others by labels. My father taught me that. You do it yourself, I'm sure. I can say words like *Aborigine* or *Amazon* and you think you know more than you do."

"Those are not ideologies that one can embrace or choose not to," he said. "Nazism, communism, fascism are different."

"You said yourself that one does not have to agree with everything his country does. In its earliest throes, did the United States not permit cruel enslavement?"

"It did," Kealey admitted. "We corrected that internally and decisively through bloody means."

"In time, I believe that the idea of the Fatherland for which so many diverse people fought would have had a similar purging," Carla said. "We will never know. What I *do* know is that my grandfather was young and impoverished and in need of something to believe in. The Reich raised him up and made him a man, but it was a man who was forged rather than grown. War gave him the tools of a man but not, in all ways, the wisdom or compassion of one. There are times when I feel very, very sad for him."

Kealey did not. Durst had made his choices and had to live with the results. But Kealey had no intention of saying so.

"Which came first?" he asked her.

She gave him a puzzled look. "Pardon?"

"The outside exercise or your interest in being a trainer?"

Carla smiled. It changed her entire disposition. "I was always a tomboy, scaling trees and swimming across ponds. I felt good doing these things. So many of my older relatives died when they were young—they were heavy, they smoked constantly, they lived in ways that even to a child seemed unhealthy. So I made it my business to keep people from needless bad health."

"Commendable," he said.

"It also gave me the freedom to make my own hours, to spend time with my grandfather. With my parents away so much, we were very close." The smile faded. "My family has always lived in fear of visits like yours, of someone coming and taking my grandfather away, even though he had done nothing."

Kealey did not bother pointing out the sickening irony in that.

"He has spent the bulk of his life wanting nothing more than to feel useful again. I think you can imagine what that's like."

Kealey nodded without conviction. Carla was too caught up in her thoughts to notice.

"That is why I came with you. I want to make sure that this happens. I want to be there when it does."

"I can understand that," Kealey said. "But it's a long road from here to there. Assuming the relic is where your grandfather left it, there is still the matter of persuading those who are following the false prophet to stand down. People, especially a mob, don't always listen to reason." Kealey wondered if there was any statement he could make that would not indirectly reference her grandfather's past.

"You impress me as a man who knows his job and does it," Carla said. "When we get this holy artifact, I believe you will know what to do. Perhaps even God Himself will guide you."

Carla settled back and shut her eyes, content to have made her case. Kealey thought for a moment about asking her more questions, this time gently guiding her to the topic of Ricardo Ramirez and whether his money was supporting their household. She was more open to him now, she might willingly divulge key details of Ramirez's operations, or accidentally reveal them, not knowing that they were important. He could come away with intel he could use later, after the Staff of Moses situation was dealt with.

But Kealey let her rest. The whole topic of Ramirez and Hernandez made him sick. And this was not a simple jaunt he was on, with a trained and trustworthy team. He was not about to hang his hat on Durst's character. He did not believe that Carla was insincere, but field operations were like combat: One never knew what he—or she—would do until they were on the ground with bullets flying. Kealey was not convinced that either Durst or his granddaughter would simply lead them to the site, then get on a jet and go home.

Which was why Kealey didn't try to imagine "what it was like" or what Carla was feeling during their conversation. He couldn't afford to. He never knew when it might be necessary, for the good of the mission, to do something for which someone would never forgive him.

He just couldn't afford to care about that. Innocent lives could be depending on him.

CHAPTER FORTY-TWO
JEBEL MUSA, SINAI PENINSULA

With just a single shot fired by a sniper, the activity on the Mountain of God hadn't been a matter for the military.

It was now.

Lieutenant Adjo slowly moved the flashlight beam across fourteen twenty-liter drums marked NAPALM. That explained the mice, anyway. Whenever men on the river wanted to keep rats from boarding their ships, they would put open pans of gasoline on the deck. Apparently, the smell discouraged the rodents from approaching. He couldn't imagine what someone was planning to do with the incendiary compound in the desert but then, they might only be storing it here.

There were also a few trunks containing weapons. The cases were unlocked. No one was expecting company. There weren't enough weapons to stage a coup or revolt; they were small arms, mostly, with a few rifles, semiautomatics, and hand grenades. He guessed it was for defense, if needed.

Perhaps they plan to move all of this out with a mass of people following the prophet, he thought. That was how jihadists and terrorists worked. They moved around among innocents, usually schoolchildren, so they couldn't be easily targeted by aerial strikes. Pilgrims would serve the same purpose. *But to what end?*

Whispered voices reached him from somewhere along the corridor. He couldn't make out what was being said, but the words were clipped, urgent. Whoever was coming probably didn't think their voices would carry this far.

Adjo checked his cell phone. Not surprisingly, there was no reception in the cave.

He had to get outside to report his findings.

He took a pair of hand grenades from one of the cases and put them inside his robe. Then he went to one of the walls and turned off the flashlight. He put his hand against the wall. The way back to the passageway was direct: it would be the first opening he'd encounter. Whoever was coming wouldn't see him.

Adjo started back at a trot, hoping to reach the tunnel before the others arrived. Watching for any sign of illumination, he soon saw a growing cone of light in the distance. It helped to light his way. He saw the opening and knew that even if he got there first, he wasn't going to be able to get far inside before the men were upon him. All they had to do was fire a few rounds down the tunnel and the bullets, even just ricocheting, would almost certainly get him.

Adjo slowed to a walk and called out, "I borrowed one of your hand grenades and will be returning it to you without the pin!" Echoing down the tunnel it sounded like the voice of God. "You have five seconds to withdraw!"

The flashlight stopped moving. Adjo resumed running ahead. The fact that the others weren't retreating suggested that they didn't quite believe him. He would have to convince them.

He withdrew one of the hand grenades and sent it hopping down the sloped floor.

He had not pulled the pin, but they would not know that when they heard it coming. The goal was to buy himself time to reach the opening.

Adjo got it. He heard shouts and footsteps receding down the tunnel when the grenade was spotted. The illumination vanished but Adjo was free to flick on his own flashlight now, and he bolted for the opening.

He stopped.

It occurred to him, suddenly, horribly, that he'd made a disastrous mistake. All the enemy had to do was recover the grenade and roll it in after him, without the pin. He'd be trapped. He couldn't believe he'd been that stupid.

Swearing, Adjo ran past the opening and fired a burst at the ceiling of the cavern. Through the cottony near-deafness that resulted, he heard shouts and more footsteps going in the other direction. That was followed by the sound of gun safeties being clicked off as orders were given to take up positions at the bend. Adjo fired another short burst at the ceiling ahead. He didn't want to kill anyone. He just needed to keep them back long enough to recover the grenade before they did.

Following the bobbing cone of his own light, he saw

the explosive lying innocently against the cavern wall two meters ahead. He heard an order given to move forward. They saw his light, too. He shut it off and dropped to his belly, scurrying toward the grenade. He felt around for it, grabbed it, and hesitated—but only for a moment. He couldn't afford to meet a larger force in a firefight.

He pulled the pin and rolled the grenade. Simultaneously turning and noting the location of the opening, he lay down his flashlight, pressed his hands hard against his ears, which were still ringing from the gunfire, and jumped to his feet. The blast should kick up a huge cloud of dust and blind the enemy long enough for him to get away.

Following the beam of light but running outside it so they couldn't shoot at him, Adjo ducked and swung into the gash in the cave wall. Behind him, the world flashed gray-white and loud. He dropped to his belly, holding his ears until the thunder died, then clawed ahead with desperate fingers while pushing along with his feet. His raw knees scraped the walls with every movement, but he didn't dare stop. He needed to reach the turn ahead before any survivors came after him.

He scrambled in a way he hadn't since trench drills when he was a new enlistee. He couldn't see and didn't need to; there was only one way to go, and this time gravity gave an assist. Adjo anticipated that the men had already radioed to the monastery and that his exit was being cut off. But he didn't intend to have to fight anyone at the base of the tunnel.

The young officer heard scraping sounds behind him, of metal—like a knife or gun barrel—on rock. Obviously, not everyone had been taken out by the hand grenade.

Moreover, someone apparently wanted his share of the glory.

It bothered him that he could die here, of course. What bothered him more was that he could die without making a report. He did not know if anyone outside the mountain would have heard the explosion. For all the MFO knew—or cared, which was even less—the muffled blasts were coming from somewhere else, perhaps artillery being tested across the Suez in Ras Gharib. In any case, it would take time for them to report the matter to the Ministry of the Interior, which controls and dispatches the Central Security Forces. By then Adjo would no longer have need of their protection.

There was a faint shine on the walls ahead, one he had seen from the other direction. It was the air duct.

Perspiring and bloody, and coughing as the fringes of the dust cloud crawled down the tunnel, Adjo flipped onto his back and crab-walked to where he was directly beneath the hole. He stood so that he was inside the narrow vent. It was just the right size to accommodate the drums of napalm. They must have been brought up individually at night, by car or cart, and lowered into the tunnel so they could be hauled to the cavern for storage.

His breathing was rapid, his movements anxious as he tore off his shirt as well as the shredded sleeves of his robe. He dropped them between his legs and used his feet to form them into a small mound that was thicker on the downward slope. Then he began to climb. It was only about ten meters to the top, but that was too high to jump. He had to find himself finger-holds, toeholds, and try to crawl upward. When he found it impossible to grip the relatively smooth walls with his hands, Adjo used his feet and knees to edge upward. He kept himself from backsliding by pushing against the rock with his forearms. It pained the already torn flesh, but it was the only way to ascend. When he was finally able, the officer threw his trembling, weary arms over the lip of the vent and pulled himself free.

The sun nearly blinded him, and he was forced to shut his eyes.

Quickly untying his belt—as fast as his shaking fingers would work—he cracked one eye slightly. He slipped one end of the sash through the pin of the remaining hand grenade and lowered it halfway down the airshaft. Then, holding the other end, he lay on his belly overlooking the opening. Adjo didn't bother waiting until the pursuers were nearer. He gave the belt a hard tug. He felt the fabric grow light as the explosive dropped off. He heard a muffled *thunk* as the hand grenade landed on the piled cloth. He needed it to stay there. If it didn't, he was a dead man.

Swinging away from the opening, Adjo scrambled down the mountainside, half rolling, half crawling, putting as much distance between himself and the air vent as possible. He was still moving when the ground shuddered beneath him. There was a muffled roar—it really did sound like distant thunder—which died quickly. He lay panting on the earth, sprawled unevenly on rocks and thistles, which were more annoying than painful. The fresh air told him just how full of paste his mouth was. He spit it out as best he could, then pinched his nose with his fingers to expel the dust with a series of snorts.

Opening his eyes no more than a slit, and still feel-

ing the sun punch the back of his eye sockets, Adjo
flopped onto his backside and slumped forward. Breathing more regularly now, he gazed toward the edge of the
vent.

It was much larger than before. As he had hoped, the
blast had weakened the walls and caused them to fall
in. A bulb of dust was filtering from within, like Al-
addin's genie not quite taking form. There was very little of it, however, which meant that the opening had
effectively been sealed.

His energy returned, the will to move took hold,
and Adjo found the strength to push himself from the
sweet brown earth. Wincing against the still-bright
glare, he knew he had to get away lest anyone —from
the monastery or the MFO—came to investigate the
rumbling in the mountain. They would probably at-
tribute it to God and stay away, but he was not going
to count on that.

He rose. His bruised feet throbbed from the pain of
just standing on them; it would have been easier to
crawl, but his knees were too raw for that. Adjo looked
around and staggered toward a slope some six meters
off, neither up nor down, hoping he could remain erect
until he could fall against it.

He succeeded, barely. He dropped his right shoulder
against it, the part of his body that hurt the least, and
gently rolled onto his back. Able to reach his water
skin now, Adjo gratefully washed out his mouth and
took a short drink, just enough to reinvigorate himself.
The drink was like an electric shock, sending little
waves of strength in all directions. He started to move
away, toward the east—away from the sun—conclud-
ing that whether the enemy came from below or on the

surface, they would converge on this spot. He wanted
to put lateral distance between himself and the explosion.

Adjo was unprepared for his legs giving out, causing him to roll down a gradual slope to a rough but
cushioned fall against a clump of bushes.

Thank you, God, he thought. Not just for the soft
landing but for the fact that none of them was burning.

He lay there limp and exhausted, in a robe more rag
than garment, with eyes glad to have the upper cliff
blocking the sun and a mind that wanted only rest. But
he couldn't. Not yet. He reached into his robe for his
cell phone. The case was cracked, but the damn thing
still worked. He punched in the direct line to Lieutenant
General Samra. It seemed the most absurd partnership
imaginable. Adjo was physically and emotionally spent,
but this little gadget was full of pep and chirpingly
eager to please.

Samra answered quickly. Adjo tried to speak, blew
out air, swallowed, and tried again.

"Sir," Adjo said, "they are storing drums of napalm
inside the mountain. Also guns and close-proximity
weapons."

"What? Who is?"

"I don't know."

"Where are you?"

"Mountainside," he answered, but his sluggish brain
was still chewing on the previous question. "Wait, sir,"
he said. He had remembered the wallet of the man he
had hit in the cave. "I took a wallet from a monk—I'm
checking."

"A monk?"

"Only dressed as one, I'm sure. He was carrying a firearm and a flashlight."

Adjo reached deep into his robe and pulled it out. With slippery, torn fingers he withdrew an identification card. He had to rub it on his sleeve to wipe away his own blood before he could read it.

"Egyptian-issued," he rasped. "Phut Eid."

"I'm looking it up," Samra said. "Are you all right?"

"A little bruised and torn," Adjo said. "Nothing life-threatening except that men are after me. I must find a place to rest. Oh, and thank you for the supplies. They were a great help."

"I'm sorry it couldn't have been more," Samra said. "Do you want an extraction team?"

"No," Adjo said, despite the exhaustion and odds against him. "We need to know more. I must let this play out."

"Only until tomorrow," Samra said. "I'm reading reports from the MFO now. They heard two explosions and informed Interior. I will tell the minister that you need more time to investigate lest these lice go into hiding. However, I can't get you more than that. The crowd out there is growing. Something has to be done."

"By us," Adjo said.

"What do you mean?"

"Obviously, someone else is doing something very, very well," Adjo said.

"I have tremendous faith in you," Samra said. "Nothing is turning up on Phut Eid. It could be a false document or he may not be on any of our watch lists."

"It would be terrible if he really was a monk," Adjo said. "I hit him pretty hard."

"I'm sure he was an imposter," Samra said. "Were there any distinguishing marks on the drums of napalm?"

"Not that I could see," Adjo said. "It was dark and I only had a moment."

"Very good. You need to rest now. Call me when you can and I'll let you know if I turn up anything on the name."

"Thank you, sir."

"Thank you, Lieutenant. Well done."

The lieutenant turned off the phone and put it back in his robe. He took another swallow of warm water, then snuggled himself as low as he could go in the wild foliage. With the sun behind the mountain, the shadow and branches should protect him from casual observers.

But his brain was still working as the rest of him quickly faded. And Adjo's last conscious thought, while not enough to keep him awake, did terrify him.

The burning bush, he thought again, his mind drifting back to the napalm. *All that burning . . . burning . . . burning. . . .*

CHAPTER FORTY-THREE
MARRAKECH, MOROCCO

It was dark but still hot when the Gulfstream landed at Marrakech-Menara Airport, five kilometers from the heart of the nearly thousand-year-old city. A sedan was waiting to take the group to their hotel; it was not a government vehicle but a private limousine.

Well, why not? Phair thought. *Anonymity had not worked very well in Caracas.*

Kealey lingered before getting into the car, pretending to talk on his cell phone. In fact, Phair later learned, he was looking around, checking passengers, porters, taxis, and police to make sure they weren't being watched. After two minutes he got in the car, apparently satisfied. Before he shut the door and the car light went off, Phair thought he saw a trace of self-censure in the twist of Kealey's mouth—as in, *That's what I should have done in Venezuela.*

They were booked in the Desert Pearl Hotel, a sandstone-faced structure five stories tall with a pool and handsome but not opulent appointments. Kealey told them not to get too comfortable since they wouldn't be there long. That was all Kealey said of their plans.

Phair wasn't sure who Kealey didn't trust. Not that it mattered. The cleric did not live for the agent's approval. In fact, in the struggle between "like" and "don't like," he was coming down on the side of the latter. The clergyman had not managed to come to terms with the events in Venezuela, or onboard the ship. He felt that Kealey had crossed a line with his good-me, bad-me routine. Everyone lost their temper from time to time, but his tirade struck him as the true, despotic Kealey punching through his Teflon veneer. Perhaps he'd deserved the rebuke, and he would try to maintain some kind of perspective. He understood that they needed the Nazi. But he felt that Kealey should have been more sympathetic to his conflict. If the larger struggle were not about morality, what were they doing here? But then, perhaps the loss of a personal god, whoever that was for Kealey, could only devolve into a loss of personal morality as well.

After checking in, Kealey talked briefly with Durst in the lobby. Phair was not invited to join them. He assumed the agent was asking for details about their next move. Durst must have provided them because Kealey left to talk to someone at the information desk.

Phair went to his room. He looked out the window at the hazy city lights beneath a low-lying mist, and the exotic moon overhead. It reminded him of Iraq, with its blend of the new and the timeless. He felt a sharp sense of nostalgia for those years, when there was so much to discover and so little to lose. Even if they took his life—and rarely did he fear that, for he never presented a threatening profile or uttered a seditious phrase—the priest had enriched the soul he would be laying before God.

Phair watched Carla walk out to the pool. He hoped she was searching her soul or praying to God for forgiveness. Not for herself so much, but for her grandfather. Before he could truly repent and save his soul, he needed to accept the fact that he had sinned.

The priest let the drape close and noticed that his BlackBerry was flashing on the night table. He looked at it. Jonathan Harper had sent maps to Kealey, who had forwarded them to Phair.

"In case anything happens to me, I shouldn't be the only one with this information," it said.

It was a tactical maneuver but also, Phair guessed, a show of faith. It was like a sip of brandy: it took a bit of the chill away but it wasn't about to make him drunk on Ryan Kealey. The cleric looked at the maps, and at one in particular, which Kealey had starred. It was a map of the desert region south of Tarfaya. A coordinate had been marked with a small X. Phair clicked on it. There was a satellite surveillance photograph with an odd-looking object causing an odder-looking shadow to ripple over the desert sand. He guessed that this was their destination.

What puzzled him was the time stamp on the photograph. It was an hour before Durst and Kealey had spoken in the lobby. Either the CIA was guessing or they'd figured it out beforehand.

Phair walked idly around the spacious room. He was tired but restless, wondering why he was being so accepting about all of this. If Kealey had the location, why continue to deal with Durst? Because the Nazi might be lying? Was Durst testing them to see if they were trustworthy? Would they get to the well only to be told the Staff was somewhere else? Did Durst even know where it was, or was this a twisted game of some kind? Is this how covert operations worked, having to trust the unreliable for results that were uncertain, at best?

Phair needed to get out. He needed to do something proactive. Maybe his problem had nothing to do with people but with structure—square rooms, timetables, chains of command. He had lived without them for so long, and so happily. He needed to taste that again.

The cleric unpacked the duffel bag, which contained the clothes and basic toiletries that had been provided for him in Florida. There was also an emergency kit, standard army issue, which had everything from a compass to chewing gum to a pocket flashlight and penknife. There was even a long-sleeved, thin, black shirt— *Where's the matching ski mask?* he thought, laughing— and he pulled it on.

Phair happened to see himself in the mirror. He didn't know the man looking back at him. It wasn't the face of a cleric or the Iraqi nomad who had barely even looked at a mirror for a decade and a half. It wasn't the instructor from Fort Jackson, a simulacrum of pedagogy who recited fact and ritual without much personality or a larger purpose, other than to turn out single-minded servants of God and country.

Who was it?

The man in the mirror was a fourth, he decided, waiting to be born. But as what? He had no idea. That was what he needed to find out.

With a determined turn from the mirror, James Phair went out the door to reflect not on where he'd been, but where he was going.

CHAPTER FORTY-FOUR
MARRAKECH, MOROCCO

All deserts swallow the tracks of civilization, large and small, but they do not always digest them. In that way, they're like history itself.

The Second World War played out in massive swells through the Sahara, what the British described as "Big Pours"—an ironic reference to a place where water never flows. Many of the artifacts that were left behind in the conflict, from personnel to jeeps, are still there. The economic and political realities of the region simply did not support memorialization or extensive excavation.

But the historical accounts and the remnants didn't paint a complete portrait. There were largely unrecorded participants, unheralded events, and unfinished stories. Durst himself represented all three.

Ryan Kealey knew something of the history of the region. He had read biographies of Rommel and General Charles "Chinese" Gordon, the British officer and explorer whose search for Noah's Ark took him to the ends of the continent. Yet Kealey knew that facts alone were largely useless to him now. He knew the muscular forces that had moved the large events forward, domino-like, but crucial information often fell through those black tiles. Witness the slipup in the background check of James Phair. Even though Jonathan Harper felt he had a good idea where the chest might be hidden, Kealey wasn't willing to go there alone. If information was missing, if they had drawn a wrong conclusion, Kealey would blow the trust of Durst and his grand-daughter and he would never get that back.

He went to bed late and rose early. After four hours of sleep, Kealey got up and, over strong Moroccan cof-fee and toast ordered from room service, studied the latest data from the CIA. It was also time to think; his sleeping brain had a way of sorting information into useful groups while freshened eyes often found new patterns or details he had missed before.

Not a lot of that happened this morning.

There was no new information, though the update from Egypt was of some concern: satellite photographs showing at least three thousand people gathered in the desert at the foot of Mt. Sinai.

The discovery of napalm inside the mountain was of even greater concern, and for the first time, Kealey ad-mitted to himself that Harper had been fully correct to send him on this mission, delaying his operation at the hospital at Basra. Suddenly Kealey realized with a jolt that Basra was moot now. The agency would keep their eyes on the Iranian doctor, but they could not interrupt his life as it was progressing or that would threaten the route of information from him to Hernandez to the CIA. Dr. al-Shenawi, the terrorist financier, trainer, and facilitator, the dupe for the death of an American mayor, was now a protected asset.

Kealey couldn't even feel rage anymore. The parts of the machine were fitted and slick with oil and already humming. From his cold, mechanistic perspective, he could even see that Harper had been right to send Kealey here instead of west to work Hernandez for intel. Napalm on the holiest of mountains brought the whole situation a few steps closer to a global concern, though the e-mail from Harper stated that no one was sure who or what the napalm was to be used against, or why. The latest satellite surveillance of the mountainside had revealed no exterior movement of interest. Nor had anyone seen anything of the supposed prophet or his activities since the Task Force 777 video.

"Hopefully, we will be able to make some educated guesses when the identity of the individuals inside the monastery has been ascertained," Harper wrote in the secure communiqué. One of the men had identification on him, but as yet, nothing had been turned up on him. "The Egyptians won't share his name," Harper noted, "which means they probably know who he is and don't want to tell us."

That could mean any number of things, Kealey knew. The man might be a monk who was suffering from what the church called "monastery fever"—isolation in a holy setting that turned men with a mission into men with visions. That was something that had to be handled by the church.

That wouldn't easily explain the napalm, Kealey thought—unless the two were unrelated. It was possible that the military secretly used Mt. Sinai as a warehouse and the low-ranking special-ops officer had simply stumbled on that fact. That would be another reason for the Egyptians to suddenly cut off the flow of information. Who knew what else might be stored there?

The prophet could be an Egyptian whose identity would be a potential embarrassment to Cairo, such as an industrialist who had "gone native" and was using his fortune to sponsor a movement of some kind. Perhaps he was a Muslim cleric with a vast following whose identity would polarize forces for and against his sect throughout the Middle East. He might even be the son of an oil sheik, another Osama bin Laden who had to be protected from capture or assassination by the army until his influential family had the chance to rein him in.

Regardless, the exponential growth of the crowd was troubling, along with the possibility that these people might be firebombed for some maniacal religious or political reason—something that wasn't on the radar of the CIA or Task Force 777. Kealey didn't have enough information to consider all that. And then there were things that could not be factored into his thinking, from a sudden sandstorm in the desert to a preemptive Egyptian military action against the cave where this man was hidden.

It was profoundly frustrating. What made it worse was that he couldn't get his hands dirty in the main issue until this preliminary step of the operation was achieved—and he couldn't even be sure when and if that would happen.

He closed his laptop and phoned the others. None of them answered. He went to their rooms and knocked on the doors.

Nothing.

Carla was easily located. She had fallen asleep on a chaise lounge by the pool and had remained there through the night, a thin blanket pulled to her chin, her legs tucked fetus-like against her belly. The sun was still too low to have awakened her. Kealey let her sleep while he looked for Phair. He found him out front, walking back from the direction of the Old Town. The priest seemed surprised to see Kealey waiting for him.

"Did I do something wrong?" the cleric asked.

"Technically, you were AWOL," Kealey said. He was careful to make it an observation and not an accusation.

"Very, very technically," Phair replied.

"You're a crucial part of this mission. If something had happened to you, I wouldn't have known where to look."

"I'm sorry," Phair said. "I couldn't sleep and didn't want to wake you."

"A message at the desk—"

"I didn't know I would be leaving the grounds," Phair said. "I was walking out front, saw a taxi, decided to take it to Medina and back. On the way I saw the Church Saints Martyrs. It was a lovely night, a night like I remembered at the best of times in Iraq, so I decided to get out, visit the church, and walk back." He thought for a moment. "If a chaplain goes to a church, that would be very, very, *very* technically AWOL, I should think."

Kealey didn't appreciate the jab. The priest had an air of smugness, of righteousness, that had no place on the team. Kealey took a deep, calming breath of the dry air. He smelled morning cooking on the wind, some kind of meat. He heard vague chanting from a minaret well behind the hotel. He did not embrace the stimulus but he recognized the sense of isolation. He was not in the arms of the agency here. There was no infrastructure other than himself, and when any element of his team was out of balance he had to pull them back to center, to stability.

"Did you find it inspirational?" Kealey asked.

"I found it haunted," Phair replied. "Churches are houses of God, but they are also houses of the anguish that's poured out there. Depending on my mood, one takes hold more firmly than the other."

"And you were ready to receive pain."

"I understand what compels flagellants," Phair said. "It isn't just penitence as a form of piety. It's a liberation from fear."

"Of?"

"Depending on the man, it differs," Phair said.

"For you?"

"Sometimes we do what is convenient or safe instead of what's right," he said.

"Are we talking about Durst?"

"Oddly, no," Phair said. "I understand why he's necessary. I even understand why you rebuked me on the ship."

"Then what?"

"When I ran off to help the Iraqis during that firefight, I was tuned to their pain," Phair said. "It mattered more at that moment than my other obligations, including the fact that they might have been responsible for killing my countrymen. I felt it was important, tonight, to reconnect with that feeling."

"So you could overlook the other challenges."

"Something like that."

That was still a little vague for Kealey's taste, but there wasn't time to question the cleric further. As long as Phair pulled his own oars, Kealey could live with a little uncertainty.

"Do you happen to know where Durst is?" Kealey asked.

"I haven't seen him since we arrived," Phair said.

"Why don't you go to your room and order something to eat," Kealey said. "I'll call you when we're ready to leave."

"All right, I'll go to my room," the cleric said, with a wry twist to his mouth.

Kealey watched as Phair eased around him. Car traffic was beginning to collect on the nearby N9, and the rising sunlight bounced from the gilt domes and clay towers of the old city, which was only a kilometer distant. The new light illuminated Phair. His black shirt whitened with windblown sand, his feet sore and legs a little awkward from his long walk, he seemed only slightly less out of place than the robed and sandaled merchants who were setting up little stands along the street.

Is it his look, or is he just accustomed to blending in? Kealey wondered. It was a real skill, the ability to not draw attention to oneself. The roll of the shoulders, the angle of the head, the stillness of the arms, the smaller, lower steps, the lack of sudden movement. It was something Kealey had never been able to train people to do. One gained it only by necessity.

Kealey also wondered if Durst had gone to Medina as well, perhaps searching for his own past. It troubled him that the German might have lied about the location of the Staff and had gone to collect it elsewhere—perhaps to ransom it. If so, Kealey would get the information out of him later. Durst would have to return, since his granddaughter was still here.

As it turned out, Durst was in the lobby of the hotel. A few members of the housekeeping staff were the only other people down there, polishing lamp bases and setting up a coffee urn. Phair was glancing at a morning newspaper, waiting for the coffee. Durst was facing the pale oak registration desk in front of a high wall of blue with large patterns of gold and green diamonds. He was dressed in jeans and his CIA-issued black shirt. Behind the counter, a woman was on the phone. Durst appeared to be waiting for something. The door to the office beyond was partly open. Inside, a Muslim was about his prayers.

"Good morning," Kealey said, walking over.

Durst turned, nodded, and looked back across the counter.

"I didn't see you here earlier," Kealey said.

"I went looking for a café that might serve milk," he said. "Failing to find one, I came back to ask for it. They are only setting up for coffee and tea."

Kealey stepped up beside Durst. The German's face was damp with perspiration, and he looked drawn.

"Are you all right?" Kealey asked.

Durst seemed puzzled. Kealey indicated his face.

"*Ja, ja,*" Durst said. "I ended up behind the hotel, in the basement, and took the stairs up."

The receptionist hung up and apologized for making Durst wait. "Can I be of assistance, sir?" she said pleasantly.

"You can," he said. "I would like some milk set out

on that cart and I would also like you to close the door in the name of decency."

The woman smiled. "Ahmed is not bothered by—"

"*I* am bothered by," Durst said. "He can pray to whatever camel god he wishes but this is not designated as a church or mosque. I would trouble you to respect the views of guests who may not be interested in his display! Or is this also a cabana where I may openly change to a swimsuit?"

Without expression, the woman turned and went back to the office, closing the door behind her.

Durst turned to Kealey and said loudly, "Bloody savages."

"You probably won't get your milk now," the agent remarked. It was a little taunt to avoid making a larger expression of disgust.

"I'll bet I do," Durst said. "That girl will want to show me that she is a devoted hostess above all. Good manners are important to these people. Or at least, they were once."

Kealey realized that in Durst's entire life, he had probably always been a guest or an invader. Entitlement was part of his muscle memory.

From a door behind the corner, the receptionist summoned the lobby attendant. The woman walked over, listened for a moment, looked at Durst, nodded, then left.

The bastard was right.

"She'll probably spit in it," Durst said, then shrugged. "In some parts of Africa that was considered a blessing."

"You've seen so much but you've seen so little," Kealey said. He felt his resolve to stay outwardly neutral cracking.

"What you mean to say is that I have embraced little," Durst said. "What is there to take from a place like this except a sad realization that the world is threatened by savages?"

"Do you actually believe these things, or is this all for effect?" the agent asked.

"I am not sure what you mean by *effect,*" Durst said. "It is not the howling of a jackal in the night, the herald of a pack that has been driven from its hunting ground. I believe, Mr. Kealey, in a standard of human conduct and the firmly held belief that many religions and cultures push us closer to the cave than to the stars. My God, isn't that the very argument we are here to make?"

"Only because it is a threat," Kealey replied.

Durst cocked his head toward the reception desk. "When it comes to choosing one day, which side will she pick? When our armies withdrew from Africa and Eastern Europe, did the liberated peoples celebrate their freedom, or fall to civil war along old tribal lines? I tell you, when we sought the sword Excalibur to keep it from the British—who were also seeking it—we came across a prophesy on a church wall from the year 700 that read, 'One land, one king.' The desire—no, the *necessity*—for purity is older than the Nazi Party, Mr. Kealey. You may criticize my beliefs, but had the war turned out differently we would not see a world still in conflict. We would see civilization on the road to immortality."

"At what price?"

"Less than you are paying now," Durst said.

His milk arrived and he took it from the attendant without thanks. She left quickly without expecting any.

"We meet here in a half hour to go to the site," Kealey said, eager to discontinue the conversation.

"I'll be right here," Durst assured him.

Kealey noticed Phair watching them. He didn't know if the cleric could hear, but he probably had a sense of what had transpired. He said nothing, merely went back to his newspaper. Which said a great deal. Kealey couldn't be bothered with his issues, either. He went to the far side of the lobby and peered into the pool area. Carla was gone and he called her room. She was not there. He left a message for her to meet them in the lobby at seven a.m., then went to his room and called Harper to confirm their travel plans. If Carla did not show up, he would leave without her. If Durst refused to go, he would tell him that he knew where the chest was and didn't need him. He wasn't fond of brinksmanship, but he could play the game if he had to.

"You sound stressed," Harper observed. "Is everything all right?"

"Intramural squabbles between myself, an unrepentant Nazi, and a Catholic priest who is having a crisis of faith," Kealey said.

"Not something that's covered in our code of conduct," Harper said.

"We'll get over the speed bumps," Kealey assured him.

"I'm sure," Harper said. "If you need help, I can have someone in from Madrid—"

"I know," Kealey said. "I'll make this work. I'm determined."

After confirming that the vehicle they requested would be there on time—a commercially rented, euphemisti-

cally named COW—a squat, bulky Cage On Wheels—
Kealey hung up. They were not back on their previous
terms of friendship, but the conversation had been
warmer than any they'd had in the past six months. The
realization that Harper was correct about how he assigned his agents, however, did not cover the profoundly
disquieting decision to work with Hernandez for, apparently, perpetuity. Kealey couldn't think about that now.
He finished his coffee in the room and emptied his duffel bag of all nonessentials. In a few hours the only
thing he needed would be inside it.

Then the real problems would begin.

CHAPTER FORTY-FIVE
JEBEL MUSA, SINAI PENINSULA

Lieutenant Adjo was awakened by a buzzing in his ear. He instinctively reached for the phone on his hip, found it wasn't there, and realized a moment later there was a dragonfly in the bushes above him. He brushed it away and listened. It was the only sound. Even the wind was uncharacteristically still.

It was dark, and he had no idea how much time had passed. It had to be a few hours at least, since there had been enough time for his muscles to stiffen and his bruises to ripen and his body to ache as it had never hurt before.

In order to get off his back, which was locked tight, Adjo had to rock himself to his left side, which was slanted down, and roll into his belly. From that position he was able to get his hands and knees under him and push himself out from inside the bushes. There was less than a half meter between where he was lying and a rocky drop down the sloping cliff. He knew that because he could hear stones that he'd dislodged tumbling down the incline. He took pains to get to his knees and stay there until his head cleared and his body grew accustomed to moving again. He swung his arms gently to and fro and rolled his shoulders. He flexed his toes. Everything hurt.

He drank a little water—there was only another mouthful left—and then he checked the time on his cell phone. It was three in the morning. He barely remembered going to sleep.

His head was still foggy and his nasal passages and throat were raw. There was a cause and effect there, he suspected. The dry desert air had sapped his insides, leaving him dehydrated.

Though the darkness made for treacherous climbing, he didn't want to waste any more time lying around. The darkness also assured him privacy. Besides, there was no reason he couldn't make part of the journey on the tourist road. It was almost certainly reopened by now.

Before setting out, Adjo checked his phone. There was a text message from a private e-mail address, BHE777. That was Lieutenant General Samra. "Call any hour," it said and gave his private cell phone number since that wasn't programmed into the phone the MFO soldier had given him.

He connected to the number. "Sir, it's Lieutenant Adjo."

"I have information," Samra said. The senior officer was alert and had obviously not been asleep. "The man you encountered at the monastery, Phut Eid. He's twenty-two years old and an archaeology student at the King Abdul Aziz University in Jeddah."

"Just a young student?"

"Nothing more. Perhaps the ID is stolen?"

Samra described the photo he had seen. It matched the image on the license.

"What's driving us all a little mad here is that there have been no communications among any of the known insurrectionist groups," Samra said. "We have spoken to the tour buses and local charter services, none of whom have any record or recollection of having brought large crates or drums to the mountain."

"Money buys selective memory," Adjo said.

"I know. But we had to try. Even so, they could have been smuggled in with shipments of supplies for the monastery. They are a very closed order and there are not many ways of getting information from the members."

Adjo was still thinking about Phut Eid. "Why would an archaeology student be recruited for this project?"

"My guess is that he knew about the tunnel you climbed and helped them to expand it," Samra said. "Incidentally, that passage was apparently cut millennia ago by volcanic activity. Perhaps that is what gave rise to the stories of it being the fiery Mountain of God."

Adjo found the subject interesting, but for another time. He did not want to waste battery power on it. "Sir, I don't see as how there's any option but for me to try and get back into the monastery."

"Out of the question," Samra said. "They will be watching for you now. So will the MFO. They have been authorized to stay an extra day because of those two explosions. Someone reported to them that a terrorist had been in the compound."

"Surely the minister can tell them the truth—"

"He does not want to get involved at this point, and he is reluctant to have the military move in until we know more about what is happening on the ground. We don't know if an incursion may trigger the men in the mountain to use the napalm. No, what I want you to do is infiltrate the mob and see what you can learn about where they are going or what this supposed prophet is going to do."

"Has there been nothing on the Internet?"

"Not that we have been able to find," Samra replied. "We believe the organizers and pilgrims are communicating strictly by phone—one to another to another. That's why you may be able to find something out by moving among them."

"Yes, sir," Adjo said.

It all made sense, though he didn't like the fact that the men in the monastery had complete control of this situation. Reactive tactics were only good in martial arts, not in crowd control. Still, though he was on the front lines of this struggle, Adjo had access to only part of the information flow.

"I am expecting a report from the American team as to their next move," Samra went on. "You will need to meet them."

"Do we know when?"

"Tomorrow night, I am told. They are in Morocco. One of them speaks several Arabic tongues."

"Very good," Adjo said. "If my phone dies or for some reason we don't communicate, I'll watch for them after sundown at the entrance to the monastery. Have one of them say something I will recognize—perhaps 'Good evening, Adjo.'"

"I'll let them know."

"What are they doing in Morocco?"

"They are looking for something to stop the prophet," Samra replied. "I should like to know what they are planning. This is monstrous, this invasion. All these people, foreigners for and against us. It must be stopped. We *must* control the situation."

Secretive Americans, radical students, gun-toting monks—it was all beyond Adjo's area of expertise. Obviously, Lieutenant General Samra was also at a loss. That made Adjo even more convinced that perhaps his superior was correct about collecting as much information as possible before doing anything more.

Adjo turned off the phone and stood. He must be a sight, he knew, with his frayed robe and bloodied limbs. But the chances were very good that if anyone saw him, they would not imagine him to be what he was.

Still stiff from neck to ankles—kicking along the tunnel floor had required muscles he had never known he had, let alone overtaxed—Adjo made his cautious way down the mountain. He knew where the tourist road was and wanted to get on it while it was still dark. If anyone was coming up, he'd see the vehicle headlights.

He picked his way across the rocks, feeling along in the darkness. Surprisingly, he did not hear the sounds of search or pursuit. The wind was up slightly, and it concealed movement from much farther than a few meters. Still, he had expected to see at least probing flashlights upon the hills or headlights. Perhaps his attackers had other tasks and decided he was not worth the chase.

He did not hurry nor, apparently, did he need to; it was still two hours until dawn and he had less than three hundred meters to go to the foothills. From there, it was roughly a half kilometer to where the pilgrims had gathered.

The sun rose as Adjo reached the bottom of the mountain, revealing cars and trucks, camels and horses, all spotted among a rainbow sea of robes and different-colored tents—from the lush green of the Kindah to the tan of the Azd. The likes of such a diverse gathering had probably not been seen since the days of the cara-vansaries a century and more before.

Adjo made his way across the gently sloping terrain below the monastery, happily trading sharp-edged rocks for hard, parched earth. As he neared the camp, he became aware of great activity. It was more than just the waking of pilgrims, though there was that, too. There was also excitement.

"Good morning to you," he said to a man who was crouched on the hood of a dusty jeep, looking at a cell phone. The middle-aged fellow was dressed in jeans and an open button-down shirt and was wearing a *kaf-fiyeh*. A cell tower outside the monastery, concealed in a tree, allowed tourists all the electronic amenities of civilization out here. "What is going on?"

"We have been promised a message from the prophet," the slender-faced man said enthusiastically.

"On that?" Adjo indicated the phone.

He nodded. "There was a text message announcing that he will appear to us on the mountain," he said.

So Lieutenant General Samra was right about how the prophet was communicating.

"I did not receive this news," Adjo said.

"Why not?" the young man asked suspiciously.

"The buses were not running, and I have walked a

long distance, as you can tell," Adjo said. "My cell phone is out of power."

"Let me see your phone," the man said. "If my adaptor fits, you can use my cigarette lighter to charge it."

Adjo realized his mistake, then. His phone was military issue, branded as such with three green stars inside a crescent moon.

"Maybe later, my friend," Adjo replied. "I am too excited now. What did the message say?"

"It said that something great is about to transpire, and that those of us who are able should take videos of the event," the man said. "We are to send it to everyone we know, everyone we care about."

"To bring them here or to prepare for the prophet to go to them?" Adjo asked.

"I do not know," said the man. "Why do you ask so many questions when you can just wait and see?"

"I've come a long way," Adjo said with a smile. "I'm so curious!"

"I understand," the man said. He had turned from the mountain to look Adjo over. "You can use a wash. Would you like some water?"

"I would like that very much," Adjo admitted. "By the way, my name is Bassam Adjo. I am from Cairo."

"I am Nayef Chalthoum of El Arish," the man said, as he went around to the passenger's seat and handed Adjo bottled water and a roll of paper towels. Adjo accepted them with a gracious bow.

There was no room to sit—a man had pitched a tent literally at the rear fender, and a small bus and a battered all-terrain vehicle flanked either side of the jeep—so Adjo remained standing as he cleaned his knees and then his elbows. "Do you know anything else about the event we are to witness?" Adjo asked, wincing from the sting of the warm water.

The man fussed over his phone for a moment and handed it to Adjo. "Now you will know all that I know," Nayef said.

Adjo set the bottle down and looked at the text message. It was simply from Caveoftheholyprophet at a local Web-mail service. It read:

> Spread the news to all you know.
> The thunder of His voice will be heard.
> The power of His mighty hand will be seen.
> And the earth will tremble.
> Send it to all

Adjo forwarded the message to his own cell phone, then returned this unit to his host. He finished washing, refilled his water pouch, thanked Nayef for his hospitality, then moved away from the jeep. When he was lost in the crowd, he forwarded the message from his phone to Lieutenant General Samra with a short explanation. From the eagerness of the crowd and the way it seemed to be growing—the horizon was dotted with pilgrims—he sensed that he would know more before Samra did.

CHAPTER FORTY-SIX
SAHARA DESERT, MOROCCO

Kealey picked up the rental car at the hotel, after which he and his companions drove to the Desert Excursion Depot in Tarfaya, on the Western Sahara. The shop was one of many designed for young and affluent thrill-seekers, in a region where windsurfing and event racing were increasingly popular tourist attractions.

There, they collected the Libyan army surplus desert patrol vehicle that had been reserved for them. Kealey loaded the duffel bag he'd brought into the back and helped Carla and her grandfather into the two rear seats of the canvas-topped vehicle. The sand-colored vehicle was de-armored for better mileage, and the storage cage had been removed from the back, leaving the vehicle open on three sides.

They all put on tinted goggles and lightweight safari hats as Kealey set off down the two-lane road. There was no conversation between Phair and Durst. While the German seemed to relish the return to his old magistracy, as the war records described it, and thrill at the memories of this familiar mosque or that bazaar—so much of it apparently unchanged—Phair seemed to see nothing around him. From the proud set of his head and sternness of his jaw the cleric seemed to be cloaking himself alternately in righteousness and indignation.

When they neared the town of Akhfenir the desert was simply there. It began at the side of a newly asphalted highway that picked up where the two-lane road ended. Following Durst's instructions, Kealey turned off the road at a triangular camel-crossing sign fringed in red. He traversed a meter of sloping gravel—crushing empty plastic bottles that littered the road as far as he could see—and kept an eye on the compass on the dashboard. Durst was directing them exactly where Harper's research said he would. There was a global positioning system in the vehicle but he didn't turn it on. He didn't want a record of where they had traveled. By international law, the United States had no business searching for a weapon of any kind in the African desert, nor did they have the right to remove it—or a historical relic—once found.

The skies were cloudy and the air was surprisingly cool as they drove across sparse, low-lying scrub. The vehicle offered an unexpectedly smooth ride on its oversized tires, and Kealey was able to maintain a steady pace of fifty-five kilometers per hour. Durst continued to be enthusiastic as he recognized landmarks. He seemed very much like a man who had enjoyed his adventures here sixty-odd years before. Carla seemed to be caught up in his excitement, holding his hand and smiling as she watched not just the sights, but his exhilaration.

For Kealey, there was no romance in the moment. Though nothing but desert spread before them, Kealey didn't feel the wonder that had inspired poets and explorers. In his journeys around the world for the CIA he had seen camels with laptops in bags by their sides and had eaten at American fast-food franchises at most of the world's great sites, from the pyramids to the Himalayas. Thanks to GPS technology, there was little danger of being stranded anywhere outside of the South Pole and sections of New Guinea and the Amazon, of discovering anything new, of finding people who did not have knowledge of and an opinion about your president or worse, current film stars. Even as he looked here and there at the increasing expanse of slightly reddish sands broken only by the occasional dune or oddly twisted, deep-rooted trees, Kealey knew that this was not the often uncharted desert of T. E. Lawrence.

Kealey did not stay on the grooved trail that had been worn in this section of the desert by the constant press of camels, very few of which were to be seen. That path was visible here and there at the whim of the winds, impossible to follow unless your feet knew the way. Instead, he journeyed southwest, sixty-three kilometers, until Durst confirmed what he already knew: they were near the site.

What Carla had jokingly described as "the caravan of one" reached a sprawling, rundown stockade that had once been used to herd horses. It looked like it hadn't been used in thirty or forty years. It was about the size of two football fields. The old chicken wire fence was torn and flapping, the metal finely pitted from years of windblown sand, and the thick oak posts were dark and brittle from nearly constant cooking by the sun. The posts sloped this way and that, victims of the shifting desert surface. The wood troughs that lined the interior of the fence were filled with sand.

Durst's lips pressed together when he saw the corral. His granddaughter took one of his hands in both of hers and held it tightly.

"The owners built it to sell horses to both sides," Durst said, leaning forward so he could be heard over the hum of the engine. It was as though he were seeking a blanket absolution for everything the Nazis had done here, since even the natives were corrupt. "The well is to the northwest, about a quarter-kilometer."

Kealey nodded. He drove past the structure, keeping careful watch on the compass since he wasn't sure how visible a landmark might be from their position. He noticed that whatever misgivings Phair had were gone now, as the chaplain sipped water and looked out eagerly at the horizon. The notion that he might be close to something that had been touched by God had seemed to have a transformative effect.

Phair turned. "Herr Durst, why didn't you bring the Staff to the castle at Wewelsburg?"

"Ah, you know of this?"

Phair nodded.

"We knew the Allies would find out about it. That is why we hid the most prized items."

"What else did you hide?" Kealey asked.

"Books, mostly, as well as the führer's personal mandrake that he used for protection."

"He believed that a plant root could protect him?" Phair asked.

"It *did*," Durst insisted, as though accustomed to

Hitler's sanity being questioned. "It saved him when von Stauffenberg detonated a bomb under the conference table in the Wolf's Lair. Erik Hanussen blessed the root in 1932 and accurately predicted the day and date it would bring Hitler to power. Hanussen also forecast that if Hitler stopped believing, the Reich would fall as swiftly. Hitler's faith in the occult faltered when the blood sacrifice fell short of his goals."

"Blood sacrifice," Kealey said. "You mean the war."

"*Ja.*"

The war was tragic enough, but comprehensible in terms of conquest. But it was demented to imagine that it had been fought as a kind of pagan ritual, that there was a quota of blood to be filled and they had simply derived the most efficient methods of fulfilling it. Kealey wanted to throw the old man from the vehicle into the sand and drive away.

"There!" Durst said suddenly.

Kealey looked where he was pointing, at a two-o'clock position. About two meters of a rusted assault gun poked from the sands at a forty-five-degree angle. Durst was right about the location and right about the fact that no one would have thought to go probing beneath that monstrosity, a twenty-ton panzer.

"It used to be the color of the sands themselves, healthy and strong," Durst said ruefully.

"I'm surprised it can still be seen," Kealey said.

"*Ach,* that is the genius of our selection of this place," Durst declared. "There is a draft from the dry well. The wind rushes up forcefully and with some regularity and prevents the sand from accumulating."

Phair was still strangely silent.

"I thought you'd be more excited," Kealey said to him.

"When the Staff has been recovered, I will be," Phair assured him.

Leaning forward, Durst was smiling as decades of age slipped from his face and shoulders. Kealey could hear and see the young *untersturmführer,* eager to serve the cause, charging through the sands in this panzer or some other desert vehicle, willing to trade for information or necessities with the locals to retain their goodwill—or crush them if they got in his way.

They pulled up to the tank, which was partly exposed on the northern side. Metal plates and gear had been removed by Arab traders or souvenir hunters before the sands had corroded and rendered them useless. Durst left the vehicle as it crunched to a halt on the dry dune beside it. His aged eyes were like those of a predatory bird, sharp and fixed on the wheel that once held the powerful tank treads. Below it was the crushed stone wall of an old well. Carla followed him and Phair swung from the vehicle. After shutting off the engine, Kealey joined him.

There was a low, constant wind that strangely enhanced the silence of their surroundings. Now and then something clanged inside the dead hull of the tank, stirred by a local gust.

"The tank was crippled and we struggled to get it here," Durst said as his granddaughter walked beside him, helping him to negotiate the thickly piled but porous sands. "We knew it would be stripped but that the heavy frame would never be moved, thus protecting our secret—"

He stopped, and while the others watched he did something that Kealey had not been expecting.

CHAPTER FORTY-SEVEN
JEBEL MUSA, SINAI PENINSULA

The sun cast long afternoon shadows among the multitude gathered in the Wadi el-Deir. Lieutenant Adjo moved among them, looking at faces that covered the spectrum from curiosity to reverence. He saw a few vehicles with people who were well dressed and seemed to have come from cities. What he did not see, which surprised him, were caravans of the sickly in search of healing, or news crews from any of the cities. Word was limited to the people the organizers had wanted to be here, and admission seemed to be restricted.

He began to be very impressed by, and fearful of, the planning that had gone into this.

He sidled up to a group of young men and women having a breakfast of bread and sun-warmed coffee in the back of a beaten-up pickup truck. White feathers were stuck on splinters of wood on the side panels.

"You were able to make it through," Adjo said to a young man whose legs were dangling over the side.

The man nodded.

"It took me the longest time."

"You took the Nuweiba Road?" the man asked.

Adjo didn't know whether to answer yes or no. He made a noncommittal face. "Which way did you come?"

"Through the Raha Plain, as someone suggested when we left Port Said," he replied. He thrust a thumb behind him, toward the cab. "My parents heard of this from a friend at church and insisted we all come."

"I thought, being on a motorbike, it was best to stay on the paved roads," Adjo replied.

"I travel Nuweiba when I carry chickens," he said. "With so many people, we were afraid that one breakdown would hold up the traffic. With two, no one would move for hours. And that would cause more vehicles to overheat and die. A nightmare," he said, shaking his head. "Is that what happened to you?"

Adjo nodded. That was the way news crews would have come. He suspected that at first, the organizers strategically blocked the road to make passage impossible. After that, as crowds grew, the MFO would have blocked the road to prevent a potential humanitarian crisis. Adjo knew from experience that the desert was impossible to plug, especially at night. The United Nations troops would also have restricted airspace around the mountain to leave it open for possible military action.

Either the organizers want any and all images of this event to come from the pilgrims, or they don't want professionally shot video that can be studied, Adjo suspected. Probably both.

As for the infirm, Moses was not a healer. He was the mouthpiece of God, a miracle-worker. The sponsors of this pageant would not want their party spoiled by cripples who remained crippled. But how did they keep them out?

Adjo gratefully accepted a piece of bread from the young man, then moved on. He wanted to talk to someone who was alone, and tired. Someone who would give unguarded answers. As he moved through the tightly packed crowd he saw license plates from Yemen, Libya, Saudi Arabia, Jordan. These people had come great distances through the sieve that was Egypt's border—holes created by geography, force of numbers, inattentiveness, bribes. He had to fight down the anger he felt. His work, the ongoing work of his team, had amounted to nothing. He wished they were here with him to form a wedge and begin to drive these people out.

Adjo swallowed his anger. He had to regard this as an opportunity to fix what was wrong; with so many people gathered here, it would be difficult for Cairo indeed, for the region, for the world—to overlook the problem such unfettered access posed to the stability of his government.

He stopped beside a middle-aged man who was sitting on a rock and wriggling severely blistered toes. Adjo took a swig of water.

"I don't know if I can move another step, either," Adjo said, flopping heavily on the ground beside him.

"The prophet will renew us, as he did for the Israelites," the man replied with a single, confident shake of his head.

"If it is the will of Allah," Adjo said with affected reverence. He was still angry about this entire operation. "Have you seen the *Gharib Qawee*?"

"He has not yet shown himself," the man said.

"I pray that he does," Adjo said. "It is the fondest wish of my poor mother to see him."

"Where is she?" the man asked, looking around.

"Alas," Adjo said, "she could go no farther. I left her back in the plain."

The man regarded him with horror.

"There were many others who were infirm," Adjo said pointedly. "She was in no danger."

"Why are you not with her?"

"She begged me to see the prophet on her behalf, and to bring her word of his divinity," Adjo said as humbly as possible.

"Did they not tell you?"

"Tell me what?"

"The Care Trucks will bring the sick to the front of the crowd at the appointed time."

"Blessings to you for this information," Adjo said. "There were so many people that I—"

Adjo never got to finish the interrogation, or to ponder why the sickly would be brought to a position of prominence. Surely they were not going to be healed. It wasn't possible.

Moving as one with the surrounding field of humanity, the man was suddenly on his feet. There was no cheering. The silence was profound. Adjo turned his eyes toward the mountain, toward the peak he had watched so clinically through night-vision glasses. If ever there was proof that it was faith that informed faith, and not the object of the veneration itself, it was the mood that washed over him as he stood there. He felt as though he were in the presence of something great, even though he could not see anything exceptional. The belief of the crowd was a real, nearly palpable thing.

On the mountaintop, obviously the result of the sun, was a radiance striking a highly polished object.

"The Staff of the Prophet," reverently muttered the man to whom Adjo had been speaking. He wasn't speaking to Adjo but to himself, involuntarily. Then he made a humming sound, a wordless prayer of thanksgiving that quavered with humility and excitement. Around him, like deep-throated birds in the grasslands, Adjo heard others say *prophet* and *Moses* with the same helpless awe.

There was no evidence that this is what they were seeing, but that didn't seem to matter. At this distance, video images from phones would show nothing substantial. It would be interesting to see if the occupant of the cave came down the mountain and, if so, whether the Staff would continue to glow.

Adjo did not get a chance to find out.

CHAPTER FORTY-EIGHT
SAHARA DESERT, MOROCCO

D urst dropped forward on his knees.
   "Ich bin hier!" he cried.

Carla gasped softly and darted after the elderly man, but he wasn't hurt. He flopped onto his chest and scurried forward, pushing with his knees, brushing sand aside with swimming motions of his arms, clearing the way to a spot across from where his eyes were fixed like little machines. He reached a place where the missing tank tread would have rested on the stone wall of the well.

"I'm all right," he said with annoyance as Carla fell in beside him. "Get me a flashlight! *A flashlight!*"

Phair and Kealey were both nonplussed by his actions. Kealey had a penlight hooked to his key ring. He slipped it off and handed it to Carla, who gave it to her grandfather. Shaking as though he were stricken, Durst probed the darkness with the light. He swept the beam left to right, right to left, then up and down. Kealey had a sick feeling at the top of his throat.

"Gone," the German said at last.

Kealey walked to Durst's side and squatted. He glanced into the well. The light was still now, as though Durst had stopped living. Kealey saw a dark rectangle among the stones, an opening in the well wall. There was nothing inside.

The agent's first and most frightening thought was that the bad guys had it. If that was the case, the problem just became different and far more difficult. His mind raced through the ramifications, none of them hopeful.

Durst just lay there, moaning, oblivious to the sands blowing over him. He had not been speaking to his granddaughter nor to the men who stood over him. He was lamenting to no one in particular.

"Come," Carla said.

Durst rose unsteadily, helped by Kealey and Carla. His eyes suddenly looked tired. With hardly any effort, as though he were all bones, they helped him to the vehicle. Kealey crouched beside him. He recovered his small flashlight, tucked it in his shirt pocket, and tried to get Durst's attention by moving his eyes to align with the German's dull, staring ones.

"Talk to me," Kealey said. "How do you know it's gone? It might have just fallen into—"

"I saw the missing stone under the opposite tread wheel," Durst said. "It had been lifted away."

"How is that possible?" Kealey asked. "Who else knew about this?"

"No one living," Durst replied dully.

Kealey rose and walked around the tank. He leaned against it, pushing to check for stability, as much as a push could determine. Then he lowered himself onto his belly and wormed underneath along the line of the other missing tread. The way the tank was positioned, he couldn't go far enough to reach the opening. The tank had obviously been damaged by a mine—there were scorch marks along a hole in the undercarriage—and then backed over the well, ending up with its tail angled down like this. The relic must have been concealed afterward. The men in the tank wouldn't have wanted to carry anything they didn't have to, walking from the desert.

A spike had been driven into the top side of the well. Recently, since the steel was still silver and unpocked by sands. The flashlight revealed hemp threads snagged by the topmost block of the well. Someone had come here, lowered himself over the side, and taken the Staff of Moses.

But how the hell did anyone know it was here?

His first conclusion, perhaps as unfair as it was instinctive, was that Durst had an ally whom he had called during the night. But the German seemed as surprised as the rest to find the hiding place violated. Kealey didn't think he was that good an actor. But who else could have done this? If this had been a professional operation, something run by Harper or someone else at the CIA—for reasons Kealey couldn't quite fathom—they wouldn't have been careless enough to leave traces of the intrusion. Everything would have been replaced and properly aged so that when Kealey and company went in, sand would have fallen from the cracks when they removed the block, suggesting that the object had been taken years before, the trail cold.

No, Kealey thought, *this was recent and nonprofessional.* Which raised an alarming possibility: that the artifact being employed on Mt. Sinai was the genuine

Staff of Moses. Not that Kealey believed it could perform miracles, but what he believed didn't matter. If
the people behind that movement had the actual Staff
and some kind of provenance to go with it, the problem
he faced just got a whole lot worse. In fact, if anyone
had followed them, photographed them, the images
could be used as evidence to support the claim that this
was the genuine article. Why else would the government of the United States be out here with the Nazi
who had stolen it?

Phair ambled over. "This could be the work of a religious organization," he said.

"What do you mean?"

"The Vatican's Safe Harbor League, the Sons of
Joshua, some group that has field operatives," he said.
"For all we know they've been watching Durst for
decades, waiting for him to make his move. They may
have picked off this information at any time since we
landed."

"Why not just go to his house and beat it out of
him?" Kealey asked, a little angry at himself. Perhaps
they hadn't been as secretive as they should have been.

"In the case of the Church, these material missionaries
are men of peace," Phair replied in a venerating tone.
"They acquire merit through patience and charity."

"Or they knew he was under the protection of a
gangster, too," Kealey said, abruptly dismissing Phair's
thick piety.

Kealey studied the well and removed a few of the
strands from the stone wall before wriggling back out. He
tucked them in his passport and walked over to the others.

"I don't understand how anyone could have known,"
Durst said. He looked as if he were in a daze.

"Could your satellites tell us anything about who has been out here?" Carla asked Kealey.

"There is so much going on in this part of the world, we're not able to keep satellites trained on every region," he said. "Absent a specific reason, we tend to watch the trouble spots, and the Western Sahara isn't one of them."

"Someone may have been here within the past few hours," she said. "If you looked now, in the surrounding region—"

"It would take about ninety minutes to make the calls and get the coordinates changed," he said. "The perpetrators will be long gone." He regarded Durst. "Are you sure there were no other records of your work?"

"I am positive," he replied, his voice catching, near tears. "*Positive!*"

"I need you to think back," Kealey said. "Tell me everything the Russians said when you told them about your work."

"How can I?" he said. "They were speaking Russian!"

"What use would the Russians have for the Staff *now*?" Carla asked.

"None that I can think of," Kealey admitted.

"It may not be the Russians," Phair said. He was standing a few paces away from the group.

"Who, then?" Kealey asked.

"There were some eighty million Muslims living in the Soviet Union, in Chechnya, Uzbekistan, Kazakhstan, Azerbaijan," Phair said. "One of those people, someone who was not a 'godless peasant,' may have read the file and grasped its value."

"Why not go after the Staff then?" Carla asked.

"To what purpose?" Phair replied. "The Kremlin would have confiscated it."

"A common soldier wouldn't have been free to go after it," Kealey said. "But there's another possibility."

The others looked at him.

"During the war with Chechnya, Muslim collaborators had access to KGB personnel," Kealey explained. "After the fall of the Soviet Union, when the KGB was disbanded, hundreds of unemployed operatives were happy to sell information about enriched uranium, double agents, pretty much anything they knew or could dig up from the files. If Herr Durst's field reports were in fact taken to Moscow, an agent who had worked with Muslims there or perhaps in Afghanistan might have sold them the information."

"That is a rather tortuous route, is it not?" Carla said.

"It is no less so than the means through which I tracked it," Durst said.

"The important thing is, the Staff isn't here," Kealey said.

He turned and looked out at the desert. The sun-bleached expanse suddenly seemed extremely large, incredibly hostile, and almost mocking in its easy, rolling tranquility.

The intelligence operative considered his options. Given how little they knew, there wasn't a lot to think about. Instructing the others to return to the vehicle, Kealey went to the other side of the tank to call Harper. He checked his watch. It was the start of the business day in Virginia. Harper would be fresh. Kealey needed that now.

The TAC-SAT signal was strong.

"What've you got for me?" Harper asked, answering on the second beep.

Kealey told him.

"Well, that's not what I wanted to hear," Harper said.

It wasn't a criticism, just fact. Kealey didn't feel the need to apologize.

"Where do we go from here?" the deputy director asked.

"To Sinai," Kealey said. "I don't see what else to do. If they have the real Staff, we need to assess what that means on-site. Have you heard anything from your Egyptian friends?"

"Only that their man at Sinai has had some trouble with militia of some kind. They're being very secretive."

"Ego or payoffs?"

"Everything's on the table," Harper said, then asked Kealey to hold on.

The phone was frustratingly silent. For several long moments, Kealey wondered if the line had gone dead.

"Ryan, I just received a heads-up from the Double-H," he said. "We've got a new situation at the mountain."

CHAPTER FORTY-NINE
JEBEL MUSA, SINAI PENINSULA

The sound arrived moments after the blast. By the time Adjo looked up at the mountain, the fireball was almost fully formed. It was a snapshot that seemed absurd and terrifying· frightening in its size, and strange in the shape it held for a long moment, like a damp, glistening red pepper balanced on its stem.

The heat wave struck an instant later, an oily blast that warmed his cheeks and caused his mouth to open and literally baked his insides for a long, long moment. He felt the warmth at the top of his throat. It took several tries before he could swallow. After hovering high above the mountainside, unaffected by the wind, the pillar of fire poured down the side of the cliff as a sudden, continuous blaze. It reminded Adjo of a horse's mane roused by the wind, long licks of fire striking out here and there in a continuous flow.

Gunfire popped around him as men who had weapons fired them into the air. Others prostrated themselves on the floor of the plain. They and others were chanting, *Musa, Musa, Musa!*

It wasn't the prophet but the drums of napalm Adjo had seen. That was why the men in the monastery hadn't followed him onto the mountain. They were busy setting up the pyrotechnics.

Feigning excitement but watching the crowd for any hint of instigators, anyone paying more attention to rabblerousing than to the event itself—he saw none—Adjo made his way back toward the thickening edge of the mob nearest the mountain. He approached a thick-waisted, middle-aged man who seemed to be by himself. The man was firing a 9mm pistol into the air, nearly hitting himself in the head with his recoiling forearm. When the man had fired his last shot, he stopped and danced with joyous abandon from foot to foot while he loaded a fresh clip.

"May I?" Adjo asked with affected fervor, pointing to the sky and then the gun when it had been loaded.

The man smiled and handed him the Beretta like an offering, on two open hands. Adjo thanked him—and ran off. The man shouted and gave chase through the tightly packed mob, but he hesitated when Adjo—still elbowing forward—turned and angrily flashed the gun at him. Adjo continued to back away and a few seconds later was lost to his pursuer.

The foothills were still bathed in the warmth of the initial blast, while the heat from the ongoing fires descended in a greasy mist. Some of the pilgrims were moving back as the fine droplets seared their skin. No doubt the unusual nature of the fire would cause them to feel even more strongly that this was no ordinary fire but the fire of God, the one who had blocked the armies of the pharaoh. Perhaps that was the intent of the perpetrators. Napalm would not be commonly known by these people. Dynamite, yes. Gunpowder, absolutely. But not this incendiary compound.

Adjo turned his face down and the conflagration dropped pinpricks on the back of his neck. He moved as quickly as he could, pushing people aside so he could get to his destination. He suspected now that the reason the monk had spoken to him in the monastery was that he was probably not a monk at all but one of the people behind this operation, someone who wasn't sure of the way clerics behaved there. More than likely he had signaled someone, either with a gesture or an electronic device, that he was being interrogated about the prophet by someone who didn't look like a pilgrim.

What Adjo didn't know was where the movement went from here. If they were following the Old Testament—and that was the only assumption he had to go on—they were going to be headed for a land flowing with milk and honey. Adjo had no way of knowing whether that was Israel, Palestine, Jordan, or somewhere else. Possibly somewhere else in Egypt. After all, they were already here. All but one of those was out of his jurisdiction. But he did know this much, from a purely strategic point of view: what was happening was well planned. And it couldn't be a vague jihad that would require years or even months to grow. First, there were too many people here, ready to do whatever they were told. Second, at some point soon someone was going to go up the mountain and find the remains of the chemical accelerant, or prove that the prophet was being backed by someone other than God. Questions would be asked about the legitimacy of the leader and momentum would be lost.

Curious and fearful, Adjo finally managed to penetrate the crowd and headed for the monastery. The air around him, however tainted by the smoke, and the soil beneath him, however many foreign feet had crossed it, suddenly seemed very, very precious to him. He did not want anything to happen to his homeland.

The tours, of course, had not resumed. They were not likely to now. The MFO would be keeping everyone from the mountain while the Egyptian military was consulted. The army would study the situation by air before becoming involved in land reconnaissance; that was their way. In any case, they were not permitted to enter the monastery. It had the status of a foreign mission, answerable to the Church.

It would take at least three hours for the aerial survey to be completed. Lieutenant General Samra confirmed that when Adjo risked a quick phone call. Adjo gave him his impressions of the blast and its cause—confirming what Samra had already suspected—and told him he was going to the monastery, then hung up quickly. He wanted to have enough battery left to report whatever he found out in the monastery.

The gunfire had stopped and the chanting had begun in earnest. The people wanted to see their prophet. Adjo had heard of mass hypnosis, of group hysteria, and he was convinced that the local world had gone entirely mad. To believe that someone with drums of napalm and a magician's wand was somehow endowed by God was a desire, not reality. Apparently—and tragically—that was enough to manipulate a horde of desperate souls to someone else's ends.

The entire region stinks of that, he thought bitterly. It was what had kept peace at arm's length for millennia. Usually, his focus was too local to worry about the bigger picture. He was suddenly very sick of it and determined to stamp it out.

Starting here.

Despite his resolve, Adjo's overtaxed limbs were beginning to stiffen and wobble. He was about a quarter of a kilometer from the monastery. Getting in wasn't going to be easy, if it could be accomplished at all. He decided to take a short rest. He didn't see any guards—perhaps they were all busy planning some other miracle?—but he had to assume they were there.

He sat on the gentle slope of the mountain, about fifty meters up. The wind was blowing away from him, carrying the stench of the napalm in the other direction. The breeze helped to refresh him. As he sat there, the phone vibrated again. It had to be important; Samra knew the situation with the battery.

"Where are you?" the lieutenant general asked.

"On the north side of the monastery, away from the crowd," Adjo replied.

"Wait there. That American special-ops team with special knowledge of this situation is on its way."

"What about our own military?" Adjo asked. "I assumed they would send aircraft—"

"That may not happen for quite a while," Samra said. "They're debating that at the Ministry. The MFO reported that there was celebratory gunfire."

"There was, but not by soldiers—"

"With all the weapons out there, they don't want to provoke a shoot-out—"

"Sir, we were *attacked*!"

"A holy site was scorched, and politically, that is a different thing," Samra said, his tone gently reprimanding. "We have no evidence that it was an act of aggression or anything other than what it appears to be."

"It comes in conjunction with my being fired at—"

"Something else we suspect but cannot prove," Samra replied. "You know, we have seen the fire. It is being sent on cell phones. We obtained a copy."

"They have very good reception out here," Adjo remarked. Most tourist sites did, in case of illness or terrorist activity. The bastards obviously knew that, too.

"We are going to study the footage to try and get proof that supports your napalm theory," Samra said.

"Sir, I saw the drums. I smelled the gasoline."

"I cannot recommend sending in the army based on the say-so of one man, you know that," Samra said. "Especially since the MFO has not been able to corroborate your claim."

"They are too far from the site and the wind is blowing away from them," Adjo said bitterly. But there was no point arguing and wasting precious phone time. "How will I know these Americans?"

"I will send them to your location," Samra said. "Three men and a woman. Look for them sometime between sundown and dawn. I'm told they will have a halogen penlight. Look for the narrow, white beam."

"That's going to keep me pinned down when I could be investigating."

"I don't want you investigating anything else," Samra said. "You were lucky to escape the first time. Stay where you are; that's an order. Do you have sufficient supplies? Food? Water?"

"I have enough."

"Very well. Call when they arrive," Samra said. "They will have fresh equipment you can use."

Adjo hung up. He still had some of the rations the MFO official had brought, and he ate those. Even his jaw hurt, from clenching it throughout the day.

He railed quietly against Samra's order. The lieutenant general was under a lot of pressure and may have been saying that for the benefit of someone else in the room. Still, it was foolish. If special-ops reinforcements were going to be arriving—with "fresh equipment," Samra had said, which suggested not just a phone but also weapons—Adjo should be able to tell them as much as possible about the foe they were facing and the terrain on which they would be meeting them. That did not mean sitting on the mountainside, looking down at the garden. It meant reconnoitering.

It also meant disobeying an order.

Maybe Samra is right, he thought. *If something happens to me, the Americans will be lost.* And he would be more use to them if he were rested.

Eating his last two date bars, Adjo waited for the sun to pass to the other side of the mountain. He slept for a while, confident that the cooler breezes of the early evening would wake him in time to watch for his teammates.

A small thrill shot along his lower back as he considered the word. He had never been part of an international coalition. He could not even have imagined the circumstances under which such a thing would happen.

That was more of a miracle than anything he had seen so far.

CHAPTER FIFTY
MCLEAN, VIRGINIA

One of Jonathan Harper's favorite resources, the Double-H, was a high-flying drone aircraft. The initials stood for Harold Hill, the hero in *The Music Man,* and it was designed to read the spectrographic signature of gunfire and isolate potential "trouble in River City" within a three-hundred-mile radius. The technology was developed by the FBI to watch for domestic homicides in troubled neighborhoods and to allow for rapid response. The program was discontinued due to potential invasion-of-privacy issues and inadmissibility of recorded data in courts. The military had no such qualms about deploying the Double-H device on drone aircraft in the Middle East as a way of helping military patrols steer clear of armed encampments, or for identifying which windows in hostile villages held snipers.

In this instance, the Double-H had recorded at least 432 instances of gunfire in a five-square-mile section of the desert north of Mt. Sinai. According to computer analysis, the bursts came from 214 distinct weapons within that area and were fired within a period of seven seconds.

Harper was still on the phone with Kealey as he reviewed the data.

"Either it was a monastery takeover, a mass suicide, or they were celebrating something," Harper said.

"A mass suicide with a lot of people who couldn't shoot straight," Kealey pointed out.

"True," Harper said when he realized how many shots were fired from how many guns. It was funny how data, crossing a certain threshold, immediately pushed buttons suggesting an explanation.

A second alert followed. This one was a red flag e-mail from Lieutenant General Samra of Task Force 777. Harper read it to Kealey as he read it himself.

"Agent reports massive explosion in Jebel Musa region," he said. "No further details."

Harper was already accessing the satellite database. Since this matter had begun, the National Reconnaissance Office had been watching the region with the Measat-3, located 36,001 kilometers above the earth in a geosynchronous orbit 0 degrees, 34° N, 46 degrees, 1° E. Harper accessed the photographic data.

"I'm showing a massive fireball over the mountain twenty-eight minutes ago," Harper said. "It's consistent with the napalm that was reportedly stored there." He clicked back fifteen seconds, the minimum interval between the images. "The blast erupted from a point about two-thirds of the way up the mountain." He magnified a section of the screen. "I take that back. It looks like it vented from several points." Harper advanced the images. "It burned along a ridge after that. It's still smoldering."

"A natural fire wouldn't have burned down, but up," Kealey said.

"Exactly, and it's down about seventy-five percent from when it started," Harper replied.

"Conditions are dry up there—a lot of underbrush that would go up quick and leave nothing else combustible."

"That's what it looks like," Harper agreed.

"Jonathan, if 777 found napalm, why didn't they move in?"

"Caution," Harper replied. "They had no evidence it was about to be used. And they couldn't be sure it wasn't wired to blow in the event they did move in."

"Are they going to move in now?"

"Not yet," Harper answered. "They don't want to agitate a bunch of armed radicals."

"Armed radicals don't need provocation," Kealey pointed out. "Look, if the bad guys have got the Staff of Moses, adherents with guns, and events that are going to be touted as miracles, we've got serious trouble."

"Do you think your German would recognize the real Staff if he saw it?"

"That would probably depend on how close he got."

"He wouldn't lie about it?"

"He's pretty blunt."

"Then we need to get him close to the prophet," Harper said. "We need to find out if they have the actual relic—and if not, who does and why."

"We can be back in Marrakech by midnight," Kealey said.

"I'll have a plane waiting that will put you in Cairo by dawn."

"I need something else, too," Kealey said. "I found some fibers on rock that had been removed from the well. We should have them analyzed."

"A courier will meet you to take them to the embassy in Rabat," Harper assured him.

Every American embassy had a sophisticated laboratory and a technician capable of performing fairly complex forensics. It was necessary in the event that explosives were somehow placed on the grounds, bullets fired into the compound, incendiary devices hurled over the wall, or even in the event of murder. In unstable regions, where workers couldn't leave the smallish compounds, homicide was not unknown. It was not always possible—and seldom advisable—to trust local police for investigations of any kind.

Harper told Kealey that he would forward any additional information, though he suspected things would be quiet for a few hours. It would take time for the pilgrims to be given instructions or inspiration, whatever the game plan was, generating some kind of response. More pilgrims, perhaps media coverage once the crowds had swelled impressively—there was no way of knowing.

As word of the activities at the Mountain of Moses spread through the intelligence community, Harper was summoned to a meeting of department heads to discuss the implications.

No one who attended that meeting—or others like it that were hastily called in capitals from Israel to Great Britain—could have predicted what was going to happen.

Not even the prophet.

PART THREE
THE TRIGGER

CHAPTER FIFTY-ONE
CAIRO, EGYPT

By the time Kealey and his team landed in Egypt, the embassy in Morocco had completed its initial test of the fibers from the well.

"They were from a rope," Harper told him as the jet taxied. "Very old, very dry hemp."

"How old?"

"Says here the natural dyes were intact, meaning it hadn't been exposed to daylight, yet the desiccation factor was ninety-eight percent. They say it had been stored in someplace dry and hot for decades."

"That could be the tank," Kealey said.

"Or else it was part of the rope that was originally used to put the box in the well," Harper told him.

"That's possible," Kealey agreed. "Though it's also possible that someone knew the rope was in the tank and used it to recover the Staff in the last few days."

"Durst? Did he have time? More than that, did he have the stamina?"

"Not likely." Kealey huddled closer to the phone.

"He was alone the night before we left, but I can't see how he would have gotten out there. He would have had to organize things en route."

"Not impossible."

"No," Kealey agreed. "But he seemed genuinely surprised to find the artifact missing."

"His granddaughter?"

"Again, I don't see how she would have organized something like this."

"The same way you did," Harper said. "Especially if her parents have resources at any of the regional embassies. Or maybe she called in Ramirez."

The other possibility was Phair, of course. The chaplain had seemed uncharacteristically disheveled when Kealey met him the morning they left. Durst hadn't said anything about what was in the tank, but that didn't mean Phair couldn't have asked him. Again, the question of "why?" was something Kealey could not answer.

As Kealey hung up, that left the other troubling possibility: that the so-called prophet actually had the real Staff. In which case, undermining him to his adoring throng was going to be much more difficult. Especially if they had the provenance to show how the Staff came into his possession. *"A vision from God told me where in the desert to find it. . . ."*

It was shortly before dawn when the jet reached the gate in Cairo. Everyone managed to get a few hours' rest and they grabbed breakfast to go from Starbucks, of all places, as they headed for the curb. An embassy car was waiting for them. They had not brought any bags, since those might have raised questions if they were scanned or searched, such as "Why is everyone wearing the same clothes?" Kealey did not want that delay. It was just as easy for the U.S. Embassy in Cairo to provide them with new gear.

Kealey watched the other members of his team as they boarded the nondescript van that would take them to Mt. Sinai. There was no conversation, no suspicious glances at one another. Maybe Phair, possibly even Durst, had gotten past their shock and were pondering the same question as Kealey: what to do if the people on Mt. Sinai had the real deal. Even if it had no supernatural powers whatsoever, the psychological impact would be extraordinary.

After the van had been underway for several minutes, Phair turned to Kealey, who was sitting beside him.

"The location is going to give the Staff added symbolic weight," he said ominously.

"How so?"

"Moses met his future wife, Zipporah, at a well," Phair replied. "Its rediscovery will suggest a new marriage, a new unity."

Kealey craned toward Durst, who was behind him. "Was that a consideration when you hid it?"

"Of course not," the man replied. "We had the damaged tank and knew that the well was a place where we could protect the chest from discovery."

"That isn't how it's going to play, not to these people," Phair said. "They'll say the tank wasn't able to destroy it."

"If 'they' were the ones who took it," Kealey said.

"It won't matter," Phair said. "Those are the facts. I'm betting there are photos to go with it."

"Who else could have taken it?" Carla asked.

Kealey thought for a moment, weighing expedience against need. "One of us," he replied.

The woman laughed. "I was waiting for that. Does that include you?"

"If you like."

"What is there to like about any of this?" she asked.

"I had no reason to lead everyone to the desert and back so they could see an empty hiding place," Durst said. "That is moronic."

"What about your people in Washington?" Carla asked.

"I can't rule it out," Kealey admitted. "But they would have come with helicopters, if they were going to get in and out before us from the nearest staging area. And I saw no sign of the dunes created by prop wash."

"Assuming any of us could have made it into and then out of the desert with no one else knowing, what could we do with the object?" Carla asked. "Neither myself nor my grandfather need the artifact or the money. Do either of you?"

Kealey responded by not responding. Phair also said nothing, though there was something restless about his mouth.

"What is it, Major?" Kealey asked.

"Nothing."

"Let's have it. We need everything on the table."

Phair thought for a moment, then said, "This isn't an accusation, simply an observation. 'The enemy of my enemy is my friend.' I just wonder who Herr Durst dislikes more—a nation of Semites whom he regards as beneath him, or the nation that defeated him in war?"

Carla tensed visibly but her grandfather calmed her with a squeeze of his hand.

"That is a good question," Durst said. "I do not have an answer for you. But I also do not have your Staff."

Phair did not press the matter. But as he faced front his twisting mouth settled into a half smile that Carla and her grandfather could not see. Kealey didn't like it. Phair's expression had an I've-got-a-secret smugness that left Kealey wondering again about Phair's loyalties. Did the cleric sympathize with anti-Americanism—and, if so, was it enough to abet the people operating in Egypt? He would have to watch the man more closely as they went forward.

They rode in silence for some time before Durst asked suddenly, "Mr. Phair, what is the worst thing that you have ever done?"

Phair angled round so he could see the German. It was not a challenging question. The man seemed to want to know.

"I don't think I should answer that," Phair said. "You might be insulted."

"To be disliked is not an insult," Durst shrugged. "It suggests that your point of view is effectively communicated to someone who disagrees. But then, I think I know the answer. Apart from collaborating with me, what else have you done that was wrong or sinful?"

"I deserted my post during combat to minister to the enemy," he replied.

"An Arab?" Durst said. He laughed. "To you they are not so bad as I am. Yet they have done more destruction to your homeland than I."

"You never got the chance."

"We never wished to destroy an infrastructure," Durst replied. "We did not do so to Paris."

"London?"

"The city itself would never have been attacked had Churchill not bombed Berlin first," Durst pointed out. "But that is not the issue. From your voice, I suspect you do not think desertion was a bad thing under the circumstances."

"No. But some in the military did."

"Then let me be more precise," Durst said. "What have you done that *you* consider bad?"

"There is nothing I'm ashamed of," Phair told him. "Nothing I have ever been humbled to tell in confession."

"You are missing something then," Durst said. "Regret builds character. What about you, Mr. Kealey?"

"I don't think I like this game," Kealey replied. "We have other—"

"Are you afraid to answer?" Carla asked.

"No. It's just no one's business, actually."

"We are a team on a mission," she said. "My grandfather has told me that nothing bonds people more than that, joins them for life. Unless, of course, some member or other feels above the unit."

"That would be the commander," Kealey said.

"*Mein Gott,* we lost commanders daily!" Durst said. "The next leader would be one of us, a boy like me, who was a commander in name. Those were our most successful groups. Everyone had a stake in it."

"I thought you were fighting the Communists," Phair said.

Kealey didn't want this to turn into another spat between Phair and Durst. "The worst thing I ever did was when I went into Indonesia with a humanitarian group after the 2004 tsunami devastated the region. My job was to find out how badly damaged the radical Islamic infrastructure was by the disaster."

"Did you help at all?" Durst asked.

"Very little," Kealey said frankly, "and only then when my conscience wouldn't let me pass by someone with two broken legs who was stranded like an upside-down turtle. I was there to gather intelligence and I felt lousy when I left two weeks later. If I had applied myself to searching for survivors or moving food to outlying regions, who knows whether more people would have survived?"

"At least you had a conscience," Phair said, now the pastor.

"And you were doing a job," Durst said. "To me, that does not seem like the wrong thing."

"It was and it wasn't," Kealey said.

"Things aren't always clear-cut," Phair said.

"No."

"Would you have done things differently?" Carla asked.

Kealey replied, "No."

There was no further discussion.

Kealey opened a pouch that contained information from Harper that had been forwarded to the embassy. There were maps and contact information for the region. He read the dossier of Lieutenant Adjo, whom they were to meet. He sounded underqualified for the kind of recon that had been thrust upon him. Men like that either died from a lack of caution or performed in an exemplary manner. It was like the old story about the chess novice who was either destroyed by a grandmaster or managed to beat him because his moves were so unexpected, unpredictable, and unprecedented. Since Adjo was still alive at last accounting, and had gathered valuable intelligence, he was obviously born to the Fifth Column. Kealey had encountered men like that. What interested the agent in particular was that Adjo had not sabotaged the napalm he'd discovered. That would have taken no time and little more than a rock-struck spark. The result would have been equally short-lived. He had been smart enough to let things play out in the hopes of uncovering the larger plan.

Or maybe Lieutenant Adjo learned from living on a river, you catch rats when they're farthest from the hole and a little bit less cautious, Kealey thought as he closed the file and put all the documents back in the leather briefcase.

The rising sun lit a chessboard of a world, with ornate minarets, shorter buildings with rook-like crenellations, and small, smooth columns supporting animal-head designs in front of official buildings or mosques. All of it was endlessly drenched in off-white, a surface that protected the people inside by reflecting sunlight and heat. Kealey had been here before. Once, ten years earlier, he had "attended" a pan-Arab seminar on the danger of theocracies here. Turkey, Egypt, Saudi Arabia, and Jordan were the only nations in attendance, which underscored the theme rather forcefully. Iraq sent no one because the feuding religious sects couldn't agree on a national position. There were times—and now was one of them—that Kealey felt the regional situation was hopeless and the world should just wall it off.

We use a third of the goddamn oil we get from here just to police the region, he thought ironically, then bit-

terly. Of course, military assets had to be used so their
performance could be studied and evaluated. Soldiers
and munitions had to be deployed to better understand
how they function in real-world combat. Ordnance had
to be used because it had a limited shelf life.

Still, he thought, *holding actions like Korea, Vietnam, Iraq, make future wars inevitable. The way to
deal with international problems is to surgically remove the problem-makers.*

The densely packed city gave way to Western-style
suburbs and then to sparsely occupied hills and plains.
Here and there he saw ruined temples and tombs, not
the familiar pyramids but no less imposing in their history if not in their size. The cars that sped by them on
the highway seemed to be time itself moving, while the
ancient world stood stately and still.

It took most of the day to reach the foothills of Mt.
Sinai, crossing the Suez Canal and skirting the Red
Sea. The driver was a local man, employed and vetted
by the embassy. He didn't say anything unless spoken
to. They were careful not to say anything they didn't
want him to hear.

Kealey didn't feel anything special when he reached
the mountain. There was no sense of holiness or history, except in a geologic sense. That did not surprise
him. He was not a spiritual man. He responded to the
fingerprints of men upon the labors of nature. What
people carved, built, left behind—that was what inspired and occasionally moved him, and his job was to
see that monsters like the jihadists didn't tear those
things down. That someone could put over a theological charade on hungry masses, then or now, did not impress him.

The sun was just going down as the group neared the mountain. The wind that had pushed away any lingering smell of gasoline had failed to stir up the fine line of fire that was still visible on the profile of Mt. Sinai. That was because there was nothing much to burn, which was probably why aerial retardants had not been brought in by the so-called peacekeepers. There was also the fear, Kealey suspected, that interfering with the "work of God" would have consequences.

"Look at that," Carla said.

Kealey looked to where she was pointing. It was the first time he had seen the mass of humanity gathered there, clustered around the edge of the mountain like algae at a dock. Kealey heard a hum. He cranked down the window and ducked his head through the opening, angling his ear so he could hear past the rush of air.

"They're chanting, aren't they?" Phair asked.

Kealey nodded.

"This is really going to pop when the prophet shows himself."

"You think he will?" Carla asked.

"He has to," Phair said. "That's the only step up from a miracle, to show the man who wrought it."

The driver turned back toward Kealey, who had withdrawn from the window.

"We're going to have to stop," he said. "There's an MFO blockade ahead."

"Pull over and let us out here," Kealey told him. "You can go back to Cairo."

The van squeaked to a halt on sand-dusted brakes. The four passengers got out in the near dark, carrying the backpacks of clothes and provisions the embassy in Cairo had provided. The van turned and coughed away, leaving them alone by the side of the road. The gardens of the monastery were to the right. They would be able to make their way around the peacekeepers by walking that way. Kealey broke out a pencil-point flashlight from his backpack.

"What are they saying?" Durst asked as they set out.

"*Musa*," Phair said. "Moses."

"They are calling for their leader," Durst said. "I have heard this sound before."

The German did not have to elaborate. Kealey felt the weight of dreadful history upon his back, the awareness that civilization hadn't progressed at all in more than seventy years.

Just then, several lights appeared at the top of the mountain. They appeared to be torchlights, sharp orange smears against the blackening sky.

"The prophet is coming from the mountain," Phair said.

"We've got to find our contact," Kealey said with a sudden sense of urgency. He didn't know what the prophet's plan was, but he didn't doubt there was one. These people were acting at night, when it was cooler for travel and their actions could be cloaked. Were they planning to move out? It was likely, since they knew they couldn't stay long without the pilgrims getting restless and the military or the U.N. moving in to avert a potential health crisis. But where would they go?

Kealey had put on his own backpack and went to take Durst's.

"I can manage," Carla said as she shouldered her own.

"It's not a problem," Kealey insisted as he hefted the packed case over his left shoulder.

"Are you afraid I will run off, or shoot you with the gun your man gave me?" Durst asked.

"Those are not in my top ten concerns," Kealey replied.

With a sweep of the light on its broadest spread, Kealey had a look at the flat terrain. There were no gullies or rocks to watch out for. Refocusing the light in a tight beam, he picked his way onto the plain beside the road.

"Here," Phair said, tapping him on the arm and offering him something.

It was a long stick.

"You can use it to poke ahead for holes," the cleric suggested. "That, and herding sheep, is really what they're for."

Kealey looked at it. A broken branch from an anonymous tree. It really was the prophet who made the staff. *Then why would they need the real one?* he wondered. Assuming they were the ones who actually took it?

"You keep it," Kealey said. "It looks better on you."

With a great many questions and no answers, Kealey started across the narrow stretch that would take them to the gardens and Lieutenant Adjo.

CHAPTER FIFTY-TWO
JEBEL MUSA, SINAI PENINSULA

As he had planned, Adjo was awakened by breezes shortly after sunset. Even before he sat up, he knew that something had changed.

There was a dull roar from the human sea just beyond his sight, an expression of oneness, of expectation.

Things were happening. He wondered what, exactly. It was eerie to hear the voices rise from the dark plain, borne on the wind like the howling of the dead. *Maybe it is,* he thought, remembering his school days and the stories of the gods and of Anubis in particular, the jackal-headed deity who escorted souls to the underworld. There was something in the crisp starlight and voices coming from ordinarily empty spaces that inspired belief in such tales.

Illumination below caught his eye.

Lieutenant General Samra had said Adjo had between sunset and dawn before the Americans arrived. He looked at his watch. The sun would have gone down some twenty minutes ago. Either the Americans were very efficient or there might be trouble ahead: He saw a thin, straight line of light some two hundred meters to his right. He ducked behind a boulder and peered around the side. The light matched the description Samra had provided, but he wasn't about to bet his life on that. The flashlight was turned to the ground, shifting left then right and back, as though looking for safe passage across unfamiliar terrain.

Or for someone hiding.

The light stopped for a moment, then began probing the gardens below methodically. Adjo watched until whoever was holding the light suddenly stopped and cast the light in his general direction.

They knew where he was supposed to be.

"*Miseh ilkheyr,* Adjo," said someone in the group. It was credible Arabic for "good evening."

The light jumped in Adjo's direction as he spoke. "Good evening," the Egyptian said in a soft voice.

The same speaker announced that his name was Phair and he was part of an American tour group.

"Let me see you," Adjo said.

The man said something in English and the flashlight was immediately turned on the man who was holding it, and the others. There were four. That was the correct number.

His legs once again stiff—but loosening more quickly than before—Adjo walked toward them. "You came earlier than I was expecting," he said.

"Sometimes our government is more efficient than any of us expects," Phair replied affably, again in passable Egyptian Arabic. "Is there any news since the fire?"

"I believe the prophet is being summoned."

"We believe he's already on his way down the hill," Phair replied. "Do you have any idea what will happen next?"

"I have no idea," Adjo said apologetically. "I know that the monastery has been used as a base by people who are not monks, but that they may be finished with it now. What is your mission—and do you have any water?"

"Of course." Phair removed his backpack and produced a bottle. He handed it to Adjo.

"Also, a cell phone," he said. "Mine is very nearly dead, I suspect, and I need to contact my superior."

Phair fished through his backpack, assisted by the man with the flashlight. That man said something to Phair, who translated.

"This is our commander, Mr. Kealey," Phair explained. "He wants to know what we're saying. I told him."

"He is a civilian?" Adjo asked, then chugged half the bottle. "Intelligence?"

Phair nodded. "I'm the only officer here. A cleric. My government seems to think I can make some sense of this. As for our mission, it was to find a way to discredit this prophet by presenting the true Staff to the pilgrims."

"You knew where it was?"

"Mr. Durst, over there, did," Phair said. "That's his granddaughter with him. But when we got to the location of the true Staff it was gone."

Phair found the secure TAC-SAT phone and handed it over.

"I wonder how much that matters," Adjo said. "These people are blinded by devotion, and I do not think they will remain here much longer. I hope to know more after speaking with headquarters."

Adjo phoned Lieutenant General Samra while Phair spoke with the others, presumably telling them what had been discussed.

The update from Lieutenant General Samra was ominous. "I was about to call you on the other phone," Samra said. "Radar has spotted fifteen helicopters coming in your direction across the Sinai Desert. They took off from Sharm el-Sheikh International Airport ten minutes ago."

"Carrying what?"

"We're trying to find out," Samra told him. "But I'm guessing you'll know before we do."

"True enough." Depending upon the kind of helicopter and air speed, they would be here in less than an hour.

Adjo hung up and briefed Phair on the latest development. Phair translated for the others. The leader of the group, the man with the flashlight—who seemed to possess a reassuring air of calm, as far as Adjo could tell from his economic movements and smooth voice—spoke with the translator for a few moments.

"Mr. Kealey wants to know what you think we should do," Phair said.

That caused Adjo a flash of consternation. He was hoping these people had some ideas. Perhaps they did and were just being polite. Or, as strangers in his country, maybe they were being smart. That was encouraging.

"I believe the monks in the monastery have either been taken elsewhere or are being held captive," Adjo said.

"If the monastery has been commandeered by rogue elements, the monks are most likely still there," Phair said. "They would be needed in case questions arose about the church's operation, or a familiar voice was required on the telephone, or a password on a computer."

"That is true," Adjo said. "Then if they are there, they may be able to tell us who is behind this masquerade and perhaps something of what their intentions are."

"So you think we need to talk to them," Phair said.

Adjo liked the man's style. He nodded.

"I agree. What about those helicopters from the Red Sea?" Phair asked. "Any thoughts?"

"Since they are not military but seem to be together, I have to assume they are coming to support the prophet, perhaps to take him elsewhere."

"Out of sight, away from scrutiny," Phair said. "As in the mountaintop video."

"I took that," Adjo said proudly. "I agree—they were very careful that he should not be seen too closely, or by too many."

At Kealey's urging, Phair stopped and translated. The cleric informed Adjo that Kealey agreed with both assessments. Then he pointed to Durst. "This man has to try and get close to the prophet, to see his staff. Mr. Kealey still wishes to know whether it is false and perhaps use that against them. But these three do not speak the language or look like pilgrims. Will that attract attention?"

"There are many people with many different dialects among those gathered here, and they will be attending the prophet, not each other. Besides, it is night so the clothing should not matter. But there will be a great deal of jostling. It will be difficult to get very close, and to see very clearly."

"Hopefully, he can tell from a distance."

Kealey asked something else and Phair translated.

"Do many of the people out there have cell phones?" Phair asked, indicating the plain.

"They seem to," Adjo replied.

"That is how they're getting word out," Phair said. "Viral terrorism. It's a new world."

"New indeed," Adjo said. "I have spent a career keeping foreign elements from disrupting my country. Yet here I am, working with foreign operatives to do just such a thing."

"I have similar issues, Lieutenant," Phair said as he slipped on his backpack. He moved slowly, purposefully, like a man who was used to shouldering loads.

"You have worked with Arabs before, I assume," Adjo remarked. "Your language skills are—"

"I have lived among Arabs and many are as brothers to me," Phair interrupted. "No, Lieutenant. That's not what I meant.'

Phair didn't elaborate and Adjo didn't press him. He assumed when the American mentioned "issues" he was referring to his current teammates, possibly the girl with the accent. Ultimately, it wasn't important. Only the job mattered.

It was quickly arranged that Phair and Adjo would go to the monastery and the leader—Kealey—would go with the others, Carla and Durst. As Phair said to Adjo when the decision had been made, "I'm a priest. I belong at church." They would stay in touch by phone. Adjo told them to try and collect intelligence about the helicopters when they arrived and get him the information so he could make his own quick assessment and forward it to Task Force headquarters. Then the three set out quickly, and Phair waited while Adjo hid everything he still possessed under a bush where it wouldn't be discovered.

"Either that is a formidable disguise or you've been through a lot," Phair told the man.

"A day ago, these were new," Adjo told him. "It's a strange thing about the desert. The new quickly becomes old, yet the very old endures like new."

The men set out along the gently sloping expanse, moving westward. A crescent moon had risen and provided sufficient illumination for their walk.

"It's humbling to be in this place," Phair said as they walked, his staff moving in counterpoint to his steps. "I wish I had time to appreciate that feeling."

"Have you ever been to Egypt?" Adjo asked.

"No. I was in Iraq for sixteen years, but never here."

"You were with the military?"

"Yes—and no," Phair said. "I chose to stay behind. I wanted to try and understand the roots of their religious strife, and to help wherever I might."

"Did you succeed?"

"I helped a little," Phair said. "As for understanding—I think a core of us are too close to the serpent and too far from God, still. Those people are angry and need to fight about something, anything. If they didn't embrace one cause it would be another, or another. They fight over theologies that aren't much different, over politics that share mostly the same ideas, over borders that don't matter at all, really. And they drag others into the struggle. It's sad."

"And yet here, today, I have seen all manner of people, all nationalities, out in the plains in peace," Adjo said.

"For now," Phair said. "They are potential zealots who need only a match. Would you prefer to wait until that flame is ignited?"

"No," Adjo said. "Though I wonder."

"About?"

"My country possesses a character that has endured for millennia, a culture and personality that is worth preserving," Adjo said, surprised by his tone that was wistful rather than proud, defiant. "Civilized nations create ways for people to share that culture with them. We have done that. My work has been about welcoming an orderly international community without changing the nature of the home I love. An assault on the desert, which may yet be inevitable, is not the best way to achieve that."

"My church is the same way," Phair said. "It creates comfort for those who are within and intimidates those who might wish to do more than visit. I don't have the solution, Lieutenant. I wish I did."

"That is what I was wondering," Adjo said. "Perhaps that is why people come to a place like this. To get to the root of things without the adornments, without the ritualized prayers or manmade boundaries. Part of me hopes that we have calculated wrongly, that all of this is about a true and innocent search."

"How do you feel, being here under these conditions—with pilgrims at the foot of the holy mountain and a prophet in its peaks?"

Adjo laughed. "As Moses did. Alone. Wondering what in the name of the Lord I am to do next!"

Phair chuckled. "I have to admit one thing, Lieutenant," he went on, quickly growing serious. "I understand your feelings about home. I would go to the smallest, dirtiest church in Iraq, with the smell of dung in the doorway and people sleeping in the pews. Yet God was still the most powerful presence." He looked at Adjo. "You saw the staff turn into a serpent. Did you believe it, even for a moment?"

"No, even before I heard what our analysts said, that it was a snake all along, drugged to muscular rigidity. They point to the fact that the object was cast down rather than merely laid down."

"What does that prove?"

"A blow would have triggered a brief, automatic reaction in what they call an enforced anti-kinesian state," Adjo said.

"Paralysis?" Phair said, apparently uncertain of the Egyptian translation.

"Yes," Adjo told him. "They couldn't afford to administer some kind of counteragent, I was told, because after the demonstration the snake would then have remained mobile instead of becoming stiff once again—as it was supposed to have done for Moses."

"Of course, if we're being true to the Bible, it was Aaron's staff that was cast down, not the rod of Moses."

"That is another point," Adjo said thoughtfully. "It doesn't matter whether this is the actual Staff. The men behind this are clearly seeking an emotional reaction, not a logical one."

"For these masses, that may be true," Phair replied. "The first wave of any religious movement is usually the blind adherents and the seekers of anything new or potentially a revelation. If their objective is to establish a new cult, the closer scrutiny will be where it succeeds or fails."

"The Staff itself."

"That's right. Which is why I wonder if that's their actual goal," Phair said.

"I was thinking of that myself, just before you arrived," Adjo said. "To thousands of pilgrims, I wonder if what they saw today was not the Burning Bush but the Biblical Pillar of Fire, the harbinger of the destruction of the army of Pharaoh."

"Very possibly," Phair said. "And the helicopters?"

"I don't know. Angels?"

"There aren't any in that story. Only chariots."

"Either way, we have some difficult hours ahead of us."

"Speaking of difficulty, do you have a plan for getting into the monastery?"

"Not as yet. I was hoping that upon seeing the enclave, an American special operative would have some insight on that."

"I believe I do. Have you a weapon?"

"Yes."

Phair was quiet for a long moment. "Where is the front entrance?"

"To the east. Why?"

"Because that is how we are going to enter," Phair replied.

"You have a plan." It was a statement that was really a question.

"Yes. It will get us inside, I hope. After that, I may be able to talk them into ignoring us."

"How?"

"By being unimportant," he said.

"And if that fails?" Adjo asked, though he knew the answer. That was why Phair had asked if he had a gun.

"It won't be by our doing if violence becomes necessary," Phair replied.

The gun suddenly felt clammy in Adjo's hand. Not like a foreign object he wished to be rid of, but almost organic.

There was apparently nothing more to be said as they left the refreshing coolness of the garden for the ominous cobbled expanse outside the monastery. Adjo noticed that the cleric had discarded his staff somewhere behind them. Perhaps he didn't want to be perceived as a prophet impersonator and brushed aside. A part of Adjo wished he hadn't done that.

Any opportunity for a miracle should not be overlooked, he thought, as they strode through the faint moonlight toward the main gate and a plan that sounded like it might get them in the door and nothing more.

CHAPTER FIFTY-THREE
JEBEL MUSA, SINAI PENINSULA

Ryan Kealey shouldered his way through the crowd, followed closely by Lukas Durst and Carla. Everyone on the plain was standing, watching the torches move along the side of the mountain. There was one light in the center of the circle, but it said nothing about whoever was holding it. Kealey guessed it was the prophet, of course, the other hand wrapped firmly on his staff. The man of the hour was probably surrounded so that someone would show him the way down or catch him if he stumbled. It wouldn't be terribly impressive for the Deliverer to drop full on his face.

The crowd was not unusually dense at the foot of the path from the mountaintop. The pilgrims no doubt assumed that the prophet would come to them. Many were probably tired from the journey and baking in the sun, and not everyone wanted to walk about the plains in the dark.

"They are all such sheep to think this could possibly be real," Durst said with disgust.

"I'd watch what I say," Kealey cautioned.

"Why? Another Nazi allusion?" Carla snapped.

Kealey stopped and glared at her. "No," he said quietly. "I'd watch what I say in English, German, or Spanish. Anything but a regional accent may draw unwanted attention. Though the shoe does fit, doesn't it?"

Carla's head ticced to the side in embarrassed little moves, but Durst nodded in agreement. The man might be a loutish fascist, but ego wasn't a large part of what guided him. He could be reasoned with.

They reached the path that ran like a ribbon along the mountainside. The torchlight was drifting down away from the smoldering ridgeline, like embers from a wildfire. The faithful had lined both sides of the road as far as Kealey could see, sometimes five and six people deep, but without shoving, no one jockeying for position. To be close to the prophet was apparently all they needed. Now that Kealey's eyes had fully adjusted to the moonlight, their staunch posture suggested they had not come to see so much as to protect. If there was a rush of pilgrims to get close to the prophet, the men lining the road would hold them back. Kealey didn't think they were part of the plot, at least not founding members. They were willing converts.

Kealey kept Carla and Durst back several meters so as not to draw undue attention from anyone in that line. There was a fidgety eagerness about the German, his head moving and pecking as he tried to keep the torches in view as they came and went beyond the heads of the pilgrims.

There was indeed a circle of robed attendants as Kealey had guessed. As they neared the bottom of the path, the surrounding circle doused their flames in the dirt. Either they did not want to detract from the prophet or, more likely, they did not want anyone to see them too clearly.

"Those monks do not look real," Carla whispered. "They're hovering near him like police, not like the devout."

"I agree," Kealey replied.

"Are they dressed that way to conceal weapons?"

"That's my guess," Kealey said. There was something sweet about Carla's manner. After her faux pas a few minutes before, she seemed eager to show she was part of the team.

In the midst of the circle was a tallish figure with a brown beard and white robe, lava red—and flowing, at that—in the torchlight. He wore new sandals with thick soles; a benevolent expression peeked from under the hood that covered his forehead. With each step he purposefully planted and replanted a chest-high stick in the ground beside him. It was straight, slender, durable, and dark—like a sapling that had been burned and hardened in a forest fire. One fist easily encircled the staff near the top, which ended in a knob worn smooth by hand labor.

"That is not the Staff!" Durst said through his teeth, a poor effort at reserve. At least he said it in English, which was probably not understood by anyone who might happen to hear.

"Are you sure?" Kealey asked.

"I wouldn't give you a Euro for that thing. And—

look for yourself. It would not have fit in that place where I left it."

That was true. Kealey motioned for Carla and Durst to follow him. He wanted to get out of the crowd before they were trapped as people clustered around the prophet. It was already becoming difficult to move, the pilgrims instinctively moving toward the light, floating in hypnotically on their chants, wanting to be a part of whatever was happening. There was a communal hunger and at the same time, an outpouring of energy and passion. Kealey tried to imagine what the prophet himself was feeling, something real or something cynical. It would depend, he guessed, on whether the man was a believer or part of the scam. Kealey also wondered if Durst was feeling a sense of longing or déjà vu. This had to be what the Germans had experienced when their führer arrived to address a rally.

Kealey was most curious, though, what the man would do next. Taking Durst at his word that the staff was a fake, that all of this was orchestrated, the organizers would not be able to leave much time for the fraud to be discovered. Whatever their plan, whatever their hand, they had to reveal it soon. No doubt the helicopters were going to be a part of that.

There was a press of people forming new layers, new lines, many, many pilgrims deep. But they did not intrude on the path that had been created for the prophet. The chanting continued, uncoordinated and personal, as the pilgrims bowed or held their hands palms-up in a show of supplication. A few went to their knees, others tripping against them in the dark. Some, here and there, took pictures using cell phones. The monks did not attempt to discourage such activity as they maintained their black-garbed bubble around the figure.

The prophet did not stop. He did not acknowledge the worshipers. Once he reached level ground he strode toward the north, toward the plain. As he passed nearer, he seemed the model of what Kealey imagined an ancient desert dweller to be like, his body lean with hunger, his eyes wide with vision and focused on some distant goal.

"Do you have any idea what he's going to do?" Carla whispered.

"If he were going to address the group, he would have spoken from higher on the mountain," Kealey said. "Look at the soles on his shoes. Solid. I think he intends to keep walking."

"Where?"

"That's the question, isn't it?" he said. "It seems clear that wherever he goes, these people are going to follow."

Things became more confusing for Kealey and the pilgrims when a low-register beating rose under the sound of the chanting. Within moments the roar had equaled and then surpassed their prayers. The multitude and the plain began to grow lighter and lighter. Turning to the east, Kealey saw the helicopters arriving. They were a formidable sight, fifteen brilliant white lights growing larger and brighter and louder as they approached.

"There's nowhere for them to set down," Carla observed. "At least, not where the people are."

"I don't think that's their intention," Kealey said, as he watched them approach at top speed some one hundred meters above the gathering.

"So they aren't picking up the prophet," she said.

"No," he said. There was a hodgepodge of markings on the aircraft. They weren't part of an organized fleet. But neither the prophet nor the former torchbearers looked up. The helicopters had been expected.

The aircraft continued west, not stopping until they were beyond where Kealey suspected the edge of the crowd might be, a bottleneck formation of mountain and brush at the far end of the Wadi el-Deir. Finally, they set down.

"Little more than a century ago those lights would have been considered gods," Durst said softly to no one in particular. "Yet they are men. I learned that. One day they will, too."

It was an uncharacteristically unguarded remark from a man who had bought into the myth of the *übermensch*. Whether it was part regret, part revelation, or simply exhaustion talking, Kealey was glad to hear it.

But this was not the time for his own introspection. The important thing was to get away from the crowd, reconnoiter where the helicopters had landed, then contact Harper and figure out their own next step.

Telling Carla where he was headed in case they were separated, Kealey maneuvered ahead, beyond the prophet and closer to the truth.

CHAPTER FIFTY-FOUR
WASHINGTON, D.C.

Jonathan Harper was eating lunch away from his desk, which was a rarity. He had been dragged away by Sarah Knute, the director of Public and Media Affairs. They were seated in a corner booth at Off the Record, a wood-paneled bar not far from the White House. Harper was picking at an order of lightly fried calamari while Knute tucked into a cheeseburger. The thirty-five-year-old woman had the metabolism of a teenager, and except for a bit of wear and tear around the eyes, she looked like one.

"Don't let those squid have died in vain," Knute cautioned.

"No," Harper said, halfheartedly dipping one in a dish of tartar sauce, watching and turning it for nearly a half minute before finally consuming it.

"I like a man who knows how to dine instead of rush, rush, rush."

He smiled thinly.

"I dragged you out so you would forget the office for an hour," Knute said. "There's nothing you can do right now."

"I know." It reminded him far too much of San Antonio. He looked at the secure cell phone that sat on the table beside him. There was only one call that he would risk taking in a public place. Not that anyone would be eavesdropping. Virtually everyone who came here knew everyone else, and knew where to sit so as not to be overheard. The women at the next table worked for the mayor of D.C. Across the aisle was a pair of congressmen from the South. Everyone was huddled so close, so paranoid, so deep in their own secretive conversations that they didn't have time for anyone else.

"We need to do something with this project you're on," Knute was saying, also sotto voce.

Her conspiratorial tone got his attention. "What do you mean?"

"Everyone says we work only against the Islamic world, that we want them only for their oil," she said. "We should be putting out the word that we're working on behalf of the stability of a sovereign Arab nation."

"We need to know more before we leak word of any involvement," Harper said.

"The press is asking questions."

"That's their job."

She made a face. "The *Post* heard from someone in the Egyptian Ministry of Defense that Israel was behind a plot to destabilize the region, and that we had a team over there helping them."

"And you said?"

"It was all a lie."

"You told the truth," he grinned.

"I concealed the truth," she said. "But if I didn't, this could help bolster our image abroad."

"Whose? The nation's or the CIA's?"

"The nation's," she said. "Who cares what anyone thinks about us?"

Sarah was right. Choose any agency, any officer or politician, and you'd find 50 percent of his or her subordinates, or the nation itself, disapproving of what they were doing. Even if you happened to be doing the right thing, that would be the wrong thing to someone, somewhere. Nations, though, had a more permanent, universally recognized personality. For most of the world, Russians would always be brutes, Frenchmen snobs, the British humorless with bad teeth, the Israelis land-grabbers, Americans greedy with short attention spans and great movies. Once in a while, though, it helped to remind the world that America was also about democratic values.

Usually.

They continued eating as the press secretary pressed her case. Harper half-listened. It was sobering to be out and about in the greatest seat of power on the planet. He sat there and considered—as he rarely did, caught up in the moment-to-moment demands of the office— that despite the tiny part they all played here, virtually everyone in this restaurant, in restaurants like it, created rippling ramifications throughout the globe and history. By extension, a good meal, an unusually pleasant service staff, a drink or appetizer on the house, could change the mood of any individual present and, through them, alter the course of history.

"The press hasn't really picked up on what's happening out there," Harper said. "Shouldn't we wait to see how that plays?"

"Why do you think they haven't?"

"Still below the radar," he said. "Too grassroots and far away."

"For now," she said. "When it breaks, though, every-one will be afraid. Until Russia invaded, who cared that there was a country called Georgia?"

"Georgians," he replied.

"Right. Not most Americans. As soon as things ex-ploded, everyone was afraid it would be the next big flashpoint. Same here. Americans, Egyptians, you name it—they'll all be afraid when they find out. That's why, if we get out in front of it, we can not only control the vol-ume of noise, but sweeten it. It's happening, yes, but your government is on top of things."

"For once," Harper said.

"Exactly."

"With the help of a Nazi. Who we kidnapped."

"We did?"

Harper nodded. "I think we need to let this play out a little longer."

"Okay," she said, "but here's another point of view. If we take someone into our confidence, they'll owe us. I don't have to say anything about the team members or what we're doing. Just about our counterterrorist work. We can make it look like a reporter did some snooping and came up with the story. In public 'no comment,' but I'll continue to be an unnamed source and spin it."

He thought about that for a moment. It was good to have the press in your debt for the times things didn't go so well. "Who'd you have in mind?"

"The *International World Journal*."

That unwieldy name had been created by the merger of three former print magazines into one online news source. They were centrist and generally accurate.

"Okay," Harper said.

"Great," Sarah said, smiling with satisfaction. "Are we going to turn over the Nazi when we're done?"

"I don't know," Harper replied.

"Don't we have a quid pro quo arrangement with the Israelis?"

"For intel, not war criminals."

As he answered, a text message appeared on his phone. The words appeared in a single space, each new one replacing the last, so that no one could read the message without seeing the entire thing.

It was from the American embassy in Egypt. There had been a three-alarm fire in Sharm el-Sheikh. The only reason he received the alert was because he had a team there. The fire did not, on the surface, seem to have any bearing on the mission.

Still, he would mention it to Kealey when he called. Just in case.

CHAPTER FIFTY-FIVE
JEBEL MUSA, SINAI PENINSULA

Kareem Galal sat at the large oak desk, waiting. There was nothing in front of him save for a laptop and a battery-powered lantern. An AK-47 sat on his lap and a walkie-talkie was looped to his hip. With alert, excited eyes, the man was watching cell phone images being flashed to various websites from the foot of the mountain.

A voice crackled from the radio. "Sir?"

Galal snatched the radio from the leather strap and raised it to his mouth. "Here."

"Two men are approaching from the garden," the caller said. "One looks like a pilgrim, the other is wearing trousers and a shirt."

"Armed?"

"Impossible to tell."

"Do they seem to know where they're going?"

"Yes, sir. The pilgrim is in the lead."

Galal considered the matter. He was thinking of the intruder who had been exploring the tunnels the day before. That man was a pilgrim, too. These two couldn't possibly interfere with what was about to take place. It was too late for that. But Galal was curious to learn whether the two visits were related. And who had sent the men.

"Find out what they want," he said. "Make sure they're not reporters wearing a camera."

"If they are?"

"Keep your gun hidden, be a monk."

"Yes, sir. If they aren't?"

"Kill them."

The subordinate clicked off and Galal went back to his Web browsing. He liked the way the events were being reported. The pictures and short videos alone told the story. Very few of the pilgrims had anything to say, and those who did expressed only awe.

It was exactly as they had expected.

Before the sun rose, the world would be changed dramatically.

It was by far too late, he smiled.

CHAPTER FIFTY SIX

JEBEL MUSA, SINAI PENINSULA

Adjo felt electrified as they walked to the front gate of the monastery. This was going to be a challenge. Pushing himself was one of the qualities that had drawn him to Task Force 777. He had never been much of a student because the risk had never been terribly high. His father would hit him with a strop for bad grades, but not too harshly because he needed the boy to help carry boats to and from his work shed each morning and evening. Adjo had never felt challenged by the river because the shore was never more than a dozen meters away in either direction and, if it was swollen or raining, one didn't go out. That was not the case here.

Unlike every other mission, there was nothing secretive or forceful about their approach. It was neutral, daring in its lack of bravado. The tactic went against his training. Unlike his previous visit to the monastery, Adjo was moving toward the enemy in the open, not running from him in a place of concealment. That went against his instincts. Adjo's one precaution was to wrap the tatters of his garment around his right hand to conceal the gun he had taken from the pilgrim. He hoped that whoever they met would think he was merely trying to keep the robe from dragging on the cobblestones, a quaint attempt at dignity.

They reached the old wooden door beside the towering gate. The MFO cordon was several hundred meters to their left, well beyond the gardens and past a downward dip in the road. That was where their jurisdiction ended—farther than the shores of the Nile had ever been. The only thing visible was the upper dome of the glow from the lights they had erected.

The American searched for a bell or knocker. He found neither and pounded one of the ancient panels with the side of his fist. They did not have to wait long for someone to appear on the wall above them. Adjo did not think they would be shot out of hand. Even if someone recognized him as the refugee from the tunnel, the "monks" would want to take them inside and find out what he knew and who he had told. Besides, the MFO would be watching the monastery. Gunfire would be an invitation for the Egyptian component— active members of the military—to move in.

"I am from the All Saints Diocese in Cairo," Phair said in Egyptian. "Father Constantelos is expecting me."

"He?" The man indicated Adjo.

"My guide," Phair said. "I had considerable difficulty getting here."

The observer on the wall stepped away. Even though he was out of sight, Adjo recognized the distinctive static of a walkie-talkie. They were obviously using very old, very localized technology so that the calls couldn't be hacked.

"Stay there!" the man said, reappearing at the top. "I will open the door."

"You see? Easy," Phair said from the side of his mouth.

"Getting inside is never a problem," Adjo observed. "Is this diocese real?"

"Very."

"So what do we do next?"

"I was sent to do research in the library," Phair told him. "If they don't accept that—"

"They won't."

"Then, regrettably, we fight our way to the archives. That's where you were shot at and that's where I saw a small downlink antenna on the roof."

"Where?"

"Behind the cross," Phair said. "I don't believe the designs changed during the time I was in Iraq."

Adjo was impressed. He hadn't noticed it before.

The men were ushered inside. Phair went first, surrendering his backpack at the insistence of one of the three men who were waiting for them. The men were dressed in jeans and sweatshirts. In the dark, it was difficult to tell their skin color. A fourth man joined them from the direction of the office. He was a monk.

"*Beati pacifici,*" Phair said to him as one of the men patted him down.

The monk stared blankly at him.

"Why these precautions?" Phair asked, though not before shifting his eyes toward Adjo. "The bishop spoke to the appropriate authorities. We are expected, to do research."

Phair's glance, slow and wary, informed Adjo that there should have been some kind of response to the Latin. As if they needed any assurance that these men were not affiliated with the monastery, this was it. Four against two, superior firepower—there was no question who the odds favored, especially with their knowledge of the compound.

Adjo couldn't afford to think like that. As they patted the cleric down, he could see Phair's expression collapse into something sad and resigned. Seeing that, Adjo fixed his attention on the goal. They had to obtain information and phone it out of here. Getting themselves to safety was secondary.

One of the men approached Adjo next. He extended his arms as the man went to search him. The gun was still wrapped in the ragged hem of the robe. The man reached out to pull it off.

Adjo didn't know what the American's follow-up plan might have been, but they were not going to be admitted anywhere, under any pretense, once the man found the gun. The cleric's ruse had gotten them inside and that was all.

His arm swung toward the man and the gun shot through the fabric. He moved his arm quickly. There were two bursts and two more men went down with wounds to the torso. Adjo had avoided head or heart shots so they'd have a chance to survive. The monk reached into his robe, and Adjo put him down with a shot to the thigh.

Phair grabbed two guns and Adjo took the other two.

"I'm sorry," Phair said.

Adjo wasn't sure who he was addressing. It didn't

matter. They needed to get to the archives, quickly. If any relevant records or monitoring equipment were here, that was the likely place.

"Will the MFO respond to that gunfire?" Phair asked in a loud whisper.

"It's likely, though they'll probably send in members of the Egyptian military for reconnaissance."

"It will be interesting to see if the phony monks try and stop them."

"The ones dressed as monks will be left alone and will probably vouch for the others," Adjo said. "We're the ones everybody wants."

There was movement along the top of the outer wall and around the other structures in the compound as the two men hurried through the darkness. A few men peeled away toward the gate. Others came in their direction. Adjo could hear the footfalls. But there was no talking, no one was using a radio. The occupants obviously did not want to give their positions away.

Adjo and Phair reached the archives without encountering any opposition. That didn't mean there wouldn't be men waiting inside. Adjo stood to the side while he reached over and tried the door. It was locked.

"The windows are barred," Phair said, having made a quick check.

Adjo motioned for Phair to get behind him, then fired twice at the wood to the left of the doorknob. He kicked the door and it swung open as he dodged to the side. When no one fired, he took a chance and stepped inside. Phair followed him in.

The young officer shined his light around the room. It appeared deserted. There was a door in the back and Phair ran toward it. Adjo turned a small desk on its side and pulled it in front of the entrance. He didn't want to shut the door and leave himself blind. The desk was high enough so that anyone coming in would either have to stop and step over it or else push it aside. He crouched behind the other desks, deep in the narrow room, and laid the recovered guns at his side.

"Let me have a light," Phair said.

Adjo glanced back and shined the flashlight on him. The inner door was locked but a quick search uncovered a key on the bookcase beside it. Phair fit it into the lock and the door opened. He stepped inside.

Adjo looked out at the compound as voices and lights started to converge in their direction. Obviously, the decision to come here had been correct. The men couldn't have known where they were going. They were simply coming to the one place that was worth protecting.

Adjo's mouth was dry, but he dared not put down his weapon to wet it. He hoped they didn't have tear gas. If they did, he'd have to surrender this position and join Phair.

"Jesus wept," Phair said, after less than a minute.

"What is it?" Adjo asked urgently, half-turning. The lights down the street were growing larger as they moved toward them.

"Anyone comes through that door, you kill them," Phair said, his voice thick with disgust. "I have to call this in."

CHAPTER FIFTY SEVEN
JEBEL MUSA, SINAI PENINSULA

Kealey's phone vibrated as he pulled away from Carla and her grandfather. It was Jonathan Harper. Other people were on phones, talking or sending video images. He would not stand out.

"Can you talk?" Harper asked.

"Yes, though I don't know if I can hear," Kealey replied, poking a finger in his left ear. "The prophet has descended and is walking through the plain to where the fifteen helicopters just landed—"

"We saw that," Harper said. "I just got the word from the National Reconnaissance Office. They have no ID on any of them, and we can't tell anything about the crew. What are you seeing?"

"Nothing yet," Kealey told him, "but we've confirmed that our own target is a fake."

"Then who took the real Staff?"

"I still don't have a clue," Kealey said, trying not to yell over the murmuring tumult of the crowd. "Phair and the Egyptian officer have gone to try and find out

more at the monastery. I'm going to check on the choppers."

"What about the prophet?" Harper asked. "Did you
see him? Was there anything to him?"

"He wouldn't turn heads anywhere else," Kealey said
as he continued to make his way through the crowd.
"There was nothing rock-star about his coming among
his followers."

"Security?"

"Small cordon surrounding him, I couldn't tell if
they were armed. But no one was running forward."

"Sniper positions forward?"

"Negative," Kealey said. "He's got people around
him and there are no elevations closer than a half mile."

Kealey understood why he was asking. It wasn't
about an Egyptian operative taking the prophet out but
one of his own people, and making it look like an official act. That's the fast road to a movement having its
own martyr.

"Are you hearing anything?" Kealey asked.

"We got an alert about a big fire in Sharm el-Sheikh,"
Harper said. "It seemed to be centered in a bakery."

"Timing?"

"Right after the choppers left," Harper said. "The
police are investigating."

"Which way did the wind carry the smoke?" Kealey
asked.

"Northwest."

"The same direction as the choppers," Kealey said.

"I don't follow."

"If they're connected, the fire was not set till after
they left," Kealey said. "Otherwise, they might have
been grounded."

Harper was silent for a moment "Good get. I just checked. There was a half-hour hold on all flights due to smoke. I'll do some more checking and let you know what I find out."

"Thanks," Kealey said. He signed off, then looked across the plain. Carla and her grandfather had caught up while he talked to Harper.

"Is something the matter?" Carla asked.

Kealey told her what Harper had reported, as much to try and process the information himself as to inform her. Connected or not, the precise timing and inexorable nature of all these events troubled him. It was like trying to stop an ocean breaker. The participants, himself included, were being swept in one direction by events as well as their own momentum.

He turned to Durst. The German was standing there in a strange posture that combined slope-shouldered defeat and fist-shaking anger. He felt this getting away from them, too.

"You really didn't take it?" Kealey asked the German. The agent practically had to yell to be heard. The chants were growing louder as the prophet moved among them, closer to Kealey. People were firing guns again.

Durst shook his head angrily, once.

Kealey faced Carla. "Or you?"

"I did not." She was not angry, just very, very insistent. "Why does it matter right now?"

"Because I don't like what I'm thinking," he said. "Look, I'm going ahead, but I don't want you with me."

"Why?"

"I have a bad feeling about whatever is going on up there," Kealey said. "Go back toward the monastery

and watch for Major Phair and the Egyptian officer. If
for some reason you don't hook up with them, go to the
MFO checkpoint. Tell them you're tourists who were
stranded here and have been lying low."

"They will believe that?"

"They're the United Nations," Kealey said. "They'll
believe anything."

Carla looked at her grandfather and repeated what
Kealey had told her. He nodded and they set off in that
direction, against the flow of the pilgrims.

"Be careful!" the agent shouted after them, but he
wasn't sure they'd heard. He decided he liked Carla. It
wasn't easy, being in her position, trying to keep her
family intact and civil, but she handled it with grace.

The crowd was thinning in that direction as the
acolytes joined the press of humanity heading toward
the plain. People had abandoned their cars for now, but
they'd left the headlights on to show the way. It was a
strange vista, ghostly pale, many of the people in silhouette as Kealey joined the sea of pilgrims.

What he had been thinking, what he didn't want to
share with Carla, was that someone on their own side
had taken the Staff—possibly someone from the CIA.
It may not have been Harper's doing, but someone who
had access to the information—one of a handful of senior-
level staff—running his own operation. Maybe someone's
idea of defusing this situation was having some professor
show up on CNN, holding the treasure and undermining the movement in one bold gesture.

*The bad guys would never let their staff be tested for
age or authenticity,* he thought. *They would lose the
public relations battle.* The story of the true Staff would

captivate the TV audience. It had religion and Nazis, two things for which viewers had an insatiable hunger.

There was just one problem with that scenario. Something was going on here and now. The CIA might not have until prime time to fix it.

Kealey had this fleeting, hopeful vision of a consortium of benevolent theologians gathered at a college campus somewhere, deciding that this was the best way to save the world, by resurrecting a figure revered by three conflicted faiths. Kealey was willing to bet that absent the unifying figure of the prophet, many of the people gathered here would turn on one another with violence, spurred by different interpretations of scripture and law and millennia of cultural schisms.

If that was the case, then bringing down the prophet would make Kealey a participant in genocidal rage.

But I don't think that is *the case,* he thought. He didn't believe there were visionaries behind this movement because he knew human nature, and it was selfish and fundamentally base.

That was his last thought as he let himself be carried by the surge of bodies, camels, horses, and blind will to what might well prove to be the gates of Paradise.

Or Hell.

CHAPTER FIFTY-EIGHT
JEBEL MUSA, SINAI PENINSULA

Adjo heard Phair speaking in English. He still didn't know what the cleric had found. When the American finished phoning his superiors, he came over.

"May I have that?" Adjo said, indicating the phone. He wanted to know what Phair had found, but he had something to do first.

Phair handed it to him.

"I'm going to call my superior, request an extraction team from the MFO checkpoint—" He was interrupted by a metallic *clunk* and then a hiss.

"Damn!" Adjo cried.

Within moments the room began filling with tear gas from a canister thrown from just outside the door.

"Close one eye, cover your mouth, drop to your belly!" Adjo told Phair as he pulled a sleeve across the lower half of his face. He knew that wouldn't protect him from the effect of the gas, but it might minimize it.

The young officer flopped onto the floor where the

air was a little clearer as the heat of the room caused the smoke to rise. The hiss of the canister died and he heard voices, feet, furniture being pushed aside. He couldn't see anyone in the thick, gray mist. He released his gun to wipe his open eye. As he did, boots charged from the fog and he felt himself being lifted by the arms. The guns clattered as they were gathered behind him.

Adjo was dragged out, blinking hard and gasping as his lungs were exposed to the unfiltered gas. The outside air pushed its way into his mouth and eyes, and he finally stopped hurting some two minutes later, at about the same time he stopped moving. He was thrust into a chair in a warm, clammy room. He opened his eyes but everything was a smear. He did not resist as he was tied to a chair.

"You shot my men," claimed a voice that came from a shape some distance in front of him.

"I wounded them," Adjo wheezed. "I didn't want to kill anyone."

"They didn't threaten you," the speaker said.

"They shouldn't have been here at all," said Phair, who was somewhere behind them. His voice sounded raw.

The shape moved away. Blinking out the clinging remnants of tear gas, Adjo tried to peer through the dimly lit room. The lantern on the table was a blur. He could hear the men shifting, the guns hitting buttons on their clothes, the scraping of a chair being pushed aside. He could even hear their breaths, tight and fast.

"Should you have been here?" the man asked.

"I'm a priest."

"A strange one," the speaker said. "You are American?"

"Yes. Why are there armed men in this monastery?" Phair asked.

"I think you know the answer to that," the man said.

"I don't!" Phair said. "I came to learn more about the prophet!"

"To learn or to stop him?" the man asked.

"Why should I want to stop him?"

The man turned back to Adjo. "I should ask you that question. You did come here earlier?"

"To find out why someone shot at me."

"Because you were an undercover military operative asking questions," the man replied. "We knew who you were."

"How?"

The man did not answer. Instead he said, "Do you know, I could release you and it would have no impact on what we are doing here?"

"What *are* you doing here?" Phair implored.

"Changing the world for the better," the man replied.

Adjo frowned. "I know your voice."

The man hesitated before saying, "Yes."

There was a shuffling of boots and a sound of movement, about waist high, level with Adjo's ears.

"You're just going to kill us, too?" Phair asked.

Adjo suddenly had a good idea what Phair had found in the locked room. He thought of getting to his feet and trying to hit someone with the chair. He could accept death, but not sitting on his ass—

"We're not going to kill you," the man replied casually, as though he were discussing his plans for dinner.

"We don't want to inflame the U.S. of A. just yet. Our enemy combatants will surely take care of you."

"I'm glad for that," Phair said. "But things don't have to play out this way."

"What way?"

"With honorable, compassionate men tied to chairs. How do you know we're working at cross-purposes?"

"I'm an informed man."

"There's still a lot you can learn," Phair said.

"I believe you," the man said. "It is a shame I won't get to spend more time with an Arab-loving American. They are rare."

There were a few whispered words and then Adjo heard the door open, then close and lock decisively. The room was very dark.

"Do you have any idea what just happened?" Phair asked.

"No," Adjo replied. He was struggling against his bonds. Something guttural rose from his throat.

"They took my phone," Phair told him.

That brought Adjo's attention back to the moment. He couldn't tell if his was gone. He assumed it was. "Does it have a record of numbers you called?"

"I don't know," Phair said, grunting. "I missed several generations of technology. Lieutenant, what could it be too late for?" The grunting sounded like he was doing something, but Adjo couldn't tell what.

"I'm guessing there is a reason they gathered these people here and it has nothing to do with faith," the Egyptian replied, as he worked his wrists up and down and from side to side.

"What can they possibly be doing?" Phair asked. "Arming them? Creating a multinational militia? Obviously there's a larger plan—that comment about not wanting to inflame the U.S. yet."

"It's possible," Adjo said. "Perhaps the helicopters will take them away, set them somewhere with specific missions, targets." He stopped struggling for a moment. "How did he know you're American?"

"My accent?"

"I would have guessed you to be Turkish," Adjo said. "You don't think your people are involved in this, do you?"

"I wouldn't put anything past them," Phair admitted. "The man who captured us obviously has allies—and there was that comment about enemy combatants."

"I know," Adjo said. "He's expecting a shoot-out of some kind."

"With—?"

"The MFO," Adjo said. "They're going to come in at some point."

"He seemed certain they'd kill us," Phair said. "Why? As you said, we're tied up, and it's not like they'd bomb the monastery."

"I don't know the answer to that, either," Adjo said.

The young Egyptian resumed his struggles with added fervor. He felt anxious, angry, wanting to be out of here and beating that man's head in with a rock— whoever he was. It enraged him that he couldn't place the voice. The Egyptian was also annoyed with himself. He had knocked around this place for days, finding information but not the right kind, not enough, not in time. He was a border patrol officer, not a spy. He shouldn't have been the one doing this, certainly not alone. Samra should have sent additional resources, the MFO be damned.

We should have moved in the very first night, when the group of pilgrims was in the cave. But then you would have been no different than the theocracies that surround you, he told himself. It was as important to retain that neutrality as it was to uphold their sovereign borders.

Adjo could feel his flesh tear and his wrists grow bloody, but the chair was solid. The struts in the back were not going to move. Perhaps if he threw himself over, the chair would come apart.

That was when he heard something that made him wonder if maybe the Christian world did have God a little bit on their side.

CHAPTER FIFTY-NINE
JEBEL MUSA, SINAI PENINSULA

As they walked toward the monastery, Carla Montilla did not know what she was doing even though she knew why she was doing it. Her life had never been all purpose and no plan. Because she had well-to-do and well-connected parents to help her, progress was inevitable. The goals varied, but never the pace. She moved quickly, decisively. Even when Carla hiked or bicycled, she knew where she was going and how long it would take.

This escapade was madness. It was an adventure when it started, like an amusement park ride. But it turned out there was no track, no car, and no one at the controls. She was going forward without support, without a specific plan, and without an actual goal once the place was achieved. She now found it stupid rather than exciting, and felt even worse because her grandfather was involved. It was likely that he would have come without her in any case, but he was a man of passion rather than good sense. She should be providing that.

As they moved through the darkness on uneven stones and gullied ground, Carla also wasn't convinced that what they were doing was worth the risk. From listening to dinner-table talk as a child, she knew there were always revolutions and mob gatherings in the third world. To try and stop them was like trying to stop the wind. It blew here and there and was part of the nature of things.

And yet.

There was something contagious about Kealey's determination. His question to her as she left, about the Staff, was as sincere as any he'd uttered. It made her want to help. He seemed to want to do the right thing, even when he did not approve of the people who stood by his shoulder.

That was the only thing that kept her going on the path to the monastery to wait for Phair and the Egyptian.

The wait was not a long one. As they neared, she heard a commotion by the front gate. Leaving her grandfather resting on a flat boulder, she eased around the intervening slope, a grassy affair that started some fifty meters above her. She felt like a fox stalking its prey, and that gave her a little thrill, perhaps because she didn't feel a real sense of danger.

She stopped and looked and saw men leaving the compound. They shut the door and walked toward a van that was just pulling up from the MFO position down the long, winding road.

Two of the men were standing in the headlights, looking down at cell phones. They were punching buttons and listening. A moment later the phone on

Carla's belt vibrated. She looked at the number. The caller ID read "Cell Two."

That was Phair's designation. She hesitated. It stopped buzzing. An instant after that the phone hummed again. She glanced at the lighted faceplate. The caller ID read "Cell Three." That was the Egyptian's designation.

She slid behind the slope and immediately called Kealey's programmed number. He picked up.

"What is it, Carla?"

"Did you receive a call from Phair or Adjo?" she asked quickly.

"No," he replied. "Wait—Phair is calling now."

"It's not him!" she whispered loudly.

"Are you sure? He sent me something less than ten minutes ago."

"I see men at the gate of the monastery," Carla said. "Some are putting wounded men inside a van—several monks, it looks like. Others are using phones, probably the ones you gave Phair and Adjo. I think they're trying to find out who else is here."

"Where are you?"

"On the southern side of the monastery."

"Were you able to see anything else?"

"There were five men leaving the compound through a door beside the main gate. They were behind the headlights so I couldn't tell what they were wearing."

"Can you get to the MFO position down the road without anyone from the van seeing you?"

She looked in that direction. It was the same way they had first approached the mountain when they arrived. "I think so."

"Go," Kealey urged. "If something has gone wrong inside, you and your grandfather need to get to safety."

"What are you going to do?"

"I still need to find out why the helicopters are here," he said. "Then I'll join you. And Carla?"

"Yes?"

"Thanks for the heads-up. You did great."

She replaced the phone, feeling surprisingly proud. She hadn't realized she'd come to respect Kealey's opinion so much.

She returned to her grandfather. "We have to go," she told him.

"I don't understand any of this," he said. "Where could the Staff have gone? Surely the events must be related."

He was oblivious to anything but the artifact. In a way, she envied him that.

"We can figure that out later," she said.

He nodded surrender, not agreement, as he rose and walked off with her. It had only been two days but she was exhausted. She couldn't imagine how tired her grandfather was.

It was just two hundred meters to the checkpoint. It would be good to get this responsibility off her shoulders, sit down, and be an observer to however it all worked out.

Of course, she told herself as they moved furtively along the slope toward the southern side of the road, *so far absolutely nothing has gone as planned. . . .*

CHAPTER SIXTY
MCLEAN, VIRGINIA

Jonathan Harper sat in his chair in the Underground. With their track record on this operation dragging, he was gratified that one part of the puzzle may have been solved. And while there wasn't time to waste, Harper wanted to be sure about the interpretation before he phoned Kealey. The ramifications of what he suspected could be severe.

The deputy director had summoned photo expert Paul Schuyler, psychiatrist Gail Platte, and CIA intelligence analyst George Nesmith to an urgent meeting in the ironically named conference room in the heart of the building. The windowless, oval chamber sat within a web of electronic hoops; the lack of angles allowed the oscillating spectrum of low- and high-frequency waves to blanket the occupants uniformly. Only one landline-secure computer and phone gave them outside access. It was double the security and twenty times the size of the Automat. It was joked that if a government cabal were ever bent on overthrowing the federal government, it would take place in one of Washington's most secure locations, such as this. Hence the name, referencing the Weathermen from the seventies.

They sat around a circular table perfectly proportioned to the room. There was a monitor set in the table, facing up, before each of the fourteen stations. The keyboards were rubber mats with pips.

The reason for the meeting was a photograph. Phair had sent it to Kealey, and Kealey e-mailed it to Harper before instructing Phair to delete it.

"Did he know how?" Schuyler asked.

"Ryan walked him through it," Harper said.

Harper asked everyone to have a look at the image. It showed bodies on the floor or slumped in chairs, in no particular arrangement.

"Off the top, Gail," Harper said. "What do you think killed those monks?"

"I can tell you what didn't," the petite woman replied, her voice rough from forty years of smoking and three years of screaming because she stopped. "As you probably noticed, there is no external trauma or blood and they apparently died where he found them, since there was no attempt to align them in some convenient way for moving or disposal."

"Asphyxiation?" Harper suggested.

"The mouth is typically open in cases like that, as they die struggling for breath," she said. "The fingers are often extended, an involuntary grasping reaction to the chest muscles expanding as the lungs attempt to inflate. Neither of those are apparent here. It looks like they died peacefully."

"Poison?"

"Again, not likely," she said. "The open water bottles on the table were set down, not overturned. Two had the tops screwed back on. Poison designed to kill acts immediately."

"So why bother?" Harper asked everyone. "A bullet would be as quick. Or a knife."

"Gunshots may have been heard by the MFO forces," Nesmith pointed out. "Even silencers in a small room like that would have a loud, distinctive pop."

"Assuming the MFO bothered to listen," Schuyler said.

"True," Nesmith agreed. "But professional killers would have assumed they were. As for knives, maybe someone had an aversion to stabbing monks. But these deaths do not suggest either."

"Why?" Harper asked.

"If they'd been attacked, Phair would have found them praying or about to. This looks entirely unexpected."

"And instantaneous," Platte added. The psychiatrist enlarged the one mouth that was facing the camera and ran an auto-enhance of the image. "But, you know, poison just doesn't fit."

Harper was surprised by that. "Why?"

"There is no distention of the tongue, discoloration of the lips, salivation, or any of the superficial indicators of poison. But there do appear to be thin, uneven, lightened strips in the flesh of their faces and hands."

"Meaning?"

"Perspiration," the psychiatrist replied. "They sweated against dusty skin, leaving trails."

"Maybe it was hot in the room," Nesmith suggested.

He was a short, thin man with a devil's advocacy nature.

"Possibly, but those water bottles are still pretty full. No," she said. "I'm guessing those men were kept in there for some time—one of the men looks like he has two days' growth of beard—and that they died feverish."

"What, locked up and forgotten like lepers in ancient Rome?" Nesmith asked.

"No," she said. "Infected. This may have been an execution *or* it could have been a test."

"A plague," Harper said.

The word hung ominously in the air, as if it were itself toxic. That was what Harper had feared when he saw the way the bodies seemed cut down.

"It would be in keeping with the Moses motif," Nesmith remarked.

The mention of the prophet brought Harper back to what else the picture suggested, what he had asked Schuyler to research.

"Paul, have you got something else?"

The bald-headed man nodded. "The photograph shows seven monks," he said, clearing his throat. "I checked with the Greek Orthodox Archdiocese in New York and they told me there should have been eight monks on duty. If one man is ill, another one serves."

"Meaning?"

Schuyler held up a finger to ask for patience while he explained. "They forwarded profiles of the current staff at the monastery," he continued. "I was able to pretty much identify everyone in Major Phair's photographs. One person was missing, though—a Lev

Kusturica, whom the archdiocese referred to as a passionate member of the monastery."

"A zealot?" Platte asked.

"The word they used, the one written in his file, was *ghazi,* which is interesting," Schuyler said. "It means a 'fighter against infidels.' But it is nonsectarian. He did not advocate his faith over another where those faiths intersected."

"Moses," Harper said.

"It's possible. What I did was use his dossier photograph to search all the SIDs in the region," he went on, typing keys.

SIDs were Security Image Databases, repositories of video surveillance that were made available to international police and security groups for the purposes of employing facial-recognition software; the digital repositories are scanned for known criminals and suspected terrorists. These files were stored and accessible so they could be back-searched for new individuals who suddenly appeared on the intelligence radar. The idea was to trigger a police response in real time if individuals of interest showed up at a landmark or transportation hub.

"By the way, Major Phair is in here," Schuyler said.

"We know that now," Harper replied.

"The monastery itself does not have security cameras on the interior, but they gave us access to the exterior recordings for the last six months."

"How long has the archdiocese been aware of a problem there?" Harper asked.

"Not long," Schuyler said. "They tried to contact the monastery after they saw the news reports of sniper fire. That was the beginning."

"That's one reason we were able to get their cooperation so easily," Nesmith added. "Never mind the staff they had at risk—the eight monks and the help that comes in from the village. With the library they have there, the church didn't want anything to happen to that place."

"We turned up twenty-nine instances of Father Kusturica going outside the walls,"

Schuyler went on, bringing up the images he had found. "Three times with the same man, whom we've identified as Col. Zeyad el-Masri of the MFO."

"Is it unusual that he should be there?" Harper asked. "The MFO has responsibility for that sector."

"El-Masri was out of uniform," Schuyler said. "Why do that unless he was trying to conceal his identity?"

"But he didn't go inside," Nesmith added. "We think that was so none of the other monks would identify him."

"Why would that matter?" Platte asked.

"The monks are supposed to have limited interaction with outsiders," Nesmith said. "It comes with the territory."

"But why an Egyptian MFO officer?" Harper thought aloud.

"A test of some kind of military chemical or bio-agent?" Nesmith suggested. "Maybe one that went wrong?"

"The MFO doesn't store or deploy any of that, which would mean the involvement of the Egyptian military, or some international unit of which he was a part," Harper said.

"And that still doesn't explain the napalm, the Staff, the whole prophet angle," Platte said.

"Look, I've got to let Ryan know about the toxin," Harper said.

"Before you do, Jon, there's one thing more I found out," Nesmith said. "Until he was transferred seven months ago, Colonel el-Masri was an officer in Task Force 777. They *do* store and deploy chemical and biological weapons for study purposes, in case they're ever attacked."

He didn't have to say more.

"Is there any evidence that our contacts Samra and Adjo are in on this?" Harper asked.

"There's no evidence they're not," Nesmith replied.

"I need to let Kealey know," Harper said.

"I think you need to tell him something more," Nesmith said. "Get the hell out of there."

CHAPTER SIXTY-ONE
JEBEL MUSA, SINAI PENINSULA

Still woozy from the tear gas, his muscles aching more than before from exertion, Adjo watched as Phair walked over.

"How—?"

"It's a precaution I took when Iraqi insurgents were kidnapping and beheading foreigners," the cleric told Adjo as he untied him. "In the videos, you could always see that they tied their captives' hands against the small of their back. I wear my dog tags around my waist where they cannot be seen—and no one who does see them notices that one edge has been sharpened to a razor point. A little wriggling and it is within fingers' reach."

"Very clever," Adjo said. He was disturbed because his vision wasn't clearing. After Phair had untied him, the young man tried to stand and found himself woozy. "You'd better go—I feel sick."

"Perhaps the gas," Phair said.

"Do you?"

"No," he said, "but you were closer than I."

Phair helped Adjo to his feet, but they didn't stay planted on the ground. He felt a faint dizziness and was beginning to perspire.

"You better leave me," Adjo said.

"God will help us," Phair said. "Just put your arm around my shoulder."

"Not outside," Adjo told him. "I need to get to a computer station—e-mail my superior."

"There was one in the back room," Phair said. "I don't think we should go there."

"The monks?"

Phair nodded. "They may have been gassed or poisoned with an airborne toxin—I've seen that in Iraq. We should stay out of that room if at all possible."

"Was there a laptop?" Adjo asked. "Wireless?"

"Good question," Phair said. "You wait here—I'll look."

Phair set Adjo back in the chair then went to the rear of the archives, looking first in the corner where the dish was located. He found a desk in a small workspace. There was a computer. He came back and retrieved Adjo, walking him to the keyboard. Phair set Adjo in a chair, then turned on the power strip. The computer whirred to life. Adjo shut his eyes and let his head fall back. He felt utterly drained.

"Trouble," Phair said suddenly as a password prompt appeared on the screen. "The computer is locked."

Adjo opened his eyes. He blinked away a clinging blur, then leaned forward and input 777OVERRIDE777. The computer became active.

"You can do that to any system?"

"Only those that use government communications

systems, which all tourist sites do," Adjo replied. He was breathing heavily now. Something definitely wasn't right. "It's part of our domestic anti-terror program."

"I don't know if I'm impressed or angry," Phair replied.

Adjo didn't move.

"What's your superior's e-mail address?" Phair asked.

"Adom-dot-Samra, A-D-O-M, at command central, one word, seven, seven, seven, dot defense. I must inform him what happened here."

Phair said, "I'm telling him that the occupying force gassed us and has left the monastery for places unknown and we're in the archives. I'm also telling him about the monks."

Adjo nodded. He sat slumped in the swivel chair, his head back. He couldn't understand what was happening. He was finding it increasingly difficult to think, his mind skipping here and there over the last few days.

"I'm copying Kealey and Carla," Phair said.

Adjo nodded, at least in his mind. His head was still reclining, his eyes watery and staring. He was sick. That had to be it. Maybe from spending cold nights in damp clothes. He couldn't think. He just wanted to sleep.

"That was quick," Phair said.

"What?"

"Your superior just responded."

"That's him, always working," Adjo said. "What does he say?"

Phair said, "'Stay where you are. We are sending help.'"

CHAPTER SIXTY-TWO
JEBEL MUSA, SINAI PENINSULA

The lights of the helicopters took Kealey back to the Indonesian tsunami, when bright lights at night, fueled by chugging generators, meant that bodies were being dug from mud, foliage, or rubble. A sour feeling rose in his throat and stayed there.

As the mob swelled forward behind him, Kealey felt his phone buzz. The chanting was so loud and the sounds from the rotors so enveloping, it would be difficult to hear. He snapped the unit from his belt. Harper had anticipated the problem and sent a text message. Kealey backed from the mob toward a small scattering of boulders. As he read the message, he felt the sounds and whiteness close in, drawing sweat from the back of his neck.

777 POSSIBLY INVOLVED IN MOSES
MOVEMENT. POTENTIAL PLAGUE
SCENARIO.

Shit.

That was the only word that came to mind. It was also the only word Kealey had time to think as he received a second message, this one from a monastery e-mail address that had apparently been hijacked by the sender:

TO LIEUTENANT GENERAL SAMRA: ADJO STUCK IN ST. STEPHEN'S CHAPEL. ILL. PARAMILITARY ENEMIES PRESENT

Shit.

That answered the first question that occurred to him: Was Adjo involved?

Kealey was about to text Carla and Phair to warn them about 777 when he received a message from Phair: that Samra's cavalry was on the way. Suddenly *shit* didn't suffice.

Kealey sent a message back: AVOID 777. He had no idea whether it would be received. There was no way Kealey could get to the monastery quickly, not with the crowd all around him. Even if he appropriated a vehicle, there were too many people.

Calm and focused, Kealey texted Carla. He asked her to respond with the name of her hometown; if she had reached the MFO position, her phone might have been appropriated.

A few seconds later he received the reply:

CARACAS

Kealey updated her concisely and instructed her to go to back to the designated rendezvous spot from earlier that evening and to remain out of sight. He added that he would get back there as soon as possible.

Kealey tried to send another message to Phair, a simple "respond to this," but received no reply. He hoped that Phair had gotten out with Adjo. That hope was crushed by a message from Carla.

LIGHTS JUST WENT OUT IN COMPOUND

Someone must have ordered the power cut to the monastery. According to the schematics he'd reviewed, the transformers were in a shed near the garden. Kealey sent a message to Carla to look out for Phair and Adjo in case they managed to get out. She wrote back:

SOLDIERS MOVING IN

So much for escape. He hoped that Adjo was alert enough. He'd been there before. Perhaps he'd reconnoitered a hiding spot.

There was nothing Kealey could do for any of the others right now, and he felt bad for allowing Carla to get in this far. With luck, they could all hunker low until things had played out and this field junta had moved on.

That's too much luck for my taste, he told himself. But it was all he had for them right now.

Luck was a quality he had never courted. He relied on planning and effort over chance. There were studies that said it was a percentage of every endeavor, but he had still refused to count on it. Not in Indonesia, Sudan, Mexico, or any of the other places he had gone undercover, airdropped with special-ops teams at night or—

where his skin color wouldn't give him away shuttled into a city or market by car or train or on foot. Even if luck were a factor, it was available to the other guys, too. Let them look for it and be disappointed.

But Kealey didn't feel like pushing it away. Not now. He didn't think it was a virtue of age or circumstance. He didn't think it was because this was the least experienced team he had ever led into danger and he felt both guilty and protective. There was something else at work, a sense that structures were collapsing around him, rotted from the inside by pockets of religion and politics and self-interest. Who were all these new groups and peoples?

Tiny, upstart mammals nipping at the toes of dinosaurs.

What had changed for Kealey was just one thing. This was the first time in his life that he was not optimistic.

CHAPTER SIXTY-THREE
JEBEL MUSA, SINAI PENINSULA

Phair didn't know who cut the power or why and he hoped it didn't matter. Adjo told him that Task Force 777 had a number of men in the MFO unit. They would be coming soon enough.

He made Adjo comfortable on the floor. The young Egyptian was sweating profusely. This was something other than tear gas and exertion. Phair wondered if it had to do with the monks he found in the room. He wanted to research the symptoms—here he was, only connected to new technology for a few months, yet he suddenly felt helpless without it.

Taking a moment to consider his own bodily functions, Phair determined that anything unusual he felt was a result of the stress of the mission and not illness. He couldn't understand why Adjo was ailing and not himself. The young man had been crawling around ancient tunnels and the mountain itself. Had he been exposed to something before they arrived?

Leaving Adjo, Phair felt his way outside the room so

he could see the Egyptian soldiers when they arrived, call them over. To the right, he saw the dim edge of a light beyond the outer wall, heard the sounds of movement outside the gate. Phair assumed that was the cavalry coming to their rescue but taking care before entering. He leaned against the ancient wooden jamb and looked up, offering a short prayer of thanksgiving to God.

There had been nights in Iraq that were this quiet, this starlit, but never one that had such an underlying restlessness. Wherever he was in Iraq, there had always been the chance of an explosion, a kidnapping, a shooting. But those events were isolated and sporadic. The sense of unrest here was palpable, as though the mountain kept alive every bit of tumult and reverence that had gone on beneath its peaks. He had heard that there were energy vortexes like that around the world, in the Himalayas, in Arizona. Perhaps this was one of them. Or maybe it was something coming from him, drawn out by the holy place.

He wondered if the Children of Israel felt that when they were here. Or were they just tired and spent and ready to return to bondage?

Maybe the new prophet has learned that you must be quick on the liberating, he thought. *People want their milk and honey now.*

He heard voices to his right, some way off. Hinges complained, and he could hear the gate itself being opened. He went back inside and felt his way with hands and toes. He came upon Adjo. The man was asleep.

Phair gently shook the Egyptian's shoulder. Waves of heat seemed to be rising from the young man's body.

"Help is here," the cleric said in a hushed voice.

"I'm not going anywhere," Adjo assured him. "You don't happen to have water, do you?"

"They took everything, I'm sorry," he said. He thought of the water bottles he had seen in the back room. If the army had not been so near he would have gone back and gotten them.

Phair went back outside. He heard a vehicle drive in, the headlights blinding, forcing Phair to look away. He waved at the driver, then stepped back inside. The reflected light illuminated the room sufficiently so that he could look around. He spotted a decanter of water on a desk and retrieved it. He knelt by Adjo's head and dribbled water on his hot cheek and forehead, then cradled his head and fed him some. The young man responded quickly.

And his eyes came alive.

He pushed the stainless-steel container gently aside. "Water," he said weakly, his eyes searching somewhere other than the room.

"Yes, water," Phair replied and tried to give him more.

Adjo's hand kept him back. "Water—on the mountain."

"What are you talking about?"

"The voice. The man who captured us—that's where I heard him. He brought me water."

Phair felt a shock go through his spine. "Are you certain?"

"I'm sure," Adjo said. "They know we've escaped our bonds—won't let us get away now."

Before Phair could figure out what to do with the information, the doorframe brightened. Boots scuffled across the stone walk and shadows stretched toward them in the headlights. The men were in the doorway a moment later.

Phair didn't know whether they'd be shot and taken away, or simply taken away and never heard from again. It didn't seem to matter. He couldn't leave now, and he wouldn't have left without Adjo. He began to pray.

"That doesn't sound good," Adjo said, with a small chuckle. His back was to the door and he couldn't see anything.

Phair laid a reassuring hand on his shoulder as the men entered. Their leader was the same man who had interviewed them earlier.

"We would have come back for you and the monks later, to give you all a fitting interment in the holy desert," the man said. "We just had to come back a little sooner."

"I drank none of your water," Phair said. "You'll have to kill me."

"You were close to him," the man said, indicating Adjo. "That was enough."

"You . . . traitor . . ." Adjo rasped.

"No, Lieutenant," the man replied, with an edge. "We are saving this country—from outsiders, from theocrats, from jihadists. What we do here may save the world."

"How?" Phair demanded.

Two men came forward with handguns.

"By destroying the enemies of civilization," the man replied.

"You call *this* civilized?" Phair exclaimed.

"I call this survival," he replied coldly.

The men with the guns stood above Adjo and Phair.

"You can't destroy everyone," Phair said. "It's been tried."

"Not by us," the man replied.

Phair suddenly did not care whether or not he lived. He felt despair deep in his soul, that nearly seventy years had passed since the last great genocide, yet humankind had not progressed.

Two shots momentarily deafened the survivors in the small room.

CHAPTER SIXTY-FOUR
JEBEL MUSA, SINAI PENINSULA

The choppers had landed in widely separated groups of five and the rotors had been turned off to protect the oncoming multitude from being assaulted with dust and foliage. Men were moving around the drop-down cargo hatches in the backs. Once again, organizationally, it reminded Kealey of the tsunami relief efforts he had witnessed in Indonesia. Crews moved purposefully but without haste, unloading crates on dollies and by hand, in teams, leaving the crates stacked behind each helicopter. The only difference was that no one was moving to unpack the cargo.

The prophet seemed to be making his way to the center of the three groups of helicopters. People followed behind and were now spread all around him as far as the light reached. They had stopped chanting and there was a general murmur. It sounded as though they were saying "manna." That would figure. Most of them had probably come carrying very few supplies. They assumed—correctly, Kealey believed—that the helicopters were unloading food and drink.

A sudden night wind, strong and chilling, swept over them from the west, rushing toward the mountain.

The hand of God pushing us back? Kealey couldn't help but wonder. He wasn't a religious man, but such thoughts were not only possible here, they were inevitable. It was no wonder the pilgrims believed in the holiness of the man who moved among them. Virtually all one had to do was look the part.

Kealey heard crowbars, then saw the bundles being pulled open by helicopter crew members. The prophet himself climbed onto a mound of earth from which he addressed the group. Kealey had no idea what he was saying, but the way he kept pointing all around him with the top of his staff, he was obviously urging the pilgrims to continue their journey with him.

As the fringes of the crowd began to cluster around the prophet and the choppers, the crewmen began passing out loaves of bread. They were yelling something in Arabic and, from the subsequent actions of the pilgrims, they had apparently been told to break some off and pass the rest back.

That was when it hit him.

The bakery fire, Kealey thought. *If the food had been made there, contaminated there, they would have destroyed the place to cover any evidence.*

Is that what this was about? Mass murder? The killing of—

People who had crossed the border illegally, he thought. *The radical fringe of 777 making a statement.*

Kealey looked down, thinking. If there were some

kind of virus or bacterium in the food, how was he
going to keep them from eating it?

He looked up. People had started to consume the
loaves. They were going to eat it and follow the prophet,
where? To Saudi Arabia? Israel? Other Arab nations
when they all went home?

Did it matter? A pandemic wouldn't respect national borders.

Kealey slipped away, behind a slope of rock. He
took out his phone and called Harper.

"They're passing out bread," Kealey said.

"Contaminated at the factory," Harper said.

"No doubt. What do I do? These people will die."

"If 777 is controlling this, we can't ask the MFO to
intervene," he said. "The Egyptian officers will shoot
us down. The most we can do is tell the neighboring
countries to seal their borders—"

"I can't accept that we're helpless," Kealey said. He
was staring into the darkness, thinking, coming up
against dead ends. "Can you post something on the websites that have been carrying videos? Maybe we can stop
some of them from eating—"

"What would they believe, the photo of the dead
monks?" Harper asked.

"It's better than nothing," Kealey said.

Harper agreed.

"What about that bakery fire?" Kealey asked.

"The fire department is still going through the ruins,
but Gail says that fires like that, where there were gas
ovens fueling it, are usually hot enough to incinerate
microscopic residue of organic matter. If you can get
us a sample of the bread, we can start working on an
antidote."

"Who knows when and how I can get back to Cairo," Kealey said. "Dammit, is that the best we can do?"

"You know as well as I do that sometimes the best isn't a helluva lot," Harper said. "We didn't set this timetable."

"No, and I'll get the damn bread," Kealey said. "But there has to be something we can do. There *has* to."

"You're on-site. You tell me."

"The goddamned Staff," Kealey muttered. "If I had it—"

"Would it make any difference now?" Harper asked. "Would it part the masses and destroy the helicopters? We needed it hours ago, to plant doubt before the prophet came down."

Harper was right. *God damn it all.* He wanted to ask if Harper knew anything about what happened at the Sahara well, but thought better of it. If the deputy director had a hand in it, he wouldn't admit it. More than likely someone let something slip to 777. They must have taken it; they had the resources.

"We'll keep working on the problem here," Harper said. "Let us know if you hear from the others."

Kealey hung up. It was ridiculous, he thought as he set out to get some bread. It only just occurred to him that if the disease were airborne, he himself could be infected. Even now, he could see that the crewmen had turned the job over to pilgrims. The team was headed back to the helicopters. The prophet was still on the mound, making benedictory motions with his hands and with the staff.

Keeping the people there to kill them. Kealey wondered if he even knew. And if he didn't, if he would believe.

Not that Kealey could communicate with him.

The American moved forward, feeling desperate and angry—at the situation but also at himself. There was a saying in special ops, "Failure is the solution you missed."

He still had time.

He had to look harder.

CHAPTER SIXTY-FIVE
JEBEL MUSA, SINAI PENINSULA

He watched Kealey from the near edge of the crowd.

He had moved with the flow toward the front of the gathering, for that was where he was told Kealey would probably be. Possibly alone, if things went that way. The man had been shown a picture, told what Kealey would probably be wearing. He had been instructed to watch for someone who moved like a police officer determined to break up a brawl. He would not be chanting or praying or acting like anyone else. The man was advised to look for the glow of a sophisticated-looking cell phone, for that would most likely be his lifeline.

Even in the dark, the man had no trouble locating the American—who was, as expected, by himself. The man had followed him when he left the group to go alone to the advance section of the gathering. He had watched, waited, followed, moving as the American did. Together—though Kealey didn't know it—they now threaded their separate ways toward the feet of the prophet.

He had been asked to stay near Ryan Kealey and, when the time came, to do what needed to be done.

The man was concerned about how he would know when that time was.

"I don't know," he'd been told.

That wasn't the best answer but it was truly the only answer. Because it did not seem that Kealey himself knew what he was doing, where he was going.

Fortunately, the man was accustomed to improvisation.

And so he moved closer and then closer still, unobserved by the crowd or his subject until he was within just a few paces. . . .

CHAPTER SIXTY-SIX
MCLEAN, VIRGINIA

"I've just spoken with the head of the El-Khabeya, Egyptian Military Intelligence," Harper said to the others as he returned to the Underground. "I had to threaten all kinds of reprisals but I got what I needed. They were testing pneumonic plague at the 777 laboratories."

"Lovely," Gail Platte muttered.

"Tell me about the strain," Harper said as he sat. His tone made it sound as if he were reluctant to hear.

"It shuts down the respiratory system," she said. "It's one of the most contagious bacteriological infections, the worse because it's communicable by air or water."

"Not bread?" Harper asked.

"The heat would destroy it," Platte said.

"Is it always fatal?" Nesmith asked.

"Not if antibiotics are administered before exposure or shortly after the onset of symptoms, which usually surface in about twenty-four hours," she told the others.

"The problem is, the damn thing will outstrip the world's ability to combat it. We don't have enough drugs stockpiled anywhere."

Harper said, "We're not only looking at hundreds of thousands of dead in the first day—"

"Millions in two or three days," Platte said without inflection.

"And infrastructures without workers, international travel halted, and the ripple effect from that," George Nesmith added.

"At a minimum," Platte said. "Because there won't be enough health care professionals to go around, families will stay with each other, infect each other, and rot where they die. Just like in the old days."

"What *possible* gain is there in that?" asked Harper.

"That's the wrong question," Nesmith said. "The people who did this are asking, 'What is there to be lost?' If you're a secular nation surrounded by nonsecular enemies, if you have no real wealth, if you can't control the constant blasts of insurrection within your own borders, what do you do? You export hell. They used the very porousness of the borders from which they felt threatened to set a plague loose on their enemies."

"Real or potential," Schuyler remarked.

"Do they know we know?" Platte asked.

"I haven't received any updates from the Task Force commander," Harper said.

"On the run?" Platte asked.

"I doubt it," Harper said. "I'm guessing he left to join his men. The MK director agreed to keep this under his hat until he could reach unaffiliated MFO units and get them to the scene."

"I wouldn't be surprised if the 777 boys are going to

be where the action is," Nesmith said. "People dropping dead in the desert or on their homeward journey—which is where I'm sure the prophet will send them at once—is going to get a lot of press and they'll want to show who is in control."

"And when the diseases erupt?" Platte asked.

"The plotters will be manning the front lines, organizing people, since they've been inoculated," Nesmith said. "They'll come out of this heroes, while one of the pilgrims gets blamed for bringing the disease into the group."

"What happens to the prophet?" Harper asked.

"He's done his job," Nesmith said. "He dies and becomes a martyr, where he's much more useful. If he *is* one of the monks, I'm betting they didn't tell him that part. They probably kept him up in that cave where Adjo first videoed him, possibly convinced of his own sanctimony."

"I wonder why they didn't ask this Lieutenant Adjo to get involved," Platte said.

"He doesn't sound like he'd have gone along with it," Harper said. His hand was on the phone. He was trying to think of what to tell Kealey.

"Sedition isn't a team sport," Nesmith replied. "The fewer people who are involved, the less the chance of a leak. I'm guessing even the chopper crews don't know what they're involved with."

"Everyone exposed," Platte said, "everyone a carrier."

Nesmith frowned. "There's something I don't get. The enemy is expecting to transmit this by air, correct?"

Platte nodded.

"So what does the bread have to do with it?" he asked. "I mean, we've allowed that the bakery fire was related to this operation somehow."

"The fire was to destroy evidence," Harper said.

"Of what?" Nesmith asked. "The microbe's gestation?"

Platte nodded.

"But you said the ovens would have destroyed the effectiveness of this particular bacterium," Harper said.

"Maybe they sprinkled it on afterward," Schuyler submitted.

"No," Nesmith told him. "That'd leave a trail of the stuff through Sharm el-Sheikh. Bread wrappers aren't hazmat containers. They'd poison their own people."

"You're missing the point," Platte said. "The bread is beside the point."

"You lost me," Harper said.

"Many large bakeries use DAFS—Dissolved Air Flotation Systems—to keep bacteria-breeding yeast out of public sewer systems. The DAFS float the host medium, the insoluble matter, to the surface of a tub where it can be skimmed off and disposed of," Platte explained.

"That's where this particular bacterium was grown, then?" Harper asked. "Using regular baker's yeast?"

"It's brilliant," Platte said. "What ferments carbohydrates in baking is the perfect medium for binary fission to create lots of little bacteria in secret."

"Then why give out bread?" Schuyler asked.

"Multipurposing," Nesmith said gravely.

"To get people to cluster," Harper said, picking up the thought that Nesmith was unwilling to finish.

"The militants are probably going to release the airborne toxin from the helicopters, most likely when they take off," Nesmith went on. "That will keep the crewmen safe."

Harper said, "The good news, then, is we've still got time. I'll get on the horn to the MFO and see what they can whip up to keep the choppers grounded."

"You can't use other choppers," Nesmith pointed out, checking his computer screen. "I just checked the MESAT-6."

"What does that mean?" Platte asked.

"According to our Middle Eastern weather satellite, the wind is blowing toward the mountain," Nesmith told her. "If the MFO tries to pin them down from above, or even surrounds the area with vehicles, 777 can still release the toxins."

"If they're to be stopped, it has to be by infiltration," Harper said. "And it has to be quick."

"Not the kind of drill the MFO does conscientiously," Nesmith pointed out as he scrolled through the phone book.

Harper was outwardly unemotional. "I'll tell Ryan. Gail, you'd better notify our people at the embassy in Cairo to be prepared for what's coming—and to make sure they have antibiotics for themselves and for our guys when they come in."

Platte nodded and e-mailed their liaison at the consulate. No one said what was on everyone's minds:

If they come in.

CHAPTER SIXTY-SEVEN
JEBEL MUSA, SINAI PENINSULA

Losing the instincts he had honed in Iraq, Phair did not hit the ground when the shot sounded behind him. He did wonder why he'd heard it, however. He should have been dead before the sound reached his ears.

His next thought—which was pumped into his brain by breath so rapid he didn't recognize it as belonging to him, as something he was capable of producing—was that the bullet had missed his head. He waited for pain to flare in his shoulder or back. It didn't come.

Then he saw the shadow on the floor in front of him kick back and drop as though it had been winched about the waist.

The entire event had taken less than a second, but it was long enough for every detail to sear itself into his mind. The message that he was alive finally reached his knees, and he moved.

Phair thrust himself forward and down as though he were diving to cover an active hand grenade. In the same movement he pulled Adjo forward and snuggled his own body protectively near, his arm and part of his chest on top, a hand covering Adjo's head. Phair ducked his own head as low as it could go, his cheek to the floor. Sometimes life or death was just a matter of inches.

A second shot cracked through the cottony deafness caused by the first. It also issued from behind. Someone else fell, this time across Phair's ankles. The victim was dead weight. The cleric didn't know if it was Kealey, the MFO, or some other savior, but he was glad they were there.

He felt Adjo wriggle beside him. The young officer was so sweaty that Phair couldn't keep him pinned. Adjo scratched his way around, like a pinwheel, and Phair had to grab the back of his robe to keep him in place. Facing sideways now, Phair saw the rest of the men react. They were running for the street. He saw a black shape take form beside him, realized it was Adjo, saw that he was holding a torn robe. Adjo half crawled, half staggered to the door. He was holding a semiautomatic one of the men had dropped. The flashes from its muzzle brightened the doorway, the coughing bursts merged into one, and then Adjo leaned against the left side of the jamb. His legs went molten and let his torso drop to the corner of the doorway.

The moment he went down and the gun fell from his limp fingers, people moved into the doorway. Phair assumed they were friends, not foes; otherwise, they would have shot Adjo.

One of the newcomers stooped beside him. He couldn't see who it was but, oddly, he recognized the smell of the man.

It was Durst.

The German set the gun aside, lit a match, and moved it over him, looking for injuries.

"You are not dead," Durst said.

"Thank you," Phair replied. The cleric's eyes rolled forward. The shadow in the doorway had to be Carla crouched beside Adjo, laying him out. "How is he?" Phair asked, and realized that the dry words didn't make it past the floor in front of his lips. He swallowed and repeated the question.

"Unhurt," she replied.

"You came back," Phair said.

"We were watching the gate," Carla said, stepping over with two handfuls of guns and squatting. She put them on the floor. "One van drove away with the wounded and another came in. We didn't think that was good. There was no one watching the gate so we followed them in."

"We did not find the Staff, but I do not like to feel useless," Durst remarked.

"Thank you," Phair said again, adding, "I'm very sorry you had to do what you did."

"They would have killed you and then they would have killed us," Carla said. She was silent for a moment. "Three days ago I was training overweight clients. Now I'm a killer."

"A savior," Phair corrected.

Her grandfather reached over and put his hand on her forearm. Was he comforting her or welcoming her to the family?

"Have you been in touch with Kealey?" Phair asked, ashamed at that last ungracious thought but unable to get out of its way or—worse—to shake it.

Carla nodded. "He believes there is a plot to poison everyone in the desert. That appears to be what is wrong with the lieutenant."

"Adjo suspected as much," Phair said. "Does Kealey have a plan?"

"I don't know," she said. "He told me he was headed toward the helicopters, but I know nothing more."

Her grandfather asked for the flashlight the Americans had given her. She handed it to him and he rose, surprisingly spry. Durst went over to the doorway and slapped one of the Egyptians who was lying there. The man started and moaned and tried to grab Durst's hand, but the German stepped on the man's wrist, pinning it.

"He's alive!" Phair said.

"As I intended," Durst replied. "We may need him."

"The others?"

Durst shook his head. "Are you able to make it to the van? I think we should be leaving here."

In response, Phair rose and, after taking a moment to collect himself, walked forward with Carla at his side. Together, the three of them half dragged, half carried Adjo and the other Egyptian to the back of the van. When they were inside, Carla called Kealey to bring him up to date.

There was a lot to digest, and a great deal more still to be done. Phair decided to concentrate on the latter, for there was more at stake than anyone realized.

CHAPTER SIXTY-EIGHT
JEBEL MUSA, SINAI PENINSULA

Kealey might just as well have been at his desk. Information was coming in from multiple sources—first Harper, and now Carla with the welcome news that she and her grandfather had rescued Phair and Adjo. Kealey was proud of them, and angry at the risk they took, although he showed neither emotion as he calmly told Carla to go to the checkpoint and get medical attention for Adjo—for all of them, since they had now been exposed to the pathogen. Meanwhile, he continued to make his way toward the helicopters like everyone else, hoping he would find something there to turn the crowd back. His eyes moved frantically, his right shoulder a wedge against the crowd as he tried to figure out some way to keep the choppers grounded. He thought back to Eagle Claw, the ill-fated attempt to rescue the Teheran hostages in 1980. At the makeshift base, Desert One, a sideways-sliding RH-53 helicopter had caused chaos and destruction among the tightly packed vehicles.

As Kealey was considering how such a scenario might be enacted here, a man stepped directly in front of him, facing him. The agent extended an arm to maneuver around him. The man stepped with Kealey, causing the agent to stop and exhale impatiently. Kealey prepared to muscle around him.

"Mustair Keeleh?"

That was a surprise. Kealey stopped. "Who are you?"

"Phair frient," he said with rolling *r*s.

Kealey squinted at him. Silhouetted against the lights of the helicopters, the man was of medium height and build, robed with his head covered by a hood, and bearded, with steel wool puffs on either side of his lower jaw. The hint of a backpack jutted above his shoulders.

"I'm listening," Kealey replied. "Quick."

"Come," the man said, turning toward the thinner outer edge of the crowd.

Kealey followed for a few hesitant steps. "I really don't have time—"

"Come."

The man didn't say anything else. Perhaps he had just spent all the English he knew. Kealey exhaled again. He had no immediate options, besides the unrefined notion of using one of the choppers as a weapon. He jogged after the man, dodging a few slow-moving pilgrims.

"What's your name?" Kealey asked.

The man didn't appear to hear, or perhaps he didn't understand. He continued walking. Kealey ran in front of him. He saw his face for the first time. It was round and swarthy, his black beard streaked with white. His eyes were deep set but not unhappy. He was probably forty but looked older. If he was a friend of Phair, he was probably an Iraqi.

"You know *my* name," Kealey said, pointing to himself and saying his own name. He pointed to the other man and shrugged. "What is yours?"

"Bulani," the man replied, then purposefully moved around Kealey and continued toward the front of the crowd, toward the helicopters, to the area where people were approaching the prophet.

Kealey knew the name but couldn't place it. He thought of texting Harper to look it up, but suspected he would find out the man's purpose soon enough. Kealey's eyes drifted to the backpack, which was in shadow. There was something poking out over the top— along the man's neck—and from below, along his leg. Kealey moved in for a better look. It was a leather bundle tied with short lengths of rope at the top and bottom.

"You bastard," he muttered.

He didn't know whether to thank Phair or damn him, and ended up doing both. His only active thought was "what next?" What could he do, what should he do? He didn't even speak the language.

But Bulani did.

As the man moved along the outside of the crowd, he reached above his right shoulder as though he were drawing a saber from a back-worn sheath. His left hand snaked under his backpack and pulled a rope free, letting it drop from metal hooks on both sides of the kit. His right hand pulled the package over his shoulder and he hooked his fingers under the top and bottom bindings in turn, undoing them. The leather fluttered open and fell away.

The monks who had come down the hill had formed a circle at the foot of the mound where the prophet stood. They formed a barrier between the crowd and the object of their adoration.

"*Musa saheeh!*" Bulani cried, proudly thrusting the aged, broken staff above his head. "*Musa saheeh!*"

All heads, including those of the prophet, turned to him.

Kealey felt the breath leave his body as he waited to see what would happen next.

CHAPTER SIXTY-NINE

JEBEL MUSA, SINAI PENINSULA

Adjo seemed to recover some of his strength as he lay in the back of the van. There were no seats, so he slid against the side, gun in hand, and pointed at the head of the wounded officer who was slid in perpendicular to him, his head facing the cab.

Carla had climbed in after him. She used a pocketknife from her backpack to cut away his shirt. She shredded the fabric and made a makeshift bandage.

Durst sat in the passenger's seat studying a map of the compound and the surrounding area while Phair sat behind the wheel and, with uncertain fingers on the small keys, texted Kealey:

TEAM LEAVING MONASTERY. HAVE YOU MET BULANI?

Kealey replied:

YES.

Phair asked:

WHERE ARE YOU?

Kealey replied:

WITH PROPHET BEHIND CBS.

CBS was military shorthand for cargo bays. Phair texted:

WE ARE COMING.

Kealey typed back:

GO TO CHECKPOINT.

Phair wrote:

BULANI MAY NEED MY HELP.

He turned off the device so there could be no further discussion, tucked it away, and drove the van out the way he'd come. Using the map and a flashlight, Durst guided him from the road to a small side path that would take them around the garden and out to the plain.

Almost at once Phair encountered the edge of the mob, which was now clustered as far as the west side of the monastery. Some may have been late arrivals, and some may have come from neighboring villages from which the fire would have been visible. Perhaps that was part of the plan all along. Local Egyptians would not have needed the main road to get here, circumventing the MFO via shortcuts and footpaths.

Which is why the borders are so porous, he thought, empathizing with Adjo.

Cruising through the crowd proved slow, and then impossible. Going around them was not an option because it led to the foothills, away from where he could be of any use to Bulani and possibly where the van could not go.

"Let us turn around," Durst said. "We don't have a choice."

"Your Staff is out there," Phair said.

The German shot him a look. "How do you know this?"

"I had someone bring it."

"You? You stole it?"

"I recovered it," Phair said.

The van was completely stopped now. Phair suddenly felt deflated.

"How?" Durst asked.

"A man I know from the region."

"Why?"

"Would these people have believed an American? Would Washington have allowed me to give it to an Iraqi?"

Phair thought he saw a half smile cross the German's lips. Perhaps he admired the deception or the hubris. In any case, judging from the abrupt change in his expression, Durst was no longer complacent about the van being impeded.

"*Die Idioten!*" the German screamed at the windshield.

Two of the captured Egyptian weapons were on his lap. He cranked down the window and stuck a P228 out the window.

"Don't!" Phair pleaded rather than warned. "Some of these people—"

Gunfire drowned out the rest of his words. "*Verschieben Sie es!*" Durst screamed as he fired over the heads of the crowd.

The throng of pilgrims parted to the right and left and as far ahead as the van's headlights could see.

Almost at once, return gunfire raked the front of the van. Pieces of metal from the fender and hood ricocheted off the windshield, shattering it. Steam rose in angry puffs from a hole in the side. The tires hissed and died.

"Damn," Phair muttered. "I was about to say that they have weapons, too. That is how they celebrate here."

Opening the door and raising his hands, Phair stepped out and addressed the mob in Arabic. "We mean no harm!" he said. "We seek the Great and Holy Prophet to help a dying Egyptian in the back!"

"We all have needs!" shouted one. "It is said he will help us all with a wave of his Staff."

Phair shook his head. It was like the game of telephone he played as a boy. In just a few days, this phenomenon had gone from a single man telling a BBC cameraman, without corroboration, that he had met the True Prophet. Now he faced a mob thousands deep, expecting that man to perform miracles. This had been a brilliant grassroots movement with virtually no input from the source other than to look the part. It became what everyone wanted it to be, without it actually being anything. That was both awe-inspiring and frightening.

"All right," Phair said. "We will wait. Let us have no more gunplay."

With a grumbling that seemed to signify agreement, accented by angry gestures from those without guns, Phair looked across the crowd. There was no way they were getting through, even on foot.

With a tremulous sigh, he stood by the door and considered his options. For a man who was big on preparedness, Kealey had brought them into a situation where everyone was busy improvising. One thought occurred to him, though. It could work. He reached into his pocket and went to the back of the van. Carla had opened the door to let in the night air.

The lieutenant was shaking and feverish. He was having trouble holding his weapon on the captive. Carla was beside him, not interfering—the task was helping Adjo to stay focused—but ready to move in case he faltered.

The captive looked at Phair. "Your efforts . . . have failed!" he laughed.

"Your efforts will fail, too," Phair said in Arabic.

The man continued to laugh.

"Your helicopters will not be allowed to take off and infect the pilgrims," Phair said.

"It is too late for the pilgrims," the man said. "It is too late for all of you."

"Why?"

The man continued to laugh weakly.

"You don't have to tell me, I know," Phair said. "The helicopters don't have to take off to release their poison. Everyone who came here is going to die. And they will carry the plague to their homes and families."

"You are all going to die like this one," he said, indicating Adjo with a weak wave of his hand.

Phair snickered. "I don't think so."

CHAPTER SEVENTY

JEBEL MUSA, SINAI PENINSULA

The change happened quickly but decisively, so much so that even Kealey was unprepared for the shift. It was similar to the way animals in a field grow instantly still and attentive at the first crack of thunder.

The silence at the front of the gathering rippled back until it was nearly absolute. The quiet was broken only by the rotors and the distant rending of bundles containing bread. Crates of bottled water were also being unloaded. Even the wind seemed to have died.

Kealey could not understand what his newfound ally was saying, but he got the gist of it by his actions and the reactions of the crowd. He was telling them that he held the actual Staff of the prophet and that the man before them held a fake.

God help us all—and You can consider that a prayer— if he is asked to make it a serpent, Kealey thought.

The monks who stood near the prophet did not look to him for guidance. Two hoods turned together in conversation, obviously trying to decide what to do. One nodded and the other moved out, motioning for two others to join him. They were probably going to remove Bulani, usher him toward the helicopter.

But maybe not, if someone were to believe—

Kealey went to his knees beside Bulani and began to pray in silence. The monks continued to approach as Kealey motioned for those around him to pay respect to the Staff by kneeling. No one moved. The expressions he saw showed confusion, doubt, indecision, and all the many shadings thereof. But no one bent a knee.

The agent rose and approached Bulani just as one of the monks grabbed the Staff and tried to wrestle it away. Bulani refused to yield. A few pilgrims moved forward and seemed to urge the monks away—their faces showed surprise at the clerical violence—but the remaining monks formed a line between them and Bulani, one which no one crossed.

Kealey was about to do just that when someone shouted from behind him. Kealey turned. The man was holding a cell phone and shouting. Soon, other cell phones began to glow among the bowed heads of the pilgrims. The lights swept backward, spotting the crowd here and there like emerging stars.

Kealey leaned toward the nearest phone. Someone was speaking in Arabic from a video image.

The monk fighting with Bulani stopped. Bulani was able to wrest himself free without difficulty. He stood where they had left him, facing the prophet and repeating *"Musa saheeh"* almost inaudibly, the Staff cradled to his chest. Kealey didn't know whether he was speaking softly on purpose or not, but it was forcing those who hadn't heard to come closer. And coming closer, they saw the Staff. Whether the relic would affect them or not, it had caused a hard stop to the proceedings.

Almost at once voices were raised, along with cell phones, demanding something—probably an explanation.

Wildfire burns both ways, Kealey thought hopefully as he felt the mood of the crowd shift. No wonder there had never been peace in the region. Each new idea was fanatically granted its moment in the sun. Kealey peered to his left to see what the prophet was doing.

He was standing there, mute and small, his staff diminished and the torch held uncertainly at his shoulder. He seemed confused.

What concerned Kealey, though, was that all the monks were departing. He wasn't worried for the prophet's safety—the mob could rip him apart, for all he cared. He was worried about the monks' destination. The monks were weaving through the outskirts of the crowd, moving toward the helicopters, shouting instructions ahead of them. He had no doubt what they were going to do.

We're back where we started, Kealey thought. All the team had accomplished was to accelerate the process.

The dishonored prophet did not seem to hear the multitude or the shouts of his own monks. He did not make any sign that he intended to go with them yet he wasn't telling the people to run.

He doesn't know about the bacteria, Kealey realized.

This man was serious about what he was doing. No doubt he believed he had been given the Staff of Moses by God. Perhaps it had been planted in the monastery by the false monks so he could discover it. It may not even have been the prophet who had cast the rigged staff to the ground, turning it to a serpent. He had been kept in isolation, praying and planning for his ministry. That meant he probably didn't know his fellow monks were dead. No doubt he thought these monks were real and were running to save themselves from the wrath of the mob—a fate to which he himself was apparently resigned.

Kealey swung around Bulani and ran toward the prophet. He hoped the prophet knew some English or maybe French. Kealey could get by in French.

The agent slowed as he neared the prophet. The man looked like a church statue, frozen in his robes where he was standing. The only movement was provided by the dancing shadows created by the torch. Kealey approached slowly.

"Your eminence," he said, trying to be respectful. "Father Kusturica—I need to talk with you. Do you speak English?"

The man didn't move. He continued to stare ahead.

"You *must* believe me," Kealey went on. "Your aides are going to poison these people."

The monk looked over warily. His face was a shallow, ruddy mask from which life and faith seemed to have fled.

"What are you talking about?" the man asked, his English inflected with a Mediterranean accent.

"The whole of this mission was not to promote peace through faith, but security through mass murder," Kealey said, reaching for his phone. "Those helicopters contain bacteriological agents. The bread, the water, was to draw the people together—the gas was to be dropped when they left."

Kealey had kept Phair's photograph on his cell phone. He approached cautiously, holding the phone before him, face out. He was unsure how the monk—no longer a prophet—would react.

"These are your colleagues at the monastery," Kealey said. "They were all infected to test the germ. They are all dead."

The monk stepped from the mound as if in a trance. He came forward, transfixed by the photograph. He held the torch toward it, as though that would help illuminate the image. Around him the crowd of pilgrims watched expectantly, their gaze shifting from the monk to Bulani, waiting to see whom to rally behind. They had to get behind someone, Kealey knew. Otherwise, their journey would have been for nothing.

"This is so?" the monk asked, his voice catching.

"It is, your eminence," Kealey said.

"They told me my brothers had been sent elsewhere."

"They have," Kealey said.

The monk looked for another moment before lowering his eyes and turning away. Kealey couldn't leave it at that. There wasn't time.

"Sir, I fear that the men who posed as monks are simply going to open the tanks that are filled with plague germs. You must tell the people to disperse in the hopes that some will survive."

The monk stopped and half turned. "The others who were with me. Will they not die as well?"

"They took medicine."

"And you?"

"No, sir. I didn't know what was happening. I came from Washington to help the Egyptians."

The monk looked from Kealey to Bulani. "That—that is the genuine Staff of the Prophet?"

"It is, found many years ago and hidden in the desert."

Tears fell along the man's red cheeks. "Lord," he said, "what have I brought them to?"

"Please, if you tell them to go now, there may be hope—"

He looked across the bobbing sea of confusion and outrage. "I see their expressions. They will not listen to me. Will anything stop this contagion?"

"We are studying it now," Kealey told him. "They burned the evidence in Sharm el-Sheikh—"

"Fire?"

Kealey looked from the monk to the torch. "Intense heat, yes."

"Thank you," the monk said. "Thank you for giving me the chance to redeem my soul."

Kusturica looked toward the helicopters, his body following his head around as he held the torch with renewed purpose, tightly gripping the staff in his right. If it had no power until now, he would give it some. The monk walked away briskly, the sudden wind lifting his robe like angels' wings, his dark form shrinking rapidly in the glare of lights from the helicopters.

There was a great deal of activity in front of him as the men rushed to finish what they had begun. Even though they had been discovered, they still had an advantage. They knew it would be difficult to evacuate so many people and, even if that were done, to administer sufficient antibiotics in time. All it would take for the plan to succeed was a few people on the fringe of the gathering to depart over the mountain, along their secret paths in the dark.

As he stood there, Kealey suddenly realized that the contagion was not the only thing they had to worry about. The monk's cure posed dangers as well.

"Bulani!" he cried, and ran back to where he had left the Iraqi. With the departure of the monk, dozens of people had gathered around Bulani, obviously moved by his own devout expressions and manner.

The Iraqi looked over.

"Get them away!" Kealey was shouting, motioning with big, sweeping, pushing waves of his arms. "Get them away *now*!"

CHAPTER SEVENTY-ONE
JEBEL MUSA, SINAI PENINSULA

"What are you doing?"

The crewman shouted down from the top of the ramp of the open cargo bay as the monk approached. He repeated the question, this time more insistently.

The monk did not reply. He stopped beside the helicopter to the left of the ramp, his eyes taking in the surroundings. Several of the monks were there, opening crates. He recognized Ngozi, Badru, and Qeb, all of whom had shed their robes. When they saw him they stopped what they were doing. The nearest of the men came toward him tentatively.

"What are you doing, my brother?" Ngozi asked him. "Go back to the others. They need you."

"What are you doing?"

"I'm finishing the job you began," he replied. "I'm protecting the homeland, the monastery."

"From what?"

"Poison," he replied. "Foreign influence, Islamic extremists, destruction of a culture as old as civilization itself."

The monk shook his head slowly, unhappily, his eyes glazed with sadness. "This is not the way."

"It is our way," the man replied. "It is God's way."

Another man strode over from deep within the belly of the helicopter.

"Go about your work, I'll deal with this!" Badru ordered Ngozi. His eyes were fixed on Kusturica.

"What you do is against God's law!" Kusturica said, gesturing behind him. "A law that was given to us *here*!"

Badru withdrew a gun from his waistband. He leveled it at the chest of his former partner. "Leave or die!"

The monk, the would-be prophet, the holy man who had been deceived by men of dark vision, stood as though he were a mountain himself. He glanced to his right. On the side of the airframe, written in slightly peeled black letters on white metal skin, was the word *banzeen*. Gripping the staff and torch tightly, the monk walked to the fuel tank and dipped the torch to the metal covering.

"Get back!" Ngozi yelled, even as he turned to run.

"For the peace of God and the salvation of our souls I pray, oh Lord," said the monk. "For the peace of the whole world, for the stability of all the holy churches of God . . ."

Badru fired at him from the middle of the cargo bay. It was an awkward shot, but he was able to catch his target in the belly.

The monk fell to his knees.

The thin metal skin was already glowing red, transferring its heat to the contents within, as Badru ran from the cargo bay and ducked under the hatch to where the monk was struggling to hold the torch erect.

The wounded man looked at him. "Thank you . . . for helping me . . . pray," he wheezed.

A moment later the fuel in the tank ignited with a roar, lifting the back end of the helicopter nearly a meter in the air before rending it into a confusion of rubber tubing and flakes of metal skin, plastic valves and structural fragments, and mixed with these among the blossoming red-and-black plume, a riot of flesh and fabric and bone.

CHAPTER SEVENTY-TWO
JEBEL MUSA, SINAI PENINSULA

Kealey and the pilgrims nearest him were pushing their way toward the mountain when the helicopter exploded. They turned and watched in blank-faced shock as the flaming cloud rose, only to be joined moments later in fiery oblivion by its neighbors on either side. The shower of flaming wreckage caused the remaining helicopters to ignite, adding more ragged blasts to the no-man's land.

Crewmen who saw the first explosion coming had fled, most of them literally diving behind rocks as the first helicopter blew up. The bulk of the men managed to survive the forest of fireballs and shrapnel that followed from the subsequent explosions, most of which were limited to the tail sections.

Even before the punishing heat wave struck, the crowd had jumped to life and was running faster than Kealey's urging could have made them move. The blast came in waves as each of the helicopters exploded. Flight created an adequate buffer. Most of the retreating pilgrims were far enough from the helicopters and somewhat protected by the cliff sides. Any danger that would have been presented by the microbes was neutralized by the flaming destruction of their containers. Chances were good that any that survived would be borne high into the atmosphere by the rising heat, where they would float helplessly until they perished.

The explosions quickly subsided into a long, clanking rain of debris. Crewmen had to scurry to get out of the way of the secondary assault from above. The remains of the ruined helicopters burned with ugly hisses and snapping, the orange flames streaked now and then with blue and green as chemicals in the components or wiring burned.

Huffing from the run, the crowd looked to Kealey like an enormous living thing. If anyone doubted that all people were the same, a brisk two- or three-hundred-meter dash would disavow them of that. Some men still ran, others walked, a number of them wisely doused themselves with water, a few crawled, and those who were all out stood with their hands on their knees and talked to people who stopped beside them. A few smoked hand-rolled cigarettes. They occasionally pointed toward the wreckage and puzzled about what had happened and, no doubt, at their own gullibility.

Panting himself, Kealey looked around for Bulani. There was no point calling his name; the buzz of voices and the cough of vehicles created a carpet of sound that made it difficult to hear his own voice. Kealey knew that because he was muttering to himself about the insanity of what had just transpired.

The agent made his way back toward the monastery, his eyes searching left and right, now and then urging pockets of people to get back, to move as far as possible from the explosion site. Here and there, small deposits of oil that had dripped from vehicles announced their presence with angry, flaming flourishes. It was possible that embers from the blasts would reach clothes, the vehicles themselves, other combustibles. After a few minutes, Kealey heard helicopters as the Egyptian military finally moved in. Obviously, whoever had been running the show for Task Force 777 was no longer doing so.

He had only gone about four hundred meters but it felt longer. As he slowed, Kealey received a call from Phair. He answered as he continued to walk.

"Ryan, are you all right?"

"Yes," he said. He had to work up saliva in order to speak. "The prophet blew up the choppers."

"Good God."

"Apparently," Kealey said. "How are you all?"

"Adjo is sick, but we're okay."

"That was a brilliant move, recording the conversation with your captive," Kealey said. "It turned the crowd after your friend had planted doubt."

"You can thank Carla later," Phair said. "She showed me how to send the file."

"And you can tell me later why I shouldn't have you court-martialed for having the Staff stolen from the desert. You could have told me."

"Would you have allowed me to call Bulani and give him the location of the Staff?"

"I don't know," Kealey admitted. "But you should have consulted me just the same."

"It needed to be done this way," Phair said. "It couldn't have been an American and it certainly couldn't have been a Nazi. It had to be one of their own people, with his own faith exposed and vulnerable."

"We'll discuss this later," Kealey said.

"Just remember that thanks to all of us, countless lives were saved."

"Like your Iraqi walkabout, the heroic ends apparently justify the questionable means," Kealey said. "Where are you?"

"At the northwest corner of the monastery," Phair said. "We're pinned now by the crowd moving the other way. We need medical attention. Adjo's hanging tough, though I'm starting to feel not so great myself."

"I'll let the embassy know we need antibiotics," Kealey said. "They can arrange for an airlift."

Kealey hung up and placed the call. He quickly briefed Harper and was not surprised to discover that the deputy director had placed medical assistance on standby at the embassy; when they saw the explosions via satellite, the team was dispatched by air. Kealey asked if the unit would wait until he got there.

"We were all exposed to the bacteria through Adjo," he said. "I'll make my way as quickly as possible."

"You won't be in much danger, nor anyone you may have encountered," Harper told him. "Gail Platte says that the bacteria requires moisture and a significant body temperature to stay active. It goes dormant and dies very quickly in dry, airborne situations."

"So the real damage would have been inflicted by people leaving here and sharing food, drink, a kiss, a handshake, things like that."

"Exactly," Harper said. "Communities that share

well water or have extended families were apparently their targets. What happened to the Staff?"

"I have a feeling it's gone," he replied. "Phair's friend took it."

"We'll have to find him," Harper said. "We don't want the real one causing these same problems."

"No argument," Kealey said. He looked out at the crowd of people that was thinning in all directions. "We'll have to have a serious talk with Phair about that. I don't think the fellow wants to be found."

"He's probably going to sell the damned thing on eBay," Harper said disgustedly.

"I don't think so," Kealey said. "Though if he did, that's one way we could get it back."

Harper snickered. "Touché. That was a shitty thing of me to say. It's just that I'm going to have to explain this to the director, who is going to have to tell the president."

"You can tell him we won," Kealey said. "That's the bottom line."

"You did do that," Harper agreed. "Helluva job."

Kealey's eyes moved toward the mountain. "Other men have done greater things here. And with the same tools."

"Ryan, you going native on me?"

"I guess this place brings it out, eventually."

"The way D.C. brings out megalomania," Harper said.

There was no disputing that. Kealey said he would call when he could and Harper congratulated him again. It occurred to Kealey that things weren't quite the same: Moses didn't need a cell phone to talk to his boss.

As he made his way across the uneven terrain, the first hint of dawn was giving him some help negotiating the pitfalls. He made himself a little bet as he neared the monastery. He wondered which of him would win: the optimist or the cynic.

Cynically, he expected the cynic would come out on top.

He was right.

James Phair was gone.

The morning had fully broken across the Wadi el-Deir when Kealey reached the van. He was far beyond tired; the sunlight hurt the backs of his eyes and he all but dragged himself the last half kilometer on blistered feet and reedy legs, his arms dead weights at his side. He was still wearing his backpack because it helped keep him from slumping forward.

Carla was watching for him and waved when she saw him. Kealey was glad of that. There were many MFO and military vans and helicopters around, and he would have had no idea which was theirs.

"Thank you," was all he could say as he reached the van and she gave him a shoulder to keep him from stopping and simply going to sleep by the driver's side tire. He was beginning to feel a little feverish now, and was happy when a medic from the embassy laid him in the back and gave him an injection and didn't ask him for the pillow back when he closed his eyes and went to sleep.

CHAPTER SEVENTY-THREE
CAIRO, EGYPT

Kealey awoke to find the floor shifting and bouncing in a gentle, lulling way. He was facing the back of the dark cabin. The only illumination was from behind, low sunlight casting an oval glow on the olive-drab wall in front of him. It was coming through a window. He was in the air—in a Chinook, he surmised; he heard the rotors thumping above and in front of him—and he was heading away from the sun, which meant they were going west. Flying to Cairo.

He looked around. His eyes stopped on his right. Carla was sitting on a fold-down chair, her grandfather resting on her shoulder in the seat beside her. The young woman's eyes were half-open, not really seeing.

"Where's Adjo?" Kealey asked.

He barely heard himself above the sound of the props. With effort, he raised his right hand so she could see. Her eyes snapped toward him. Gingerly, she moved her grandfather's head so it was leaning on the canvas seatback of her chair. She waited a moment to make sure his head stayed there; helicopters, as she had discovered, were not airplanes. They tended to dip and torque. At least the chest harness would keep him in place.

She squatted beside Kealey and he repeated his question.

"The Egyptian army airlifted the lieutenant to a nearby medical facility," Carla told him.

"Will he be okay?"

"They think so, but they wanted to get him into a proper care center. We stayed a little longer to help treat some of the people who had helped the lieutenant and Major Phair."

"Was Phair treated?"

Carla nodded.

"Did he tell you where he was going?"

Carla shook her head.

"Are you two all right?"

"My grandfather is tired—we both are," she said with a smile as she yawned.

"You both did really well," Kealey said. "Thank you."

Carla handed Kealey a bottle of water that was tucked in a mesh pouch at the side of her seat. He took it gratefully and propped himself on one elbow.

"We made a difference here, didn't we?" she asked Kealey.

"Very much so," he replied. "How does it feel?"

"Honestly? Futile," she replied after a moment's thought. "We saved lives, but these people will not be stopped. War here will never end."

"Old enemies can become friends. You've seen that."

"Not blood enemies," she said. "Those battles do not end until there is no more blood."

"I don't want to believe that," Kealey said.

"Believe what you wish. It is that way. You all had trouble with my grandfather's views, but he was able to work with that man, Lieutenant Adjo, because his hate for these people and their squabbles is in his brain, not in his bones, not in his blood. When it is that deep, nothing can dislodge it."

Kealey drank half the bottle, then capped it and lay down. "Adjo fought his own kind to protect outsiders, outsiders who it was his job to stop. That would seem to dispute your claim."

"It is true he acted as a man, not an Egyptian," Carla said. "We will see if that lasts."

"We were all human beings today," Kealey told her. "Ideally, it will last for all of us."

Carla seemed sad, but it flashed away quickly, replaced by concern.

"Let me know if I can get you anything," she said comfortingly.

He squeezed her hand as she walked like a tightrope walker back to her seat. He stared at the ceiling, randomly reviewing what had gone wrong and what had gone right over the last few days. Very little of the latter. Catastrophically little, in fact. Yet somehow—

He thought of the mountain, he thought of the Staff, and then he thought of the implications of what he was *thinking*. Phair would say it was the hand of God that shaped their success, or at least nudged it.

Maybe God nudged Phair, too, Kealey reflected. The army might accept that explanation once but not a second time. He hoped that if the major were gone, this time he stayed gone.

Perhaps that was how the prophets and saints really got their strength. Not from God per se, but from the conviction that this or that was what God wanted them to do. In a way, that made the task seem more heroic. With God came certainty. Without Him, there was only one's inner resources. Without approving of what Phair did, Kealey could not fault the conviction and courage that drove him.

The agent drifted in and out of a dreamless sleep. When they arrived at the airport in Cairo, they were transferred to a van. Kealey was able to walk, hindered more by the lingering effects of the drugs than by exhaustion or injury. The van stopped first at the Venezuelan consulate. The American ambassador had called ahead. Here, Carla and her grandfather would be able to obtain the documents they needed to get home. That wouldn't be difficult with the elder Montilla's help.

"I can't remember—did I ever apologize for that chaotic departure?" Kealey asked as they stood outside the iron gates of the sand-colored structure on Mansour Mohamed Street.

"To tell you the truth, I don't remember," Carla laughed as two members of the Venezuelan guard helped her grandfather inside.

Kealey scooted over to him before the gates closed. He offered the elderly man his hand.

"Thank you, Herr Durst."

The German looked at him. "Where do you think my Staff has gone?"

"I wish I knew. It's home, though."

Durst regarded him with sad gray eyes. "The Staff and I—*wir sind weg zu langes gewesen.*"

"I'm sorry?"

"We have both been away too long," Durst said. "Home."

Durst stepped inside, followed by Carla, and a heavy electronic latch clanked shut behind them. Within moments, and without a backward look, they were lost in a turn of the path.

Kealey got back in the van, closed the door, and settled into the seat. It struck him, then, that he would probably never see any of these people again—Phair, Carla, her grandfather. It was a strange thought, but reassuring. They shared nothing, not even the same reasons for having undertaken the mission, yet they had worked together and pulled it off. Whether that was luck, determination, or fate, it did give him hope. Contrary to what Napoleon had said, God did not, apparently, favor the side with the most battalions.

CHAPTER SEVENTY-FOUR
CAIRO, EGYPT

Lieutenant Adjo was not feeling his best. The medicine the doctors had given him, the injections and intravenous fluids, had drained him more than the illness itself. But his focus had never been sharper, not even when he was trapped in the tunnel in Mt. Sinai with armed men in pursuit.

He could not call Lieutenant General Samra a traitor. The more he considered it, the more he realized the man was a patriot. A zealous, misguided patriot, a would-be mass murderer, and a megalomaniac, surely. A lawbreaker, absolutely.

But not a traitor.

The men who had served with Samra—Adjo did not yet know who all of them were, and he might never know—were simply misguided by Samra or his ideas or the notion of doing something secretive. Men were drawn to 777 in part for that reason. They liked the idea of knowing something that others did not, of some impending raid or surveillance or arrest.

But this. . . .

Adjo sat in the back of the Russian-built Hip-C helicopter as it soared over the 777 airfield headed west beyond the Nile. They were headed toward Giza, passing only a few hundred meters above well-traveled roads, the edges hidden in what looked like chew marks caused by the beating desert sand—or the Sphinx, depending on what one believed—traffic thinning as cool night drives gave way to sizzling daytime traverse. They were looking for the road Samra was said to have taken. Not all of his allies had been loyal, especially when their own lives or freedom were at risk.

The key piece of information was provided by the scum who had poisoned Adjo in the mountain. He confessed what he knew under the effects of drugs administered and questions asked before he was taken into surgery. He hadn't known much—only that after the success at Sinai, Samra had intended to hold a rally at the pyramids, a gathering to support a new military government in what was expected to be a time of confusion. Once that information was in hand, other members of the plot had come forward. Samra had planned to go there regardless. In the event of failure, they were to rendezvous and plan their next move. In the event of failure and discovery, that was to be their escape route.

Samra's staff car was visible on the side of Pyramid Road. The officer had stopped within view of the Great Pyramids and left the vehicle to walk toward them. In the distance, tour buses were arriving by the manned barricade that prevented tourists from entering until the appointed time.

Adjo told the pilot to set the helicopter down in the

sands beyond the wall, between the Great Pyramid of Khufu and the officer. Samra continued to approach, either unmindful or uncaring of the obstacle. Or maybe he felt that Adjo might be sympathetic to his cause, if not his means.

Adjo got out. He carried his MISR assault rifle angled down across his chest. Samra wore a P228 in his holster. Adjo walked toward his former superior officer, the defense minister having removed him from his post by emergency order at six a.m., two hours before. He wondered if Samra knew.

"You have been relieved of command," Adjo said as he approached. "And you used me."

"Would you have helped willingly?"

"You know the answer to that."

"Then your wound is self-inflicted," Samra said.

"My only wound is having trusted a man who was not worthy of that trust," Adjo told him. "Will you come back with me?"

Samra did not reply. Adjo looked past him. Samra's driver had opened the door but he was still in the car, both hands on the wheel. He was looking at Adjo, his posture indicating that he was not going to be a part of any gunplay. Either he knew the back of the plan had been broken, or he had remained at his post because news of the discharge had apparently not been delivered to Samra and the driver lacked orders to the contrary.

Adjo continued forward. "I am here to arrest you."

"That will not happen," Samra said.

"I assure you, it will."

Samra unbuttoned his holster. Adjo's heart pumped

harder and he felt the rifle become more real in his hands. He did not stop.

"Think about what you're doing," Samra urged.

"I am not the issue."

"But you *are*," Samra said. He was just a few meters away. "All I needed you to do was record our mechanical trick, our own staff. My intention then was to keep you out of danger. When we learned there was a real one, I needed you to bring it to us."

"Why not one of the people who was already working on your scheme?"

"Everyone had a role," Samra said. "I had to keep the MFO away, which meant involving my men in the local operations."

"'Your' men," Adjo said. "They were Egypt's men."

"And we were serving that master, all of us," Samra said. "We have a long history together, a history of impressive accomplishments."

"I hope the court will consider those when they sentence you. Now—"

"No!" Samra barked. "I will not go with you."

"One way or another, you will."

"Please, give me this. Allow me to go forward, into the shadows of a time when we were great. Permit me my dignity, at least."

Samra withdrew his gun. Adjo raised his.

"I will not fire on you nor will I run," the disgraced officer assured him.

"You had those monks murdered—"

"And I accept punishment," Samra replied. "I only want to die with honor."

A shot cracked from Adjo's gun. Samra dropped backward like a storm-blown tree.

Blood from a hole through his forehead soaked the sand to a slushy consistency.

Adjo looked at him. "No," he said, and turned back to the waiting helicopter.

"The Mukhabarat el-Khabeya found the remains of the fake staff in the ashes," Harper said.

Kealey had him on speakerphone as he sorted through his drawers and closet, tossing clothes onto the bed.

"It worked like one of those magicians' wands," Harper went on. "You know, the kind where the magician holds one end and when he hands it to you the wand droops?"

"We had very different childhoods," Kealey said. "I never went to a circus."

"A birthday party?"

"Not where there was entertainment," Kealey said.

"You never had trick toys, like gag chewing gum or fake dog poop?"

"No, I had these rubber-band guns made from the slats of shipping crates. You attached a rubber-band to the muzzle, then looped it back over the trigger."

"If it was attached—"

"You didn't fire the rubber band," Kealey explained.

"You slipped things about halfway along the barrel, like thumbtacks or little squares of cardboard. When you released the back end of the rubber band, the object went flying"

"I'm impressed, but not," Harper replied.

"If you weren't good with your fists, and weren't ready for a switchblade, that was pretty much all you had."

Kealey reached for an upper shelf of the closet and winced as his shirt pulled across his back. He had gotten burned in the Sahara and his skin was still sore, along with the rest of him.

"I heard Adjo is getting a promotion," Harper said. "Not for what he did at Sinai, but for killing Samra in a gun duel. Samra's own driver testified that his superior drew first."

"He's a fine soldier," Kealey said. "He has a lot of initiative and heart."

"We had to talk the Israelis out of going after Durst," Harper added soberly. "All former SS are on their hit list."

"I don't like his worldview, but it didn't sound as if he hurt anyone back then, and I don't think he will in the future," Kealey said.

"I had to lie and say he was helping us, and them, in order to atone for his sins," Harper said.

"The son of a bitch," Kealey said. "It never occurred to him that anything he thought or did was wrong. His granddaughter was different. I'm assuming they got back okay?"

"No snags," Harper told him. "It actually worked out for us, too."

"How do you mean?"

"The Venezuelans regarded this as a kidnapping, of course," Harper said. "They didn't make a fuss because they didn't want to publicize the fact that we were able to pull it off despite the presence of their police. Ramirez might have had a word with them as well."

There was a pause that lasted until the phone sounded dead. Harper knew the name was unwelcome to Kealey. Kealey hadn't realized just how much.

To break the silence Kealey asked, "What do we do about Phair?"

"'How do you solve a problem like Maria?'" Harper said. "You can't say we didn't ask for this, sending him back. Do you think he was playing us all along?"

"I don't," Kealey said.

"He wasn't homesick?"

"For what, poverty and the desert? I don't think so. I believe, based on nothing concrete, that he was reminded of why he became a priest and a soldier. To bring comfort where it was needed in a battlefield."

"Whose?"

"Apparently, anyone's. He's certainly not running away, he's not a coward," Kealey said.

"I didn't mean to imply that," Harper said. "I guess— I just don't understand how a man can come home— *home,* to the United States—and leave again. He could have found a way to work with his friends through us."

"After taking the Staff the way he did?" Kealey asked.

"Point taken," Harper said. "I'm still not sure why he did that."

"Because he thought it would work and was afraid we'd say no," Kealey said. "I'll admit, I felt a little like a sucker when I found out, but I can't fault his thinking. He may even be the vanguard of a new way of doing business over there."

"How so?"

"Morocco, Egypt, Iraq, the United States—the major doesn't seem to care about borders. He cares about people. That's how he survived all those years."

"You said he didn't get along with Durst."

"No, I got along better with Durst. Phair couldn't get past the confessional aspect. He wanted the guy to admit his sins."

"Doctrinaires make poor conversationalists," Harper said. "Everyone shouts, no one listens."

"I don't know," Kealey said. "Phair was different with Adjo. In the major's defense, none of the people he appears to have associated with in the Middle East espoused genocide."

"This is all Gail Platte territory. Me? I had enough trouble explaining to the president how we lost the Staff of Moses. I tried, 'Well, sir, technically we never had it . . .' but he wasn't buying that."

"Where did you leave it?"

"I told him the truth," Harper said. "He wasn't happy, but he understands how it happened. His concern is not that a holy relic was lost but that it could surface again in a similar scenario."

"That probably won't happen," Kealey said.

"I agree," Harper replied. "Terrorists don't like to repeat themselves. They figure, correctly, we'll be watching that route."

"That wasn't what I was thinking," Kealey said. "The people who have it won't *let* that happen."

"Oh? All they need is one greedy SOB to turn, go

for the cash. That's how most of the terrorist leaders get found, you know that."

"This is a matter of God," Kealey said.

"Matter of fact," Harper murmured.

"Is the army going to go after Phair?" Kealey asked.

"I don't know," Harper told him. "I don't see how they can. They're too busy finding guys who are shooting at us. If they do find him, though, the Internal Investigator's Office won't go easy on him. Not this time. Nor should it. He could have asked to go back, through channels. He could have resigned and gone back as a civilian."

"Phair obviously doesn't put much faith in channels," Kealey said. "He measures time in souls rescued and lives saved. His own security just doesn't matter in the face of that."

"I'm not impressed," Harper said. "Impulsive people worry me."

"Oh, he's not as impulsive as all that," Kealey said. "He just follows a different book of regulations."

"Sorry, I need to get off the phone now, Ryan," Harper said. "I've got a scheduled call, West Coast."

Kealey could tell Harper was dangling bait. Did West Coast mean Hernandez?

"No problem, I think we've covered everything," Kealey said.

"See you Monday," Harper said.

"See you Monday," Kealey lied, and tapped off.

He sat for a moment, thinking about Chaplain Major Phair. Kealey didn't believe in praying, and he didn't think he had the rank to ask God to shuttle a good luck message to Phair. But he did wish the cleric well. He wanted to believe that humanism and patriotism were compatible, and there wasn't a better ambassador than James Phair.

As for himself, he had another mountain to ascend. This one was in Connecticut.

Kealey was doing one last check of his bedroom when his phone buzzed. It was an e-mail, and Kealey glanced at it out of habit. He stopped reading as soon as he saw the sender's name: Dina Westbrook. The Ice-breaker. Was she calling about Phair? Or had she been pulled onto the Hernandez carousel?

Kealey shut off his phone and dropped it in the bottom of his duffel bag, then started piling clothes on top of it. Maybe he wasn't coming down off this mountain, except for supplies now and then. Or maybe someday, he'd come down with some new ideas and a few clear messages.

EPILOGUE
BASRA, IRAQ

Phair and Bulani parked the thirty-year-old Volks-wagen Beetle down the street from the mosque. It was twilight, the darkness hiding the scars of an explosion that had damaged the face of the ancient structure. There were no streetlights, only the here-and-there glow from windows along the ancient street. Most of those were candles, since electricity was sporadic and temporary.

Phair was nervous. Through family, Bulani's Shiite wife had made arrangements for him and her Sunni husband to get together with elders of a moderate wing of the local religious community. The meeting had been organized quietly. Radicals would not have hesitated to kill both men out of hand just for being within eyesight of these sacred grounds.

An old Ford Galaxie pulled up behind the Beetle. A man stuck his arm from the driver's side window, palm down, and the headlights faded off.

"That was the signal," Bulani said. His tone told

Phair more than that. It indicated that Bulani was anxious about getting out of the car and going over.

Phair popped the door and stepped onto the worn-out asphalt of the narrow street. He wore a stubble of beard and a *djellabah*. Under his arm he carried something wrapped in terrycloth. He walked over to the Galaxie and stopped beside the open window.

"Good evening," Phair said in the local dialect.

"Let me see it," said the driver.

"Come with me."

"Where?"

"Into the mosque," Phair said.

The two men in the car sat upright in alert, unhappy silence.

One of them said, "If you are found out to be a Christian and he a Sunni, you will be killed, and him along with you."

"Either this is the Staff of the Prophet and God will protect us, or He will not and we may die," Phair said. "I am willing to take that risk. How better to prove it is what I say?"

"Part the waters," the passenger said. "Show us a miracle."

"We of three faiths are here talking—is that not a miracle?" Phair asked.

"It is simply good manners and the urging of my mother," said the man in the passenger's seat.

"She wants her son, and her son's sons, to survive," Phair said.

"The men in the desert—they lied about possessing such a thing," the driver said to Phair.

"The men in the desert were liars," Phair replied. "I am not."

The men fell silent, their eyes on the Volkswagen.

Phair turned, saw that Bulani had not yet left the car. Phair motioned for him to do so. The Iraqi obliged and stood facing the others.

"We are here to seek common ground at the request of those who are dear to us," Phair went on. "If the four of us can find that, then there are even greater miracles in store. Let us take the first step."

The men continued to look ahead. Apparently convinced that neither the priest nor Bulani was a threat, they got out of the car. The three men of Islam looked at each other with suspicion. It was not the fear of arms or violence that concerned them, Phair knew, but a fear of concessions and compromise, a dread of the changes they might bring.

"'None of you has faith unless he loves for his brother what he loves for himself,'" Phair said.

The driver regarded him. "You know the holy text."

"I respect it as I respect my own," Phair said.

The man acknowledged the honor with a slight bow. In response, Phair displayed the bundle he had held under his arm. He removed a stick, charcoal with age, jagged from wear, physically unimposing. The two Shiite men looked at it. Even in the dark it seemed to become part of the cleric's hand and arm and made the flesh more than it was just a few breaths before.

It seemed to make them all a little greater.

"Lead the way," the driver said.

"I will be proud to," Phair said as he walked across the chipped curb through the darkness toward the mosque.

www.julieberryphotography.com

ANDREW BRITTON was born in England and moved with his family to the United States when he was seven, settling in Michigan, then North Carolina. After serving in the Army as a combat engineer, Andrew entered the University of North Carolina at Chapel Hill where he pursued a double major in psychology and economics. Visit his website at www.andrewbrittonbooks.com.

UPC

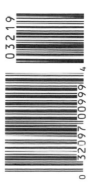

Ryan Kealey has no doubt that the forces seeking to tip this teetering world into chaos are just getting better. Better equipped, better organized, and, most terrifying of all, more patient. And despite all the ELINT, the all-seeing electronic intelligence gathered at Langley, nothing stops a devastating attack from ripping through the heart of San Antonio, Texas.

Wrenched from retirement to work the Texas tragedy, Kealey learns of a far greater threat in the Middle East. A radical terrorist group claims possession of a powerful ancient relic, the Staff of Moses, which they will use to unleash plagues across the globe. To avert unimaginable devastation, lone-wolf Kealey, armed with ̶n̶o̶t̶h̶i̶n̶g̶ ̶b̶u̶t̶ ̶h̶i̶s̶ intuition, must prevent a disaster of bibli̶c̶a̶l̶ ̶p̶r̶o̶p̶o̶r̶t̶i̶o̶n̶s̶ that may well be inevitable.

Visit us at www.kensingtonbooks.com

ISBN-13: 978-0-7860-3219-8
ISBN-10: 0-7860-3219-7

50999

EAN

9 780786 032198

PRINTED IN U.S.A.